NET
FORCE
THREAT
POINT

Also in the Net Force series
created by Tom Clancy and Steve Pieczenik,
and written by Jerome Preisler

NET FORCE
THREAT POINT

A NOVEL

SERIES CREATED BY
TOM CLANCY and
STEVE PIECZENIK
WRITTEN BY
JEROME PREISLER

HANOVER
SQUARE
PRESS

HANOVER SQUARE PRESS™

Recycling programs for this product may not exist in your area.

ISBN-13: 978-1-335-14311-2

Net Force: Threat Point

Copyright © 2021 by Netco Partners

This edition published by arrangement with Harlequin Books S.A.

Hanover Square Press
22 Adelaide St. West, 41st Floor
Toronto, Ontario M5H 4E3, Canada
HanoverSqPress.com
BookClubbish.com

Printed in U.S.A.

FOR SUZANNE

Bears, dragons, tempestuous on mountain and river,
Startle the forest and make the heights tremble.
Clouds darken beneath the darkness of rain,
streams pale with a pallor of mist.
The gods of Thunder and Lightning
Shatter the whole range.

—Li Bai, 701–762 AD

PART ONE

ASSASSIN'S MACE

1

The South China Sea
April 10, 2024

"You're at two-zero-zero meters on the button," said Murph.

Murph was John Murphy, the dive supervisor topside aboard the cable-laying ship CS *Stalwart*.

"Roger," replied Zak through the pipe.

Zak was Isaac Tinian of Warwick, Rhode Island. He had been on the job five years, longer than most guys. Before that he was a police scuba diver, a solid line on a saturation-dive applicant's résumé. But even with that unique level of experience, he'd needed multiple referrals to qualify for the training.

There had been twenty-five men and women in his class. Zak was the last still with the company. That was a ninety-six percent attrition rate.

Now he was nearly in the dark, with a whole lot of water on top of him. It meant a whole lot of depth pay on top of his salary. With good reason. He knew all the risks. But he also knew the thrill of it. That, and the big bucks, kept luring him back to sea.

Two-zero-zero.

For the average person, two hundred meters translated to about six hundred fifty feet underwater. At that depth, the pressure bearing on Zak was over twenty times what it would be on the surface. At *half* that depth only one percent of the light made it down. It was like being in outer space but with poorer visibility. Space was sterile and empty. The ocean was an organic soup swirling with particulate drift. Decaying aquatic plants and animals, an endless blizzard of fish poop. With all that gunk floating around, even high-intensity lights couldn't reach very far. It played tricks with your mind. You felt lost in all that darkness.

But Zak had no room in his head for fear, uncertainty and doubt—FUD in sat-diverspeak. His ability to push all that aside was largely what made him one of the tiny percentage of people who could do what he did over the long haul.

"Systems look good from here," said a second voice in his ear. "How you feeling?"

"Nice and steady."

"Let's keep it that way."

"Check, Rawl."

Rawl. Everybody on a dive crew was called

something for short. Zak liked to joke that they all might as well be baseball players. Andrew Rawlings was his partner and the man in the diving bell. After a month in storage breathing heliox instead of normal air, they both sounded like ducks in some old cartoon. In Rawl's case, a duck with a noticeable Southern twang. His hometown was Bartlett, Tennessee, and he still lived there between gigs.

Zak continued to descend on his umbilicals. The bell—known as *Beebe* after the famed inventor of the bathyscaphe—hung from a cable about three hundred feet closer to the surface. As it had neared its working depth minutes ago, he'd exited the floor hatch, taken a short ride on the guide weight beneath it, then jumped clear and dropped toward the seabed.

Now he could no longer see its egg-shaped contours. He was descending through a pitch-black void, with only the faint, smeary glow of *Beebe*'s exterior lights above and the blue ghosts flitting around him. Bursts of luminescence emitted by various deep-sea creatures, they were like living fireworks, sparking and curling and braiding out in every direction. They had no pattern, no predictability. Without visual landmarks for reference, it was impossible to even guess their distance from him. The blue ghosts could be ten feet away or a hundred. A hundred or a thousand. They were hypnotic, beautiful and very dangerous if he let them become distractions.

He shot a quick glance down at the bottom. He had two head mounts: a high-intensity LED underwater lamp on one side of his hat, and a digital video camera on the other. Both were powered by his umbilical lines and would run without interruption throughout the dive. The digicam feed was streaming up to Rawl and the support crew on the *Stalwart*'s deck, so they could inspect the site in real time.

Below Zak, clear in the light beaming from his helmet, was the thirty-foot-wide trench *Stalwart*'s sea tractor had recently plowed into the sea bottom. The trench had yet to be backfilled by the tide, leaving its excavated center—where the cable was buried—lower than its margins.

"I'm right above the cable trench," he said. "Eyes wide open."

He wasn't expecting any problems. The site had been chosen for its geological stability. There were no underwater canyons, no slopes, no reefs or fault lines. Just mud and gravel, the terrain a flat, level expanse running off toward the Spratly Islands… China's Dangerous Ground. So named because that was where the aquatic terrain got rough.

Zak descended a little further. His augmented reality HUD said he was at exactly two hundred seventy-three meters—almost nine hundred feet. Which put him just west of the exposed cable connection and about a mile upstream from the landing station at Palawan.

After a few moments his boots touched down beside the trench. He hopped across the bottom, following its southern edge. His helmet's A/R was a more sophisticated version of the dashcam system in his car, but not much. Basically, it served the same purpose, overlaying his video input with arrows, colored lines and data readouts. It would guide him to the juncture he wanted to inspect and sound an alert once he reached it.

Zak was about ten yards along when he heard the beep. He hadn't really needed it. The *Stalwart* had installed a multiplexer here two weeks back, ahead of laying several branching lines of cable, the first of which was already buried in its own trench. He could see where it forked eastward from the splice, stringing out to its own endpoint.

He looked down at the shallow furrow defining the original cable's path toward shore.

"Odd," he said over his radio. "Everyone getting the vidstream?"

"Roger." That came from Murph. "Hang on a second. I'm going over your coordinates."

"You must be in the right place," Rawl said. "You see the cable sticking up out of the bottom."

Zak did not reply. His dive partner was right on both counts. This was the only cable nexus for miles around. And the Positioning System for Deep Ocean Navigation—POSYDON—was as dependable as terrestrial GPS. There was no doubt in his mind he was on point. But what confused him was that he didn't see anything all. At least, nothing unusual.

He waited. Maybe there was a mistake. But he didn't see how it was possible.

"Zak?" Murph again.

"I hear you."

"Your location positively checks out."

Which came as no surprise. And which also confused the hell out of him.

"I can scoop out the sediment," he said. "Inspect the cables and SDM to see if anything's funny."

"Sounds like an idea," Murph said. "Give me a minute. Fried's on his way to Control."

Fried was Bill Friedlander, the dive team's project manager on the *Stalwart*. Calling him in was SOP. Everything had to be logged and subject to approvals. They would need his green light before digging up a segment of line.

Zak waited. Blue ghosts spun and danced around him like fireflies. No one really knew why so many organisms down here emitted a glow. He'd heard they used it to confuse their prey. Or stun them. But he'd also heard that some of them used it defensively, sneezing out light trails to send stalkers off in the wrong direction. Whatever their purpose, they put on a stunning show. It was like they were all scribbling on a huge three-dimensional blackboard at the same time. With phosphorescent chalk.

Zak was watching one such manic display to his right when he noticed a separate and distinct radiance some distance off. Exactly how far off he couldn't tell. At first it looked like a small sphere of light. Not blue but white, with a diffuse halo around it.

Zak stared for a long five seconds, puzzled. The light grew in size, its corona and inner circle quickly resolving into a single disk of brightness. It appeared to be coming closer and was moving at a rapid clip.

"Does everyone see what I see?" he said.

There was no answer from above.

"Murph? Rawl? Do you two copy?"

He waited. Then waited some more, frowning behind his mask.

There was still no answer.

The dive-control van was a modular unit in the center of the four-hundred-fifty-foot *Stalwart*'s main deck. Situated near the moon pool—the well through which the diving bell was lowered into the water—it was nothing fancy on the outside. Not too big, not too small, a single door, a couple of windows. The sort of corrugated aluminum trailer where the foreman might slug down his morning joe at an ordinary construction site.

The interior of the DCV was another thing. There were two side-by-side stations, one with specialized video-monitoring and communications panels, the other with the gauges, dials and switches used to regulate the life-sustaining gas mixture inhaled by the underwater team. A third console, on a separate wall, controlled the scrubbing and filtering of gases *exhaled* by the divers, removing carbon dioxide, moisture and biological contaminants, then mixing the leftover oxygen with helium for recycling to the bell. The Gasmizer made for an efficient, closed system that ensured the supply of heliox would be without interruption.

All three technicians in the van were dead. Grigor Malkira had shot the men at the side-by-side stations as he entered, using a single subsonic bullet for each. They never knew what hit them. The third tech, seated with her back to the door at the Gasmizer console, lived long enough to register his presence, swiveling toward the door. Grigor put one round in her heart and one in the middle of her forehead. She had sprawled backward over the console, her blond hair spilling over its controls and readouts in a bloody fan.

Now Grigor stood behind the dead man at the dive-control station, holding his sound-suppressed FN Five-seveN against his thigh. Eight seconds ago, he had cut all communications between the surface and the bell and between the bell and diver. His next matter of business was at the saturation-control station beside it.

It proved fortunate that the window was between them. Grigor was sidling past it when he glimpsed a man outside on deck, approaching the DCV in the shadow of the crane. He immediately recognized him as Friedman, the project manager.

The van was close quarters, but Grigor moved with fluid, unconstrained ease. He was unusually tall and thin, his limbs disproportionately long, giving him an odd, stretched-out appearance—

like he was made of soft putty or taffy instead of meat and bones. As a boy at the Russian *detdom*, the other orphans had joked that if he stood sideways, he disappeared.

He returned to the door, two quick steps, flattening his back against the wall alongside it.

A moment later Friedman reached the van. Grigor waited for him to swipe his finger under the biolock scanner, listened for the click of the dead bolt and brought the Five-seveN up in his clenched fingers.

He was stronger than his rubbery appearance suggested. As the door swung open and the project manager stepped inside, he grabbed the man's arm above the elbow and flung him toward the Gasmizer station. Friedman stumbled toward the dead woman but managed to catch his balance before crashing into her body.

He spun around toward Grigor.

"Gelfland?" he blurted. His expression was quizzical.

Grigor used up two more bullets, and the project manager crumpled lifelessly to the floor, his forehead a red smear. Then he kicked the door shut behind him and mouthed a simple order in Southwestern Mandarin. The mild Sha County inflection was a brushstroke that would have delighted his Pinnacle instructors. Old Anna in particular.

"Ji. Kin leh."

"Si."

He slid over to the sat-control station, shoved

the man slumped over the console to the floor and took his seat, holstering the pistol under his windbreaker. He'd familiarized himself with its gas distribution panel over the past few months and was able to reset its critical life-support values in seconds.

Grigor was looking over the gauges when he heard the rat-a-tat of automatic gunfire outside the van. There were multiple bursts, then a pause. Then more short bursts.

He glanced at his watch. Ten minutes to go.

He rose from the chair, stepped over and around the bodies on the floor and went out onto the deck, turning quickly toward the helm of the massive ship.

Zak knew he was in serious trouble.

There should have been an alert. It was supposed to be automatic. A series of urgent beeps in his earpiece, simultaneous warning messages on the HUD. But it didn't happen. The cascade of system failures was so rapid it felt like everything shut down at once. He was suddenly cut off from his life support, the bell and the dive-control crew.

Zak opened the valve for the bailout tank on his back. The cylinder's emergency supply of heliox would buy him four minutes, maybe a couple more if he regulated his breaths. That wasn't enough to get him to the surface. He would need a slow ascent to prevent his internal body tissues from exploding. Hours, not minutes, of decompression.

But if they were aware of the situation topside—and they had to be—they would be working like hell to restore the connections to him. The same for Rawls. And there were built-in fail-safes in case of critical system malfunction.

Zak urged himself not to panic. They weren't going to let him die down here. Not if they could help it.

He breathed. Almost sipping from the bailout tank. Wanting to conserve the precious gas mixture.

Then the light shone in his eyes. That circle of light in the darkness. It was coming on fast, about ten feet above the seabed, slightly above him.

The light fanned out. The detritus in the water refracting and dispersing and attenuating it. Zak stood there, baffled. Then saw the craft take shape underneath it.

He realized it was some kind of deep submersible. A bubble capsule in front under the light, a large arm on either side of the capsule. There was something vaguely crab-like about it.

It slowed, drew closer still, then stopped. Hanging there above him, its lamp shining through the black.

Zak's mind raced along three parallel tracks. He was acutely aware his bailout canister was emptying with each breath. Aware he'd heard nothing from Rawl or the control van. And he was aware of a human form looking out through the bubble.

Blurred. Barely visible. But there.

Watching him.

He was mystified and afraid. Those were alien feelings on a dive.

"Rawls? Murph? Do you copy?"

Silence. The submersible hovered motionless for another long second. Then a sudden burst from its thrusters sent it flying forward.

At first Zak thought it would shoot past him. But it didn't. It stopped again. This time directly overhead, its metal grapplers snatching at his umbilicals. He felt a hard tug as they clamped shut over the lines, sinking into them, clipping them like giant wire cutters.

The second tug was even harder. It lifted him with a jerk, hoisted him upward. And then his feet were no longer anchored on the seabed. The submersible was carrying him away, dragging him through the pitch-black water like it was a hungry predator and he was its helpless prey.

He hung below it. He couldn't see anything. He was cold. Terribly cold.

Zak was swept through the water for what felt longer than it must have been. Dangling from the severed lines, he struggled desperately to breathe as the submersible carried him along. His heliox was running out. There was a pressure gaining behind his eyes, in his head, his chest. Like they were all bursting from within.

He felt his consciousness departing in a muddled rush and tried to hold on to it. But he couldn't. It was slipping away from him. He was no longer able to think, no longer struggling to fill his lungs, no longer feeling much of anything. There was only the cold and an increasingly vague sense of movement.

Soon Zak's awareness let go of them too, and he belonged entirely to the darkness.

Grigor strode from the elevator onto the bridge and almost tripped over a dead body. He paused and lowered his eyes to it. The crewman was sprawled in his own blood, his white uniform shirt stained the color of the red puddle around him.

"Women yijing guding hao jiash shi, Zhe chuan shi women de."

Grigor glanced up at the man who'd spoken to him. Tall, bearded and muscular with thick Mongolian features, Jochi stood on the opposite side of the leaking corpse, wearing the tan shirt and reflective yellow vest of a ship's engineer. In his hand was a compact Brügger and Thomet TP9 submachine pistol, suppressed with a thirty-round magazine.

"Nin shifou yi yu chedui qude lianxi?" Grigor answered in the same coastal Mandarin he'd finessed earlier.

Jochi motioned toward the wide curve of windows around them. Outside, the ocean rippled blue and reflective in the midday sun.

"Shi," he said. *"Tamen zai lushang."*

Grigor nodded his satisfaction. The fleet was on its way.

He looked about the room. There were nine others in it besides himself, Jochi, and the dead man lying faceup between them on the floor. Four belonged to the bridge crew, and they were lifeless and bloody in their rotating chairs. Another dead man was slumped against the wall under a window, his shirt dotted with bullet holes. A fifth, the *Stalwart*'s captain, was at the command station. His throat had been cut. The gash looked like a grotesque lipstick smile.

The rest, four men in total, were alive. It was no fluke that they were members of Jochi's strike team. All carried weapons identical to his TP9. One had taken the helm.

Grigor immediately strode up behind him. The dimensions of the bridge were expansive, and the *U*-shaped operations console occupied most of it. He saw rows of radar, sonar and navigational touch screens, joystick controls and panels with clusters of lighted indicators and industrial buttons.

He studied the navigation displays over his helmsman's shoulder. The main screen showed the *Stalwart* in stationary position off Palawan. But that was a fake. A chimera. A second nav screen gave a different picture—and the real one. The ship had already left the vicinity of the Philippine archipelago and was bearing toward the Spratly Islands at its top speed of fifteen knots.

Grigor trusted the Wolf's location-spoofing software would be masked from the most sophisticated counteranalysis. What he'd seen of his work in New York had easily cemented his reputation as dark prince of the *technologie vampiri*.

But he would have felt confident regardless. The average car had over a hundred fifty million lines of software code. How many powered the ship? Trillions? A few malignant lines slithering into its system would be hell to detect.

The digital conning binoculars on the console were Wi-Fi-tethered to the ship's nav system. Grigor lifted them to his eyes. As the fleet appeared in the lenses, they noted its exact coordinates and measured the distance. It was less than ten miles to the southwest.

He counted ten unmarked boats...eighty-foot trawlers with high bows and stern wheelhouses. The sort of aging rust buckets that were mother ships for poachers of sea cucumbers and reef clams.

Grigor nodded to himself, lowered the binoculars. He saw that Jochi had come up to the console and handed them over to him.

The bearded man peered through them across the miles of glittering sea. *"Tamen you henduo caihu,"* he said. "They have many talents."

Grigor gave a thin smile.

"Zongguo nan ti," he said.

Jochi nodded his understanding. It was truly and literally a Chinese puzzle.

The submersible returned to the trawler's launch bay with the diver still dangling from his umbilicals. His body was a gruesome sight.

When a person died and circulation ceased, the gases in the cells and blood vessels became static and formed thousands of tiny bubbles. When a person who died during a saturation dive surfaced too fast—without proper decompression time— the pressurized bubbles grew in size until they became very large.

The result was like shaking a can of carbonated beverage and then popping the tab. But with a human body instead of a can, and blood and fluid instead of soda.

The three deckhands who removed it from the grappler's clasp wore their biohazard suits gladly.

As they removed the diver's suit on a plastic tarpaulin, they would have unanimously agreed the most disturbing sight wasn't the blood foaming from his pores and orifices, it was the eyes. They had ruptured in their sockets and then liquefied to the consistency of custard, which caused one of the men to vomit on the spot, inside his hood.

Undressed and wrapped in the tarp, the body would be carried off for cremation. But the trio would still need to sanitize his helmet and wet suit before passing them along for analysis.

The technicians had it easy, they grumbled. In all accomplishments they took full credit, leaving it for others to clean up their ugly messes.

2

Mother Nature was responsible for the weather. The theatrics were Carol Morse's.

As director of operations for the fledgling US Department of Internet Security and Law Enforcement—Net Force—Morse was intent on marking her territory. She knew her probe would irritate the CIA and likewise chafe its old-guard intelligence agency partners. With the world's largest e-commerce site also party to the deal, a major dustup was clearly over the horizon.

Especially if things were even half as wrong as she feared.

She had sent her team to CloudCable's Portsmouth, New Hampshire, headquarters in *Dragonfly*, a sleek, long-winged hovercraft that looked like it could have been a scout craft for intergalactic invaders. She had also dispatched a mobile cyberlab from the Bedford field office, a half hour's drive from Portsmouth Harbor.

Call it overkill, but Morse was adept at shaping perceptions. She wanted a splashy entrance, and she meant to leave behind a big, bold organizational footprint.

Except it didn't entirely turn out that way.

Mother Nature.

Normally, *Dragonfly* would have drawn all eyes skyward on its approach. But here on the coast right now, those eyes were indoors with their owners. Blame the once-in-a-century storm that had raged through northern New England the night before, flattening trees and utility poles from Massachusetts to the Canadian border. With large chunks of the grid out and a stay-at-home order in effect throughout the state, the only people out were emergency repair workers…and they were much too busy to look up.

It was a different story in *Dragonfly*'s passenger cabin, where Amenjot Musil, Net Force Investigations, sat at his window looking down at the ground. The aerial hop from Manhattan's West Side took about an hour. He had spent the first thirty-five minutes of that hour staring at his tablet and reviewing what was known of the cable-layer CS *Stalwart*'s disappearance.

Given how little that was, Musil could have been done in five minutes. But he was a thorough man. Moreover, his companion on the flight seemed in no mood for friendly chitchat. Assuming it was just a mood, which by definition was transitory. It might be her usual disposition. Musil could not know, since he had only met her before boarding the aircraft.

Whatever the reason, Kali Alcazar wasn't at all talkative. Not to Musil. Certainly not today. In fact, she had seated herself on the opposite side of the aisle from him, even though they were the only two in the cabin. Which had left him with nothing to do besides puzzle over the missing ship.

Until a few minutes ago when he'd looked out his window.

The devastation below had filled him with simultaneous awe and sadness. There was wreckage everywhere on the water's surface. Musil saw damaged and capsized boats, entire wharves that had broken free of their fastenings, all kinds of floating debris. He had assumed some of that newly created driftwood came from homes and businesses and found it incredible to think this area had dodged the worst of the storm. What must it have been like farther north in the areas that took its brunt?

"Seat belts on, back there," said Lucas the pilot over his intercom. "We're landing in five."

Musil buckled up and glanced across the aisle, where Kali sat quietly aloof in a flowing black trench coat with a large, deep hood raised over her head. Or was it a cowl? Whichever, her look and manner made him think of a wandering sorcerer—an association many people would consider fitting. Her software coding *was* almost magical. And it wasn't necessarily white magic, if her reputation was to be believed. In fact, Interpol blamed her for one or another notorious hack on all four continents. Also, Colonel John Howard at the Force's military outpost in Romania. Though, he had merely voiced his suspicions. Or so the organizational chatter went.

Musil himself bowed to the wisdom of the sages. *I am not good; no one is bad.* Judging others was a waste of one's time on earth, and he chose to ignore the gossip. He would keep an open mind about Kali. Whether or not she ever decided to speak to him. Or in his presence.

He felt his stomach lurch as the air taxi began its descent. It had crossed the harbor after its approach over the Gulf of Maine, banked left over an old-fashioned arch bridge and then turned inland.

CloudCable's corporate and manufacturing headquarters looked like any other industrial park—security fences, flat, gray concrete buildings, a blacktop employee parking area divided by narrow greenbelts. The helipad at one end of the parking lot didn't quite fit the ordinariness of its appearance. But it also wasn't extravagant for a company of its size, with major government and corporate contracts.

Musil observed a lot of people in hard hats milling about a dock outside the complex. Some were on forklifts and wheeled yellow cranes. Most were gathered around a kind of tunnel—it resembled an airport Jetway—that ran from the facility to the waterfront. All the workers looked busy. Large panels of metal had been torn or partially detached from the sides of the tunnel. Storm damage, probably. A curved rail track that emerged from the tunnel mouth near the waterfront seemed to have withstood the high winds. Either that or it was already put back together. The storm had barreled quickly through the area, allowing the crews to get an early jump.

Dragonfly angled away from the dock and overflew a low rectangular building on the west side of the facility. About a dozen vehicles were nosed up to it, among them a long white van with the Net Force emblem on its sliding panels. The mobile digital forensics team from Bedford.

Above the helipad now, the air taxi's rotors went vertical, and its wheels deployed with a slight bump. Moments later it made a smooth landing on the rubber.

Musil unbuckled and shrugged out of his harness. Kali did the same. Then Lucas appeared from the forward cabin.

"We're here," he said.

"We want to oblige your request," Jack Olsen said from behind his desk. He was CloudCable New Hampshire's managing director. "I just need to ask that you present the appropriate warrants."

Musil sat across the desk, looking at him. Olsen was a fit, clean-shaven man in his fifties with wire-framed glasses and horseshoe male-pattern baldness. His hair was cropped short on the sides to make his bare pate less conspicuous to the eye.

Musil admired the artful camouflage. Fortunately, he had no personal experience with that particular litmus of male vanity, owing to the thick, uncut black mane of hair piled under his *dastār*, the traditional peaked head wrap of Sikh religion. Whatever potential his genes denied him in height—he stood five foot six in shoes—seemed to have been channeled into his follicles.

But hair was not the issue here. His or Olsen's. The issue was Mr. Olsen's surprising uncooperativeness at a juncture when he should have welcomed help with open arms.

Musil wasn't sure what to make of it.

He sat looking thoughtful, Kali in a chair to one side of him. The room was warmer than *Dragonfly*'s rear cabin, and she had lowered her hood—or cowl—to reveal her own jet-black hair, which was short with scarlet streaks. Standing behind them near the door was a young forensic technician from the van named Jase Hudson, his hands clasped in front of him.

"Mr. Olsen, your ship is missing," Musil said after a moment. "We're trying to learn what happened to it."

Olsen's gaze suddenly moved away from him. The office was modern minimalist in its layout and design: clean lines, white walls, soft lights, wide windows, a spacious white filing credenza the only furnishing besides the desk and chairs. Atop the credenza was a big cutaway replica of a cable-laying ship. Also on it was an enlarged cross-section of an undersea fiber-optic cable segment. Beside that in a transparent display cube were what looked like several authentic lengths of cable or cable connectors. Otherwise, the room was free of decoration.

Musil realized Olsen was staring at the model ship. It didn't seem a conscious look. His eyes had just gone there and lingered. After a moment he seemed to catch himself.

"I know most of the people on board," he said, shifting his focus back to Musil. "The officers and crew. The divers. Seventy-seven men and women. Finding out what happened to them isn't just a company priority. For me it's personal."

"Then, respectfully, what is the problem?"

"I don't understand."

"You knew my team would be coming today."

"Yes."

"You said you would cooperate with our investigation."

"Yes, certainly."

"So what changed?"

Olsen shook his head.

"Nothing at our end," he said. "Possibly we had different expectations for this visit. My sense was it would be introductory. CloudCable does not give outside parties access to our servers without a court order. The same applies to data about specific individuals. It's strict policy."

Musil considered that a moment, then gestured toward the model ship.

"Sir," he said, "is that the *Stalwart*?"

Olsen nodded. "A perfect reproduction. Given to us by its designers when it left the yard."

"It's an impressive vessel."

"We're very proud of it," Olsen said. "The *Stalwart* was built to spec. It carries nearly five thousand miles of cable when fully loaded. That's almost four *thousand* metric tons. It can deploy a deep diving bell with a crew of four, an unmanned submersible and what's known as a sea tractor to lay the cable. All three are reproduced on the model, if you want to take a look." He paused. "Everything on the ship is state of the art."

"Then, how can it have simply disappeared?" Musil asked. "If there was an emergency, wouldn't someone call for help? Send out a message? I would think there would be automatic distress signals. GPS-locating systems for the ship."

Olsen looked at him. "All true, Agent," he said. "We've wondered the same things."

"And you have no answers?"

"I wish we did."

"Then, why not let us do our work?"

Olsen took a breath.

"Our industry is highly regulated," he said. "You're asking us to open up documents, emails, connection logs and potentially personal employee information. There are confidentiality issues. Potential liabilities. We have financial obligations to our corporate partners."

Musil was quiet a long moment. He was thinking Olsen seemed evasive rather than untruthful. Which sometimes came bundled together, but not always.

The CS *Stalwart* had been laying cable for a multibillion-dollar, hybrid government–civilian project. A trans-Pacific cable and cloud-computing system financed by the CIA, NSA, National Geospatial-Intelligence Agency and, last but not least, Olympia.com, the world's largest online e-commerce, cloud-service and media-streaming enterprise. The deal had been in the news for months, as had the opposition to it—led by Net Force's director-in-chief, Alex Michaels—on grounds of national security.

Musil tried to put himself in Olsen's shoes. The contract was likely key to CloudCable's future. And here in his office this morning were members of the agency whose cyber director was its most outspoken critic. As a top company executive, he was in an unenviable spot.

The agent decided to change tacks. "Sir, understanding your position, can you confirm the *Stalwart*'s whereabouts when it disappeared?"

"Generally, yes," Olsen said. "We're establishing a direct undersea fiber link between our country's West Coast cities, the Philippines, Taiwan and Japan. I'm not able to provide the exact location of the lines. That, again, is confidential absent a warrant. But it's no secret that *Stalwart* has spent months operating in the South China Sea."

"In what Beijing insists are its sovereign waters."

"The Chinese have made that claim for decades. No one takes it seriously." Olsen shrugged. "I doubt they believe it themselves. They've blustered at times but never acted on it."

Musil looked at him. "Are you at all concerned they might have this time?"

He was silent. Musil waited.

"I don't keep my head in the sand," Olsen said after a moment. "I've thought of it. I've also frankly thought about piracy. Or an accident at sea. Different scenarios. Right now we only have questions. CloudCable has put all its internal resources into finding answers."

"Then, let us help."

"We would welcome that…but, again, the paperwork has to come first," Olsen said. "Look, Agent, I'm sorry for the pushback. Bottom line, secure communications are our company's stock-in-trade. If we didn't follow strict procedures, we'd be buried in lawsuits. And eventually put out of business."

Musil smoothed his beard. He'd tried. But as the proverb went, there were worlds and more worlds below them, and a hundred thousand skies over them. His current approach had led nowhere, and he would have to change it. For now, that required a tactical retreat.

He took a business card out of his wallet.

"All right, Mr. Olsen," he said, and handed him the card. "We'll be in touch."

He got up to leave. Kali stayed seated, looking across the desk at Olsen.

"Did you speak about this to anyone else?" she asked.

He hesitated. "Such as?"

"The CIA," she said. "The other agencies. Did you speak to any of them before we came this morning?"

Olsen hesitated another moment.

"They're our partners. That's all I'm at liberty to say."

Kali finally rose from her chair, her eyes still on his face.

"Thank you," she said.

Olsen got up, stepped to the door and opened it. Kali went out first, then Musil, followed by Hudson. Olsen nodded and smiled but didn't say another word. They turned down the hall toward the building entrance, the office door closing behind them with a soft click.

The techs headed back to FBI Portsmouth in their van, a straight ten- or twelve-minute drive south. But *Dragonfly* would have a much longer trip down to New York, and Musil had anticipated more than corporate stonewalling from Cloud-Cable. It left him disappointed.

He walked across the blacktop with Kali. She

had spoken perhaps a dozen words all morning, none to him. But it did not escape him that they might be the most significant words of their meeting with Olsen. Aside from Olsen's response.

The tilt-rotor's side panels were wide open, its propellers vertical to the ground but not yet spinning. Musil saw Lucas waiting on the rubber outside.

"News flash, Jot," he said as the agent approached. "There's a last-minute detour."

"What do you mean?"

"We need to head up to Maine," the pilot explained. "*Way* up. A place called Chacagua Island. Couple of our wireheads got caught in the storm last night."

"Do you know who they are?"

"One's Natasha Mori. The other is Bryan…not sure I caught his second name…"

"Ferago?"

"That's it."

Musil looked puzzled. "What were they doing here?"

"No clue." Lucas spread his hands. "They say Mori's OK, but Ferago needs some medical attention."

Musil knew them a little. Especially Bryan, who had interned with FBI Cyber in the old days. A nice young man, very intelligent. Musil had thought him merely introverted before finding out he was on the autism spectrum. Both he and Natasha had been grad school students at Director Michaels's Columbia University cyber lab and were presently instructors at Net Force boot camp.

"How long a flight is it to the island?" he asked.

"Half hour on the hop," Lucas said. "We need to add a little time for a stop at the Coast Guard station in Boothbay Harbor. They have a new hospital facility and vertiport, and I want to pick up a paramedic. It'd also be a good place to get a refuel/recharge for *Dragonfly*. Though, if we're dropping Ferago off there, I might wait till the return trip."

Musil nodded.

"We should get going," he said.

Kali was already climbing up into the cabin. He hurried to enter behind her and strapped in. Then Lucas started the engine, and they were up in the air.

Olsen waited two or three minutes before following the small group out of his office, then stood in the glass lobby as they crossed the parking lot toward the vertiport. He watched until their little air taxi took flight, shooting skyward straight as a string.

As it zipped off toward the north he went over to the entrance and pushed through into the sunshine.

It was a beautiful spring day, New England weather at its finest. The storm had sucked all the moisture out of the air as it spun past, and it was mild and dry out with a calm, fresh breeze. He strode from the building, his shoe bottoms crackling down on scattered twigs and branches that had been swept across the concrete walkway by last night's winds.

Olsen stood in the mild breeze, smelling the nearby water. Gulls were gliding over the harbor just north of the office complex. The air taxi was gone.

He stood there in silent reflection for a long five minutes. He thought about those people on the *Stalwart*, wondering how their loved ones would feel if they learned the truth. Then he thought about the consequences for him.

Sometimes, he thought, it was too late for the truth. Sometimes secrets needed to stay secret. At any cost.

Olsen suddenly felt his heartbeat become hard and rapid. He closed his eyes and stood with the warm sun on his face, trying to settle himself down. But it didn't work. His heart wouldn't stop racing.

Finally, he gave up, reached into his pocket for his global smartphone, and made the call overseas.

3

It was ten at night in Beijing and therefore ten in the morning in Washington, DC, where President Annemarie Fucillo was thinking that, in one major regard, she would have preferred to switch time zones with China's leader for their telecon. The famously insomniac Fucillo was at her peak of alertness after dark and knew she would have to be razor-sharp dealing with him. So minus other considerations, she would rather he had taken the morning slot.

But she had prioritized strategic positioning, political gamesmanship or whatever else one chose to call it. In the protracted negotiations leading up to their scheduled conversation, President for Life Tsao He Feng had strongly conveyed his desire for the morning. Fucillo had therefore insisted on the opposite despite her own preference for the night. She had known her fellow Harvard alumnus for years, and he was as spoiled, egotistical and chauvinistic as Chinese leaders could be. Allowing him to be chronologically ahead of her—when his Zhongnanhai executive complex was aggressively revved for its daily business, and her West Wing was quiet and dormant—would translate into a sense of dominance for him.

No go. Fucillo intended to be in the driver's seat. Her preference be damned.

Now she sat in the Oval Office with her tablet in front of her on the Resolute desk, Celia the First Coon Cat warming in a splash of sunlight in the middle of the rug and her three top foreign policy experts in their customary seats around the room. These included Secretary of State Tanner Woodbridge on the sofa, National Security Advisor Josh Urias in the leather armchair to Fucillo's right, and the NSC's Indo-Pacific Affairs Coordinator Yen Lee Greenberg parked at a wing table to the left of the fireplace. All had phones and headsets. As usual, Greenberg's laptop was on the table so she could take personal notes. The rough memcon—or memorandum of telephone conversation in unabbreviated English—would be written by professional notetakers down in the Situation Room, then combined with a transcript generated by the White House computer servers for a single document exclusively available to CIA Intelligence and the director of national intelligence. Also in Sit was the communications staffer who had made the actual phone connection, for a grand total of thirteen officials and White House aides placing or listening in on the call.

"Madam President," Urias said, "we expect PPRC Tsao on the phone in three minutes."

Fucillo gave him a vague nod while looking down at her tablet. She was reading over the talking points that Greenberg had drafted as part of her call package and that she'd already discussed with everyone in the room in a caffeine-fueled six o'clock prebrief. Besides being known for her all-night work marathons, Fucillo was legendarily big on prep.

The goals of the call were clear and fundamental. The US chartered CS *Stalwart* had vanished in the South China Sea along with its crew of seventy-seven. In calm weather. Near reefs and islands over which the Chinese were asserting territorial claims beyond any sane or reasonable limits. With satellite data indicating the waters had teemed with Little Blue Men, a maritime militia that Tsao refused to admit was anything more than a civilian fishing fleet.

It wasn't just baffling. It was suspicious in the extreme. Tsao had claimed to know nothing about what happened to the *Stalwart* through diplomatic channels, and maybe he didn't. Fucillo was not one to jump to conclusions. But she wanted to put him on notice that she expected his government's cooperation and had no threshold for its typical secretive bullshit when it came to American lives.

"Thirty seconds," Urias said.

Fucillo nodded. She lifted her coffee cup to her mouth, sipped, lowered it back onto the saucer and grabbed the phone.

SECRET/ORCON/NOFORN

EYES ONLY

DO NOT COPY

OFFICIAL MEMORANDUM OF TELEPHONE CONVERSATION

SUBJECT: Telephone Conversation with President Tsao He Feng of People's Republic of China

PARTICIPANTS: President Annemarie Fucillo of USA, President Tsao of PRC

Notetakers (Situation Room): Shawn Heyward, Carmen Seager, Andrew DeVito

DATE, TIME: April 15, 2024, 10:07—10:27 a.m. EDT

PLACE: White House Oval Office

"Hello, President Tsao. I hope you're well. And I appreciate your scheduling this conversation on short notice. As you can imagine, I'm deeply concerned about the cable-laying vessel that went missing near the Spratly Islands."

"I certainly understand, Madam President. On

behalf of the Chinese people, I want to extend our sincere best wishes for those aboard the ship."

"That's very kind of you. Learning what happened is my focus right now."

"Of course. And I am confident your country will have answers."

"Hopefully. Though, I do have to say some troubling reports have reached my desk."

"Oh? How so?"

"If I may be direct, they relate directly to the presence and activities of your maritime militia in the vicinity of the *Stalwart*'s last known position."

"Madam, my government has emphatically stated that there is no such entity."

"I'm aware of that. But we have information that over two hundred of your distant-water fishing boats were observed massing around Yongshu Jiau—we call it Fiery Cross Reef—prior to *Stalwart*'s falling out of communication. That seems a large number, wouldn't you say?"

"Only taken out of context. Some fishing boats have sheltered near the reef due to maritime wind conditions. This is typical. I would again emphasize a patient and rational examination of the facts."

"Agreed. But I won't mince words. Those vessels were moored in the area for over three weeks. That's a great deal longer than ordinary fishing boats generally stay in one spot. Particularly when there's excellent fishing somewhere else."

"I know nothing about that. But I can look into it."

"Thank you, Mr. President. There are also reliable

findings that these boats have reinforced hulls and top speeds of eighteen to twenty-two knots. Which far exceeds the speed of an average trawler. Finally, I've heard reports about men with automatic weapons aboard them."

"In waters infested with pirates, our civilian fishers are wise to arm themselves. I should, moreover, remind you these are designated Chinese territorial waters. We have the right to dictate the rules of safe passage."

"That claim is disputed by most of your international neighbors. But to reiterate, my pressing concern is the *Stalwart*."

"Madam, I'm sure you don't mean to imply that my country is involved with the loss of your ship."

"*Possible* loss. We're optimistic about a positive outcome."

"As are we. Naturally."

"And to your point, we're just trying to figure things out. So I would ask that you share whatever information you might receive about the *Stalwart*. It would be a step in advancing accountability and transparency between our countries."

"Of course."

"Then, you'll keep us updated?"

"We will do our best."

"Thank you."

"And Madam?"

"Yes?"

"One final word. If I may. On the subject of transparency."

"Certainly."

"I would caution your nation about exploiting undersea cable networks in latitude fifteen-five, longitude one-hundred-fourteen-five for future intelligence operations."

"Excuse me?"

"I think you understand. But let me plainly summarize. My government has no knowledge of any actions against your cable ship. There is no Chinese naval militia. We have sufficient maritime assets without using fishing boats as projections of our national security. However, we see this as a humanitarian situation and will try to be helpful."

"Whatever you can do, Mr. President. And thank you. I know it's late in Beijing and expect you're getting ready for bed."

"In fact, I rarely sleep. Matters of state occupy me day and night."

"Well, then, OK. I won't keep you. We'll be in touch."

"Goodbye."

President Fucillo looked directly at the secretary of state through her new progressive lenses. They enabled her to see him across the room without fumbling off her reading glasses. Peachy. They had also inspired a popular, loudmouthed television opinionator to take some obvious and predictable jabs at her. *The president's always been a closet progressive. Now she wears it on her face.*

Not so peachy. Fucillo didn't give half a damn

about his idiotic grade-school punditry. Call her what you wanted, she did not view herself as a political ideologue but a hard-core, dead-center pragmatist. Labels annoyed her because they made it harder to put across her ideas to the American people.

Still, she could live with it. As long as she got things done.

"What was Tsao talking about?" she asked Woodbridge.

He leaned forward to scratch behind Celia's ear. "Beats the fuck out of me," he said. "I guess nobody ever told the son of a bitch not to kick a fresh cow turd on a hot day. You gave him three chances—or was it four?—to outright spit on the idea that his boats are mixed up with whatever's going on with the *Stalwart*. He didn't take a single one of them."

She shook her head. "That isn't what I meant. You heard his remark about the underwater cable networks."

"It's the usual crap. His people have been playing that tune so long I can hum it in my sleep. A legacy claim to over a million square miles of sea and every rock sticking out of it. Going back thousands of years to the Western Han dynasty. And then there's the stale, old chorus about us spying on them. I'd dismiss it."

"No. I've known Tsao since I was with State and he was minister of foreign affairs. He's measured. Precise. He doesn't escalate on reflex."

Woodbridge shook his head. "I didn't hear escalation in his comment. Not to say he knows anything. And not to say he doesn't. But I took it as a defensive swing. Just in case."

"In case of what?"

"He finds something out internally that could be problematic to him. You give those crazy fishermen guns and set them loose to patrol a million-mile tub, things can get out of control pretty fast."

"I'm with Tan," Greenberg said. "The Olympia–CIA deal's been publicly discussed and dissected. One of your own cabinet members has been hammering it on his podcast since last year. *Stalwart* was out there laying cable. It wasn't conducting espionage operations. And Tsao knows it. This is all open-source information for God's sake."

Fucillo was silent. The cabinet member Yen had spoken about was Alex Michaels, the director of Net Force, and she was thinking she needed to meet with him. Probably with her CIA chief too…but Alex first.

"OK, everyone. More to come," she said. "It's been good to see your sunny faces. Let's get on with what promises to be a long day."

Woodbridge smiled pleasantly. Fucillo noticed Celia had gotten her way with him. She had that knack.

"All rise!" he said, lifting her gently off his lap.

Tsao He Feng's executive residence at the Zhongnanhai enclave was a restored Qing dynasty palace west of the Forbidden City. Through the open parlor window to his right, he could see lights from Precious Moon Tower above the South Gate illuminate the stream that wound through nine gradual turns in the ancient palace grounds, eventually feeding the great man-made lake at their center.

Tsao had taken President Fucillo's call alone in the room. The single transcriber was his trusted nephew Kim, his sister's eldest son, who had listened in and made his handwritten notes from a secure white room two floors below. Kim had also enabled the phone connection. There was no other record of the conversation between the two leaders. At a time when leaks and computer intrusions could undermine all government secrets and objectives—even the presidency itself—Tsao was intent on keeping tight control of what happened around him.

After hanging up the phone, he sat in thoughtful silence for several minutes, massaging his smooth, heavy cheeks with one hand. It was a pleasant spring night, and the breeze carried the scent of flowers and soil through his window.

He lifted the receiver and dialed. The minister picked up immediately.

"Have you any news from Fiery Cross?" Tsao said.

"Not yet. General Wei's flight is slightly behind schedule."

"I should have the rogue on that island executed," he said. "I don't know why I've held back."

"He claims to have a gift horse."

"We'll see. And even if so, it's a horse that's liable to trample us."

"Or kick the Americans in their ribs for their attempted espionage."

Tsao said nothing for a long moment. Then he grunted into the receiver.

"Alert me when the plane lands," he said. "Whatever the hour."

"Yes. You'll know."

Tsao kneaded his cheeks again. He could hear the stream of nine slow turns trilling like musical chimes over its rocky bed. The sound did not relax him tonight.

"I'll be waiting," he said, and hung up the phone.

4

The Terminal, New York City

Carmody dove headfirst from the overhang like a falcon, plunging hundreds of feet straight down into the ravine. Its stone walls were sheer and vertical, the narrow Black Sea inlet below winding between them in slow, snaking curves. Then the lock branching off into the cliff wall, a tunnel cutting deep into the mountain slope.

He hovered above the inlet. He could not see its western bank. He could not see the tunnel entrance. That side of the channel was washed out and distorted, like a smeared watercolor painting. It disoriented him.

After a moment Carmody shot back upward,

soaring high toward the top of the cliff, then higher, until he was above the distorted area and gliding over the escarpment. The sirocco was hot and dusty but not yet strong, and he could scan the rugged landscape for miles around. He saw the two ancient towers guarding the inlet's mouth. He saw the railway line coiling around from the far side of the mountain. But the west bank of the inlet remained an unnatural blur stretching as far as he could see to the left and right, and for a hundred feet up from the mountain's base.

He'd had enough. For now, anyway.

Carmody snapped off his V/R headset and was at a desk in an air-conditioned office. He was sweaty, out of sorts and a little nauseous, his brain and body adjusting to real physical space.

He grabbed a bottle of water on the desk and drank. Then he crushed it in his big hand, dropping it into the trash under his borrowed desk.

He had a meeting with Carol Morse in ten minutes.

Morse's office was on the eighth and uppermost floor of the Terminal, a converted nineteenth-century warehouse that stood like a brick-and-mortar fortress in New York's Hell's Kitchen.

She was at her desk facing the door when Carmody entered. A slender, blonde woman in her midforties, she wore a charcoal blazer, white blouse and platinum necklace with a small blue sapphire pendant. From his side of the desk, Carmody couldn't tell if she had matched a skirt or slacks with the blazer. Whichever, he knew she would look snazzy, put-together and situationally appropriate. Morse was never anything less than fully poised.

"Mike," she said. "Please, come in."

Carmody pulled up a chair, sat opposite her and waited. All in a second or two, he noticed the Hudson River through the high casement window behind her, and the digital-photo frame on her desk with her kids and dogs in the randomly looping pictures. He did not see any shots of her husband, but maybe they would come up. Or not. Carmody didn't frequent the water cooler. He didn't listen to rumors. Her personal business was none of his. But he did have eyes and ears and got the sense there were problems over her move from Virginia to New York.

"Coffee?"

Morse gestured at the machine with the cup in her hand. She took hers black, no sugar.

"No, thanks," he said. "I've hit my new morning max."

"How many cups?"

"Three."

"That's a lot."

"It's down from five. But I'm inching up on my cigarettes."

"Balance."

"The secret of a healthy mind and body."

She lifted her coffee cup to her lips. The sapphire hanging from her neck was a half shade darker than her eyes.

"Don't mind me," she said and sipped. "I indulge as I see fit."

Carmody watched her and said, "When you called me in, I was running a HIVE scenario."

Morse nodded. HIVE was short for Highly Integrated Virtual Environment, a kind of online training ground with an infinite number of settings that authorized users could access from anywhere in the world.

"Crimea," she said.

"How did you guess?"

"There's no morning max on how often you can run the scenario," she said. "So I assumed you were running it."

Carmody nodded. "Our man's been hunkered down there for five months."

"I know."

"He could be cooking up anything."

"I know."

"We can't wait forever to move."

"Agreed."

"So?"

"We need more information."

"I got plenty from his lapdog, Gustav Zolcu."

"Yes," she said. "But it isn't enough."

Carmody looked at her. The Wolf was the most dangerous hacker in the world. He had accomplished knocking Manhattan off the power grid, killing hundreds and almost taking out the president. All on his own string, as far as anyone knew. But according to Zolcu, he had since become even more of a threat.

"Drajan Petrovik has Russian sponsors now. He's a state actor. Bad news for the human race."

"You're convinced we can believe Zolcu?"

Carmody nodded, slowly. "He's too scared of me to even think of lying. Besides, his boss wouldn't leave home for some secret Crimean base without an official ticket in. And Russia controls Crimea."

Morse sat there a minute.

"The Soviets built hidden installations throughout Eastern Europe," she said. "They were literally small cities. Some with miles of underground passageways. Railroad lines, tunnels, laboratories, living spaces for hundreds, you name it. And oh, by the way, they were meant to withstand direct nuclear hits." She exhaled. "Everything that ends begins again. The surprise is that Russia restarted the program and has been constructing new facilities right under our noses. Somehow they've blinded our surveillance satellites."

Carmody looked at her. "*Somehow* isn't usually good enough for you," he said. "What aren't you telling me?"

"Only what I'm unable to."

"That's bullshit."

"It is what it is," she said. "The Wolf knows we're on his trail. He won't leave his new den. He's too protected. So you'll have to get inside."

"Agreed."

"You've hunted and wounded him before," she said. "This time you have to kill him. And for that you need a team."

"I already have one."

She shook her head. "It's divided between the US and Romania right now."

"Your call. Not mine, Duchess."

Morse smiled a little. Until a few months ago, they had mostly interacted across thousands of miles, over secure channels. He was accustomed to using her code name.

"It was necessary," she said. "We're growing fast. We need to train our recruits here in the US. And your men are the best."

"Because they learned from the best," Carmody said. "It still leaves me short."

"Then, I repeat, assemble a new team," Morse said. "It has to be large enough to get past a numerically superior, well-armed force. But small enough to be fast, agile and covert. Also, there will be total deniability for our government. No records, no outside contact. If you screw up on the ground, it's your problem. If you succeed, I'll grab most of the credit."

"And won't feel guilty about it?"

"Not one iota."

He grinned. "Is that it?"

"A plan would be nice," she said. "And for that you'll need more information."

"You already said that."

"I think it bears repeating." Morse put down her coffee cup and meshed her hands on the desk. "Mike, do you get disoriented using the HIVE's V/R? A mild headache?"

He looked at her. "How did you know?"

"It could be a lucky guess," she said. "Or that I've had a similar experience."

"Or that you monitor my sessions," he said.

She shrugged.

"We get biometric feedback from HIVE users. It helps us to improve things."

"Cute."

"Necessary," Morse said.

"That your word of the morning?"

She shrugged again. "Those symptoms…the experts call it cybersickness. They believe it happens when you don't have enough real world detail in a given scenario. Your eyes are looking for all the tiny little sights that seem to be imperceptible but are really picked up and registered by your brain. And that are hard to recreate in full. It isn't virtually flying over mountains that makes you airsick. It's flying over mountains that don't cast the right shadows or have snowcaps in season."

"So what are you saying?"

"We need a clearer picture of the Wolf's new den. And that means cracking their security long-distance."

Carmody was quiet for several seconds. Then he nodded. "OK," he said. "That it?"

"Yes and no," she said. "We should have a conversation about your friend Kali."

He looked at her. "I'm listening," he said.

Morse tossed her coffee cup in the trash receptacle and stood up.

"Not here," she said. "It's a glorious spring morning. Let's take this outside."

South China Sea

Major General Wei Shun Zeng was dead tired and bone sore. Dead tired because of his long, drawn-out trek from Beijing traveling incognito as an ordinary citizen. Bone sore thanks first to his shoddy overnight accommodations in third-tier Nanjing, and now to the cheap rattletrap jet flying him on the last leg of his fool's errand. He was only glad to have a skilled military pilot at the controls to make the island landing at night.

The aides who had met him at the airport for the second leg of his trip—both also traveling in civilian clothes—were wise to sit far to his rear in the cabin. In his current mood, he wanted no one in his personal space. Cramped as it might be.

Until last week, he had never heard of Captain Zhou Kexin. Nor should he have. Zhou was a mere field officer. Born in Xinjiang Province, with the majority of his service across the border from Primorsky Krai, Russia's Far Eastern Federal District—two marks against him right there. But he had become Wei's central focus virtually overnight. And the government's. With one brash and irresponsible action, Zhou had brought China to the edge of a mind-boggling crisis.

Wei was in a classic no-win situation. He'd known it the moment he received his orders. What he did not know was the reason the supreme leader had sent him as a glorified messenger to someone of vastly lower rank and inarguable lunacy. It might well be taken as an insult…but only if he failed to consider the mission's gravity.

Still, it left him wondering. Was he eminently trusted or exceedingly dispensable? Or both?

He had no good answers. And so he'd sat staring out his window as the sun dropped over the western sea, trying not to think more than necessary, taking advantage of his last period of calm within the chaos. He would need all his wits upon arriving at his destination.

The aircraft rattled and shook through the night sky. After a while it passed high above the booms and derricks of the Haiyang Shiyou deepwater oil platform, turning westward toward the Spratly archipelago. Wei knew then he was finally close. There was another expanse of blue, and soon he was over the group's outer islands, all clumps of green forest and sapphire atolls and white sandy coastlines.

The plane nosed down, leveled, rolled left and right, then nosed down and leveled again on its approach to Yongshu Jiau, Fiery Cross Reef, which in fact went by many names. The fishermen had called it *tuwu*—meaning *unexpected*—back when it was a half-sunken slab of rock that would tear the keels off their ships if they relaxed their guard.

But that was a different era. Now the fishing fleet guarded the reef, armed and ready, the boats anchored around it in a defensive ring. This was Dangerous Ground in more ways than one.

As his pilot shed more altitude, Wei suddenly became oblivious to the rattling and shaking of the plane. Even his tired achiness seemed to fade. What he saw below held him captivated.

Fiery Cross's transformation into a man-made island was breathtaking, a marvel of Chinese invention and industriousness. The semisubmerged rock had become an island a mile across and two long, with multiple landing strips, groupings of air defense towers, barracks and four hexagonal concrete structures around the edges—its *technical complexes*, as they called them.

Wei's gaze fell on the enormous dome at the northwest side of its harbor. *There. That's where it is.*

He leaned back in his seat, closed his eyes and waited to land. Minutes later, he felt his stomach lurch from deceleration as the plane hit the ground.

A reception party was waiting with three black BJ80 SUVs parked nose to tail behind them. Four sailors in dress whites on the tarmac, two more ceremoniously outside one of the cars. General Wei trotted down the stairs behind his aides, exchanged salutes, and was led toward the vehicles. He smelled salt in the breeze and heard the ocean all around him. It seemed to breathe quietly as he strode across the tarmac.

Calm within the chaos.

Wei's aides got into the last vehicle. One of the white-uniformed men outside the middle SUV held open its rear door for him. He made certain not to look stiff as he slid in and adjusted his legs, exhaling with relief only once the door was shut.

The convoy drove off toward the dome.

Captain Zhou stood waiting outside it in full naval regalia, his stars and bars on gleaming display in the 2500-lumen brilliance of the island's light towers. He was flanked by a guard detail of six or eight men.

As his motor escort pulled to a halt, Wei immediately matched his face to the one in his computer files. Zhou was short and square-built, with dark skin, flat features and a strong jaw. A mix of Han and Uighur traits that told of Turkish migrations, European origins. Few in the military would admit to those ethnic roots: the vast majority of Uighurs were Muslims and rarely rose to the rank of officer.

Wei had not yet gotten a chance to fully probe the captain's background and connections. But he would. Zhou had seemingly beaten the law of averages. In Wei's experience, however, a man rarely advanced on merit alone. Least of all a man from Xinjiang Province.

He smoothed down his jacket and trousers,

shrugging the carryall onto his shoulder. Then the sailors in white exited their vehicles, and one of them pulled open his door, and he got out.

Zhou stepped up and saluted. "General." He added a bow to his ceremonious greeting. "This captain is honored by your presence. How was your trip?"

"Long." Wei glanced up at the dome. "That's quite a sight, captain. Even from high above."

"It's the rounded shape that fools the eye," Zhou said. "The structure measures almost a thousand linear feet and can serve as a berth or dry dock for two corvettes at a time."

"But it isn't holding a corvette right now."

Zhou said nothing. He looked unruffled.

The general thought suddenly of a professor he once met at a Beijing dinner. He'd been expelled from Singapore amid accusations of spying for the Ministry. What was it he said? *The Chinese expand like a forest, very slowly. But once they get there, they never leave.*

Zhou did not recall any boastfulness in the statement. It was delivered in a dry, factual tone.

The island was magnificent. A wonder. And it was just one of many solidifying his nation's claim to these waters. For a decade they had spread like lilies in a pond virtually without interference, so why stir up the Americans now? Mercilessly attack one of their assets while they were still turning a blind eye?

He nodded at the dome.

"Bring me inside," he said.

New York City

Carmody and Morse crossed the West Side Highway at Twenty-Sixth Street and then walked through the greenway to the river. There was an outdoor food court at the foot of Pier 66, and Carmody stopped to order an espresso.

"I thought you'd reached your quota," she said.

"For lousy pod coffee," he said. "Want something?"

"I'll take a sparkling water," she said. "Strawberry if the guy has it."

He had it. Carmody paid, and they found a vacant bench. *A glorious spring morning.* The previous night's storm had done its damage, scattering twigs and branches all across the walk, but the air was clean and vibrant in its aftermath.

They sat looking across the Hudson at New Jersey.

"I grew up there," Morse said, nodding vaguely toward the opposite shore.

"You and your surly ex?"

"Me and Leo Harris, your superior, yes," she said and turned to him. "Where in Hawaii are you from? I forget."

"Lanai City."

"Really? Once the pineapple capital of the world. Now where Leland Sinclair, king of Olympia, hangs his hammock."

Carmody nodded. "He owns eighty percent of the island. The other twenty's a public trust."

"His tax write-off in other words."

He nodded again and drank his espresso. She took a sip of her strawberry fizz. Pigeons perched on the guardrail in front of them, seagulls wheeled overhead, and bicyclists blurred by in sporty riding gear that showed off their toned physiques.

"I'm thinking six degrees of separation," Morse said.

He grunted. "Sinclair's behind the CloudCable project. The project is why the missing ship was wherever it was. And the missing ship is why Kali flew to New Hampshire today."

"And she's the reason we're sitting here right now."

Carmody was silent a moment. "All right," he said. "Talk to me."

Morse stared out at the opposite shore again. Hoboken, Newark, MetLife Stadium, Atlantic City. Carmody had never been to any of them. Unless he counted Newark airport.

"I'm getting pushed about her," she said. "Hard."

"By?"

"Docs it matter?"

"Might to me."

She shrugged. "Our closest international allies consider her a wanted criminal. Interpol wants her extradited. And some within the Force want the same thing. They don't like her working with us. They suspect she's complicit in the attack on Janus Base. Specifically, they think she subverted our robot sentries' defensive protocols."

"*They* meaning John Howard."

"The pressure's coming from all directions."

"Including Howard, then. He's the commanding officer at Janus."

"You're a stubborn ass."

"Thanks," Carmody said. "How about Alex Michaels?"

She expelled a breath. "The director's been silent about her. So far."

Carmody drank his coffee.

"Kali got us into the Wolf's castle," he said. "She saved my life twice."

"There are layers of cover. Save your life, gain your trust. All the better to fool you."

"I don't fool easy."

"I know. But it doesn't mean you know her intentions. Or can be objective," Morse said. "You've been living with her for three months."

"I sleep on her couch."

"But you know what people think."

"I don't care what they think," he said. "She's here because she wants to be. If she wanted to give us the slip, we couldn't stop her. Not me, not anyone. She'd be gone in the blink of an eye."

Morse leaned forward and turned the bottle of mineral water in her hands. A bird stared at her from the rail. She stared back at it over the bottle.

"Look," she said, "we don't know what's around the bend with this *Stalwart* situation. Maybe it miraculously shows up unharmed. Or maybe we find out whatever happened to it was an accident.

Or maybe it escalates into some unthinkable predicament with the Chinese."

Carmody followed her line of thought. "You're saying people are distracted."

"I'm saying Kali isn't Director Michaels's focus. Which means she isn't mine right now. But that will change. At some point she will be. Maybe sooner rather than later."

"And when it happens?"

Morse straightened up and looked at him.

"I don't trust or distrust her. That makes me agnostic. She isn't my fight."

He sat there in silence. The pigeons fluttered their wings in unison and took off.

"Quitters," he said. "They had enough of us."

"Do you blame them?"

Carmody shrugged and cracked a smile.

"They aren't my focus right now," he said.

South China Sea

General Wei craned his neck back to its limit, looking up at the colossal bulk of the CS *Stalwart* raised on blocks inside the dome. It was long and white in the floodlights, with a thick armored bow, towering superstructure and an array of radio-satellite navigation and communications masts bristling from the bridge deck. On the main deck from bow to stern were lowered cranes, girders, elevated walk ramps and various pieces of machinery and equipment Wei couldn't identify. The fantail was wide and flat, the housings for the bow thrusters like tunnels. Its rudders were so huge, a tall man could have stretched out lengthwise on each blade.

Wei turned to Zhou. They were on the concrete piers, their escorts waiting a respectful distance away.

"A question," he said. "How did you bring it here?"

The captain did not hesitate. "The pirates had already ravaged it. We believe they were out of the Sulu. Unaffiliated criminals, those waters are thick with them. Our maritime militia observed the ship well outside the safe transit corridor. It seemed adrift, and they went to investigate. When their hailing signals were ignored, they approached for a closer look. Soon afterward, they discovered the crew had been slaughtered."

"And the fishermen boarded it? Were able to pilot it here?" Wei motioned expansively at the steel hull of the colossus. "A monster like this, without any problems?"

"They are skilled sailors," Zhou said. "Not to be underestimated."

Wei thought the captain was like an actor auditioning for a role he disdained. His lines spoken without even a superficial attempt at believability.

"The murdered crew members you say were left aboard," Zhou said. "What became of them?"

"Honored superior, I will not claim we abided by strict convention. As you know, our inspection of the vessel uncovered extraordinary things. Sophisticated American spy technology most vitally among them. The remains were handled in a way I concluded was in our nation's best interest. I can show you privately if you wish."

Wei looked at him for a long minute.

"Yes," he said. "Do that."

The harbor on the seaward side of the dome was wide and deep, its facilities like those of any mid-size working port. There were cranes and forklifts and shipping containers the size of trucks.

Wei looked out over the water. The batteries of high-powered lights on each side of the dock cast a bright skin on its surface. He saw wavelets sloshing up against the wharf. He saw the silhouettes of the militia's fishing boats in the outer harbor. He smelled the ocean and, faintly, gasoline and machine oil. He turned to Zhou. His men had brought a small cooler and set it down beside him. They had opened its lid and stepped away and disappeared, leaving only the two of them on the quay. Inside the cooler was a thick mound of bullet-shaped silver fish, all about four inches long.

The two officers stood in silence for a while. The wind came from the north beyond the anchorage, blowing straight into their faces.

Zhou motioned at the cooler. "The fishermen call these trash fish," he said. "They are inedible and virtually worthless. The boats trap them in their nets while trawling for more valued catch. They're used as bait or sold cheaply to the Thais, whose slave laborers use them in stew. Or to the Americans, who feed them to their pets."

Wei looked at him. "I've had a draining trip, captain. Show me what I'm out here to see."

Zhou nodded, bent, and lifted the cooler by its handles. He took two or three steps to the edge of the quay, tilted down its open end, and swung it back and then forward so the fish went flying out into the water, striking it with a hail of little splashes.

Wei immediately saw the sharks slicing beneath the surface. They were like pointed torpedoes. Their dorsal fins broke the water as they converged on the bait fish. They showed no fear of the light shining over them from the dock.

"The ocean has its own efficient means of trash disposal," Zhou said. "Tiger sharks are nocturnal feeders. They eat anything. Whatever they see or smell. They will even devour other sharks."

Wei inhaled. The sharks spun and lunged a few feet underwater. "How many bodies did you say were on the ship?"

"There were seventy-seven."

"And you really think we're done with things? They were civilian sailors, Captain."

"They were spies. Saboteurs. And now they're gone. Lost at sea. No one can be accused of anything."

Wei looked at him sharply. "You're delusional. The Americans will never let this stand."

Zhou watched the roiling water a moment. Then he lowered the empty cooler to the cement dock and turned to Wei.

"Respectfully, we've built the greatest naval battle force in the world. Yet we turn a blind eye when foreign powers defy our boundaries. They cross our sovereign waters. They send armed vessels within striking range of our shores. And now tap our undersea cables with impunity."

"Where is your proof?"

"There is more than enough."

"Then, I want to see it. I'll also require a written account of the incident for the chairman. By tomorrow morning."

The water off the dock had stilled. Wei heard the steady, insistent beat of the sea.

After a minute Zhou said, "I'll have a report ready. And all the evidence you need."

"Good." Wei stared at him. "A word of warning. Some ambition is desirable in a young officer. But you might want to go easier for the sake of your future."

Zhou was expressionless. He nodded toward the settled water off the quay.

"The tiger sharks have eaten all the food I threw them. Or perhaps they're simply exhausted," he said. "I've observed that the stripes fade in the older ones. Eventually they vanish altogether, the creature's best years behind it."

Wei looked at him. "I'll leave the sharks to you, Captain. I know men. There is a difference between bluster and true inner ferocity."

Zhou remained silent a long moment. Then he nodded. "My guards will show you to your sleeping quarters. They're soft and comfortable. I think you'll find them suited to your needs."

General Wei pretended not to pick up on the insult. After a moment the men reappeared and escorted him back inside the dome and out through its south entrance to his waiting vehicle. As his driver looped around toward the far side of the island, he thought of those he served in Beijing, many cannibalistic sharks in their own right. He hoped they would not soon be making a feast of him and his faded stripes.

5

Dragonfly climbed into the air over New England for the third time that morning, having looped back to the Coast Guard medical facility in Boothbay Harbor after its unexpected trip to Maine's northern extreme.

Only one of its two pickups remained aboard. One was the instructor at the Net Force CyberOperations Training Center named Natasha Mori. Her companion, Bryan Ferago, had been left at Boothbay for emergency treatment of his hand injuries.

Now Natasha sat in the far rear of the passenger compartment, her large pale blue eyes staring off into space. In her late twenties, she was a partial albino, her skin strikingly white and almost translucent, like frost on a windowpane. Tall, thin, almost spindly, she looked worn and tired and desolate from whatever she and Bryan had gone through on the island.

The aircraft reached its cruising speed and entered level flight. Two rows in front of Natasha, Kali shrugged out of her harness, stretched unobtrusively, slid into the aisle, then made her way past Musil toward the back of the cabin. Her hood was down, and she was carrying a paper restaurant bag she had brought on board during their refuel at the Coast Guard station.

She stopped alongside Natasha, holding on to the back of her seat with her right hand. She could not have failed to notice the bruises on her face and the caked mud and dirt in her hair.

"It's clam chowder," she said, raising the bag in her left hand. "You wanted something to eat."

Natasha's gaze pulled in from its vast distance and settled on her face.

"Where'd you get it?"

"A stand outside the Coast Guard station."

She gave a nod. Kali took two foam soup cups out of the bag, passed one to Natasha along with a plastic spoon, and sat down beside her with the other container.

They ate in silence a minute. Natasha swallowed hungrily. The chowder was steaming hot.

"Good stuff," she said. "Thanks."

Kali looked at her. "The Chez Leon in Brussels is known for its mussels steamed in garlic and butter," she said. "I visited it once, alone. Near the main plaza, I found a bench, sat and ate. A big bucketful of mussels, with a couple of plates for the empty shells. There were cats everywhere, friendly ones. They belonged to the restaurant."

"Awesome."

Kali nodded.

"I lost track of time. The sun went down. The cats wandered over and begged some off me. But I wasn't overly generous. I kept eating until the shells were piled high on the plates."

"Were you starved or something?"

"I was tired."

"Of?"

"Moving from place to place, I suppose," Kali said. "And I liked the spot."

"So is there a moral to the story?"

Kali shook her head.

"It's just a memory," she said and paused. "Your friend will recover, Natasha."

"I didn't like leaving him."

"He needed surgery. His hand was badly torn up. There was damage to his bones and tendons."

Natasha looked at her over the steaming chowder. "I won't talk about what happened to us."

Kali nodded.

"I'm sorry," Natasha said.

Kali nodded again. "You shouldn't be," she said and lowered her voice a notch. "We'll talk later. About other things."

Natasha sat quietly for a long moment, her blue eyes studying Kali's brown ones.

"Thanks again for the grub," she said.

Kali smiled and went back to her original seat. The aircraft whispered through the sky, its flight almost completely without engine noise or vibration. She strapped in.

Across the aisle, Musil pretended not to have been paying attention to her. All these hours together and she hadn't said a word to him. But her gesture to the girl was very kind. Perhaps she was opening up somewhat. He didn't know. But he did know the aroma of the chowder was tantalizing. He wished he had also gotten something to eat before takeoff.

He sat back and wondered about CloudCable's missing ship and Kali, two unsolved mysteries that kept his mind busy for the entire flight back to New York.

The Terminal

Carmody smoked a cigarette, his bicolored eyes watching *Dragonfly* lower to the roof. One was dark brown, the other greenish-gold, with faint brown lines radiating from his pupil like the spokes of a wheel. Back in the day, his boys in 22nd Special Tactics had called it his ocelot's eye, and the name had stuck.

The VTOL's wheels kissed the vertiport's rubber dead center in the yellow ring. There were two aircraft already on the pad: *Blackbird*, a large modified Bell V-280 with synthetic blackest-black stealth skin, and *Lulu*, a hot and high MD 500 single-rotor chopper recently moved from Lower Manhattan's FBI heliport, now belonging to the Force's Cy-Eye Surveillance and Aviation arm.

Dragonfly settled down with barely a sound. Its rotors stopped spinning, and the cabin door opened. Carmody crushed out his stub, glanced around for a trash can and dropped it under its metal bonnet. He didn't like leaving behind messes, large or small.

He stood between the pad and the building's rooftop access door, watching the passenger compartment empty out. Musil, Kali, then their pickup. The three of them walked toward Carmody on their way to the door, Musil with a nod hello, the pickup walking straight past him. He looked at Kali, who had dropped back a few steps.

"She didn't notice me," he said.

"Is your ego hurt?"

Carmody smiled a little.

"I'll live," he said. "I've seen her around."

"Natasha Mori. She's an instructor. Among other things."

"What happened to her on that island?"

"She and a friend were stranded there. In yesterday's storm."

"That friend have a name?"

"Bryan Ferago."

"Don't recognize it. He one of ours?"

"One of yours."

Carmody grunted. "Is the storm why she's so beat-up?"

"I don't think so. Not altogether."

"Then, what happened?"

"She wouldn't talk about it. But Ferago's hand was injured. Deliberately."

"You sure?"

"Yes," she said. "It was impaled. His fingers have multiple fractures. Their tendons are in shreds. As if someone wanted to maim him."

"And she hasn't said what happened to them?"

"That's the fourth time you asked."

He grinned. "But who's counting?"

Kali looked at him.

"Why were you waiting up here?" she said.

He stood quietly a moment, then lowered his head to hide his lips from the vertiport's surveillance cameras.

"It's Duchess. She called me into her office to talk."

"About?"

"The Wolf," he said. "And you."

Kali stepped closer. "Does she suspect anything?"

"She could, I guess. I don't know. It's hard to stay ahead of her."

They stood there another second or two, barely an inch between them. The breeze whipped the bottom of her coat around her legs.

"We have to leave here," she said.

"Not yet."

"But soon. We need to be ready."

"Like in baseball."

Kali gave him a questioning look.

"Long waits, sudden bursts of action," he explained. "You prepare to be quick."

"Yes. Like that."

He raised his eyes to hers. "See you tonight. Your turn to spring for dinner."

Kali was silent for the time it took the sun to slip in and out of a small passing cloud.

"Tonight," she said, and strode past him to the access door.

It was two o'clock in the morning on Fiery Cross Reef, where Captain Zhou sat at his computer typing out a brief core-encrypted message. He'd been prepared for Wei's arrival, or the arrival of some other decrepit member of the old guard from Beijing. His game was one of high risks, and the general's visit underscored the stakes. It changed things. And the thoughts leaping about his mind had kept Zhou awake in his bathrobe since he'd returned from the dome.

Which was not to say he would second-guess himself. He hadn't acted blindly or impulsively. He had made his calculations, aligned with the right players. The best political chess masters in the world. Zhou believed the possible outcomes were likely in his favor, but the game was still at an early stage. A bold opening move could be wasted without shrewd, decisive follow-throughs. He would have to be fearless and unflinching every step of the way. Nothing would come of timidity and caution.

Zhou imagined Wei and his peers making their reasonable, considered decisions about Xinjiang Province not so many years ago. How safe and secure they must have felt. How comfortable. They did what was asked of them without hesitation. All in the name of stability, as if anything solid could be built on a mountain of a hundred thousand dead. Of the reasonably and safely slaughtered.

Zhou drank from a glass of ice water and moved his cursor to the send button. Well, he thought, the general would not feel so comfortable tonight. Or in coming days and nights. And the same would be true of Wei's white-haired comrades. They would trip over their own feet while the ground trembled, rocked and finally crumbled beneath them. They would learn—too late—that the world was not as easily controlled as they believed.

As for the good General Wei… Zhou would not want to be in his shoes when he returned to the capital.

He took another drink of water and shot his message off to its recipient. Then he yawned, stretched his arms and neck, and yawned again. His tiredness had suddenly caught up to him. He supposed it was the release of tension. A click of the mouse under his fingertip had ratcheted up the game to another level. A two-sentence email, and pieces would move over the board. He supposed that was it. The tiny click like a mental exhale.

Zhou switched off his computer. He stood up, carried the half-empty glass to the kitchen and set it down in the sink. Then he went to the bathroom, urinated, hung up his robe and got into bed.

Three minutes after his head touched the pillow, he was sound asleep.

Russia

Two o'clock Tuesday morning on Fiery Cross Reef was ten o'clock Monday night in Moscow's Sadovoye Koltso suburb, where Urban was out walking his Caucasian shepherd when he heard the email alert. He jerked the dog's leash, and it obediently heeled beside him in the neat public garden. He had just recently set the unique tone on his smartwatch.

Urban glanced at the screen and saw the message was from Zhou Kexin. He did not open it. The coded subject line told him it was strictly need-to-know, and he was a man of faithful and exacting discipline. The position he occupied in the Directorate was a high one, but some things were still above his head.

He tapped the touch screen and forwarded the email. It would jump through several proxies over the next forty-three seconds before popping into a secure cloud vault, which in turn triggered the next alert tone fifteen hundred miles to the southwest.

Crimea

The alert sounded for Koschei while he was in his armchair sipping a nightcap of Grand Marnier.

At the familiar beep pattern on his computer, he set his tulip glass down on the stand beside him, lifting his tablet off it with his free hand. Then he opened and scanned the email, raising a dark, bushy eyebrow.

Moments later, he called Grigor Malkira on his satphone.

"We need to meet tonight," he said when he answered. "Midnight sharp. At the usual spot."

"I think you enjoy these last-minute appointments."

Koschei laughed. "Habit, I suppose. I'd almost forgotten the last time."

"I don't forget anything."

"Yes. You are *ruchnaya lisa*. A tame fox."

"Not my favorite term."

"Blame the scientists," Koschei said. "At any rate, you can expect to see a third person there."

"Who?"

"A very *un*tamed Wolf," Koschei said and disconnected.

New York City

Kali had owned the tiny West Village walk-up for years, paying for it in cash during an extended stay in the city. She had not returned since, until agreeing to accompany Carmody from Romania. Home for her was very far away, but this was a place to stay in her travels, somewhere she could do her work, and she kept it clean and uncluttered and sparsely but comfortably furnished.

Back from the Terminal, she hung her coat on a peg near the door, took a bottle of cold water out of the refrigerator and went to the dining area.

Her laptop was on the table, and she sat down behind it, touching the fingerprint scanner to unlock its hard drive. After a moment she typed in a decryption key to enter Access Mundi, the cloud vault she shared with Lucien Navarro.

Navarro had been Kali's dear friend and confidant since childhood. He, along with a handful of other internet activists, had cofounded a community of millions in cyberspace that was preparing to declare itself a nation free of geographic borders, with sovereignty equivalent to any physical country on earth. A cybernation. It was an increasingly dangerous business, as several of the world's authoritarian powers had declared any affiliation with Cybernation a jailable offense, labeling Lucien and his collaborators radical threats and instigators of rebellion.

Kali stayed in close contact with him, touching base on a regular schedule. But now the Access Mundi interface showed no messages from Lucien. No deposited files or digital stamps to indicate his recent entry. He had dropped out of touch, and that was more than a little odd to her.

Where are you? she thought. He would not go silent. Not at any time. But of all possible times, certainly not now. Too much was at stake.

Kali sat at the computer feeling Navarro's absence. It worried her. Deeply.

Crimea

The pier jutted straight out into the water from the road rimming the mountainside. It was narrow and concrete and within eyeshot of where the submarine pen cut into the high stone face. They stood at its head as the clock struck midnight, facing each other in a tight group: Koschei, squat and bearish in a charcoal-gray trench coat, the pale Grigor, and a third man, tall and thin with long black hair and dark, piercing eyes.

"This won't take long," Koschei said. He turned to the black-haired man. "Face-to-face contact is still the most secure, no?"

"In contrast to what?"

Koschei chuckled, looking amused. He turned to Grigor. "You'll be returning to the United States," he said. "New York first."

"And then?"

"Hawaii."

Grigor seemed surprised. "Five months ago, when I wanted to stay in America, you insisted it was too hot."

"Circumstances change. We need you back there in the short term. You'll take care of something for us alone, then rendezvous with the same group you led aboard the cable ship. They're already en route."

Grigor looked at him. "Why wasn't I given time to prepare?"

"One needs to know what one needs to know. I'm not here to negotiate. Or make a request. You are a prime investment of the Main Directorate. You've enjoyed the privileges your entire life. I would expect you to carry out your orders with gratitude."

Grigor stared at him, his expression frozen. "When do I leave?"

Koschei reached inside his coat for a plain white six-by-nine envelope and handed it to him. "Your instructions cover it. Read them later tonight."

Grigor put the envelope in a carryall slung over his shoulder. After a second, Koschei's hand went back in his coat, then reappeared holding a small thumb drive. He held it out between himself and the other man.

"Here. In case you think I forgot your gift."

The dark-haired man's eyes narrowed. "You have the files."

Koschei nodded. "I wouldn't think of calling you out here this late unless I'd brought them. They came via email tonight. Captain Zhou's people finally pulled them from the onboard system of the cable ship."

"And they've since been scrubbed?"

"Yes. And not only from the ship's computers. I've purged them from my email folder. The temporary drop vault from which I received them no longer exists. There's only what's on that drive in your hand and a second one I've kept for myself."

"What of the captain?"

"I'm sure he's made his own copy." Koschei

shrugged. "Call it a practical risk. There isn't anything we can do about it."

The dark-haired man looked down at the drive and held it in his open palm like a rare gem. His other hand went up to his neck, touching the soft flesh behind his ear with a single fingertip, an unconscious gesture.

Koschei had seen the small tattoo there before. It was a wheel or circular maze, like an ancient, artistically carved chariot wheel, with a six-pointed star in the center. He thought he understood its significance to the man, or mostly understood it, and had stashed that knowledge away for safekeeping. The more one knew, the better. Right now, though, he was enjoying the hungry expression on his face.

"So now you have it," he said. "The key to everything."

The dark-haired man dropped the drive into his pocket.

"For both of us," he said, raising his eyes to Koschei's.

Koschei gave no response. The truth being the simple truth, he had nothing to add.

New York City

Midnight Tuesday in Crimea was five o'clock Monday night five thousand miles away on Manhattan's Lower East Side, where Carmody had just reached the small apartment building sandwiched between two larger ones on Mulberry Street. Tapping the fingerprint reader outside its entrance, he pushed through to the tiny lobby and then rode the elevator to the fifth floor.

There was a single apartment on the floor and Carmody picked up a rich, bready scent in the hallway outside. Hot dough, cheese, parsley and pork: *pogaca*. He stepped up to the door, tapped a second reader, entered, and poked his head into the living room.

Kali was at the table in front of her laptop, sitting sideways to the door. She gave him a slight nod, and he nodded back, even though she wasn't looking. Then he hung his jacket on a peg and followed the aroma into the kitchen. A tray of the Carpathian biscuits was warming in the oven. He took two oven mitts off a hook, carried the tray over to her, set it down on the table and spun a chair around so he could sit with his legs spread around its back.

"Hi," he said.

"Hello, Michael."

"You've got your work cut out," he said, nodding at the computer.

"I'm not alone," she said.

Carmody handed her a biscuit in a napkin, took one for himself. He was wearing a black short-sleeved T-shirt. A rising phoenix tattoo covered his entire right arm. On the left were stylized runes in shades of blue.

"Super," he said, eating.

"They're from a Hungarian bakery around the corner."

He made an appreciative sound deep in his throat. "The baker didn't use yeast. It's how authentic *pogaca* is made. Also the more difficult way to prepare the dough."

"You know these things. I realized that back in Italy."

He shrugged. "I grew up in a restaurant kitchen."

"You told me you grew up in a traveling carnival."

"That was later on. From when I turned sixteen till I enlisted."

"And then?"

"I was through growing up."

Kali held her napkin with both hands. They were small with long, slender fingers and did not seem capable of taking down a three-hundred-pound bruiser built like a tank. But Carmody had seen her do it before he could count to ten.

He glanced at the computer screen as she ate the *pogaca* in silence. Lines of multicolored source code ran across it.

"How does it feel not to be alone?" he asked.

"The premise of your question is wrong," she said. "I have people I trust."

"Like Franz Scholl. The guy in Munich who helped you take down Gunther Koenig's outlaw geomapping operation."

"He's one."

"And whoever you send messages to in cyberspace."

Her brown eyes locked on his. "You didn't learn that in a kitchen."

"I was hunting you for over a year."

"And you tracked me down."

Carmody nodded. "My proudest moment."

She was silent.

He said, "So, Scholl the web activist. Your other friend in cyberspace. Or friends, plural. Are they all connected?"

Kali didn't answer. She finished her biscuit, dabbed her fingers with the napkin and slid it aside on the table.

"We have work to do," she said.

Carmody grunted. "True," he said. "Duchess wants me to put together a team."

"Did you tell her you're already doing it?"

"I'll tell her when I'm ready. Right now I want to keep this off the grid." He pulled a folded sheet of notepaper out of his breast pocket and opened it. "I made a list."

"Handwritten," she said.

He saw the glint in her eyes. "What's so amusing?"

"Your concept of modern information security."

Carmody shrugged. "A pad and pencil can't be hacked," he said. "Want to hear what I've figured out?"

"Yes."

"Schultz and Dixon are here in New York training recruits. Which means they can leave with us."

"The band stays together."

"Cranking out the hits," Carmody said. "I've got Wheeler and Long in this too."

"Aren't they in Romania? We can't launch from Janus Base."

"I know," he said. "But Janus is close enough to where I want to deploy. I'll work out the logistics."

She nodded. "Who else?"

"A couple of kids who were with us in Transylvania. One's Begai. He's a sapper. A demolitions man. The other's named Sparrow. Wheeler tells me he can hit a fly on the side of a barn at a thousand yards. That makes six."

"They're Colonel Howard's men."

"I got them reassigned to me a couple of months ago," Carmody said. "But I haven't ruled out using his guys. One of them especially."

"Julio Fernandez."

"No one knows AI better."

"I agree. But he and Howard are close."

"I'll figure it out."

"Then, that's nine. Counting you and me."

"Right," Carmody said. "Fernandez might want a man of his own. So ten. Plus, we need a pilot. Eleven. But none of it happens without more intel. And I'd like it fast."

"I'm not a magician, Michael."

"Contrary to popular opinion."

She looked at him. "I've been trying to access Sentient. It's the largest intelligence gathering tool on the planet. Designed for omnivorous data collection and analysis. On the Dark Web they call it the key to everything—hackers are racing to find a way into the network. But it isn't a single system. It has an incredibly complex architecture. One level builds on the next. Like a tower. I've found unique web beacons."

"Put the CIA and Geospacials in bed together and out comes their secret baby."

Kali nodded. "They're constantly monitoring it. Patching vulnerabilities. And I think they've had help."

"From?"

"When I know, I'll tell you. We have to tread lightly."

Carmody reached for another *pogaca*, took a bite. "OK," he said. "I'll shut up and eat."

"One thing. I have another for the team. A twelfth."

He looked at her with mild surprise. "Who?"

"Natasha Mori."

"The instructor you picked up in Maine?"

"Yes."

"Why her?"

"Because she's exactly what we need. An expert in predictive analytics."

He shook his head. "I won't bring in a member of the geek squad. Even if I was convinced she could keep a secret. I'm not going to nursemaid her."

"She won't need that."

He looked at her. Then he said, "So what do you know that I don't?"

"There are deep files," she said. "Natasha Mori is special."

He nodded. "Keep going."

"She was born in Russia. They had a human breeding program. Advanced genetics. They called it Pinnacle, and Natasha was trained to be a spy and an assassin. Alex Michaels helped bring her to America as part of a confidential deal."

Carmody sat motionless, astonished, staring at her over another biscuit.

"Whoa," he said.

Kali looked at him for a long moment.

"It goes deeper," she said.

6

Various Locales
April 16, 2024

New York

It was nine o'clock sharp Tuesday morning when Musil entered the office of Leo Harris, the director of Net Force Investigations, also known as the Cyberdogs—every single branch of every last intelligence, law-enforcement, and military organization on God's green earth apparently needing a tough-sounding handle or else.

Musil found Harris at his desk, fully done up in an expensive-looking tuxedo. Black satin peak lapel, black satin pocket trim, black satin buttons, black satin inner lining. A white bib shirt with a pointed collar under the jacket. Completing the ensemble—and adding some whimsical flair, Musil thought—was a blue bow tie with a yellow-and-green paisley pattern that on second glance revealed itself not to be paisley at all but turtles.

Little turtles with little yellow shells, green heads and legs, and round green flat-bottomed feet.

Musil took the seat opposite him, smiling, a file folder in his hand. However curious it was to see his boss in formal evening attire here at the Terminal—this early in the day, no less—he *did* look impressively crisp, clean and dapper. It was a positive sign. Harris's famously colorful, if questionable, dress had been heavily drabbed down since he'd returned from injury leave, leading some to grow concerned about his physical and mental well-being.

A positive sign, indeed.

"Good morning, sir!" Musil said from across the desk. "You look fantastic! Is there a happy occasion?"

Harris pushed the question aside with one of his own. "That a hard copy of the *Stalwart*'s crew list?"

Musil nodded. "It was emailed to me late yesterday afternoon. From CloudCable's human resources department."

"Fast."

"Yes, sir."

"Not that I'm shocked," Harris snorted.

Musil wasn't either. As a huge corporation, CloudCable paid an army of in-house and outsourced public relations people. The missing ship cost two hundred million dollars. The subsea cable on board additional hundreds of millions. And its contract with the CIA, National Geospatial-Intelligence Agency and Olympia was worth billions. There were investors and brokers and politicians staking their fortunes and reputations on the cable deal. The company did not want to appear uncooperative, even while being so. It could not afford to have a storm of negative news headlines flying around it amid the mounting crisis.

Thus, its HR department had complied with Musil's request for a set of crew records, made after he returned from New Hampshire the day before. It was a smart move. The documents were obtainable from other sources, anyway. The US Customs Office for one. Probably the Department of Transportation's Maritime Administration. Also, the project's insurance underwriters. Insurers had entire subdivisions specializing in cybertechnology. A project of the scope Cloud-Cable had undertaken required that it be indemnified for a small fortune. Besides the ship itself, and all the expensive machinery and high technology aboard, there were divers, machinists and other crew members with inherently hazardous jobs. The company needed to limit its liability.

"OK," Harris said. "You got anything so far? And what the hell are you looking at?"

Musil realized he'd been staring at the bow tie. Some of the turtles appeared to be walking. Others, swimming. Others just seemed to be placidly looking around. He thought them all lively and cheerful and wondered if he should mention it to Harris. But then he decided better of it and opened his folder.

Inside it were four or five sheets of paper that had been clipped together after his printer kicked them out, the text on each divided into columns. He had highlighted several blocks of information beginning midway down the first page in yellow or green marker...which by chance were the same colors as the turtles.

"A few things, sir," he said, and held up the printout for Harris. "As you can see, the crew names are in the left column. Their positions aboard the ship are in the middle. The right column shows the date each person was employed by CloudCable. In most cases."

Harris grunted. "What about in the other cases?"

"I'll explain in a moment," Musil said. He pointed to the upper half of the first page, highlighted in green. "This listing is for the permanent crew. As it says at the top. That would be the captain, mates, watch leaders, and chief and second engineers. Also the head cook and doctor...just under twenty names total."

"And the rest?"

"They fall into three categories." Musil moved his finger down to the wide yellow block of data running from the middle to the bottom of the page. Then flipped to the second page, which was entirely yellow. "All these names belong to members of the voyage crew. They're the majority of the ship's personnel. About forty people under short-term contract with the company. Divers, cable and freight handlers, engineer assistants, repairmen, boarding agents, maintenance workers..."

"Jot, skip the movie credits." Harris wound his hand. "I've got me an appointment downtown in an hour."

Musil nodded. Harris was definitely acting more like his old self.

"The second group of contract employees would be the scullery and mess hands. The ship's kitchen staff, food servers and dishwashers."

He flipped to the third page and tapped a single green line at the top. The right column read *The Seven Winds Group*. There were no individual personnel listings or dates of employment in the second or third columns.

Harris looked at him. "So the kitchen's run by a third party?"

"It's outsourced, yes," Musil said. "I estimate there are a dozen staffers."

"No names?"

"Not yet."

"But you already contacted this Seven Winds outfit."

"Yes. There's a corporate office in San Francisco."

"And *they're* giving you names?"

"They say they're working on it."

"What's that supposed to mean?"

Musil shrugged. "They're a transnational company. The M&S staff, as they call it…that stands for *Mess and Scullery*—"

"No shit. Let's hustle it up," Harris cut in, glancing at his wristwatch.

"Yes, sir," Musil said. "The M&S staff doesn't stay on board the entire five-month cruise. They rotate. Usually, replacements come aboard each time the ship enters a port for refuel, reload and maintenance."

"Do we know where the *Stalwart* pulled in before it disappeared? And when?"

"Not yet."

Harris pretended to look around. "Am I hearing echoes?"

Musil adjusted himself in his chair. "Sir, Cloud-Cable's HR department claims to have no information about the ship's itinerary," he said. "But Seven Winds does have an employee database. It would tell us when its kitchen personnel rotated, at what harbors and onto which vessels. We can find out about the *Stalwart*'s port calls. Their times and dates. And of course, the names of the kitchen staff. But their personnel files aren't centralized. The US office has to contact its overseas branches and wait for them to answer. It's a process."

"That's for damn sure." Harris exhaled. "All right. What else?"

Musil flipped to the last sheet of paper. The five rows were highlighted in blue.

"These are the rest of the crew members," he said. "All are listed as special advisers. There are no job descriptions. No hiring dates."

Harris studied the printout a second. Then looked at Musil.

"What's that tell you?"

"I would guess they're CIA and NGIA."

Harris nodded his agreement and sat quietly a moment.

"I think you should check out the short-termers," he said. "What'd you call them?"

"The *voyage crew*, sir."

"Right," Harris said. "Could be nothing there. Probably isn't. But you never know."

"Yes, sir."

"I'd also like to find out if those advisers really are spooks." Harris tugged his ear. "I'll handle that one myself."

"Yes, sir." Musil gave him a look. No question about it, he had not seen his boss look so engaged since he'd nearly gotten blown to pieces by a car bomb last August.

"What is it?" Harris said.

"Nothing, sir."

"Then, why in hell are you smiling at me?"

"I didn't realize I was, sir."

Which was the truth. They sat there for a long moment.

"OK," Harris said. And peeked at his watch again. "I've gotta run."

Musil nodded, gave him another look, and returned his printout to the file folder. Then he went to the door, opened it, and glanced back over his shoulder at Harris.

"Sir?"

"Yeah?"

Musil held the door half open and beamed him another smile. His teeth white, his eyes full of sincerity.

"Many blessings to you! *Whatever* the event!" he said.

And flew out into the hall like a bullet.

Thirty minutes later, Musil was at his workstation in the small second-floor office he shared with his partner Jimmy Fahey, who was out getting his tooth either drilled or root-canaled or perhaps simply yanked from his tormented mouth. Musil couldn't recall which, but Fahey had complained about his toothache for weeks before finally acquiescing to a dental visit. And even then, Musil had needed to refer him to his brother-in-law Harjinder's practice out in his home borough of Queens, not far from that Romanian restaurant they once canvassed to ultimately break open the New York cyberattack investigation. In fact, Musil had gone a step or two further than a referral, making the appointment with Harjinder himself, and then coaxing Fahey into keeping it.

At any rate, Musil had the whole office to himself this morning as he methodically fed *Stalwart*'s crew list—the names of the four advisers included—into LATTICE, the Force's still-under-construction portal to a wide pool of law-enforcement, military and criminal justice system databases. LATTICE was a deep dish of records and would be the deepest in the intelligence community once it was fully up and running.

But even in its present limited capacity, it would tell him if the *Stalwart*'s crew members were among the thousands who were indicted for an illegal offense or had been the subject of a criminal complaint or gotten into some sort of documented trouble with the United States armed forces in the last seven years or so. The excluded records held by nonparticipating agencies left a sizable info gap. But overall, it was a productive use of the data masher. Sometimes it wasn't what you found out, it was what you eliminated.

Musil wasn't looking for anything specific right now. He wasn't necessarily thinking anything would come of his search. He was casting the widest electronic net at his disposal and seeing if it pulled anything in. It was a logical starting point.

After a few minutes, he looked at his computer screen. The progress indicator in its top right corner said the search was eighty percent complete. Waiting, he thought back to the previous day's visit to CloudCable. Olsen's stonewalling had made it largely a waste of time. Until Kali asked her question, and it wasn't a waste of time at all.

"Did you speak about this to anyone else?"

"Such as?"

"The CIA. The other agencies. Did you speak to any of them before we came this morning?"

"They're our partners. That's all I'm at liberty to say."

Musil replayed the exchange in his mind. He could see and hear it all. Olsen's immediate qualifying question and defensive body language. How he'd sat up straight at her follow-through, locked his hands together on the desk and tacitly admitted he'd been in contact with the CIA and possibly the rest. Olsen might as well have stated it outright.

Musil checked his computer screen again. The progress bar was at eighty-four percent. He wondered what the intel agencies were all hiding. When it came to the CIA and Geos, secrecy was an ingrained reflex, and it was hardly surprising they had declined invitations from Director Michaels to share their resources on LATTICE. Not that Musil necessarily thought they or CloudCable knew what happened to the *Stalwart*. But he had a feeling they knew something.

A few more seconds passed. The search was ninety-eight percent complete. Musil waited. Then his computer beeped, and he sat up straight. LATTICE had scored a match.

He moved to the edge of his chair and looked hard at the screen, reading all the relevant data over twice. Then he quickly reached for his desk phone.

* * *

"Ki," Musil said into the receiver. "Jot here. I need you to do something for me."

Ki was Ki Marton, a digital media specialist and Musil's friend and former colleague at FBI Cyber before the great migration to Net Force. Back then, Ki had doubled as an operational support tech for their cash-strapped unit, a glorified term that meant he'd handled communications between Leo Harris, the field agents and other involved parties during major investigations. He often blamed losing his formerly lush head of black Korean hair on the stress level of handling both assignments.

"Do this, do that," he said now. "You ever think of actually calling to say hello anymore? I'm two floors up and haven't seen or heard from you in weeks."

Musil considered that. It was true that they hadn't interacted much lately. Perhaps because Ki no longer manned the switchboard during operations.

"So," Ki went on before he could answer, "what am I doing for you today?"

"I have the name of a crewman from the *Stalwart*," Musil said. "Stephen Gelfland. Place of residence, Teaneck, New Jersey. He was hired by CloudCable as a boarding agent trainee last November and sailed with the ship in early February. The fourth, to be exact."

"OK."

"Nine days later, on the thirteenth, a cousin filed a missing person report for him with the Teaneck Police Department. The report was forwarded to the state police. They maintain a centralized MP database."

"You pull any details?"

"Yes," Musil said. "The cousin is Clara Hughes. She lives in Pennsylvania with her husband and children. The last time she spoke to Gelfland was just before Thanksgiving. She invited him for the weekend, but he declined. He told her he was scheduled to train at CloudCable's corporate office in Massachusetts before shipping out and wanted to stay home and prepare."

"And?"

"Hughes became concerned when he didn't call her on Christmas or New Year's Day," Musil said. "She claimed he always phones for the holidays."

"Uh-huh," Ki said. "I'm guessing there's more?"

"Yes. Gelfland has been a professional sailor for years. And his cousin usually checks on his home when he's away on a cruise. She knew when he was scheduled to leave and expected to hear from him ahead of time. To make arrangements."

"And he never called?"

"No," Musil said. "She kept trying to reach him by phone but only got his voice mail. Finally, she and her husband drove to Teaneck and let themselves into the house."

"When was that?"

"The middle of February."

"Took a while."

"He's a grown man. She thought he might have gotten busy."

"All right, go on."

"When he wasn't there, they decided to file the police report."

"I assume the cops would've contacted Cloud-Cable right off."

"Yes," Musil said. "They were told Gelfland reported to the New Hampshire shipyard for orientation in January, then left with the *Stalwart*. That ended the matter for them."

Ki said, "So what's the problem? That Gelfland didn't call his cousin? I haven't spoken to mine in years."

"Really?"

"Really."

Musil frowned. "I'm sorry," he said. "Is there an issue?"

"You try being openly gay in an immigrant Korean family. Then ask me."

Musil considered that. He *had* neglected his friendship with Ki and would have to rectify it. But first things first. He wanted to stay on track about the missing sailor.

"Clara Hughes has the key to Gelfland's home," he said. "They always exchange calls on holidays and sometimes spend them together. And he was leaving for five months. Why wouldn't he get in touch with her this time? Even to say goodbye."

A pause on the line. Then an audible sigh. "All right," Ki said. "If it'll make you happy, I'll do some data mining. Run a search of social media platforms. Maybe the guy had a wild-ass going away party in January and didn't want his cuz to know. Somebody might've tagged him in a pic. You have his photo?"

"No," Musil said. "For the police, the case was a nonstarter. They didn't see a need to include one in their file."

"How about CloudCable?"

"I requested photos of the entire crew, but so far it hasn't provided them. I'll try again."

"Don't bother," Ki said. "Gelfland must have a passport image on file. Driver's license. Something. I'll dig it up. Give me a few hours."

Musil was quiet a moment.

"You're a good friend, and I value you immensely," he said. "We should have lunch later this week."

"Not dinner?"

"My wife is visiting her family in Wisconsin. The girls are with me. But if you don't mind having them along, dinner would be fine."

Ki cleared his throat. "Uh, that's OK. Lunch is cool. That Pak buffet down on Fifty-First Street?"

"Yes."

"A little bit of guilt goes a long way."

"What?"

"Nothing. You're on," Ki said and disconnected.

* * *

Musil's next call was to Clara Hughes at the phone number given in the New Jersey police reports. She answered on the second ring, and he identified himself as an investigator with Net Force.

"Can you please tell me who you're with again?" she asked.

"Certainly, Ms. Hughes. *Net Force*. The Department of Internet Security and Law Enforcement."

"I'm not sure I've heard of it…"

"You might recall President Fucillo's speech in New York. Back in August…"

"Yes. Of course. Now it rings a bell. How could I forget that terrible craziness?" She paused a second. "The funny thing is that *your* name sounded familiar right away."

Musil heard that a lot these days. It was the boy he'd managed to save from the killer. Anton Ciobanu. The FBI had used what happened to get positive press after a difficult incident earlier in the summer. One in which he'd also been involved, unfortunately. A young man had accidentally died when Musil tried to bring him in for questioning about an online banking crime, falling off a Brooklyn rooftop while trying to run from his family's apartment, and nearly taking Musil down to the street with him. But Jot was uncomfortable with both the praise and criticism. He did his job to the best of his ability and tried to make the world a little better. That was all.

"Ms. Hughes, on another subject, I'm calling about your cousin."

"Steve?"

"Yes. I—"

"Is he OK?" she interrupted. Her voice was suddenly anxious—the voice of someone who had been bracing for a bad-news call. "Have you heard something about him?"

"No, ma'am."

"Oh. Forgive me. I didn't mean to cut you off. But he's aboard the *Stalwart*. That ship that went missing near China."

"Yes."

"It's been a nightmare since I heard about that. Like he disappeared twice."

"Yes, I can understand—"

"You know about the first time?"

"Yes, ma'am."

"The police insisted he was on the ship. So I took their word for it. I had no choice. But I've been worrying for months." A pause. "Detective… you say you don't have new information?"

"It's *Agent*, ma'am. And no, I'm sorry. I don't."

"Oh." A pause. "Then, why are you contacting me?"

Musil was thinking it would be difficult to explain his reasons over the phone. "Ma'am," he said, "can we arrange to meet in person? I would like to follow up on your police report."

"Certainly," she said. "But, please, tell me…is Steve in some kind of trouble?"

"Not that I'm aware."

"The two of us grew up together, you know. We've been tight our whole lives. Like brother and sister."

"Oh?"

"I always watch his place while he's gone. Come by once a month just to make sure it's OK. That's why I never believed he would leave without a word. And even if he *did*…he's had two months to contact me from on board the ship. Why wouldn't he?"

Musil thought it was a very reasonable question. "Ms. Hughes, do you still live in Pennsylvania?"

"Yes. East Stroudsburg."

"That's in the Poconos, isn't it?"

"Yes."

Musil cradled the receiver between his neck and shoulder, took his smartphone out of his pocket and tapped the location into a map.

"I'm in Manhattan right now," he said. "If you're home, I can be there within ninety minutes. Would that be all right?"

"Yes," Hughes said. "But I think we should meet at Steve's house. It's just over an hour's drive for me. And even closer to the city."

Musil didn't have to be sold. He checked his watch and saw it was ten forty-five.

"Could you be there between noon and twelve thirty?" he asked.

"Yes. I'll walk my dog and then head out."

Musil felt gratified and eager. He'd gotten something accomplished.

"Thank you, Ms. Hughes," he said. "I'll see you soon."

People's Republic of China

Eight thousand six hundred miles around the globe and thirty thousand feet up in the sky, Wei heard a ringtone in his Bluetooth earpiece, took his satphone from his pocket and glanced at the display with surprise and curiosity.

His caller was General Huang Li, one of the CMC's seven chairs. At sixty, Huang was the panel's longest-serving member. As secretary of the Commission for Discipline Inspection, he was probably its most intimidating one after the president himself, being the Army's highest-ranked authority in charge of chain of command and its breaches.

But while Wei would not quite say they were friends, he and Huang were close in age and had known each other since their military academy days. As cadets they had often joined in idiotic practical jokes and cooked up schemes to slip from their barracks together for nocturnal carousing and gambling. Huang had spent years building up a fearsome aura, and it was well warranted. Still, it helped to remember him drunk and falling ass over tits to the floor in his piss-soaked underwear.

"Hello," Wei answered quietly, and checked his

watch. "It's close to midnight. I'd think most people would be sound asleep."

A brief scrape of laughter. "I rarely sleep at all these days, and when I do it's never sound," Huang said. "You're over Haishin."

"How did you know?"

"I know," Huang said. "You should be arriving within the hour."

"If a strong wind doesn't blow this flying death trap to another time zone."

Huang was silent a moment. "I want to meet with you."

"Surely. Say, nine tomorrow morning?"

"No. Tonight."

Wei lifted a gray eyebrow. "It will be past one o'clock before I'm home."

"Don't worry about that," Huang said. "I'll have a car waiting for you. You'll come straight to the Ministry."

"In the middle of the night?"

"I want us to meet before the full committee gathers." A pause. "You should know I've decided to recommend the harshest penalty for Captain Zhou."

Wei found himself nodding. "An example must be made of him. Any benefits that may be gained from his wild actions are a separate consideration."

"I rely on your frankness, Wei. Let's talk when we talk. I'll make the rest clear to you then."

Wei listened to the sputter of barely cooled air from the nozzles over his seat.

"I'll see you later," he said.

Huang ended the call without another word. Wei sat thinking hard and soon felt gravity and centrifugal force nudge his stomach. Then he heard the knock of the landing gear being deployed and buckled his seat belt. The pilot had begun his rattling descent over Beijing.

New York

Grigor Malkira landed at JFK a few minutes past noon, clearing the facial-recognition scanner at the gate without any problems. On the Crimean Peninsula, it would be seven o'clock at night. The sixteen-hour flight and the time difference had left him mildly disjointed, but he did not feel any jet lag. His body's internal clock adjusted easily.

In his new identity, Grigor was Wendell Balen, an importer, exporter and distributor of artisanal foods from North Carolina. He was thirty-six and divorced, with no children. Balen, who had flown directly into town after a business trip to Ukraine, was here to arrange for distribution deals between a bee honey producer in Simferopol and several high-end US retailers in New York and Hawaii. Crimean mountain honey was a centuries-old delicacy, set apart by the local subspecies of bees, their unique diet of high forest nectars and regional beekeeping techniques. Grigor had thoroughly versed himself in the subject during his flight.

Outside the terminal now, he hailed a yellow cab from the queue and set his single travel bag on the seat beside him.

The driver half turned. He was a young Black man with a small red lightning bolt tattoo on his neck.

"How are you today, sir?" His accent was West African. Senegalese French.

Grigor studied the neck tattoo. It closely resembled the Russian body marker worn by Krovavaya Molniya, or Blood Lightning, a Russian strike force made up of three elite military units with neural implants. Though recently the brainport computers had become popular throughout Eastern Europe, where cheap implant clinics were everywhere.

There hadn't been any in the States when he left five months ago.

"I'm fine, thank you," Grigor said, then gave the driver his Manhattan destination in Balen's Virginia Tidewater accent. The Westin-Marriott Grand Central, but first a stop in Greenwich Village. He provided the address. "You'll wait? I won't be five minutes."

"No problem, sir."

The route to the downtown location appeared on the taxi's GPS screen. Then its meter reset.

Grigor noticed that the driver never lifted his hands off the wheel.

A Bluetooth neurolink.

He sat back as the taxi pulled from the curb and slid into the thick crawl of vehicles leaving the airport. Neurolink vogue in America, he thought. Change swept the mighty. And it was nothing compared to what else was coming in with the tide.

Twenty miles west across two boroughs and the East River, Leo Harris was in a taxi heading toward an office building on Lower Broadway. As the driver pulled to the curb, Harris swiped his credit card—contactless skimming being a personal taboo given his knowledge of its vulnerabilities—then added a tip to the fare and pushed out onto the street.

The address at which he'd arrived was an old-style limestone edifice mostly occupied by long established legal and financial firms. The glazed entrance was set back from the street and had a lot of polished brass around its frame. So did the neat rows of windows climbing the twenty-five-story facade.

Harris stood on the pavement a full three minutes, motionless. Pedestrians bumped past. Some of them glanced back at him and swore. He ignored them and didn't budge. When he'd last been in this neighborhood it was a dark zone, the power grid down, the air thick with blast soot, people flooding the street in a mass panic. He didn't recall being scared that day. Horrified and angry, yes. Wanting to find whoever was responsible and take them apart with his bare hands. But not scared.

Today, he was scared as hell.

He took a deep breath and held it as long as he could before he slowly exhaled, a habit he'd picked up while rehabilitating his damaged lungs. He took a second deep breath and held it and released it. Then he smoothed his tuxedo and forced himself across the sidewalk and through the glazed front door.

A uniformed security guard sat at a small marble reception desk a few steps in and to the left. On the wall to Harris's immediate right was an old-fashioned lobby directory. The company names and offices were listed alphabetically in white on a glassed-in black letter board. He paused and found the name of the attorney he'd come to see. The office was on the seventeenth floor.

Harris turned to the reception desk, presented his identification and told the guard where he was going. The guard called up to confirm his appointment and tapped a touch screen on his desk. Along with a small printer, it was the only visible conccssion to modernity in the lobby. The printer spat out a guest badge and the guard handed it to Harris with a clear plastic clip-on holder. Then he pointed him to the elevator.

Harris did not wear the badge and instead put it in his right inside breast pocket. He hated adding it to the bulk of his wallet, but his phone was even bulkier and already in the tux's left inner pocket. He thought the alternative better than clipping it to the satin lapel.

At the elevator, Harris pushed the button and waited. The door was shiny brass with ornamental panels that distorted his reflection. He took his long, practiced breaths, hoping to God he wouldn't start to perspire. He didn't want to use his carefully folded pocket square to mop his broad, endless expanse of forehead.

The elevator came. Harris got in, studied himself in the security mirror and patted a few straggles of thinning hair into place.

The doors along the hallway on Seventeen were some sort of rich dark brown wood. Mahogany, probably. The floor was smooth polished marble. He followed the signs to the attorney's office, inhaled and exhaled, pressed the buzzer. The door opened and he went in.

A middle-aged receptionist at the desk. Graying hair, neatly dressed, a gold brooch on her blouse. She looked at him a moment. Looked at him some more. Gave him an efficient and amiable smile.

"I came to see John Gordon," he said nervously.

"Yes, he's expecting you." She was still looking at him. "Mr. Harris, forgive me, but did we drag you away from an affair of some kind? If that's so, we can reschedule—"

"Why would I reschedule?"

"Well, I only asked because—"

Harris thought he'd seen her eyes go to the front of his collar.

"They're turtles," he interrupted and tapped a finger to his bow tie. "I live with a box turtle."

"Oh, ah…"

"He's my *pet*. I picked him up off the road before he could get squashed."

"Oh, that's so sweet…"

"I don't want to reschedule."

"Yes, sir. I'd just thought of it because you're—"

"I came about Charlotte Pemstein's will. The *late* Charlotte Pemstein."

"Yes, sir. I know…"

Harris inhaled, exhaled. "I'm her daughter Rachel's godfather," he said. "The judge's daughter, I mean."

"Yes, I'm aware of that." The receptionist smiled. "I knew Judge Pemstein for many years. She was a fine woman."

Harris nodded.

"I don't want to reschedule," he said for the third time.

"Right, sir. I understand. And I do apologize for any confusion. If you'll take a seat, Mr. Gordon should be ready in—"

"I want to adopt Rachel Pemstein," he said. "That's why I came. I want to be her dad."

The receptionist smiled again. Harris reminded himself to breathe slowly. But it was no good. He was gasping for air and as terrified as he had ever been in his life.

Crimean Peninsula

Crimea was seven hours ahead of New York on the world clock, making it seven thirty at night inside the submarine bunker where Drajan Petrovik stood with Koschei on the concrete dock, the glow of the high overhead lights struggling to reach them through the shadows. It trickled down from the ceiling arches, weak and yellow, as if through some denser medium than air.

A small handful of technicians and mechanics in coveralls moved about the bunker's outer bay. Some were on the dock tapping on handheld devices. Others stood on the gangways extending out to the sub. A few with lighted helmets were doing their final inspections atop its narrow upper deck.

The vessel was sleek and tubular. It had no conning tower but a communications mast that could fully retract into the hull when not in use. The titanium alloy hull had been shaped while the metal was still ductile and then strengthened by heat treatment. Its outer skin was jet-black and smooth as silk, like the wings of a bat. There were no external markings.

"When I was young the boats traveled in slow motion," Koschei said. "In the water they made a racket like cement trucks. Their compartments stank of sweat and diesel fumes."

Drajan was quiet. The air was heavy and moist. He heard water sloshing beneath the lip of the dock.

"Those were the days," he said. "Is that what you're telling me?"

Koschei grinned. "I should bottle my sentimentalism around you," he said. "But I tell you sincerely…

give me the rest of the night to admire our miracle, and I wouldn't budge."

Drajan turned to him. "I define my own miracles. No one else."

"And you don't think we're looking at one? A submarine that can travel like this beauty?"

"Ask again in a few days, and I'll tell you."

Koschei was silent. He had noticed some workers hoisting in a gangway to his right, then glanced beyond them to the hinged carbon-steel floodgates at the mouth of the bunker. They were presently sealed and watertight. In a few short minutes they would swing wide open to fill the submarine bay with water.

"Well, then, let's go," he said. "We should get out of here before the dock is submerged."

Drajan nodded, slid his hands into the pockets of his trench coat.

"On that," he said, "we can agree."

They walked deeper into the mountain, turned from the dock into a corridor blasted out of solid rock, walked through into a second corridor, and then entered the control room. It was lighted and filled with monitors.

Half an hour later, they watched the massive floodgates open, the boat stealing out of the bunker into the dark channel water. At the console next to Koschei, Drajan brushed a glance over the other man's face. What had the Chinese poet written? *Bears, dragons, tempestuous on moun-*

tain and river. Startle the forest and make the heights tremble.

Koschei seemed enthralled, lost in his old dream.

Which was right where Drajan wanted him.

People's Republic of China

It was half past midnight and pitch-dark out when General Wei's plane taxied to a halt at Beijing Xijiao airport north of the city center. The segregated runway was typically used for government charter flights taking off or landing under a blanket of secrecy.

Wei struggled down the lowered airstairs to the tarmac, his hips and knees swollen and tender from all his hours in the sky. His long trip had taken a toll.

Like Wei, the driver who would take him to the ministry wore civilian clothing, a navy blue suit. Wei had expected as much. His mission had not been official when he'd left the capital days before. It was not official now that he was at its end.

The driver approached, took his bag and walked him to the car idling on the apron, a Hongqi H7 limousine. Wei moved beside him with a wooden, stilted gait, then got into the back seat just as rigidly and slowly. It was rare that he had days without pain in his joints, and changes in air pressure had a toxic effect. But he was also slowed by the weight of his thoughts. Their heaviness was palpable.

He had barely squawked at General Huang's call to meet at this hour after a mentally and physically long and depleting trip. What could he possibly have said? Huang's rank and status demanded obedience. Yes, he'd used a suede flogger tonight. The sort that left no telltale marks. But the good show horse—and the smart one—still knew to prance at its crack.

And of course, Huang had license to summon him wherever and whenever he chose. As head of the CMC's disciplinary committee, he would bear prime responsibility for the extent and nature of Zhou's punishment. And the severest punishment was unquestionably warranted. The files Wei had sent from Fiery Cross Reef last night and this morning contained information so combustible it was likely to ignite a war with America.

So timing was urgent. Wei wouldn't split hairs. But he remained puzzled. For all their youthful adventures, Huang had never sought him out as a confidant. Never consulted with him before making a decision. Never since rocketing past him in rank and station. Not once in thirty years. Why insist they meet ahead of the full committee? The secretaries were completely aware of his mission. And Wei's residence in the Jinsun neighborhood was midway between the airport and the August 1st Building. Why not give him a few hours to rest and prepare?

Let's talk when we talk.

That they would, Wei thought, and settled back

as the limousine turned onto the 4th Ring Road heading west.

It was an exponentially smoother ride than his flight in. For that, if for little or nothing else, he was thankful tonight.

7

Various Locales
April 16, 2024

New York

The shop was Kosov's Imports on Sullivan Street. Grigor was no stranger to it. He had been there more than once during his earlier stay in the city.

The cab he'd taken from the airport pulled up front. He got out, went to the door and entered the place.

It was long and narrow with wooden counters, a hardwood floor and old-fashioned balance scales. Sausages and smoked meats hung beneath the tin ceiling. There were dried herbs and seasonings in hand-labeled apothecary jars, shelves of fruit preserves and pickled vegetables, piles of canned pâtés, and barrels of sweets, grains and nuts sold by weight. The scent in the air was an odd mixture of staleness and spice.

A man in an apron was bagging items at the cash register. A handful of customers browsed about deeper inside.

Grigor waited as the man finished the sale and came around the counter. He was thick, wide and florid, with a gut that strained the straps of his apron.

"I have your order boxed up," he said.

Grigor followed him down the center aisle, boards creaking underfoot. Toward the back he passed a display case of *matryoshka* dolls. They reminded him of the White One, Natasha. She had clung to hers when she arrived at the secret city as a child, five years his junior, youngest of the tame foxes. He recalled her holding it closer to her chest whenever he came near her.

Against the rear wall, a floor-to-ceiling rack of Russian wines and spirits. Next to it, a door. The shopkeeper opened it, motioned for Grigor to follow and closed the door behind him. They were in a small, square stockroom. The shelves were crammed with merchandise. On a table was a plain brown carton sealed with packing tape.

The shopkeeper lifted it off the table.

"Here you are," he said. "*Obo vsem pozabotili.* Your full order."

Grigor took the box from his hands and tucked it under his arm. "Always a pleasure," he said, using the fictitious Wendell Balen's accent again. "You look fit."

The shopkeeper snorted a laugh.

"I'm alive," he said. "One moment. I have a little something extra. For a good customer."

His hand dipped into one of his apron's front pockets and produced a folding knife. It was a little over six inches long with a black handle. He thumbed the lock stud, flipped it open to display the blade, then closed it.

"It's ceramic…nice curve, eh?" he said, holding it out. "Won't get through airport security these days. But most other places still don't use those CT scanners. And the spring isn't usually enough to set off metal detectors."

Grigor took it with his free hand and slipped it into his jacket pocket.

"Thank you," he said. "I'll use it as a box cutter."

Another snort of laughter. "Try it on a nice filet mignon at your hotel. The blade cuts meat just fine."

Grigor smiled fractionally. "I'll remember," he said.

The shopkeeper nodded and opened the door. They both left the little stockroom. Then Grigor turned and carried the carton out to his ride.

It was not at all lightweight.

New Jersey

Musil drove his Acura across the river into New Jersey. It was a slow crawl through heavy traffic and took an hour and twenty minutes. About halfway there he wondered if he could have jogged to Teaneck faster.

Stephen Gelfland owned an ordinary, single-story ranch house on a quiet suburban street. A small square front yard, evergreen shrubs, an attached two-car garage. As he pulled up, Musil noticed a white Kia Sorento in the driveway behind a pearl-blue Toyota sedan. The Sorento had a Pennsylvania license plate and presumably belonged to Gelfland's cousin.

Musil swung in behind it and parked with his tail end almost sticking out onto the road. He noticed heaps of decaying brown leaves on the driveway and early season grass. Mixed in with them were a few windblown food and candy wrappers and a couple of yellowed, rain-cockled pages from a newspaper. Signs that the place had been vacant since autumn.

No one was in sight.

He left the car, looked around outside the garage a minute and still didn't see anybody. Then the front door to the house opened. In the entryway was a sandy-haired woman of about forty wearing jeans and a lavender sweater. She gave him a high wave.

Presumably he'd found Clara Hughes.

"Agent Musil." She came outside. "Nice to meet you."

He bowed his head slightly. "The same, Ms. Hughes."

"Please, call me Clara."

"Clara." Musil motioned back toward the driveway. "Does the Toyota belong to your cousin?"

"Yes, it's Steve's." She paused. "CloudCable gave him a corporate rental for his training in Massachusetts. They say he drove it up to meet the ship last January."

"Just before it sailed."

She nodded. "The car was dropped off at their New Hampshire headquarters. Where the *Stalwart* was docked."

Musil gestured toward the Toyota. "I wonder why he didn't pull into the garage. He would have known he was leaving it here for quite a while."

"All winter," Clara said. "The car isn't even two years old. But Steve didn't bother to lock it up."

Musil smoothed his beard but said nothing.

"Would you care to come in?" she asked. "I can give you a look around."

He nodded and followed her through the door.

The house was small but tidy, with a cookie-cutter interior layout that would have been some suburban-tract developer's idea of an average middle-income home. A combined living room and dinette, a kitchen behind it. Just before the kitchen was a hall running to the right and another to the left. Each probably led to a single bedroom. There would be a full bath in one, a second bathroom off the master bedroom. The sofa, chairs and tables looked ordinary and inexpensive. The sort of furniture that almost faded into the walls.

Musil turned to Clara. "When did you first check on the house?"

She had the slightly distant expression people got when flipping back mental calendar pages. "My guess would be the tenth or eleventh."

"Of February?"

"Yes. It would have been a Sunday. When my husband's off work."

Musil was thinking that roughly matched the timeline she'd given him over the phone. As he recalled, her missing person's report was filed on the thirteenth. "Is this how it looked that day, Clara? Everything in place?"

"Yes," she said. "Well, the kitchen was a mess. That bothered me. And still does. It isn't Steve."

"What do you mean?"

"I found a box of Kellogg's on the counter that was all torn up. Cornflakes everywhere. Not to mention squirrel poop. I think one might've gotten in through the chimney, worked its way down and gone after the cereal."

Musil looked at her. "That can happen when a home is vacant for a while."

"Maybe," she said. "If they got into the cupboards. But it surprised me that Steve left the box out. And left things to go bad in the fridge. Cold cuts, Swiss cheese, eggs. Some oranges and vegetables. There was a half-empty bottle of soda. Apple cider too. Also, food in the freezer. Pizza, TV dinners. Though I suppose they could last a while."

"Is all that really unlike him? Single men aren't always known for their neatness."

"My cousin doesn't fit the stereotype," she said. "He lost his mom when he was young. His father—my uncle Bob—was a delivery truck driver. He usually came home late. Steve was responsible for their meals, keeping the apartment clean, laundry... basically the household chores. He wouldn't leave food rotting in the fridge."

"Did you mention this to the police?"

"Yes. They were here before I tossed everything out. So they saw for themselves."

"What did they say?"

"Pretty much what you did, Agent. That he's a single guy. Like they're all the same."

"My apology. I meant no offense."

"It's OK," Clara said. "I appreciate that you're listening to me. When I told the police about Steve usually visiting my family for the holidays, their eyes glazed over. I think cops blank out when they hear things like that. I think *they* think you're painting a rosy picture for their benefit. Or just forgetting a disagreement." She shrugged. "It's understandable, I guess. Steve's forty. An adult. There was no sign of a crime. And the cable company confirmed he showed up for the cruise. He has every right to ignore his relatives."

"Except you don't believe he would."

"No, I don't."

Musil stood thinking a minute. The house was quiet. A musty, vacant silence. Anyone who walked in the door would sense it hadn't been lived in for months.

"Clara, do you recall when you and Steve last spoke?" he asked.

"Yes," she said. "To the day."

"How is that?"

"When his father was alive, Steve always had Thanksgiving dinner at his place on Long Island. After Uncle Bob died three years ago, he spent the holiday on a ship somewhere around Australia. I think he just wanted to get away for a while. Then the next year, I talked him into coming over, and it was fun. So I called to invite him again last November. It was the first Thursday of the month. Exactly three weeks before the holiday. I wanted him to have time to decide."

"And he declined?"

She nodded. "Steve can be solitary. But he's not unsociable. He told me once that he spends so much time crammed into a hold with other sailors he kind of likes staying home. Reading, watching television. With the *Stalwart* cruise around the corner, he said he'd take a rain check, fix himself Thanksgiving dinner and conference us."

"And he never did."

Clara shook her head. "That's what I mean when I say none of this is like Steve."

Musil smoothed his beard between his thumb and forefinger. "Would you mind if I have a look around the premises? I won't take long."

She smiled a weary smile.

"I'm glad you're actually here checking things out," she said. "Please, go ahead. Take all the time you need."

New York

John Gordon, Esq., was about fifty-five, a chubby, agreeable-looking man with thick brown hair, a neatly trimmed brown mustache and very white teeth. Seated behind a huge wooden executive desk, he was wearing a short-sleeved pin-striped shirt, no tie, and had draped his sport coat over the back of his chair.

"It's a pleasure to meet you, Mr. Harris," he said, rising as Harris entered the room. "Have I taken you away from something important?"

Harris was thinking that seemed to be the question of the day. "No," he said. "Why?"

"Well, you're, ah, very dressed up."

Harris looked at him. "I'm here to adopt a little girl," he said, plainly. "I figure that's as important as it gets."

Gordon smiled, motioned him into a chair and settled back into his own.

"Well, I'm glad you weren't inconvenienced," he said. "When we spoke on the phone, I probably should have made it clearer that we didn't have to do this in person."

Harris wasn't sure what he meant. "You told me you wanted to talk about Rachel Pemstein."

"Yes," Gordon said. "But we could have scheduled a video conference. If you were too busy."

"Rachel's ten years old. She lost her mom."

"Tragically, yes."

"How could I be too busy?"

Gordon looked at him a moment, offered another smile. "That's just what I like to hear," he said. "And by the way, sir, it's an honor to meet you. Really, how often does one get the opportunity to sit across from someone who saved the president?"

"Thanks," Harris said. "About Rachel—"

"Unfortunately, everything's been on hold because of your hospitalization." Gordon smiled his personable smile. "You're doing well, by the way? Because your health goes to your ability to care for a child her age. It will become critical throughout the application process."

Harris wondered if he'd missed something.

"I'm not here to apply for anything," he said. "Charlotte made me Rachel's godfather. She wanted me to adopt if something happened to her. It's in her will."

"Yes, she was very clear about it," Gordon said. "But you'll still need to go through the process. There are rules and requirements. Comprehensive steps you'll need to take. It's all in the packet."

"Wait." Harris looked at him. "What packet?"

"The adoption packet. Did I forget to mention it?"

Gordon opened a file drawer, pulled out a large manila envelope and held it across the desk in both hands.

"Here," he said. "I prepared this for you."

Harris took it from him. It was thick and hefty.

"This feels like a book by one of those thriller writers," he said.

Gordon chuckled. "It contains all the paperwork to be filled out. Also, literature that explains what's required of you in terms of documentation. References, a psychosocial evaluation, federal, state and local criminal history checks—"

"Criminal history?"

"Yes," Gordon said. "You'll need to be fingerprinted."

Harris looked at him. "I'm director of investigations at Net Force."

"Yes, I know—"

"I headed the FBI Cyber unit right here in this city."

"Yes."

"Plus, everybody knows I saved the president's *life*. You just brought it up yourself."

"Yes. And again, I'm honored to—"

"So how come you need my fingerprints?"

Gordon looked at him. "I don't," he said. "But an adoption will have to go through a New Jersey state agency. The laws are strict, and rightfully so. Again, it's a process."

"And how long does this process take?"

"Six months. Give or take."

"Six?"

"If things go smoothly."

Harris looked at him.

"OK," he said. "Anything else?"

"An unsolicited piece of advice. If I may."

"OK."

"You should hire an attorney. One specializing in adoptions. And licensed in Jersey, of course," Gordon said. "Believe me, you don't want to enter this process unrepresented. It is full of land mines."

Half a minute passed. Harris remembered his breathing exercises. He inhaled, exhaled. Inhaled, exhaled.

"Don't you think maybe that's another little something you could've mentioncd to me beforehand?" he said finally.

Gordon scratched under his chin.

"Now that *you* mention it," he said, smiling, "I do."

New Jersey

Musil did a full walk around, saw nothing unusual and decided to retrace his steps in case he'd missed something. Partway through his second circuit, he heard branches rustling in a tall blue spruce alongside the house.

He paused, glanced up toward the noise and saw a squirrel with pouched-out cheeks leap from the tree to the roof and then disappear over its sloping side. Possibly he had found Clara's cereal-eating culprit. It could have established a nest in the attic.

He didn't notice anything else of any interest. The cereal box aside, Gelfland had left the premises in good shape. Of course, he had been gone four months. The whole winter. Wind, rain, snow and the other elements would have obliterated most signs of…

Of what?

Musil really didn't know. But he sympathized with Clara and wouldn't dismiss her concerns. Based on what she'd told him, Gelfland did seem to have acted out of character by not calling her before traveling to Massachusetts—and later leaving on the *Stalwart* cruise. But that didn't make him the victim of a crime. People were complicated. They did things for all kinds of reasons. There might have been some personal issue he didn't want to share with his family. Or maybe he'd just been busy or forgetful. The mundane explanations most often proved to be the right ones.

Still, Musil was intent on being thorough. Clara had given him the Toyota's key fob. He would look inside the car and see what he could find.

He walked across the front yard to the driveway. As he neared its paved edge, he once again noticed the pile of unraked autumn leaves alongside it on the grass. Gelfland's trees and shrubs all seemed to be evergreens, so Musil guessed they had blown onto the lawn from the road or a neighbor's house. Out of curiosity, he crouched to pluck up one of the rain-warped newspaper sheets. The paper was discolored and the print washed out, but he was able to read the December 4 date on the top left.

He pulled a second sheet of newsprint out of the moldering leaves. It was dated February 19 and plastered with ads for long-expired President's Day sales. But that only meant Gelfland had been gone a while. Which Musil already knew.

He rose, went over to the car, unlocked it. Then opened the driver's door and poked his head through. Everything looked normal to him. In fact, the interior was immaculate. He saw no empty water bottles, coffee cups, coins or food wrappers. No clutter or junk of any kind.

Musil knelt for a cursory look under the driver's seat. The carpet was meticulously clean, its napping free of grit or soil tracked in from outside, which was exceptional for a two-year-old car. It fit Clara's portrait of Gelfland. Probably he vacuumed it on a regular basis.

Musil was about to pull his head out of the car when something caught his eye. A white slip of paper between the bottom of the center console and the driver's seat. He guessed it must have dropped down there unnoticed.

He got in behind the steering wheel, slid his hand under the seat and groped for it. After a few seconds his fingers found the slip and pulled it out.

It was a sales receipt. A cash register printout. Crisp and clearly legible. The name of the store was Rany's Market Basket. A nearby address. The date stamp was November 22, 2023. The time read 19:00:35. Seven o'clock at night.

He checked the calendar on his watch and then

read down the list of grocery items. A frozen turkey breast, stuffing mix, cranberry sauce, two sweet potatoes. A pumpkin pie. Canned whipped cream. Beer. A pack of paper towels.

Musil sat there looking at the receipt for several minutes. He wasn't sure what it meant. Or that it meant anything. But he folded and deposited it neatly into his jacket pocket before locking up the car.

He walked back up to the house, stopping a few feet from the door to think. He'd suddenly remembered the squirrel up on the roof. Its cheeks full of nuts that it had gathered to stash away for a later date.

He went back into the house. Clara was waiting for him in the living room, the look on her face equal parts anticipation and dread. Musil had seen it countless times on the families of the missing. *Did you find anything out about my son? Daughter? Wife? Anything at all?*

He decided to show her the register receipt.

"Your cousin went to the market the Wednesday night before Thanksgiving," he said. "It's close by. A five-minute drive from here."

She nodded, reading the list. Then her brow creased. "So Steve fixed Thanksgiving dinner. Like he told me he would."

"He certainly bought the groceries." Musil paused, curious. "Didn't you tell me he left right after the holiday weekend?"

She looked up at him. "Yes," she said. "The police say he picked up his rental car the Monday after Thanksgiving. His training in Massachusetts started around December first, so it makes sense he'd take a week to drive up and get settled there."

Musil was thinking he would double-check the dates for himself. The rental pickup, the start of Gelfland's training and orientation. Records of where he stayed while he took it. Likely a corporate apartment.

"Clara," he said, "were you being specific about the items in the refrigerator?"

"Yes." Her eyes lowered to the receipt, returned to Musil. She shook her head slightly, puzzled. "None of these things were inside when I emptied it out."

"You're positive? He bought a lot of food for one person. It would seem he'd have leftovers. The turkey, pie, beer—"

"They weren't in there, Agent. I would remember. It would have reassured me that Steve was telling the truth."

"About staying home for the holiday."

"Yes."

Musil was thoughtful. The distance to Boston was about two hundred miles. A three- or four-hour drive depending on traffic. He supposed Gelfland could have packed some leftovers or prepared sandwiches to eat along the way...

"Something else doesn't make sense to me," Clara said.

He waited.

"The receipt says Steve bought paper towels," she said. "But I hardly found any when I cleaned up. There were a few sheets left on a roll in the kitchen. That's it."

Musil glanced at the receipt. "This says he bought a pack of six."

"Yes."

"Might he have stored some away? In a closet, possibly? A kitchen cabinet?"

"I looked everywhere around the house, Agent. All his closets, the garage, the basement. I told you how Steve is very organized. So when I noticed the roll in the kitchen was low, I expected he'd have some fresh ones around."

"And you couldn't find them."

"Not one," Clara said. "Who uses up six rolls of paper towels over a single weekend?"

Musil had found himself wondering the same thing. Then he pictured the squirrel with its cheeks full of foraged food. It seemed to have gotten them stored away inside the house. He wasn't so sure about Gelfland's groceries on Thanksgiving eve.

Back out on the walk, Musil thanked Clara for her helpfulness and promised to be in touch. He was eager to get back to headquarters, put his turbaned head together with Ki Marton's bald one and see if they could figure anything out between them.

"If there's anything else I can do, please give me a call," she said. Then sighed, a long string of breath that seemed to pull her shoulders down as it left her mouth. "I feel kind of selfish, you know."

He shook his head. "I'm not certain I understand."

"Those people on the *Stalwart*. Aren't there seventy of them? They're all missing. The whole crew. And here I'm worried about my cousin as if he's the only one."

He smiled, gently. "How can caring be selfish?"

She started to answer. Hesitated, as if reconsidering. Then nodded.

"I did an online search after we spoke on the phone," she said. "You saved that little boy last summer...went into that park after him alone. I read an article about it."

His head dipped and rose. "I was just doing my job. That's all."

Clara smiled a little.

"I knew you'd say that. You said the same thing to the reporters," she replied. Then paused a beat. "Agent, you thanked me a minute ago. But I want to thank you for listening to me. For coming out here. It means a lot."

Musil stood there in silence. He didn't know what to say. Her words had made him feel awkward.

"I'll be in touch," he replied finally.

As he drove away from the house a few min-

utes later, he glanced in the rearview mirror to see
Clara still out front.

It occurred to him that she looked very sad.

The Terminal

Every so often, Ki Marton found himself thinking back to a pandemic lockdown fad called the
Walk-In Naked Challenge. The name said it all.
Someone would walk in on his or her partner stark
naked while said partner was working from home,
record the reaction and slap it up on social media.
Maybe the best video won a prize. Probably not.
He didn't recall. Months of being stuck between
four walls had left everybody bored and depressed
and primed for cheap thrills. Strange days, indeed,
to quote Jim Morrison.

Be that as it may, Ki was sure the challenge
wouldn't have turned out well for him. He'd been
too compassionate to victimize countless unwary,
languishing strangers with a glimpse of his bare,
scrawny, plucked-chicken physique. Things had
been hard enough for everybody. Why up their
misery? Besides, Mark had been a very reserved
person. He wouldn't have appreciated the stunt
one bit. Ditto for Ki's old bosses at the FBI.

These days, Ki sometimes felt his job was the
flip side of that craze. As a social media specialist with the Force, he spent long hours creeping
through a public gallery of exhibitionistic Facebook, Instagram, Chirp and ClickChat users. Lit-

erally and figuratively barging through their open digital doors while *they* were naked. The accounts were vast, fertile and largely unguarded fields of useful information waiting to be harvested. But for all the time he'd put in over the past few months and all his legitimate reasons for poking around in people's lives, the job still felt uncomfortable and voyeuristic. He didn't know what compelled them to expose themselves to the whole wide world. He didn't get how they could be so reckless putting things out there for anyone to see…until they were hurt or embarrassed by it.

At his workstation on the Terminal's third floor Cyberdogs division, Ki had started out digging up info about Stephen Gelfland with a routine, methodical set of procedures, entering Gelfland's biographical info into his search tool, then stealthily tracking mentions of his name across a plethora of different online sources—employment agencies, public records, LinkedIn, e-sellers, online dating sites and, of course, social media platforms.

It turned out Gelfland was a very private individual. His only SMP was a Facebook account that had been inactive for years. He therefore didn't have many online contacts.

Still, Ki managed to get hold of a few web images. One was about a decade old and scraped from the State University of New York Maritime College's *Eight Bells* yearbook, which was archived in the school's digital library. Another was a much more recent US State Department passport photo. Since passports were public record, Ki hadn't needed court permission to pull it.

Ki's next step was uploading the pics to his Mirror Image face recognition app. The AI-powered search engine found and compared visually similar images of people using facial geometry, converting it into mathematical algorithms. It then measured how alike they were and served out the best matches. Mirror Image was intelligent enough to compensate for the filters people used when they posted photos on the internet, providing direct links to the sites where it found them.

Easy-peasy. As the app kicked out its photos and background data on Gelfland, Ki started belting out a tune from his extensive mental playlist. His current selection being "The Irish Rover," he let loose in his best Shane MacGowan growl, feeling he was on a productive roll. It was a habit he'd picked up at home after Mark died, though he supposed the Terminal's odd acoustical properties had encouraged it at work. His office was small, bare and square. It had exactly enough room for a desk, with three computer screens, some file cabinets and a couple of chairs. Plain and unadorned, with the notable exception of its high tin ceiling, which the interior designers had left as a decorative touch when they converted the building's original store-rooms into modern workspaces.

That ceiling was where the quirky acoustics came in.

Ki had noticed its ornate panels and moldings

immediately after being assigned the office. Not long afterward, he also noticed they would vibrate sympathetically when he sang to himself, almost as if humming along. Meanwhile, the building's thick brick walls tended to mute most sounds, so no one around him seemed disturbed.

All told, Ki found it great for singing while he worked, and he was taking full advantage right now. His eyes on his monitors, the ceiling resonating overhead, he was about to launch into his favorite line—the one about Johnny McGurk being scared stiff of work—when somebody somewhere uploaded something to Facebook that changed everything about his thus far routine search.

"What the hell's this?" he whispered under his breath, the song abruptly clipped off his tongue, the ceiling panels no longer humming.

He got only his own puzzled silence for an answer.

Grigor's twentieth-floor room at the Westin-Marriott was big, bright and bland. A midrange reservation, no conspicuous suites, nothing to draw attention to himself.

As soon as he arrived there, he put his suitcase and carton down on the bed, unzipped the suitcase and got his scanner out of an inner compartment.

It looked like a cross between a smartphone and a pocket transistor radio. Black with two antennas: a stub and a collapsible. It had a display screen, some LED indicator lights, some button controls. A tiny camera lens on its upper right.

The antennas would detect any radio signals emanating from hidden cameras or microphones. The camera lens was for an AI visual inspection. Its high-definition computer eye could pick up finer details than any human eye and would not be fooled by camouflage. As the scanner processed the video images, its software would analyze them in real time with machine learning, looking for the shapes and characteristics of the surveillance devices in its database. A library in the hundreds of thousands. If it recognized one, it would show an alert, identify its manufacturer and give precise factory information about its settings and operation.

Grigor was still in his jacket as he switched on the scanner and swept the room. He moved it across the walls and ceiling, pointing the scanner's antennas at them. Then he passed its face across them as if taking photos or a video.

He gave the bed, dresser, nightstands, chairs and desk a thorough sweep, opening all the drawers to scan inside them. He bent low to scan under the furniture, then swept the entire floor from corner to corner. He checked out the lamps, electrical sockets and USB connector ports. He swept the windows, curtain and temperature control unit. He opened the wardrobe closet and ran it across its interior. Did the same with the minifridge, microwave and coffee maker. He went into the bathroom and skimmed the tub, toilet, sink and cabinets. Then he took the folded towels down off the shelves, swept the wall behind them, neatly replaced them and stepped back out into the main room.

He gave it a quick second pass. The scanner didn't beep, flash or vibrate. Its display showed nothing out of the ordinary. Satisfied the room was clean, Grigor returned the device to his suitcase and pulled the ceramic knife out of his jacket. Unfolding the blade, he slid it over the carton's shipping tape and lifted its flaps.

A box cutter.

The guns were in a backpack with specially designed sleeves, panels and pockets. He removed one to look it over, a Glock 43X with custom upgrades: an extra-long slide, extended magazine receiver, three-sixty stippling and modular reflex optics cutout. He brought it up to firing position and peered down the barrel and hefted it in his hands. It felt solid and balanced. Everything done to spec.

Grigor set the pistol down on the bed and lifted out the other gun, a tiny, lightweight Czech Scorpion EVO 3 carbine. He had requested only two changes from its original configuration, reducing the trigger pull from nine pounds to five, and replacing the original rigid brace with an adjustable one. He inspected it carefully, tested the pull, opened the brace and tucked it against his shoulder. The fit was snug and comfortable.

He put the carbine down on the bed next to the Glock, then went through the rest of the backpack's contents. In its various compartments were a pair of fiber-optic sights, two 9 mm suppressors, five 17-round magazines for the Glock, five 20-round clips for the carbine, and a fabric concealed-carry holster. Also some other specialized items he had requested from the old Russian shopkeeper.

He took out the holster, slid the Glock into it and strapped the holster around his waist inside his pants. Then he returned the Scorpion to the backpack and stashed the empty carton in the wardrobe closet.

Grigor checked his watch. Half past noon. He was hungry from traveling thousands of miles and briefly considered room service. But after a minute he decided to wait. Instead, he took his laptop out of the suitcase to review some files that he had hesitated to open on the plane, where it might have caught the eye of some bored and prying fellow passenger.

At the desk, he brought up one of the files, a dossier gathered from both confidential and open sources. FBI Field Agent Amenjot Musil had gained international attention after the cyberattack on New York. He was the heroic rescuer of a helpless child, the man who chased down the president's would-be assassin. His face had been everywhere in the media, and a fair portion of the file's contents was public record. His home address and the names of his wife and children were from hacked FBI personnel files.

Grigor studied all the photographs and read all the information and committed it all to memory. Within minutes he had learned enough to get started hunting Musil.

People's Republic of China

The Hongqi H7 limousine was China's answer to the Rolls Royce Phantom 300 or the Mercedes-Maybach S-Class Pullman Guard. A fancier of luxury automobiles, Wei had been told the president commissioned its antique design after seeing his Russian counterpart primp through Red Square in the Mercedes-Maybach. He thought the rumors were likely true.

Whether General Huang had sent it for him in gratitude for a successful mission, he couldn't say. The Committee certainly hadn't indicated any such feelings until now. In fact, he had been asked to travel to Fiery Cross Reef as if it was a routine errand for a man of his senior rank.

Still, he mused, old military hounds like Huang weren't prone to random gestures, and the fleet of H7s was usually reserved for honored officials. So he chose to take a sanguine view and label it a compliment. Provisionally speaking.

CMC headquarters was about ten miles from the airport, and his driver took the 4th Ring Road west across the city. Its three wide traffic lanes were mostly clear at that late hour, and the limousine skirted the technological parks and expansive campus of Beijing Medical University, sailed onto the western ring, and then dipped down south and glided off the exit less than a mile above the Ministry.

The car had turned onto the dark street running up to its gate when Wei's phone rang in his pocket. *Huang*, he thought.

A glance at the display proved him correct, but it was hardly supernatural prescience. He had lived alone since his wife died of breast cancer half a decade ago. His daughter was grown and married and the mother of three children. No one was waiting for him at home. And it was well after one in the morning. Who else would it be?

"I'm minutes away," he answered. "I can see you up ahead."

Figuratively speaking. What he saw, in fact, was the shadow of the August 1st building, where Huang would be waiting for him in his office above the square. A massive, blockish central structure with two low, flat-roofed wings, its main section stood high above the monuments and administrative buildings around it.

"Wei," Huang said, "I want you to listen carefully. It is very important."

He sat up. "Go ahead."

"You will be buried among the martyrs in Babaoshan Revolutionary Cemetery," Huang said. "The president will attend with a delegation of Party officials. There will be lavish wreaths of white flowers. You have been an honored servant of the people, and I promise your family will be treated with dignity and respect."

Wei stared over the driver's headrest. He was already turned halfway around in front, a gun in his left hand, his right hand on the steering wheel. There was a recoil compensator on the weapon's barrel.

Wei lunged forward from his seat and automatically shot his hands out to wrest the gun from him. But it flashed before he could extend his arms.

A bullet leaped from the muzzle into his forehead and blew out the back of his skull. Blood, bone and soft globs of cranial tissue sprayed the rear window. The driver fired twice again out of thoroughness. This time Wei didn't see the muzzle flashes. He sagged in the back seat, lifeless, his head a ruin.

The driver faced forward, lowered the gun onto the front console and continued along the empty street, once again with both hands on the wheel. As he neared the compound's west gate, he heard an odd scratching noise in the back and glanced in the rearview mirror.

Wei's fingers were groping at the seat leather. Opening and closing, opening and closing, though the brains were dribbling out of his skull. They still wanted to grab the gun, animated by firing neurons, trace signals from his brain's last command.

The driver watched them claw at the leather upholstery and felt a momentary chill. He had heard of such things before. But he had never seen it with his own eyes.

He gave an uneasy shrug and drove on past the gate. The dead man clutched at the seat for another half a mile.

When he finally stopped, it was to the driver's great relief.

8

The HIVE, Cyberspace

Carmody launched from the outcrop on the east side of the ravine, soaring as if on an updraft. The sky was gray and cloudy. Below him the inlet curved northward like a slowly uncoiling serpent. He saw the rough grain and contours of the ravine's sheer limestone walls, their surfaces cracked and pitted by ages of erosion and geological upheaval. He saw the folds and wrinkles of the rock faces, saw subtle gradations of color in the veins of iron ore lacing through them. He saw clusters of bare, stunted oak trees clinging to the slopes, and leaning firs with gray, resin-blistered bark. As the steppes marched to the west and inland there would be miles of towering pine woods. But not here.

He was above the inlet now, looking down, casting only a brief glance at the pixelated smudge of its western shore. The water's surface was as dark and smooth as glass in the overcast. On either side of the inlet's southern entrance were the two stone watchtowers. High up the mountain slope to the north were plain concrete structures that looked like industrial buildings. Outside them, piles of gravel, tractor-like vehicles and a spur of the rail line. The ravine became a narrow cleft there, the channel water running fast and rough, foaming white over its rocky bed. He could see that it was without bottomland, no banks or roads or bridges.

Carmody glided north for a closer look at the rail line spooling around the mountain's shoulder from the west. But as he dropped low, he hit another patch of unnatural distortion, like an aircraft flying into heavy fog. The air around him warped and became nearly opaque.

"Damn it," he said. "Enough."

The HIVE's immersive environment vanished. He was sitting next to Kali at her dining room table. He lifted off his headset and turned to her.

"The scenery's better," he said. "I don't feel so much like puking. But does it help us?"

She looked at him. "No."

"And it won't."

"No," she said. "I can continue to refine and sharpen the virtual environment. Pull current satellite transmissions from the distortion field's periphery. Interpolate imagery from older classified archives."

"But without real-time satellite recon, it's just a glorified video game."

She said nothing.

"Why are you looking at me like that?" he asked.

Kali said nothing, her eyes on his face.

Carmody frowned. "OK, I'll say the words," he said. "We're done in the States. We have to make ourselves scarce and finish what we started. Off the grid. You satisfied?"

Kali nodded.

"Yes," she said.

New York

"About time you showed up. They move Teaneck to the moon?" Ki said, sitting in front of his computers. He cranked his head around toward the office door as Musil stepped through. "We need to talk about Stephen Gelfland."

Musil pulled a chair up alongside him. It was now almost three in the afternoon. His slow, inching drive back to Manhattan had taken over twice as long as the crawl out to Jersey.

"What's this?" he said and nodded at the three-screen setup.

"You tell me," Ki said. "Then I'll tell you."

Musil studied the monitors. The middle one showed a collection of photographs. All were portrait shots of a man he didn't recognize, someone with a long thin face and light brown hair. He saw a school graduation picture, a few others that looked like ID photos. They probably spanned more than a decade and were arranged in two horizontal rows. From oldest to most recent, he guessed, although the man's features didn't change significantly from one to the next.

Musil's eyes went to the right-hand screen, then to the monitor on the left. Each displayed what appeared to be a screenshot of the same Facebook post—a photograph and text—with one very strange and glaring difference between the photos on the left and right. Both photos showed a group of four men posing spontaneously in a bar or restaurant. Three were sitting down at the end of the table, gathered close for the shot. The fourth stood behind the others, casually resting his arms on one of their shoulders, a redheaded guy with a mustache. All were smiling. On the tabletop were empty plates, half-filled glasses, scattered pieces of silverware, rumpled cloth napkins, the photo obviously taken after their meal.

The post had been made by someone named Garrett Schmidt, and his profile photo to its left matched the red-haired man in the group shot. The text entered underneath the post read:

Better days. A bunch of us from the CS Alliance in Glasgow two years ago. My buddy Steve Gelfland is the guy standing up. He's with the 77 missing in the SCS. Praying for the safety of all. #FONOPS #Shipmates #Stalwart77

Ki watched Musil studying the screen.

"The second and third hashtags are self-explanatory," he said. "That first one, FONOPS, stands for *Freedom of Navigation Operations*. It's DoD lingo for US Navy ops challenging other countries' marine territorial claims. In the real world, the policy's meant as pushback against the main international offenders. Namely the Chinese in the South China Sea."

Musil gave a vague nod, thinking hard. "The *Stalwart* is a privately owned vessel. It wasn't on FONOPS. Or connected to the Navy."

"Not directly, anyway."

"What do you mean?"

"Just that the CloudCable deal has the CIA and NGIA mixed up in it. So we can't really say *Stalwart*'s activities were strictly commercial." Ki shrugged. "Look, it could be Schmidt's just supporting our right to navigate those waters. I don't know. But that isn't why I put up those group shots."

Musil studied them in silence a minute. *Better days.* Sailors having a good time during a port call. Nothing out of the ordinary. Except for the one striking and unavoidable discrepancy. In the shot on the right, the man standing up was in fact Stephen Gelfland. Musil had recognized him at once from Clara Hughes's smartphone photograph. But he was equally certain the man standing in the left-hand version of the shot was *not* Gelfland. His clothes were the same in both. His body and posture. Everything the same until Musil looked at his face. Then, he stopped being the same. His face became altogether different, its shape and features clearly matching those of the man shown in the portrait photos.

"One of these posts has been manipulated," Musil said, pointing to the right-hand photo. "That's Gelfland over there." He brought out his own phone and showed him Clara's picture of her cousin. "You see?"

Ki studied the phone image. "Check," he said. "How about the guy in the other screens? Who's he?"

Musil shook his head. "I don't know."

Ki looked at him steadily. "What if I told you those photos in the middle are supposed to be Gelfland? The ID shots, the school pic. Every one of them. Plus, the guy standing up in the group shot on the left."

Musil's eyes widened. "Did you pull them from the same source?"

"No," Ki said. "That's the catch. Different organizations, different databases. Varying levels of network security that go from low to maximal protection. But it looks like somebody hacked *all* of them to change Gelfland's real face to a fake. And there's more."

"Tell me."

"The fake faces were created by a gencrative

adversarial network. A GAN. That's an artificial intelligence that tests itself to improve its results. Like blue-teaming and red-teaming in cybersecurity. They work together. The blue team sets up a computer system. The red team tries to penetrate and expose its flaws. Blue team patches them, red team attacks again. Over and over until the system's as secure as it can be." Ki paused. "The GAN does the same thing with its fake faces. It essentially red team-blue teams itself. Puts together a face, then analyzes it with facial-recognition algos. If it identifies any characteristics that might distinguish it from a real face, it reworks them until the fake is perfect. But what's incredible is that *these* are the same fake face at a different age. There's a Fake Gelfland face in every public database and online source that has information about him. One that's been aged properly in every instance. That takes some kind of special image-simulation technology."

"But you spotted them as fakes."

"No," Ki said. "I didn't. I wouldn't have been able to. They're indistinguishable from actual pictures of someone. Good enough to fool Mirror Image. And every other program I've got that's designed to reveal manipulated photos."

"Then, how did you know?"

"It was a total stroke of luck. When I got hold of Gelfland's college yearbook photo from the school library, I had no reason to assume it wasn't authentic. So I scanned the internet with Mirror Image to pull up any other pics along with links to social media sites. One of them was to Schmidt's post. The version on the right."

"The real Stephen Gelfland photograph."

Ki nodded. "You see when it's logged as having been posted?"

Musil read the tag off the screenshot.

"Two hours ago," he said.

Ki nodded again. "I clicked for the exact time and it was one fifteen. About ten minutes before I found it. It had *just* been put up."

Musil looked perplexed. "I don't understand. Where did the doctored photo come from?"

"The same place. That's the unbelievable part. And the lucky one too," Ki said. "Timing's everything in life. I saw the real Gelfland face *change* to the fake face on-screen while I was looking at it." He tapped the frame of his glasses. "Right before my myopic eyes."

Ki stopped talking and waited.

Finally, Musil said, "Someone is trolling images of Stephen Gelfland and changing them into counterfeits."

"You mean some*thing*," Ki said, nodding. "Let it sink in. Nobody's going to make a 24/7 career out of monitoring and changing Gelfland photos across the web. It has to be one powerful AI programmed for that single task. A dedicated Gelfland faker. Probably it cycles every few minutes or half hour or whatever. My guess is that it's to assure somebody posing as Stephen Gelfland isn't exposed by background checks."

Musil was staring at him with incredulity. "The fake face must belong to the impostor," he said. "I think he's the man that left New Hampshire with the *Stalwart*."

Ki gave another nod. "In my opinion as a humble analyst, you're dead-on, bro. But this is way above my pay grade. I wonder who would go to the trouble of setting all this up? Who'd have the *ability* to do it? And why?"

Musil sat there thinking about those questions. Then he shook his head. Not a single answer had come to him.

He needed to talk to Leo Harris right away.

New Jersey

Clara was back home from Jersey half an hour before she expected the school bus to pull up with the girls. Leaving her SUV in the garage, she went straight into the kitchen to prepare their snacks. She'd baked apple peanut butter muffins the night before and had some ready-to-drink chocolate milk in the fridge.

The landline rang as she was setting the muffins out on the little nook table. She rushed into the hallway to answer, hoping everything was all right with her parents. Only their mulishness about calling on it had prevented her from getting rid of the phone and its monthly charges ages ago.

"Hello?"

"Hello, I'm Tom Basile, Internet Security and Law Enforcement. Clara Hughes, please."

"Speaking." She cradled the phone against her shoulder and scooted back into the kitchen. "I'm kind of busy right now, so excuse my jostling around while I talk."

"No problem. This won't take long," he said. "I just need to verify your name and contact information for Evidence Control. Based on a new ticket."

Clara reached to get a couple of dishes out of the overhead cabinet. Her knocking around aside, the guy's thick New York accent didn't make him any easier to understand.

"Sorry to keep making you repeat yourself… but did you say 'Evidence Control'?"

"Yes, Ms. Hughes."

"Oh," she said. "I'm surprised. Agent Musil really didn't take anything from the house."

"That's Mr. Gelfland's residence? In Teaneck? I'm reading off the agent's notes."

"Yes, right. My cousin's place."

"Ms. Hughes, how it works is that items taken during an investigation go directly to Storage. My office has no way of knowing what they are initially. But every contact generates a reference code. So personal property can be tracked and returned. I'm guessing the agent did collect something from there."

She set the dishes on the table. "Well, he asked for a photo of my cousin, which I texted him. And he took a cash register receipt out of Steve's car. But I wouldn't think either counts."

"Actually, Ms. Hughes, everything is logged. I'll give you the reference code now, if you want to jot it down. Also, is this your best contact number?"

"Better if you use my cell," she said and gave it to him. "With two girls in middle school, I'm usually trying to be everywhere at once. Can't you tell?"

He laughed. "And you're at the East Stroudsburg address?"

"Right." She looked around, found a pen on the counter, scribbled on a napkin. "OK, I'm ready for that code."

Basile rattled the digits off to her, then repeated them in his Yankee Stadium bleacher-creature accent.

"Feel free to call if you have any problems," he said.

Grigor clicked off the line with Clara Hughes and in doing so wiped Basile and the disposable VPN phone number he'd used out of existence.

He stood at the hotel room window staring out between its parted curtains. The sun had moved west across Manhattan, and Lexington Avenue was awash in shade and shadow. The automatic climate control had lowered his air conditioner a tick as the weather cooled outside, leaving the room a little stuffy. He turned to get a bottle of water out of the fridge and reviewed what he'd learned.

His call to Hughes had lasted exactly four minutes and twelve seconds. In that time, he'd learned Musil had left Stephen Gelfland's home with two items. One was Gelfland's photograph, which would be a problem. The Wolf's image manipulation software was like a probing eye searching the internet for photos of the real Gelfland. Spot his face on a website, find it in a database, and Grigor's face would replace it. But for all its applied artificial intelligence, the software couldn't eliminate wild-card variables like the photograph on Hughes's phone. And digital space was too vast for real-time capabilities. It was fast, but not instantaneous. There would be a lag, a short gap in time between an image popping up online and its detection and substitution.

All of which Grigor had anticipated. The Gelfland deception was designed to have built-in obsolescence. The store receipt was the only surprise.

He closed his eyes. He remembered Gelfland leaving his car in his driveway the night of the kill, then walking across his lawn to his front door. Hidden in the darkness, Grigor had called out to him as he crossed the yard, mimicking Gelfland's responses, making himself *sound* like Gelfland, fine-tuning his vocal impersonation in case it was needed in the future…

"Steve, hi."

"Hello? Who is it? Hello?"

Grigor had waited until he reached his front door to take him out. Had come up behind him and locked one gloved hand over his mouth and brought his Walther up to the base of his skull.

"I'll be a fine version of you, Steve. Promise."

There had been a noisy clatter. Grigor could hear it now in his mind. He was Level Three Pinnacle with a trained photographic memory and could replay it all in clear and perfect detail. Could slow it all down and speed it all up and freeze it where he wanted a closer look.

Gelfland had carried a full grocery sack from his car, and its contents spilled out onto the ground as he struggled for his life. Glass bottles, other things. Then Grigor had put two .22-caliber bullets in his brain, and his thrashing stopped.

He drank some water, remembering, his eyelids pressed tightly together. As Gelfland had sagged out of his arms, he'd gathered the groceries off the lawn and walk and loaded them into the bag. *Turkey. Loose potatoes. Three bottles of ale. Paper towels and some canned and boxed food...*

Grigor had returned to the rental car he'd parked up the street. Hastened over to it with the grocery bag, dropped it onto the back seat and pulled into Gelfland's driveway to collect his body. Afterward, he transported it to an abandoned barn and left it in a bath of sodium hydroxide, burying the groceries and Gelfland's clothes deep in the heavily wooded Pine Barrens.

But he was sure there hadn't been a cash register slip. He had picked up the scattered grocery items and thoroughly emptied Gelfland's pockets. He was meticulous with his cleanup.

There was no receipt.

Unless Gelfland had left it in the car. It could have fallen out of the grocery bag, or he might have set it aside when putting change or his credit card into his wallet. Not that it made any difference. The important thing was that Musil had found the receipt and taken it with him. Probably for the date stamp. Which was only days before the start of Gelfland's training for the CloudCable cruise, when Grigor had assumed his identity. Add all that to Clara Hughes's picture of him and missing person report to the police, and it left no doubt Musil had sniffed a connection between Gelfland and the *Stalwart*'s disappearance.

Fake Gelfland's expiration date had come due. Musil's visit to New Hampshire set the clock ticking a little sooner than anticipated, but it really wasn't too big of a deal. Everything was still following the script Koschei had written months ago.

A moment passed. Grigor opened his eyes and went to get his backpack. He would take care of business here, finish up ahead of schedule, then move on to Pearl Harbor and prepare for the fireworks.

Crimea

On the south side of the villa's rooftop turret, a door opened onto a small, flat promenade where

Drajan sometimes came to breathe the night air and think. The balustrade and rail were carved from local marble, and he had stood leaning against it in his black silk robe for some minutes, listening to the pulse of the sea. The hardware for Assassin's Mace would be installed within days. But it had to be completely reprogrammed before it became operative.

He went back into the turret, where his laptop sat on a long, draw-leaf table in the center of a three-hundred-year-old Turkish rug. A tulip glass filled with amber liquid stood beside the computer. He hadn't left it there.

He walked over to the table, lifted the glass and sniffed above its rim. *Medovukha.* The Russian still mead, prepared from fermented honey, water, herbs and spices. Its aroma was sweet and flowery.

He glanced at the computer screen. Its wallpaper was a crossed dagger and sword, silver blades on a black background. The image a symbolic reminder of the story of Giuliano de' Medici, murdered in Florence Cathedral at High Mass. An old score and a power play with ten thousand witnesses to his nineteen cuts under the Duomo on Easter Sunday. The Pazzis, with their brazen public assassination, had meant to strike fear into the ruling family.

Niccolo Machiavelli had been arrested, interrogated and tortured as a suspected conspirator without evidence. Repeatedly hoisted by his wrists on the strappado, he composed sonnets to the Magnificent Giuliano when not hanging from a rope and pleading his innocence. The tactic worked to secure a pardon, and years later he wrote his classic *The Prince* with Giuliano in mind. It was anyone's guess whether he had in fact helped plot his death.

The new ruler must determine all the injuries he will need to inflict, he penned. *He must inflict them once and for all. The timid are always compelled to keep a knife in hand.*

"Drajan."

The voice was female, quiet and calm. He turned toward the archway that opened to the stairs.

Quintessa Leonides stood barefoot in the soft light. Her shift was loose and sleeveless, the sheer white fabric clinging above her knees. Her carefully manicured toenails were a translucent pearl color. She wore a diamond bracelet on her left ankle and held her own glass of the amber mead.

"Thank you for this." Drajan motioned slightly with the glass, then nodded toward the computer. "Give me a moment."

Quintessa shook her head once, left to right. She had the long neck of a swan, and her blond hair brushed smoothly over it.

"We need to talk," she said.

Drajan stood very still as she entered the turret, stepped onto the rug and approached him.

"I'm going to Paris," she said. "I leave in three days."

He looked at her. "How long will you be away?"

"I don't know," she said and shrugged her shoulders. "I may do some traveling afterward."

Drajan could see nothing but night through the windows behind her. Yet the escarpment in its massive dimensions was a tangible presence.

"You know what's about to happen," he said. "This is no time for strolling Le Marais."

"I've already made my reservations, Drajan."

"And they can't be postponed?"

"I don't want to postpone them."

He looked at her.

"What of the cryptocurrency transfer?"

"It can be arranged from wherever I may be." She nodded behind him. "Computers, Drajan. What is it you call them? *Portals*."

He took a step closer to her. "Tell me why you're leaving."

"I expect you know."

"Tell me anyway."

Quintessa regarded him with her glacial-blue eyes. "Things aren't what they were when we met."

"Is there too little excitement here? Do you miss the stim clubs?"

"Don't reduce me to a simple caricature," she said. "I miss who you were, Drajan. The Wolf. Dark prince of the *technologie vampiri*. A force alone."

He looked at her.

"I am the same."

"No," she said. "Not since the Russians."

"Their money is good. Should I refuse it?"

She shrugged. "Profit was the icing before. It never drove you."

"And you think I've become their tool?"

"The term is *state actor*," she said. "Koschei's plan is madness. Yet you work toward it day and night."

Drajan extended his hand. Touched her arm lightly with the tips of three fingers.

"Stay," he said. "You told me you were happy. I remember. That night, out on the breakwater."

Quintessa shook her head again.

"I said I was not unhappy. But that was months ago," she said. "You're right about one thing. This place is drab and gray and lonely. And you're rarely with me these days."

Another silence. Longer than the first. Drajan's fingers stayed on her arm. He noticed she did not draw it away.

"That night…you asked about a name."

"Yes."

"Kali."

"Yes. You spoke it in your sleep."

He nodded. "She is someone from long ago."

"You were lovers?"

"Yes. At the University of Madrid. And for a time after we graduated. And then it ended."

"Why?"

Silence. A smile ticked at the corner of her lips. It was without humor.

"You sleep with me and think of her."

He shook his head.

"Not in the way you believe. She was with the Americans in Bucharest. The ones who shot me. And killed Emil."

Her gaze locked on his.

"The woman outside Club Energie? Who left your bodyguard shattered on the sidewalk?"

Drajan nodded. "You know Matei. You saw what she did to him. He's three times her weight and a trained operative." He paused. "Matei told me he'd seen her at Castle Graguscu."

"With the Americans again."

"Yes."

"He's certain?"

"Yes. She tried to run him over on a motorcycle. And nearly did."

Quintessa looked at him. "Drajan, Drajan. What did you do to provoke such wrath from a woman?"

"It isn't relevant."

"I'm capable of deciding that for myself."

He looked at her for a long moment. Then shrugged.

"She is a code writer," he said. "I incorporated her scripts into the Hekate malware."

Her eyes widened. "You stole them from her. And she knows."

"She knows."

"And wants to punish you."

He nodded.

"Make no mistake, Kali will lead my pursuers to me. She won't be stopped."

Understanding spread across her face.

"You're setting a trap here," she said. "Is that it?"

"I won't hide for the rest of my life," he said. "It needs to end."

"And you'll start the whole world on fire to bait them?"

"And kill her, yes. Whatever it takes. The world can burn."

Quintessa stood there looking at him. Drajan stepped closer to see if she would back away. She remained motionless. He lifted his glass to her lips.

"Give me two weeks," he said. "I won't need longer."

She took hold of his wrist and steadied it, and drank, and he leaned forward and kissed her neck, his lips light against the pale skin.

His head fell between her breasts, the fabric of her shift smooth against his cheek. He felt her breathing rapidly and took her glass from her hand, sank to his knees and moved his hands up and under the shift.

The new ruler must determine all the injuries he will need to inflict.

Drajan pressed his lips to Quintessa's yielding body. His weapons subtler than the knife and sword, but no less effective.

9

New York City
April 17, 2024

Carmody awoke on the couch, head hurting, and checked his smartwatch. It was a quarter past five in the morning, and the apartment was dark and quiet. Kali was asleep in the bedroom. He wanted to be there with her, headache be damned. But so far his overpowering charm hadn't gotten him out of the living room.

He pulled off his blanket, yawned, sat up in his T-shirt, and massaged his eyelids. He had done a lot of virtual reconnoitering the night before and at first had blamed the dull throb in his temples on that. What had Morse called it? *Cybersickness*.

He rubbed his eyes again. Maybe he did have a kind of allergy to V/R. In a way, that would suit him fine. He felt caged and restless and had done enough playing pretend. He was going to have to get things rolling today, head out to Teterboro Airport, talk to his guy there and then deal with something else that was on his mind.

He got up. His head felt thick and swollen. He had roped out of helicopters under fire without even a touch of vertigo but couldn't handle a glorified video game.

"Cyber *bullshit*," he said under his breath. And stalked into the shower.

It was eight twenty in the morning when Jot Musil double-parked his Acura outside the Woodmere Middle School in Queens to drop off his daughters for classes.

Raysa was ten and in sixth grade. Jani was fourteen and in eighth grade and graduating at the end of the year. Both girls had inherited their mother's slight build, fine features, glossy dark brown hair and chestnut eyes.

Musil got out and opened the back door. Jani popped out of the car first after spotting some friends in the schoolyard. He helped her slip into her backpack, waited for Raysa, and got her pack on.

"OK," he said, adjusting the straps. "Remember about your phones."

"We will."

"And call me from home after the bus drops you off."

"We will."

Musil bent to kiss their cheeks.

"I love you, *mittha*," he said to Jani.

"Love you, Daddy."

"I love you, *phula*," he said to Raysa.

"Love you, Daddy."

He looked her in the eye, then lowered his voice. "Don't forget what I always tell you."

"I won't."

They dashed off across the sidewalk. Musil watched until they were inside the yard and then got back into the car for the drive to the Terminal.

Parked across the street and about a third of the way down the block, Grigor watched from the Subaru Outback he had rented using the Wendell Balen identity. His hair was dyed black, and he was wearing sunglasses. As Musil drove off, he pulled out of his spot and cruised slowly past the school-yard, staring through the chain-link mesh at the girls.

Then somebody behind him tapped the horn impatiently, and he sped up toward the corner.

At exactly nine forty-five, Harris stepped across the hall for a ten-o'clock meeting with Carol Morse. He had arranged for it late the previous afternoon after Musil brought him up to snuff about the Fake Gelfland business.

Harris figured his being fifteen minutes early would aggravate Carol, who was a compulsive overpreparer. But he wasn't big on talking points and notes. Also, she was both his ex-wife and higher-up at Net Force. Though he felt they worked well together, his theory was that regularly getting on her nerves made for a healthy, balanced post-marital and professional relationship. Like daily vitamins. Lousy tasting but good for you. Otherwise, they might get along even better, a worrisome proposition. Namely because she was long remarried, and Leo had spent years struggling to convince himself that he didn't wish it was still to him.

So he had the whole thing hashed out. Or thought he did. Except that when he entered the room, Carol was at her desk looking past a guy who was already seated opposite her, his back to the door.

She said, "Leo, glad you're early. We've been waiting for you."

He frowned in defeat. Then he noticed the guy's thick red hair.

"Prof?" he said.

Alex Michaels shifted around in the chair. He was whip thin, bearded, with clear, intelligent eyes.

"Leo," he said and stood up. "You look great."

"Last time you saw me I was on a ventilator."

"True."

"No wonder you say I look great."

Michaels faced him and smiled. "Well, you're definitely snazzier out of a hospital gown."

Harris looked down at himself. He was wearing a blue plaid blazer with an orange striped shirt. He looked back up at Michaels.

"What are you doing here?" he said. "I thought they were keeping you busy in Washington."

Michaels came across the room. Leo put out his hand, but he didn't stop to shake it, and instead clasped him in a long-armed bear hug.

"Good to see you again," he said.

"Same, Prof." Harris briefly hugged him back. "How's the pooch?"

"Julia's fine. She misses you."

"Misses my treats, y'mean."

Michaels smiled. "Leo will be Leo."

They stood there facing each other.

"OK," Harris said. "Why the hell *are* you here?"

"He's not," Morse said from her desk. "Neither are we. This meeting isn't taking place."

Harris looked at her. "Uh-huh. Got it. So, what now?"

"Now we talk," she said.

Leo was quiet. After a minute he turned back toward Michaels.

"You up to speed on Stephen Gelfland?"

"Carol sent me the info last night," Michaels said. "But Gelfland isn't specifically the reason I flew in."

"So, what is?"

"I have to tell you things about the Seven Winds Group, the CIA and the CloudCable deal. And why the *Stalwart*'s disappearance should put the fear of God into us."

Harris looked at him, took a deep breath and exhaled.

"Lovely," he said.

* * *

Carmody rode out to Teterboro on a BMW Motorrad R 18 that Kali kept in a small, reserved garage spot on Greenwich Street. The motorcycle was a long, smooth-running beast with a double steel-tube frame, sweetly balanced boxer engine and wide curved handlebars.

A few blocks west of the garage, he took it across Tenth Avenue onto I-495, wound through Jersey traffic along 95 south of Union City and West New York, then continued east for several miles onto Route 46, where he could finally lace it open on the narrow strip of Industrial Avenue heading out to the field.

The hangars belonging to Great Circle Charter were at the northwestern edge of the airport. Carmody had called ahead and saw Nick DeBattista waiting in front of the low prefab office building when the bike swung into the parking area.

DeBattista waved. Carmody cruised into a space a few feet away from him, braked, got off and walked up.

"Nice bike," he said. "What bank you rob?"

"It belongs to a friend."

"She know you're riding it?"

"How do you know my friend's a *she*?"

DeBattista just shrugged.

"She must be crazy," he said. "Or crazy about you."

"Probably neither."

The corner of DeBattista's lips slanted upward

a millimeter. He was tall, thin and about thirty, with a trio of small gold rings in his right ear and a perpetually wily, brazen expression on his face. During his Company days, Carmody had run insertions and extractions through his uncle in Italy and seen the old man flash the same larcenous half smile. Like the fox that ate the kitchen leftovers, then came back to eat the cat food. And maybe the cat.

They shook hands.

"So," DeBattista said, "where you want to go that you couldn't talk about over the phone?"

"Romania," Carmody said. "Then Crimea."

"Just a little ways off, huh?"

"If I was flying to Disneyland, I wouldn't come to you."

"True that," DeBattista said. "This round-trip?"

"Maybe."

"What's it depend on?"

"We'll get to it later."

DeBattista grunted.

"We're talking a heavy jet," he said. "My base rate's two hundred grand. Could go high as double."

"I can't afford two hundred grand. Or one hundred for that matter."

"Exactly how much can you afford, then?"

"Exactly nothing."

DeBattista's smile crept a little higher up the side of his mouth. "Now, there's an offer I can't refuse."

Carmody shrugged his shoulders. "I did your uncle a big favor a while ago. I'm asking for payback."

"Didn't his pilot fly you out of Amalfi about a year, year and a half ago?"

"Yeah."

"I thought that was the payback."

Carmody shrugged. "A bunch of freelance operators were waiting for me at his airfield. With guns."

"Not his fault. Besides, his pilot took you where you wanted to go."

"Only because my boys had guns too. And were faster with them. In my book, he still owes me."

"And who wrote these fucking fair-trade rules?"

Carmody just shrugged again. They stood listening to the drone of planes landing and taking off.

"You still smoke?" DeBattista asked.

"Sometimes."

"When the girlfriend with the hot bike isn't around?"

"I didn't say anything about a girlfriend."

"OK, whatever. I'm bumming a smoke for listening to your bullshit."

Carmody reached inside his leather jacket for a pack of Marlboros and a disposable lighter. He shook out a cigarette, lipped it and handed the pack to DeBattista.

"Keep it," he said. "I'm feeling generous."

"Thought maybe you were trying to put a dent in my fee," DeBattista said.

"At what these things cost nowadays, it'd be a deep one."

Carmody fired up the lighter, held it to the tip of DeBattista's cigarette, then lit his.

"You traveling alone?" DeBattista asked.

"No."

"How many of you?"

"Four. Maybe five."

"How soon?"

"Day after tomorrow."

"That's lots of notice right there." DeBattista took a drag and puffed. "I can see if something's available. Talk to a coupla my pilots and get back to you."

"Not good enough," Carmody said. "I need an answer right now."

"For your grand total of nothing."

Carmody held up his cigarette between them. "How quickly you forget my generosity."

DeBattista grinned. Carmody grinned back. They stood there smoking as aircraft droned, whined and throbbed nearby with the palpable vibrations they made on takeoff and landing.

"OK," DeBattista said after a long minute. "I'll get you a plane. Then, we're square for whatever you claim my uncle owes you."

"Almost."

DeBattista looked at him. "What else?"

"I want you to fly us."

"Me. Not one of my pilots?"

Carmody nodded. "I need somebody I can trust to bring us in and out of a very dangerous place. And keep a secret."

DeBattista tilted his head up and blew a chain of smoke rings into the air. Then he tilted his head down and faced him.

"So?" Carmody asked. "What do you say?"

"I suppose I could swing it. But not totally free. And don't give me your crap about my uncle. This goes above and beyond, bro."

"What's the asking price?"

DeBattista was quiet a moment, holding the cigarette, that wily half smile on his face.

"I'll think of something," he said.

"One Belt, One Road," Michaels was saying. "It's where it all starts, a policy that's driven Chinese foreign and economic policy for over a decade. The goal is for their government to have financial investments in everything, everywhere in the world…especially in the West. It's how they gain political influence. It extends their reach."

"And extends how they conduct their spying and launder their money," Harris said.

Michaels nodded. They were sitting side by side in front of Morse's desk, Harris to his right. The sky and river merged blue and bright in the window behind her.

"Until a few years ago, they could open an anonymous shell company in the United States in about the time it takes to get a library card," Michaels said. "The money they took in was untraceable. It was washed through the shells, offshore banks, House Leonides in Latvia…take your pick. You don't hear too much about it, but it's also how crooked Chinese bigwigs use it to siphon money into their personal accounts for private investments. Congress banned those shells, and a few other European and Asian countries have cracked down. But not many."

"So where's Seven Winds fit in?"

"On the surface it's a legitimate Frisco-based food service operation for commercial and cruise ships," Michaels said. "Dip down under and you find out its real headquarters is located in Malaysia. That's how easy it is to loophole the legislation."

Harris balanced his foot over his knee and impatiently waggled it up and down.

Morse noticed. They had been high school sweethearts long before they were ever married. Drag him to a romantic movie and he would do the same.

"Take a deep dive, Alex," she said. "I want Leo to see how everything falls together."

"China's global enterprises are a deliberate tangle. There are all kinds of offshoots and joint ventures, and they had years to make it impossible to sort out who owns what. But I first came across Seven Winds about a year ago. Back when Leland Sinclair bullhorned that trans-Pacific cable and cloud-computing contract between Olympia, CloudCable and two or three of our intel agencies. I never liked the deal. From a national security standpoint, I thought it was asking for trouble for top secret information to flow though the same digital pipelines as internet shopping and movie streaming. I also thought it opened up too many potential civil liberties abuses. The Olympia Plus e-services and shopping package has almost two hundred million subscribers in our country. Another hundred million worldwide. That's a lot of big data. And big data's like candy to our spooks. I don't expect them to be able to resist it. Not over time. It's too tempting. Eventually someone will reach deep into the bowl and binge."

"Which is why digital things make me puke," Harris said. His foot was still going up and down. "For the record, Prof, I know all this. I'm a fan of your podcast. I was a captive audience in the hospital."

Michaels turned to him and smiled.

"What're you gawping at?"

"Believe it or not, I missed you, Leo."

"I'm touched," Harris said. "Seven Winds. Remember?"

Michaels nodded. "After the deal was announced, I thought I'd look into its details. Or whatever details were out there. A project that enormous isn't just about its signatories. There are always other companies providing support and materials. One of CloudCable's loudest boasts—and top selling points—is that its submarine line is made entirely in the United States. Which is true as far as it goes. But how about the joint boxes and splitters used to repair damaged segments or splice them into other undersea networks? The couplers that connect it to the repeaters? The *accessories*. Any idea?"

Leo shook his head. "I figure I can always count on you for it, Prof."

Michaels smiled a little.

"There are several foreign companies that produce those items. CloudCable uses a few for different components. But its biggest supplier is a Chinese firm called Jinggu Technologies," he said. "Jinggu manufactures the steel conduits that house fiber lines when they make landfall. They're essential to network infrastructure and can run for miles." He paused. "Now, follow this. Jinggu is owned by a businessman and government official named Deng Yannan. His wife, Deng Jing, has a brother, Zhou Bohai. Those three names—Deng Yannan, Deng Jing, Zhou Bohai—appear on the filings of at least *thirty* companies over the past quarter century. Everything from electronics to energy to rare earth minerals." He paused. "Some are anonymous shells, and a few were even doing business in the United States or our allied countries before the congressional ban."

"If you're a crooked official, they're what you use for money laundering, smuggling drugs…all kindsa crap."

Alex nodded. "It turns out Seven Winds is a

Malaysian *subsidiary* of what used to be a Chinese shell. But after the crackdown, that paper tiger had to disclose its owner's name to continue operations here," he said. "Deng Jing is listed as its co-owner and chief operating officer. Her *husband's* components company, Jinggu, is a silent partner, with minority shares of both the former shell and Seven Winds."

Harris mulled that over a few seconds. "So CloudCable cuts a deal with Jinggu, and its owner recommends the kitchen services company his wife runs for the *Stalwart*. What's so suspicious about keeping it in the family?"

"Nothing, on its face," Morse said. "Until you check out Deng Jing's brother, Zhou Bohai. And *his* family connections."

"They're originally from Jilin City, right across the border from Primorsky Krai in Russia," Michaels said. "The clan's import–export trade goes back to the time of czars and emperors. Fruit, vegetables and textiles flow out of China to the Krai. Russian seafood and building materials come in. And Zhou Bohai controls the flow."

"He's what they used to call a merchant prince," Morse said. "Immeasurable wealth, economic and political clout on both sides of the border. His trucks roll back and forth across it, day and night, with millions in goods."

Harris looked from her to Michaels. "Either of you gonna explain where all this ties in to the *Stalwart*?"

Michaels nodded.

"Bohai and Deng Jing aren't the only siblings," he said. "There are several brothers. The youngest is named Zhou Kexin. He's a Chinese naval officer."

"And?"

"And his current command is Fiery Cross Reef. An artificial, militarized island. He's also thought to be in charge of a Chinese fishing militia fleet that anchors off the reef. Which our satint tells us sent trawlers into the immediate vicinity of *Stalwart*'s operations before it fell out of contact."

"Which now gives us *three* family members who can be either conclusively or plausibly linked to either CloudCable or the missing ship," Morse said. "How's that for making your spidey-sense tingle, Leo?"

He looked across the desk at her. And kept looking at her.

"About the Seven Winds kitchen and scullery people," he said finally. "There were a dozen of 'em on the *Stalwart*. Musil told me the ones who sailed out of New Hampshire would've rotated out when the ship pulled into port for maintenance."

"And been replaced by a crew out of Seven Winds Malaysia," Morse said. "*If* it made a port call there. We still don't know."

Harris brought his eyes to rest on hers. "You already dragged my ass down the rabbit hole. So I'll keep going. Say Deng puts her men on the *Stalwart* to make sure it can't send out an SOS.

Then say her brother, the captain, sends his boats to haul the ship off to that reef. It'd be a perfect inside job."

Morse nodded. "Perfect."

"Except for me the question's still *why*?" he said. "I get it that the Chinese think they own half of the Pacific. I know they like to strut and act tough. But that's a long way from an outright attack on an American ship."

Morse held up a finger and reached for the low stack of paper on her desk. There were three stapled copies of a single thin document. She gave one to each of the men in front of her.

"Two days ago, POTUS spoke to President Tsao on the phone. She provided me with a call transcript."

Harris thumbed through the pages. They had been prepared with a manual typewriter as a precaution against anyone hacking the file. He saw three security designations above the header: Secret/ORCON/NOFORN.

The first was nothing exceptional for a conversation between heads of state. It meant the transcript might contain information that was damaging to national security and was usually applied as a general precaution before a full State Department review cleared it for release. The ORCON—*Originator Controlled*—grading was a little rarer. It tightened access to the doc a few notches, restricting it to members of the intelligence community specifically authorized by the

White House. Not even personnel who normally saw top secret documents could read it without the president's nod.

The NOFORN—*Not Releasable to Foreign Nationals*—classification raised Harris's eyebrow. It would have been tagged on by the Secretary of Defense or some other upper-echelon intelligence official. But it was only supposed to be used for hush-hush field reports and analyses from the CIA or other agencies. He couldn't remember it being applied to any other type of document.

"President Fucillo personally overrode the DoS so we could see this, Leo," Morse said. "The most remarkable excerpt is on the last page. Alex is already familiar with it."

He flipped to the page. A single exchange toward the bottom was marked with a yellow highlighter.

President Tsao: On the subjects of transparency and reciprocity... I would caution your nation about exploiting undersea cable networks in latitude fifteen-five, longitude one-hundred-fourteen-five for future intelligence operations.

The President: Excuse me?

President Tsao: Madame President, I think you understand...

"Don't tell me," Harris said. "These coordinates cover the spot where the *Stalwart* was operating?"

Morse nodded. "They pinpoint it," she said. "The tenth parallel crosses the Spratly Islands midway between the Philippines and Malaysia. They're spread out over about a hundred sixty thousand square miles. And China asserts sovereignty over every one of them."

"Based largely on a journal written two hundred years before Christ," Michaels said. "It describes their locations and geographical features very accurately, so they didn't just pull their claim out of thin air."

"Maybe," Morse said. "But somebody else can worry about it. Our problem involves the *Stalwart*. I think it was out there spying for the CIA."

"Hold it," Harris asked. "You telling me the pres wouldn't have known about that?"

Morse looked at him.

"Not if it's black-boxed as an unacknowledged special access program and someone conveniently forgot to tell her. It happens, Leo. I know the funny smell. Some people in the Company breathe it every day, and it's one reason I'm no longer with them." She paused. "Those four CIA advisers—" she made air quotes "—are the giveaways. When you sent me the info about them, it put that cruise in a whole different light. *Stalwart* was conducting espionage ops. And I'm guessing the Chinese found out and did something about it."

"You mean hijacked it," Harris said. "You think

they outright grabbed a United States vessel and crew as hostages."

"Or worse."

He looked at her. "We need to find out what the ship was doing out there."

"Yes."

"And get into Seven Winds's computer system. Find out who came aboard at that port call."

"Yes."

Harris shook his head. "If you're right, I'm thinking this is gonna be bad."

"As bad as it gets."

"Then, we damn well better hope you're wrong."

Morse sat looking at him and Michaels for a long moment.

"We'd better," she said, nodding. "Because it looks like a recipe for war if I've ever seen one."

The North Pacific

It was four in the morning over the Pacific Ocean five hundred miles northwest of Oahu, where the merchant ship *Xingyun Liwu*, or *Lucky Gift*, plodded toward Honolulu Harbor in the reddish predawn twilight.

Sailing under Chinese flag, the vessel measured seven hundred feet in length and almost two hundred feet from port to starboard at its widest point, roughly the dimensions of two football fields. Double-bottomed with a bulbous bow, it carried thirty thousand tons of large-diameter, hot-rolled steel pipes for delivery to American buyers. The seamless corrosion-resistant pipes had been manufactured in Cangzhou, China, and shipped in climate-controlled intramodal containers that could be easily transferred to trucks, rail trains or even cargo planes and then shuttled to their endpoints all across the mainland.

At about four thirty, the crankshaft that drove the *Xingyun Liwu*'s gargantuan two-stroke diesels hissed and shuddered to a halt. The ship was just north of where the submerged Hawaiian Ridge and a line of undersea rock formations called the Necker Ridge crossed the Tropic of Cancer, their outcrops infamous among seamen for creating treacherous passage. But here the bottom was flat and silty and the calm blue surface clear of natural obstructions.

Soon after coming to rest in the water, the *Xingyun Liwu* released its covert passenger. It was a quick exit, a hatch door retracting on the underside of its modified hull, the egg-shaped, manned deep-submergence vehicle drifting out and downward like a sluggish amphibian on a cold morning.

The pilot was called Li Quang. Three years ago, with a team of researchers aboard, he had parked a submersible at the bottom of the Mariana Trench. The deepest place on earth. The mission was hailed as a scientific triumph by his government and livestreamed on China Central Television. The entire country had watched it.

In stark contrast, today's dive was being conducted in secrecy. Only those who needed to know, knew.

Cradled in a sphere of darkness, Li was six minutes into his dive when he switched on the thalium/iodide metal vapor lamp above his forward viewport. The T/I emitted a high-wattage beam in the blue–green spectrum. Green light was the radiance to which the human eye was most sensitive. It was also the wavelength least absorbed by water. With the lamp beaming out in front of him, Li could visually gauge his rate of descent. If he was going down too slow or too fast, he would need to add or subtract ballast.

So far, Li's uniquely experienced eyes told him he was descending at about one hundred feet a minute—his desired speed—and his visual estimate matched the readings on his control panel. The deep submergence vehicle felt stable and even. All systems were functional. He felt reassured but would not relax his vigilance.

There were many hours of work ahead of him in the enduring midnight of the abyss.

PART TWO

SILENT DRAGON

10

New York

Carmody rode straight back into Manhattan from Teterboro. It was the second warm, bright day in a row. The sort of weather that got people daydreaming about summer vacations and barbecues.

Not that he could remember the last time he'd had either.

Riverside Drive was jammed with vehicles. While rumbling south through the gluey traffic, he made a pair of calls to the Terminal on his helmet's Bluetooth. A quick one to Dixon, then Carol Morse.

"Duchess," he said when she answered. "You free?"

"What's that noise?"

"Wind drag. I'm on a bike."

"Some guys have all the luck."

"You're welcome to ride with me."

"Sure, with very large training wheels," she said. "What's up?"

"I need to talk to you. In person. Say, in half an hour? I've got a stop to make first."

A pause. He imagined Morse checking her calendar.

"It's your lucky day. I have no appointments," she said after a minute. "I'll be in my office."

"Better if it's our bench."

"Except you know motorcycles aren't allowed on the Esplanade."

"I'll leave it at the Terminal. That's my next stop."

A pause. "What's going on, Mike?"

"I'll explain."

There was another beat of silence.

"OK," she said. "Don't wipe out on the way over."

Carmody grinned behind his visor. Then he split the lane and throttled open, blowing past the slow-moving cars ahead of him.

At the Terminal a short while later, Carmody touched his thumb to a bioscanner, waited as a thick, stainless steel sliding door retracted into the wall, then stepped through into the gun training area.

He stood looking down its length as the door whispered shut. The long interior space was divided into two sections. Its physical range had a dozen firing lanes, four stretched out to one or two hundred yards for rifles, the rest at thirty and fifty yards for handguns and carbines. There were lighting controls, moving targets and other programmable features, but it was fundamentally no-frills, the kind of setup Carmody used for his practice shooting. If you wanted to earn your quals, you had to do it here at the scored-target physical range.

The other section, separated from the lanes by a floor-to-ceiling acoustical partition wall, was a three-hundred-degree, interactive firearms training simulator. The sort Carmody rarely used for himself. Its five huge, high-definition laser projection screens, arranged in a surround-theater configuration, thrust the trainee into a realistic shooting scenario. The weapons were authentic, though adapted for CO_2 cartridges and fitted with laser-guidance attachments.

Carmody found Scott Dixon at the sim room's control station throwing virtual bedlam at a group of three recruits. One held a Benelli M2 12-gauge, the others MP7 submachine guns.

Dixon was brown-haired, thick-featured and squarely built. He wore a snug navy blue T-shirt and had a Navy SEALS trident medallion hanging over its collar on a short gold chain. On his left bicep was a tattoo of a General Electric television with color bands on the screen. The name *Else* was written across the bands in looping graffiti-style letters. Else was his girl in Munich.

Carmody came up to him from behind and stopped to his right. Dixon's station had an angled dual display, a gooseneck microphone, a joystick control and a computer keyboard. The display showed a scaled-down mirror of the scenario on the projection screens: winding stone-and-mortar corridors, ornate rugs, mounted suits of armor. Shooters in helmets and armored vests sprang out from behind corners, their weapons chattering. The walls swept past, and then the recruits were plunging down a set of worn granite stairs into darkness.

"Castle Graguscu," Carmody said.

Dixon nodded.

"You ought to remember."

"They know it only gets worse at the bottom of that stairwell?"

Dixon shook his head. "I like to keep 'em guessing."

Carmody was quiet a moment.

"The reason I came is to tell you to be ready," he said. "You and Long."

"For?"

"We're heading back to Romania."

"When?"

"Day after tomorrow, hopefully."

"Thanks for the generous notice."

Carmody shrugged. "I could have told you tomorrow."

"Or the day after, I suppose."

"There you go," Carmody said and cocked a finger at him. "Don't spit at me for being considerate."

Dixon looked at him.

"I thought we were done with Romania," he said.

"Almost," Carmody said. "Let's call this trip in honor of the good old days."

"Uh-huh."

"Also, we have to stop there before heading to Crimea."

"Well, hey now, Crimea," Dixon said.

Carmody's face grew serious. "I'm assembling a strike team," he said. "This will be a lot for us to handle."

Dixon was quiet a minute. He nodded at the training theater. "They're heading down to be ambushed in that pit under the castle. What'd Wheeler call it?"

"An *initiation well*," Carmody said. "It was built by the Knights Templar."

"Right," Dixon said and laughed ruefully. "Romania. Christ."

Carmody looked at him. He motioned to the television tattoo on his bicep.

"There's extended leave waiting for you when we're done," he said. "You and Else in the Bavarian Alps."

Dixon was quiet a minute. "It's gonna be bad, huh?"

"Yeah."

"Now you're scaring me."

Carmody shrugged his broad shoulders.

"Better you know than have to guess," he said.

Grigor stayed one or two car lengths behind Musil after watching him drop his daughters off, following along as he drove toward the Manhattan-bound Queensboro Bridge. When the agent turned onto the entrance ramp, he continued past it on the busy avenue for a short distance, then swung onto a side street and found an empty parking spot.

Cutting his engine, he took out his phone and navigated to a home buyer's website. The search bar asked for a preferred zip code, address or neighborhood for the desired purchase, and he typed in WOODMERE MIDDLE SCHOOL.

Five listings instantly came up. The third one down the screen read: "Beautiful bungalow at the end of an incredibly private cul-de-sac. 3 bedroom, 2 bath, elegant sunroom. Short walk from Main Street, Flushing. Situated near subways and intermediate school. For sale by owner. Available for immediate occupancy. Call: 718-555-7834."

Grigor looked over the photos of the property, then reviewed its position on the GPS map inset that accompanied the listing. The home was a few blocks away from where he was parked.

He pulled out of the spot and drove over. The

street was called Meadows Court. He rolled up past the bungalow, giving it a quick scan as he went on toward the dead-end sign, then cut the engine again.

The place was vacant. The street was quiet and tree-lined. Scrub brush and weeds had overgrown the metal rail marking the roadway's terminus. Looking out his windshield, Grigor could see that he was at the crest of a low hill.

Perfect.

He dialed the number on the listing. A male voice answered on the third ring. "Hello?"

"Good morning," Grigor said. "My name is Wendell Balen and I'm calling about your home ad. Forgive me for bothering you this early."

"No worries," said the man on the line. "I was just about to leave for the office, so it actually isn't a bad time."

"Ah, excellent."

"I'm Fred Kaplan, by the way. I take it you're interested in the place?"

"Believe it or not, Fred. I'm outside it in my car right now. I saw it online last night and thought I'd drive over first thing to take a look. It's as advertised…beautiful."

"I'm very fond of it," Kaplan said. "The bungalow belonged to my late mother. She kept it in immaculate shape, as you can see."

"Yes, absolutely," Grigor said. "Mr. Kaplan, I realize it's an imposition…but would I be able to look inside while I'm here? I'm very serious about it, or I wouldn't ask."

A pause. "Tell you what. I'm not far. If you'd like a quick tour of the property, I can stop by and give it to you before heading into work."

"That would be tremendous, thanks a million," Grigor said. "I really appreciate it."

"No problem. I want the place to go to someone who really loves it, Mr. Balen. Say we meet out front in about fifteen minutes?"

Grigor smiled, pleased.

"I'll be waiting," he said.

New York

"We should really stop meeting like this," Carol Morse said.

"Now, there's an original line," Carmody said.

She smiled. They were on the bench on the river walk, where he had been waiting with his espresso and her strawberry mineral water in a cardboard take-out tray.

"I'm boring but prudent," she said. "We're within eyeshot of headquarters. Someone could see us here. It might give the appearance that we're discussing something inappropriate."

"Things that bad at home?"

"I meant professionally."

"But are things that bad?"

"Let's stay on point." She took a breath, nodded back toward the Terminal. "I don't want it to seem like we're keeping secrets from anyone there."

"Even though we are."

She didn't reply. Carmody handed her the bottle of fizz, then took his espresso out of the carrier and peeled back the tab on its lid.

"On point," he said. "I have a big ask."

She looked at him. "It's been that kind of morning."

"Already?"

"Yes," she said. "OK, you go first."

"What do you mean?"

Morse drank from her bottle.

"It means I have one too," she said.

Fred Kaplan arrived at the Meadows Court bungalow in a Nissan Altima, stopping outside its attached garage. Grigor waved from the front lawn and instantly sized him up. He was in his fifties, short, balding, glasses. Average build, a bit fleshy around the neck. He wore a dark blue suit, white shirt and striped necktie.

He approached with his hand extended. "You take a look around while you waited, Mr. Balen?"

Grigor smiled as they shook.

"Call me Wendell, please," he said. "And yes, this is quite a nice plot of land. Very set apart."

Kaplan nodded, cocked a thumb in the direction of the dead end. "Being on this hill, you'd think you were somewhere way out in the country. But right on the bottom's a street that connects with the busiest neighborhood in the borough." His smile broadened. "As a kid, I had it made. I could mess around on the hillside and pretend I was lost in the forest. But when I got hungry, I'd climb down to the bottom and head over to the pizza joint up on Main. It's a five-minute walk."

Grigor laughed. "Ideal," he said.

Kaplan looked at him.

"That isn't a Queens accent I'm hearing," he said. "You from down South, pardon my nosiness?"

"North Carolina," Grigor said. "I'm a distributor of imported food, and eighty percent of my business is right here in New York. So I've decided to relocate."

"Wife? Kids?"

"Maybe someday," Grigor said. "Right now I do too much traveling around."

"Guess it makes the move easier."

"Exactly."

Kaplan nodded and gestured toward the house. "C'mon, I'll give you the once around. As I said on the phone, my mom kept it in great condition."

They went inside. The front door opened into a large, bright sunroom with a wide picture window. The room was empty except for a lowered window shade.

"I've cleared out all the furniture," Kaplan said. "Some I kept, some I sold. If you decide to come back for another look, I'll get a couple lawn chairs out of the garage so we can have coffee."

Grigor nodded. He followed Kaplan through the house, committing its room layout to memory.

In the kitchen, he asked, "Is there a basement? I don't remember from your listing."

Kaplan gestured toward a door to his right. "I'll show it to you," he said. "My parents never finished it, but Dad used it as his workshop. It's partially aboveground, so it stays really dry."

He went to the door, held it open.

Grigor smiled. "After you," he said.

Kaplan switched on the lights and started down. Grigor counted twelve stairs over his shoulder. They were fairly steep and ran along the wall on the left, with a basic wooden rail on the right side. The floor below was concrete.

Grigor waited until Kaplan took the first step, then pushed him hard with both hands. Kaplan's feet left the tread and he went flying down to the bottom with a wordless exclamation of shock and surprise. He hit the concrete floor with a dull, meaty thump and Grigor hurried after him.

Kaplan was flat on his face, groaning, blood already running from his forehead. Grigor crouched over him grabbed his head with both hands, and smashed it against the concrete once, twice, three times before turning it sideways with its cheek against the floor. Then he got a knee on his neck and pressed.

Kaplan flailed. Some wheezing noises escaped his throat as he gasped for breath. Grigor kept his knee in place. After three minutes, he shuddered and voided his bowels and died.

Grigor went through his pockets and took his

keys, wallet and phone. Then he dragged the body over to a corner and left it behind the water heater. The blood from his broken skull left swipe marks on the concrete.

Grigor was careful to avoid them as he returned to the stairs.

The North Pacific

Li Quang was in the final stage of his hour-long descent, his vertical lift thrusters rotated downward, their propellers stirring up a fine cloud of sediment as he hovered thirty feet above the seabed.

Thus far the dive had been happily uneventful. Hoping that would continue, he switched on the DSV's incandescent belly strobes and overhead floodlight in preparation for touchdown. Their brightness devoured the softer radiance of his driving lamp, casting a column of blazing light onto the bottom. Small underwater creatures scuttled into the carpet of silt, fleeing the sudden brilliance.

Li checked his instruments. The water's density reduced and distorted his depth perception, giving him what pilots call a two-and-a-half-dimensional field of view. Hazardous objects could seem nearer or farther, and larger or smaller than they were. He would keep one eye on the terrain and one on his digital panel.

At the moment his visual input and electronic readouts were in sync. The terrain below him was flat and regular. There were no discernable ridges or rocky protrusions in the immediate vicinity. No long lines of seamounts as he had seen in the Trench, some forty feet tall and spewing super-heated white water like chimneys. The *huoshan-shi*, or volcanic stacks, would have melted the PVC on his cameras and probes had he gotten too close.

Li skimmed forward, a hand on the joystick. After several hundred yards, he jogged to his right, northward, and went on in that direction until the fiber-optic cable trench came into sight below.

Hovering above it, he nodded to himself and typed a message into his computer for the technicians aboard the *Lucky Gift*. Then he cut his thrusters and released ballast.

At 05:17 Pacific Daylight Time, Li settled onto the ocean floor with a soft bump. The mission was right on schedule, his tiny vehicle perpendicular to the lightwave cable. He could see it straight ahead through his bubble-like viewport, stretching on seemingly without end.

Now he took his hands off the controls, reached into a compartment for an electrolyte drink and took a few tiny sips of the sugary fluid through a straw. It sharpened his alertness and gave him a needed physical boost.

He had much to do over the next six hours. With no margin for error.

Grigor was back at the midtown hotel after being out all morning. He had driven Fred Kaplan's car to a neighborhood lined with abandoned factories, removed the license plates and thrown them into a trash can several blocks away. Then he had called a rideshare to take him back to Meadows Court and his rental vehicle.

A minute or two after entering his room, he got a fresh bottle of water from the little fridge, opened his laptop and launched a Google search for the website of the Woodmere Middle School in Flushing, Queens. A link appeared on his results list and he clicked on the home page, then clicked again on a menu tab that took him to the monthly class calendar. It confirmed that school would end at 3:00 p.m. the next day, with no early dismissals scheduled.

Grigor clicked the Contacts tab. It brought him to an alphabetized list of names and email links for the principal, vice principal, student counselors and teaching staff. Also on that page was a number for the school's main telephone switchboard.

He committed the number and relevant names to memory and drank some water. His first bit of learning was finished. The second part would be more complex.

Opening a new window, he clicked on the YouTube icon and typed "Musil interview New York cyberattack" into the search bar.

A long column of posts came up. Most were repeats of a single four-minute video clip—a segment of a televised FBI news conference given weeks after the strike.

Grigor clicked to play it. The agent looked awkward on camera.

"Agent Musil, July 27 is a date no one in this country will ever forget. How does it feel when some call you one of its most heroic figures?"

"That's very kind. But I don't consider myself a hero."

"You saved a little boy's life. And in doing so had to chase a trained assassin, a man who tried to kill the president. Can you appreciate why people are taken with your story?"

"Respectfully, sir, I was doing my job. A child was in danger, and I responded."

"Agent, as member of the Sikh faith, a group that's widely misunderstood, is it gratifying to see your actions bring such goodwill toward your community?"

"When you say community... I'm a husband, a father, a devout Sikh, a New Yorker and an American. These are all one. I believe teaching others is part of being alive. If people learned from that terrible day, then perhaps some good came out of it."

The clip went on for another two minutes. Grigor watched it to the end, silently mouthing Musil's responses, syncing up with his speech patterns. With the second and third replays, he began answering along with Musil in a normal voice.

"I was doing my job. A child was in danger, and I responded... When you say community... I'm a husband, a father, a devout Sikh..."

Grigor studied the video several more times,

breaking the agent's voice down into all its components: its pitch and formants, its phrasing and articulation, its emphases, intonations and rhythmic and melodic changes. There were two or three additional interview clips, and he again went through multiple replays of each, mimicking the agent's answers to reporters' questions, copying and refining the man's vocal characteristics.

An hour passed before he got up and went over to the dressing table. He was ready to test the quality of his impersonation.

"Hello, this is Amenjot Musil," he said, standing in front of the mirror. "I'm calling about my daughters, who are students at your school."

He grinned, satisfied.

His reflection grinned back.

Kali was at her laptop when Carmody got back to her apartment. She heard him come through the door and quickly shut its lid.

"Everything's set," he said as he entered the dining room.

"When do we leave?"

"Day after tomorrow."

She looked at him. "I still have to speak to Natasha Mori."

"Yeah."

He pulled out a chair and sat beside her at the table.

"Your BMW's a sweet bike," he said.

"You managed not to crash?"

"No fair. Last time I was chasing a souped-up car in the snow. And there were major haystacks."

She laughed. It rose up from deep inside her, throaty and thick as syrup. Carmody realized he had never heard her laugh like that before.

"I saw Duchess on the way back from the airport," he said. "I've got a favor to ask you."

"In exchange for?"

"Her doing me one," he said. "It's tied to the missing cable ship. I'll explain later."

Kali nodded. "Go on," she said.

"There's a company called Seven Winds based out of Penang," he said. "I want to grab some files from its human resources system."

"How soon do you need them?"

"Before we fly."

Kali met his gaze.

"There's a twelve-hour time difference," she said. "If I'm to do this, I would have to start now."

Carmody gave a small shrug.

"I'll try to stay out of your hair," he said.

Leo Harris slouched at his desk behind a tall stack of adoption forms. It was now an hour after his meeting with Morse and the prof about the *Stalwart* situation, and he'd placed some calls to hustle along the CloudCable warrants.

With that done, he had decided to work on the forms for a little while. This after first tackling them at home the night before, sitting at his kitchen table, and scarfing down a frozen pizza while Mack the turtle chomped on some fruit salad in his bowl by the sink.

He'd figured the best way to deal with it was in shifts. Go for an hour or two checking boxes and answering questions. Then take a fifteen- or twenty-minute break before getting back to it till he reached his upper limit.

The first two pages mostly concerned his intentions and he got all that out of the way pretty fast. Next came his personal information. Basic stuff.

The third page was a speed bump. They wanted his full medical history and physical condition and whatever medications he was on, and they wanted the names, addresses and phone numbers of his doctors. Leo had looked everything up and written it down and then paused to take a hot shower.

The next section mostly asked for information about Rachel, including his written assessments of her personality and mental health. *What is the child's understanding of why she has separated/ moved from the parent(s)? Explain. Do you observe the child to be well-adjusted? Explain. What would make the child feel most at home? Does the child have favorite toys, naps, habits, etc.? Explain. What is the child's religious background, and what will it require?*

Explain, explain, explain.

Leo had sat thinking a while. He'd known Rachel since she was born. By then, he and Charlotte had been fast friends for over a decade, going back to the first investigation they'd worked together.

She had nicknamed him her Double Mitzvah Man—mitzvah meaning *good deed* in Yiddish—after that one.

The Dr. Midnight child-porn ring was a collection of rich, politically connected sickos, and Leo had busted it up like a balloon filled with ooze. Mitzvah One, Charlotte had called it. When reflecting back, he always felt it was the biggest and most rewarding accomplishment of his FBI career. Besides saving the president, of course. But that came later.

At the time of the arrests, he was with the Internet Crimes against Children Task Force, and Charlotte was a first-year US attorney for the Eastern District of New York. Cool, sharp and tough-minded, she had leaned on him heavily throughout the courtroom proceedings. If she'd felt any pressure as a newbie going up against a high-powered legal defense team—and she must have—he never saw it. She was with him every step of the way, matching his determination to get max sentences for the creeps. It had spurred Leo to keep looking for additional evidence to shore up the case against them.

He'd found it in one of the head pervert's alias email accounts. A Dropbox link, a trove of encrypted files and finally a video of the guy sodomizing his own nephew. That sordid bonanza had compelled him to cut a deal and flip on his partners in slime. It also enabled Charlotte to keep all the kids he'd abused from having to recount their horrific stories on the witness stand. Mitzvah Two in her book.

Hence, Double Mitzvah Man.

Leo had met Charlotte's husband, Drew, at a dinner to celebrate the conviction. Nice guy, told bad jokes, taught criminal law at John Jay College. As Leo recalled, he would be diagnosed with stage four pancreatic cancer two months afterward. Right around when Charlotte learned she was pregnant.

Drew Pemstein never got to see his only child. He would know it was a girl, and he and Charlotte would name her after his grandmother. But he died weeks before she came into the world.

Leo recalled seeing Charlotte come apart at his funeral, and then in her home at the shiva, the seven days of mourning and prayers after the burial. But never again. After maternity leave, she just went back to the AG's office with her usual unconquerable attitude. She had told him and Carol that she owed it to her unborn child to stay positive, that it could be harmful to the baby if she gave in to depression while carrying her. Leo would never forget that.

Nor would he forget when Charlotte asked the big question. Rachel was probably eighteen months old, and they had teamed up on another case, a gang of drug traffickers that had been reeling in teens on social media. One day during pretrials, she just put it to him over lunch in Chinatown. No lead-in, no warnings, no hint she was going there with the conversation. They had been comparing notes on the evidence and gotten their dumplings delivered to the table, and out it came.

"I want you to be Rach's godfather. Would you consider it?"

Leo had been lifting a dumpling off the plate with his chopsticks. It stalled under his chin.

He asked, "Why me?"

She said, "Who better?"

He'd shaken his head.

"Charlie, I'm not Jewish," he said. "I thought it's all about teaching the kid religion if something happens to you."

"Not for me," she said. "For me it's about someone having her back and teaching her right from wrong. And it doesn't hurt that she adores you. So I repeat...who better?"

He had sat there with the dumpling suspended below his mouth. "Rachel won't need me to teach her anything," he said. "You're gonna stick around long enough to be a great-grandma."

She had smiled at him. "I'll try, Leo. But I need some peace of mind. You know what they say. *Hope for the best, plan for the worst.*"

In Leo's memory, the silence that followed had lasted several minutes. Probably it wasn't that long.

At last, he'd shrugged.

"Say I do this," he said. "Would it make me a Triple Mitzvah Man?"

Charlotte's smile grew larger, but her eyes had been very serious.

"This mitzvah's mine," she said. "I'm giving my only child something special. Some*one*. If he agrees to be her godfather. And promises to take care of her if I can't."

Another silence. Leo had swallowed hard. Taken a deep breath. And nodded once.

"OK, I will," he said. "I promise."

That was eight years ago.

Where are the child's parents? Will the child maintain an active relationship with them? Will they call or visit? Explain.

At his kitchen table last night, Leo had felt his eyes go hot and wiped them fiercely. Then he'd stood up to get Mack, carried him back to his tank in the bedroom and hit the sheets.

And this morning in Carol's office there had been China and all its secrets. And the CIA and NGIA and all their secrets. And all of those secrets adding up to what Carol had rightfully stated could be a recipe for war.

Leo grabbed a pen from the cup on his desk. He was used to writing reports the way every other cop or investigator wrote them. Nothing but the relevant and observed facts of a case.

The form in front of him was different. It wanted him to spell out his thoughts and feelings, and he wasn't sure he even knew how to do that.

What do you observe to be the child's under-

*standing of why she has separated/moved from
the parent(s)? Explain.*

Leo breathed, hesitated, breathed again, tapped
the paper with the pen. And wrote,

*Rachel Pemstein's parents are both de-
ceased. Her father died before she was born.
Her mother died in a car accident during the
cyberstrike of '23. Her understanding of it…*

His hand suddenly froze. He realized he had no
clue about Rach's understanding of their deaths.
He'd never asked.

There were plenty of reasons. He had been in
the hospital for months while a distant aunt took
care of Rach. Afterward he spent several more
months on a breathing machine at home. And then
he went back to work, and there was the attack
on Janus Base. And now there was China and everything else.

Reasons. Good ones, he thought.

But were they, really?

Leo sat there a little longer. Thinking about
Charlotte. Thinking about Rachel. Thinking about
what he needed to do.

"OK, I will," he said abruptly into the silence.
"I promise."

A minute later he reached for the phone.

The hack wasn't difficult or complicated. She
just had to be patient, methodical and orderly.

Kali started by running a web search with the
keywords *Seven Winds Group Malaysia Human*

Resources. The fourth in her thread of results was a LinkedIn page for the corporate branch's HR manager, a woman named Farah Tan.

A click of the touchpad and Kali was reading the public information Tan had up on the site. It included her profile photo, work experience, education and academic degree. On the right side of the page under the heading *People Also Viewed* was a list of some twenty names and profile photos whose links had come up in related web searches. Four of them—three women, one man—also belonged to employees of Seven Winds Malaysia's HR department.

Kali copied and pasted the five hits to her digital notes, then continued down her original list of results. She found two more staffers within the department on the second page, both women. One had a public LinkedIn profile, like Farah Tan. The other had posted a similar profile on a site called ZoomFind. She again found and copied the related search links.

Within half an hour, she had assembled a list of eighteen employees within the company's HR department. She then logged in to LinkedIn under an alias to access their members-only contact information, such as their work phone numbers and email addresses.

She was halfway done. A few sips of tea, a brief stretch to work the kinks out of her neck and she went on to the next step.

Which was to try to find her eighteen human

resources staffers on the major social media platforms. She did this in-app each time, again log-
ging in with a false username and password and
then typing their names into the search bar.

It produced a hefty catch. Fourteen of the eighteen were members of Facebook, Instagram or
Chirp. Twelve of the fourteen had accounts with
multiple sites. Only three had high privacy settings.
The rest were completely public.

Kali ignored the three secure accounts and
browsed the rest. The most interesting ones for
her purposes belonged to the HR department's
generalists and assistant hiring managers, since
they were usually the first to receive job applications and résumés.

There were six women and three men within
that group. Four of the women and two of the men
listed their romantic statuses as *single*. All were
under thirty-five, and three under twenty-five. The
ideal demographic, since it was the most vulnerable to phishing expeditions.

She spent an hour carefully examining the photographs and videos posted on their personal timelines, narrowing in on the type of people they
found romantically or physically attractive. She
studied photos and videos of boyfriends, girl-
friends and favorite celebrities: actors, musical
artists, athletes and other popular figures. She
read through the user's accompanying comments
and innuendos about their looks and physiques.
Where possible she noted the user's stated or ap-

parent sexual orientation. She went as far down their timelines as possible.

After two hours Kali got up with a nod of satisfaction, brewed some more tea, poured Carmody a cup and sat quietly sipping beside him on the couch. He didn't ask how she was doing. He didn't ask how much longer she might need. He just sat and drank and gave her a chance to relax.

She liked that about him.

After a short while she returned to the computer and studied her targets. All six made good candidates for her spear-phishing expedition. She would compose two emails with embedded links to web-based résumés, one for the men, one for the women. Each résumé would be detailed and realistic and include an expandable profile photo as clickbait. Like the identities of the applicants—one male, one female—the photos would be counterfeits, deepfake images Kali would create using an AI-powered image generator.

Three hours later, she cast her line.

Now she would wait to see who bit.

The Chinese food cart outside the Terminal's Tenth Avenue entrance was one of Jot Musil's favorites, and he was about ready for lunch. Harris had applied for an emergency search-and-seizure warrant to gain access to CloudCable's electronic records, and Musil was optimistic the urgency of the *Stalwart* situation would speed them along. The information he and Ki Marton had dug up about Fake Gelfland was critical in establishing a probable, imminent threat to national security; hopefully it would convince a judge to expedite the request.

Musil was eager to fly back up to New Hampshire once the warrant returned with a judge's signature. Assuming there were no delays, he thought that would be soon. In the meantime, he could only wait.

And grab some Chinese, the waiting having made him very hungry.

He left the building on Tenth and turned right on the sidewalk. The cart was at its usual spot on the southwest corner of Fifty-Fifth Street, a half block down from him. There were only three people waiting in line.

Musil stepped up behind them and read the posted menu. At the counter, he ordered sautéed chicken and broccoli, fried rice and an egg roll. As he carried the bag back to the Terminal, his empty stomach rumbled a little. He was thinking the food smelled delightful.

In a crowd across the avenue, Grigor sipped some cola through a straw, watching Musil through his sunglasses. Once the agent reentered the building, he decided to spend a few minutes getting the lay of the neighborhood.

He walked up Tenth Avenue past a short stretch of restaurants, pizzerias and groceries. At Fifty-Ninth Street, where Tenth narrowed to become Amsterdam, Grigor saw a large home-goods chain

store and decided to stop in. He found a roll of
Gorilla industrial tape in the adhesives section,
browsed the aisles for a pack of white men's hand-
kerchiefs, and paid, slipping the items neatly into
his pack.

Grigor gave the cashier a pleasant smile as he
left the store and turned back downtown. He re-
traced his steps along the avenue, staying across
from the Terminal, passing its main entrance along
with the food cart where he had seen Musil pick
up his lunch.

He was scouting the area a couple of blocks
south of the building when he noticed a row of
yellow cabs parked at the curb up ahead. Five,
altogether. The traffic lanes on Tenth only ran
north, uptown, so the taxis were all nosed in his
direction.

Grigor paused on the sidewalk. As he stood
there, a sixth cabbie pulled up in a Toyota passenger van, double-parked alongside the last car
in the row and got out. He was dark complected
with close-cropped hair and a full beard, wearing
a knitted white *taqiyah*, or Muslim skullcap. He
went around to the curb and walked north, toward
Grigor. After fifteen or twenty feet he entered a
storefront or restaurant to his right.

Grigor continued walking downtown toward
the taxi stand. As he got closer, he noticed a cluster
of small Indian, Pakistani and Bangladeshi restaurants and spice shops along the street. The door the
taxi driver had gone through belonged to a place

called Share Punjabi. A sandwich board sign in front said *LUNCH BUFFET 12–5 PM.*

He strode up to it and paused on the sidewalk again, glancing through the large front windows like a potential diner making up his mind whether to eat there. Inside to the left was an extensive buffet counter. In the center, a long cafeteria-style table. He saw a few smaller tables along the right-hand wall. Then, toward the rear past the tables on the right, a corner niche where three men knelt on a decorative prayer rug. Grigor noticed that one of the men was the double-parked taxi driver.

He looked at his watch, saw it was just past noon. They had answered the Islamic call to prayer. Specifically, the *dhuhr salah,* or midday worship.

He stood thoughtfully on the sidewalk. New York City cab drivers typically worked twelve-hour shifts. The first shift was five o'clock in the morning till five at night. The next ran the subsequent twelve hours. So the men in the restaurant were roughly in the middle of their shifts. The usual break time. They would finish their devotions and then eat together in the restaurant. Given the location of the cab stand, it was probably a regular gathering. Assuming twenty minutes for the prayers, then lunch, they would be inside an hour. Then return to their taxis at about the same time.

Grigor walked on a few yards, then paused once again when he reached the cab stand. He briefly looked them over and saw two Toyota hybrid sedans, a Tesla Model 3 electric and two Nissan passenger vans. Three vans counting the double-parked vehicle at the end of the row.

After a minute he shifted his gaze to the flow of northbound traffic. The taxi fleet was fairly homogenous. In New York City only a handful of makes and models were certified for medallions. They all blended together to the casual eye.

Grigor watched the traffic.

"Almadi shabah, al mustakbal hilmun," he said under his breath in Gulf Arabic.

The past is a ghost, the future a dream.

He stood there watching. Thoughts raced through his mind like the rafts of yellow cabs barreling along between the trucks, buses and passenger cars on Tenth Avenue.

After a long moment, he nodded imperceptibly to himself and picked up his pace, mingling with the crowd on the street, heading downtown.

The North Pacific

Li Quang had expected to sit on the ocean bottom for six hours, but he was ready to surface in just over four. The operation had gone off without any technical hitches, cutting the length of the dive significantly.

He credited its ease of success to his own preparation and the DSV's advanced onboard technologies, especially its eight dexterous, tentacle-like gripper arms. Bionically modeled after the limbs of an octopus, their artificial muscles were made of soft, contractile polymers that allowed them to elongate, curl and even change shape, replicating the creature's agile reach and grasp. Generations removed from traditional robotic claws, they were optimized for precision clasping and manipulation.

Targeted, delicate, precise, it was the definition of a surgical procedure. Under his careful control, the six-foot tentacles stretched out over the trench, threaded down into it and pulled up the cable segment with minimal disturbance of the sand cover. He had practiced his splice, and the damper's installation, multiple times in an augmented reality training room, using physical versions of the grippers in a virtual undersea environment. The simulation had reproduced the conditions under which he would be working in accurate detail, even duplicating the range and brightness of his halon lights.

Everything done now—the cable neatly laid back to the trench, the trench refilled with silt, the submersible's tentacles coiled in against its metal curvature—he again typed a message to his support team and then launched into his careful preparations for surfacing.

Minutes later, he activated his thrusters. The craft trembled as it left the bottom and then yawed and trembled some more, gradually stabilizing, climbing slowly but steadily against the almost unimaginable pressure bearing down from countless thousands of tons of seawater.

Li settled back in the pilot's seat, doing his best to get comfortable for the ascent.

It was a long distance up to the ship.

11

April 18, 2024
Penang, Malaysia

Amina Nor checked her office email and voice messages fairly often throughout the day. First thing in the morning, she would pick at her regular take-out breakfast of chicken congee while looking over the previous day's unopened messages and job applications. If she saw something urgent, she would respond. If she had no extra assignments or fires to put out, she might open some lower priority emails. Otherwise, she would wait until after lunch for them.

That was her routine, and she rarely deviated from it. Amina was a creature of order and habit.

It was now nine in the morning on Thursday, April 18 in Penang, and all was peace and quiet in the human resources office at the headquarters of Seven Winds Malaysia. That had not been the case for the past week or two, and Amina knew it was because of the lost cable ship. Her company had provided its kitchen staff, and she'd heard its executives were under pressure from the US to either release or not release their personnel files. One friend, a director's assistant, had told her there were conflicting requests from *different* parties in America. And she'd heard a rumor that the company's Chinese owner had instructed that they hold off on cooperating with any of them until further notice.

Now, Amina used her plastic fork to mix the congee's topping and porridge and thought how she was grateful to have no part of the cable-layer mess. As a generalist with HR, her main job was to screen new employment applications. She would see that they conformed to company guidelines, sort them according to the desired position and forward them up the line. If there was a problem with a submission's format or content, she might return it to the sender for revision. If the issue was minor enough, she would often call or email the applicant and straighten it out herself.

Amina went through dozens of résumés a day at peak hiring times, this being one such period. She was pretty quick reviewing them and sending them along to the appropriate recruiters. Still, she was facing quite a backlog today.

She forked a small mouthful of her breakfast from the container and went down her queue. The first three résumés had arrived as attachments to standard cover emails, and she reviewed and routed them within five minutes. The fourth email she clicked on was addressed specifically to her and had been sent by someone named Yasmani Rodon. Rather than including the résumé as a file attachment, it contained a simple note.

April 17, 2024

Amina Nor
amina.nor@SevenWindsGroup.my.net

Dear Ms. Nor,
As a Ship Steward with 7 years of experience, I believe I would be a strong asset for the Seven Winds Group.

    I am a self-motivated, versatile worker and have served on both commercial and passenger cruises, as well as privately owned yachts and superyachts. My most recent position was Lead Steward for a 128-day, 23-country tour beginning in Los Angeles and concluding in London.

    Please click on the hyperlink below to review my full professional background and contact information.

    I look forward to hearing from you.

Sincerely,
Yasmani Rodon

    Amina followed the link, scanned the résumé and instantly decided Mr. Rodon was a model candidate for employment with Seven Winds. She also found herself looking at his photograph and allowing herself a momentary fantasy. Rodon was dark-eyed, handsome and thirty-six years old. Four years her senior, and unmarried.

Clicking on the photo to enlarge it, Amina sighed wistfully and forwarded the email to the hiring manager.

She had just been successfully spear-phished. The moment she clicked on the photo, Kali Alcazar's sophisticated backdoor Trojan had loaded and detonated inside her computer.

Within hours, its stealthy crawlers would spread throughout Seven Winds Malaysia's human resources network.

New York

Nine o'clock Thursday morning in Penang was still nine o'clock Wednesday night in New York, where Kali shut her laptop, stood up, meshed her hands and stretched her arms over her head.

Carmody was looking at her from the couch.

"So?" he said.

"We have a hit."

"That was fast."

"It only takes a single person, at a single desktop." She lowered her arms to her sides and turned to him. "The packet still has to penetrate the network's defenses from the perimeter inward. There could be threat alerts."

"Threat alerts don't sound good."

"How very astute."

He smiled a little. "What if they go off?"

"It isn't likely. Most of them should be disabled. Others will look like false positives to the system administrators. But nothing is foolproof. There's a slim chance a breach will be discovered."

Carmody thought for a second. "Say it is. What then?"

"The crawlers propagate laterally."

"English, please."

"They jump from computer to computer in the network. A machine just has to be turned on to be infected."

"So the ITs would have to *dis*infect every machine in the department?"

She nodded. "I should be able to exfiltrate the files before that's done."

"When will you know?"

"Hopefully by tomorrow morning."

Carmody digested that. She strode over to the closet and reached inside.

"Going for a ride?"

"A walk."

"Company?"

"Not tonight."

Carmody heard the distance in her voice. She was already barely present in the room. He watched the door close behind her and heard the click of the lock. Then he sat there in silence, curious about where she had gone. Technically she was in his custody. If he had wanted to know badly enough, he could have followed her. But he wouldn't, and she knew it, though she would still be keeping an eye peeled for him.

He suddenly smiled. It surprised him a little, because he couldn't pinpoint the reason. But he knew it had everything to do with Kali Alcazar, and that much was no surprise at all.

Kali entered Washington Square Park through the marble arch on its northwest side. The night was cool and pleasant, and people were out strolling and gathering in clusters around the musicians, magicians, jugglers and balancing acts in the fountain plaza.

She found a bench and called a number on her world phone, using a dedicated IP VPN.

A male voice answered. "Ah, here you are. I'd started to think I might not hear from you."

"I waited till I could speak freely," she said. "Have you been able to reach Oarsman?"

"I've tried dozens of times. He doesn't respond."

"I don't like it."

"Nor I. But he could be preoccupied. It's possible."

"No," she said. "That isn't it."

"We shouldn't jump to conclusions. There's a great deal going on—"

"All the more reason he would stay in touch."

"So you're convinced he's in some sort of trouble."

Kali paused.

"We have an arrangement," she said. "If more than a week passes without any communication from one or the other, it means something is wrong."

"Then, what's next?"

"It depends."

"On?"

"Who you know you can trust."

"Assuming you're correct about Oarsman? I don't have to tell you the answer."

Kali silently watched the buskers around the pool. A young man walking a small dog smiled at her as he passed the bench. She gave no indication that she noticed, and he moved on.

"Can you travel to Paris?" she asked after a minute.

"Under the circumstances, of course."

"How soon?"

"Later this morning. I can book a flight that will have me there in two hours," he said. "I'll have to rush and make plans. The inventor's fair is in just two weeks. Can you believe it's been a year?"

Kali thought for a long moment. "The days run together," she said. "I haven't stopped to breathe."

"Who you are…it must be a heavy weight."

"I see it as a gift," she said and paused again. "No gifts are free."

"*Ja*, I do understand. But the old days seem a lifetime ago. I miss you, *Einglien*. And still look forward to hearing your story of the fishermen's wager."

She smiled.

"I'll tell it to you in person, I promise."

"Gott will Rechtzeitigkeit."

"Safe travels," she said. "We'll talk."

"Yes."

Kali disconnected, put away the phone and sat watching a juggler throw colored balls in the air. Three, four, a fifth, a sixth as he himself spun in circles.

She lingered for some minutes admiring his skill at the trick. Then she nodded thoughtfully, stood up, dropped a tip into his cup and left the park.

Crimean Peninsula

It was four o'clock in the morning when Drajan heard his smartwatch vibrate on the nightstand.

Across the room, he and Quintessa were awake in their robes, eating at a small limewood table in the throw of a silver candelabra. From the beginning, they had recognized in each other the look of nocturnal creatures.

The watch hummed quietly again. He wondered who it might be.

"One moment," he said, resting his fork on his plate.

She nodded slightly, her cool blue eyes trapping the candlelight. Famished after a night of lovemaking, they had ordered a servant to leave a tray at the door. Something to eat, sweet toast and Almas caviar, the golden roe extracted from a rare albino sturgeon between sixty and a hundred years old and found only in Caspian waters.

The cryptoprincess's tastes were as expensive as her appetites were inexhaustible. Over the past months, Drajan had come to appreciate them all.

He rose, went to pick up the watch and saw the notification on its display.

There had been an intrusion in the Seven Winds Malaysia human resources network.

"Is something the matter?" she asked from the table.

He turned to her, noticing her eyes, enjoying how the orange light flickered within them.

Fire and ice.

"On the contrary," he said.

At 9:07 p.m. on Thursday, Ki Marton was in his office on the third floor of the Terminal, indulging his current Pogues kick through his enormous headphones.

He was also exactly five minutes from the most important, surprising and perplexing discovery of his entire law-enforcement career.

Outside the sonic environment of his phones, Analytics was as quiet as a library reading room… so quiet, in fact, he could keep the door wide open and warble along to the music without drawing baleful stares from the hallway. At that hour the vast majority of Forcers were home with their partners, children, dogs, cats, or whomever or whatever usually waited for them at day's end.

Making it a perfect place to work for someone who had nobody waiting for him at home and no desire to be there with only the four walls for company. Better to put in some overtime and make himself useful. His gut told him that Fake Stephen Gelfland was at the very core of the disappearing cable ship mystery and that finding out his real identity was therefore crucial to moving the investigation forward.

And so he had stayed late to do what he did best. Which had the fringe benefit of helping him keep his head above the deep, sucking swamp of loneliness that was life without his best friend and partner.

The plan was simple. He would run a photo of Fake Gelfland scraped from the internet—a *probe* photo, in law-enforcement lingo—against the hundreds of millions of photographs stored in classified government identification systems and databases. *Candidate* photos, in the same lingo.

Among the agencies to whom he had reached out, the FBI was by far the most cooperative, probably because he still had a lot of contacts within its sprawling organizational bureaucracy. It gave him quick access to NGI-IPS, the Next Generation Identification-Interstate Photo System that served the agency and state police departments. The rest presented varying levels of resistance but gradually came around to some degree of helpfulness.

By late afternoon, Ki had obtained provisional authorizations to search the CIA's Guardian image repository, the Department of State's TIP/PISCES, and the NSA-sponsored TIDE, or Terrorist Identities Datamart Environment, a master list of known and suspected terrorists. He also gained access to the Immigration and Naturalization Service's biometric database, leaving only Interpol, which he had emailed earlier. But the six-hour time difference between New York and Lyon, France, where it was headquartered, probably meant a lag of a full day.

In each instance there were stipulations and constraints. None of the agencies allowed him to run a direct line into their databases. All required that he put his digital signature on a Memorandum of Understanding, which meant they had total and absolute oversight of his probe, as well as the discretionary power to restrict it on grounds of informational security. And he had a strong hunch the CIA—a party to the CloudCable deal—would give his searches its close scrutiny.

Still, four out of five wasn't too shoddy. With the single exception of Interpol, he had secured all the permissions he would need. Additionally, Net Force's Mirror Image system contained its own candidate pool of cybercriminals and cyberterrorists. But with the organization not quite a year old, and budgetary scuffles in Congress putting the brakes on its funding for the servers and routers and technical personnel, the search engine was not yet as extensive as the rest.

At six o'clock, Ki decided to have something to eat, went out for a burger and asked the waitress to bag his dessert. An hour or so later he returned to the Terminal to get started.

He had led off with the FBI's face-rec system. The number of images NGI-IPS kicked out could be set for a minimum of two, a maximum of fifty and a default of twenty potential matches. Requesting the max, he submitted his probe photo and then let the software evaluate it against the candidate pool. The search was an automated process: once he fed in the photo, there was nothing for him to do but crank up his music and wait.

Ki got his results within minutes, and they were a letdown. Not a single match out of all those many millions. He frowned, unwrapped the cheesecake, poured some coffee from the maker and dug in his fork. When Mark was alive, he would not have eaten compulsively. Certainly not after his former six o'clock cutoff for snacks. He was only five foot six with a sluggish metabolism and had struggled to keep trim. But in the past ten months he'd developed a bulging waistline. It wasn't going away anytime soon.

Several bites of cake later, he logged into Guardian with his visitor credentials. The time stamp on his screen said 19:37 p.m. He waited less than fifteen minutes and again was disappointed. There were no potential candidates.

He tried TIP/PISCES. No luck.

TIDE was likewise a washout.

At half past eight, Ki went to stretch his legs in the hallway, then returned to his office and put on a fresh pot of coffee. While the machine gurgled and hissed, he returned to his computer, opened the INS database, scanned in his Fake Gelfland image and clicked Enter.

The coffee maker beeped. At the same instant, his computer screen flashed:

NO RESULTS

It was ten minutes to nine.

He poured some coffee and carried it back to his cake. He had exhausted every outside search engine and felt discouraged. His last shot was Mirror Image, and he wasn't expecting much out of it. It had not been designed as a repository of criminal photos, and its galleries weren't nearly as inclusive.

Ki finished the cake, balled up its wax-paper wrapper and overhand-lobbed it into the wastepaper receptacle. *Trashetball*. Then he submitted his photo, turned up the volume on his phones and sat back to wait.

It was nine o'clock on the dot at that point.

At four minutes past the hour, his result appeared on-screen. It read:

TOTAL MATCHES: 1
PROBABILITY RATING: 98%
FILE PINNACLE: ACCESS DENIED
CODE 8752 RESTRICTED D/DISLE
APPROVAL REQUIRED

Ki stared fixedly at the monitor.

"Access denied," he read aloud. "This is bizarre."

He turned off his music and leaned forward in his chair. He had found his first match for Fake Gelfland's photo using Net Force's own unfinished search engine. And at the same time run into his first brick wall.

Access to the file was blocked.

D/DISLE stood for *Director, Department of Internet Security and Law Enforcement.*

Blocked.

By Alex Michaels.

"Why would he do that?" Ki asked aloud. "And what the hell is Pinnacle?"

There was a flat, unanswering silence in the room.

It was 9:12 p.m., and he had just made his ultimate discovery.

After a large dinner of prime steak and vegetables, Grigor was taking a long, hot shower before bed. Tomorrow he expected to be finished in New York. Though his plan had some flexibility and movable parts, it fell within the limits of a broader, overriding schedule. One with very hard, very inflexible borders.

So he had ordered from room service, wanting a solid meal before he moved on. Then he had sent an encrypted phone message to Jochi and gone into the shower.

Rinsing off now, he dried himself and wrapped the towel around his waist. What else was there to do? A final check of his weapons and gear, but that could wait. First, a good night's sleep. He needed to be sharp when he awoke in the morning. He did not expect to return to the hotel after he left.

Grigor got into bed, turned off the light and closed his eyes. Then he lay still on his back with his arms folded across his chest, his physiology autoregulating, his heart rate slowing down to forty beats per minute, his breathing becoming so shallow as to be imperceptible. For him there was no transitional stage between wakefulness and sleep. No segue. His eyes did not move under his lids. He never dreamed and rarely moved or turned under the sheets. He simply shut down and detached from consciousness.

In a state of deep repose, Grigor slept soundly.

Six hours later, he would awake rested and ready for Musil.

Hawaii

It was four o'clock in the afternoon when the *Lucky Gift* lumbered into Mamala Bay southeast of Oahu.

Bearing west, going a steady three knots at dead slow, the container ship rounded Diamond Head and Waikiki's white crescent beach on its starboard side. Sunlight gleamed and speared and starred off the residential towers and hotels at Kewalo Basin Harbor as it passed the waterfront marinas heading toward Honolulu Harbor. Armstrong Island sat in the middle of the harbor, where the sun was also bright and hot over its wharves, storage sheds, container terminals, skyscraping cargo derricks and acres of open freight yards.

The city's busy downtown area was less than two miles to the north. Westward around the barrier reef was the lagoon known as Wai Momi, *waters of pearl*, so named by Indigenous islanders for the coveted oyster pearls that the tide swept into it. At the head of its narrow inlet, Pearl Harbor was homeport to the nine destroyers and cruisers of Naval Surface Group Middle Pacific (NAV-SURFGRU MIDPAC), SUBPAC's fifteen nuclear submarines, and HSM-37's Easy Riders and their squadron of MH-60R Seahawk marine attack helicopters. On the leeward side of the lagoon was a landing field for a fleet of huge C-47A logistics and support aircraft called Windjammers.

With its small complement of five hundred service members, the Naval Computer and Telecommunications Area Master Station was situated three miles inland of Pearl Harbor, roughly at the island's center. Its stated mission was to provide command, control, communications, computers and intelligence to all naval, joint, agency and coalition forces afloat and ashore in the Pacific and Indian Oceans' areas of operation.

NCTAMS PAC had many outlying departments across the island. These relied on six fiber-optic landing stations along the coast from which tens of thousands of miles of underwater cable, shared by civilian telecoms and the Navy, rose up from the depths.

Outside Honolulu Harbor's main channel now, a pair of tugs made fast their towlines to the *Lucky Gift* and escorted the giant ship toward its berth in the island's foreign trade zone. There it slotted in across the inlet from the Sand Island breakwater, dropping anchor alongside the long, concrete quay wall at Pier 2.

In his billet under the stern deck, Jochi took the equipment he expected to need from his locker, laid it across his mattress, then carefully assembled and organized it for his advance scouting expedition. He could hardly wait to be free of the ship. After weeks of idle confinement and periodic seasickness he felt bored, blunt and sluggish.

But that was about to change. The target had to be carefully reconnoitered, and there was no sense wasting time. Grigor would arrive within forty-eight hours. From that point on, things would rapidly accelerate.

Jochi took his safety vest and helmet off a hook and set them on the bed with his gear. He and a small group of his men would leave the ship as members of the cargo gang and avoid drawing attention to themselves.

They had slipped in under the Americans' noses. Now they had to prepare for their mission.

12

New York

Carmody awoke on the couch with a start. Someone was shaking him. He raised his head and looked up into the dark.

Kali.

She stood there leaning over him, a hand on his arm.

"Something wrong?" he said.

"Yes," she said. "I'm in the system."

"Seven Winds?"

"Yes."

"How deep?"

"As deep as we need to go," she said. "I think I've found what you wanted."

He sat up and massaged the back of his neck.

"What time is it?"

"Four in the morning."

"Early bird," he said. "So what's wrong?"

"It was too easy," she said.

"I love you, *mittha*."

"Love you, Daddy."

"I love you, *phula*."

"I love you, Daddy."

"And don't forget…"

"Call you from home after the bus drops us off!"

Musil stood on the sidewalk outside his Acura, sending a bright, white smile to the girls as they bubbled with laughter. He saw sparks of their mother's playful humor in their eyes.

"You know your dad too well," he said.

"You think?" Raysa said and glanced at her older sister.

They giggled again, then stepped forward together and hugged him around the waist.

"Don't worry," Jani said. "We're careful."

"We are!"

"And you're the best dad in the world."

"You *aaare*!"

He wrapped them both in his arms and drew them closer.

"Thank you for putting up with me, girls," he said. "See you later."

Musil watched until they were in the schoolyard, then returned to the Acura and started it up. As he pulled into the street, he glanced at his dash display and noticed Ki Marton had called and left a voice message. He'd left his phone in the car while standing outside with the girls.

He pressed the voice command button on his steering wheel and played the message.

"Jot, it's the Ki-Man. Get back to me ASAP. I have major news."

Musil was thinking it would have to be major for him to phone this early. It wasn't even eight thirty in the morning. At a stop sign, he signaled a left turn and pressed the V/C button again to call him.

Ki answered on the first ring.

"Dude, there you are," he said. "Listen. It's about Fake Gelfland. I was going to tell you last night. But it was kind of late, and I figured you're alone with the kids—"

"Ki."

"Yeah?"

"What were you going to tell me?"

"Right," he said and rattled it all off in his manic way, explaining about his database search and then the blocked file.

When he finished five minutes later, Musil realized he had distractedly driven straight past the bridge while listening to him. Worse, he'd gone a full five blocks past the entrance ramp, a turn he made every morning on his way into Manhattan.

"Call Harris right now," he said. "I'm on my way in."

"Right."

"And Ki?"

"Yeah?"

"Today is the day."

"Zowie," Ki said. "What day?"

"Your day for lunch," Musil said. "On me."

"Seriously?"

"You will feast on limitless Punjabi."

"Wow!"

"Be ready, my friend."

Musil got off the line. The rush-hour traffic on Queens Boulevard was too thick for him to make a U-turn, so he abruptly swung up the nearest side street to double back.

Major news, yes.

Even though he didn't have the foggiest idea what it meant.

"Boss?" Ki Marton said over the phone.

Leo Harris held the receiver to his ear and glanced at the office wall clock. It was still a little before nine in the morning, his chair not even warm, and the phone was already goddamn ringing. He felt cranky and desperate for caffeine, having been awake until the wee hours thinking alternately about the pending CloudCable subpoenas and his plans with Rach.

"Technically I ain't your boss anymore, but let's leave that aside for now," Leo said. "What's up?"

"I stayed here late last night trying to find a match for the Fake Gelfland photo. Got conditional permission from the CIA and Twenty-Six Fed to access their classified databases. A couple other agencies too. I ran a full dragnet."

Leo grunted. Twenty-Six Federal Plaza was the location of the FBI's New York field office, where he had been Ki's direct superior once upon a time. Apparently, his former ASAC still had a gift for jumping over the procedural bogs that could normally stall investigations for weeks.

"Any luck?" he said.

"Yeah. Well, in a different way than you'd think. It's weird. The searches were all busts. Until I wound up getting a hit. Sort of. On Mirror Image."

"*Our* database?"

"Yessir. That's the weird part."

Leo straightened slightly out of his tired slouch.

"OK," he said. "How about the *sort of* part?"

"I can't pull the image for a look at it."

Harris frowned.

"Why not?"

"It's locked up tight. Priority A status. Only the person who assigned it can open the file."

"You know who that person is?"

"Yessir. It was right on my screen."

"Then, how about you stop fucking around and tell me?"

Ki told him.

He sat there looking surprised.

* * *

"Carol? It's Leo."

"Hi, I just walked in. What's up?"

Which was exactly what Leo had asked five minutes ago, and one link back on the lengthening telephone chain Ki had started.

He held the receiver in his hand, his eyes straying to his watch. It was just after nine thirty.

"You ever hear of something called Pinnacle?" he asked.

She didn't answer.

"Carol?"

"I'm here."

"No shit," he said. "What's Pinnacle, Carol?"

She didn't answer.

Leo Harris was an experienced investigator. But he didn't need to be one to know that if you asked somebody the same question twice and got silence both times, chances were that person was holding back on you.

"Listen," he said. "There's a locked file in Mirror Image. And I think something's in it about that guy on the *Stalwart*. Fake Gelfland."

"Are you sure?"

"No. But only because I can't open the file."

"Who locked it?"

He told her, then listened to more dead air.

"I have to call Alex," she said after ten long seconds. "Stay tuned."

"Hello, you've reached the voice mail of Alex Michaels. I'm away from my desk right now. But if

you'll leave your name, number and a brief message, I'll return your call as soon as possible."

Morse hesitated with her fingers tight around her phone.

"Alex, it's Carol Morse," she said. "Call me ASAP. It's urgent."

She hung up and glanced impatiently at her watch.

It was a quarter to ten.

At that moment in Langley, Virginia, Michaels was in the office of Deputy Director of the CIA Lane Kildeer at the agency's headquarters compound, having arrived for what was anything but a routine visit.

Kildeer looked at him across his desk. "I'm surprised to see you here, Alex," he said. "Sorry I kept you waiting outside—I wish you'd called ahead of time."

"We spoke yesterday," Michaels said. "I told you I planned to come by."

Kildeer was tall and slim with thick, silver hair that was swept back over his forehead and carefully sprayed into place. His suit was blue and tailored. His shirt was white, starched and crisp, and his red necktie was perfectly knotted. Everything about him gave of an air of tight, deliberate control.

"I must have misunderstood," he said. "I thought it possible but no sure thing. Or I would have checked my calendar."

"I don't buy that, Lane. I think you intentionally kept me cooling my heels."

The DD briefly studied his face. "Forgive me if I wasn't able to drop everything. But it's been one call after the next, followed by a meeting. For almost two weeks now. I've been answering questions about the *Stalwart* to everyone here and on the Hill. Up to *and* including the president."

Michaels gave himself five seconds. He wasn't looking to butt heads.

"Fair enough," he said. "Believe me, Lane, I would rather not be here right now. I'm trying to get an organization off the ground. Neither of us has time to waste. But I want to ask you something point-blank. And it had to be done in person."

Kildeer didn't answer at first. Then he nodded faintly.

"Please," he said. "Ask."

Michaels looked at him across the desk. "Was the *Stalwart* installing Sentient spy technology as part of its activities?"

"Not that you want to put me on the spot."

"It's a straightforward question," Michaels said.

"That wasn't my point."

"Does something about it bother you?"

"No, not at all."

"Then why think I'm putting you on the spot?"

Kildeer gave a vacuous smile.

"With all due respect… I don't owe you an answer."

"Do I take that as an affirmative?"

"I'm sure you'll take it however you choose, regardless of what I say. You've been openly critical of the CloudCable effort all along."

"For domestic security reasons," Michaels said. "I don't like the idea of our intelligence agencies sharing their vital data flow with a privately owned online marketer. If I've wondered whether there might be more going on, it's never slipped into my public comments."

"And privately? You haven't speculated?"

"That isn't relevant. Though, frankly, it's reasonable to wonder."

Kildeer nodded his head.

"While we're being honest," he said, "I've never understood why establishing Net Force was necessary. I'm not disparaging it. I'm only telling you that I feel the president was misguided in pushing it through Congress. Our existing intelligence groups—the agency among them—did a fine job of anticipating and counteracting threats to our electronic infrastructure without an additional layer of jurisdictional haziness."

"Is that why New York happened?"

"New York was an exception. The cyberattack had unprecedented elements. We've since plugged all the holes in our defenses."

"Except for the holes you can't see," Michaels said. "We're here, Lane. Like it or not, Net Force is here to stay…but how about we stick to my question? I want to know about the *Stalwart* being potentially out conducting espionage operations.

Using new Sentient technology. In Chinese territorial waters."

The room was silent. Kildeer's fingertips came together under his chin again. This time his eyes were fixed on the ceiling, as if looking for the right answer there.

"The CIA is chartered as an independent intelligence agency. It has been for almost eighty years. And we have to retain that independence to do our job. As I suggested a minute ago, I'm not required to loop you into our operations. Specifically or generally. You don't have oversight."

"But the president does," Michaels said. "No one can go snooping on China without her knowledge and approval. That applies to all of us."

More silence. Kildeer brought his hands down to the desk and sat up straight.

"Is this why you've come, Alex? As Annemarie Fucillo's personal errand boy? You'll forgive me, but I thought you would be more circumspect about your special friendship."

Michaels stared at him. "You're losing me."

"I don't think so," Kildeer said. "Rumors fly in Washington. As a member of the cabinet, you really wouldn't want that. It opens you—and POTUS—up to all sorts of uncomfortable questions about conflict of interest. Not to mention candor and integrity in your dealings within the government. Fair enough?"

Michaels stared at him for a long moment but said nothing.

"I think we understand each other moving forward," Kildeer said. "Is there anything else you'd care to discuss before we both get on with our morning?"

Michaels shook his head.

"No, Lane. Not right now," he said. "But it doesn't mean we're finished. If I find out you're keeping secrets about the *Stalwart* that resulted in harm coming to the civilians aboard that ship… and that threaten our national security… I promise you'll be hearing from me."

Kildeer looked at him and smiled his white, neutral smile.

Michaels stood up and left.

"Something funny?" Carmody asked.

"No," Kali said.

"Then, why are you smiling?"

"You always ask questions twice."

"And more often if needed," he said. "Why the smile?"

The apartment was quiet. He was sitting at the table in front of her laptop. She had come up from the kitchen with a steaming cup of tea.

She looked at him for a long moment.

"Your hands are too large for the keyboard," she said. "It gives you trouble when you type."

"This the first you noticed?"

"I noticed a long time ago," she said and nodded at the computer screen. "The list of names. You've sat there looking at it for hours."

He nodded. "It's got me thinking."

"About?"

"A few things," he said. "Like you not trusting it."

"I don't trust how few barriers there were to getting hold of it."

"Explain the difference."

"The integrity of the file is a separate question from how it is or isn't protected," she said. "Imagine a museum that posts signs that its exhibits are protected by a security system. But the surveillance cameras aren't connected. The alarms aren't monitored. The guard dogs have no teeth."

"And no bite," Carmody said. "A thief could make off with the goods without any real trouble."

Kali nodded.

"I assumed the system would have defenses," she said. "I also expected my crawlers to penetrate them. But the shields were barely adequate. It's as if someone only wanted to make it *appear* that safeguarding the data was a serious matter."

"So you think it's a setup."

"That's your word. I won't rush to conclusions."

He looked at her. "OK," he said. "But let's work it from that angle a second. Back to your museum. If the security's a sham, how do we know the exhibits aren't too? Maybe they're all forgeries and worthless junk. Bright, shiny lures."

"It's possible," she said. "It's also possible Seven Winds is lazy about updating its internet security. Or looking to save money. Or just negligent."

"You have a favorite pick?"

"I wouldn't discount any of them."

"But say somebody planted the list. Made it nice and hackable. Who would do that? Who is it that they want to find it? And why?"

She looked at him. "I believe we should focus on things we know."

"About the list."

"Starting with the list."

Carmody was quiet. That was sound deductive reasoning. Test the things you know so you're sure about them. See what connections they might have. Then separate them from the things you don't know and move on to examine the connections.

The list. She had hacked it from the Seven Winds human resources employee records. Twelve men, all employees of a no-name Chinese corporation who had been transferred to its subsidiary, the Seven Winds Group, on the third of April. Four days before the same dozen men boarded the CS *Stalwart* as replacement food workers during a port call in Penang Harbor. That was the seventh of April.

Three days before the ship vanished from the face of the earth.

After extracting the human resources file, Kali had prowled online for information about the parent corporation. While the Anti-Money Laundering Act of 2020 did not quite prohibit companies from operating namelessly in the United States, it did require their owners to provide *their* names, birth dates, addresses and other documents to the Treasury Department.

Its public database quickly revealed that the parent was co-owned by a husband and wife, Deng Yannan and Deng Jing. Yannan, the husband, was also sole owner of a business called Jinggu Technologies. Both were born and bred residents of the People's Republic of China. Furthermore, Yannan was a government insider. The brother-in-law of the Chinese president and an international trade representative for the Chinese Ministry of Commerce.

"I'll tell you what bothers me," Carmody said. "This group comes aboard the ship. They aren't really hired by Seven Winds. They don't have résumés in its HR system. They all work for the no-name and just show up at the dock one day as kitchen help. What's that about?"

"We don't know, Michael."

"Right. But it's the timing. And the guy who owns the no-name. Yannan has some serious political connections." He paused. "Morse thinks China's keeping secrets and may even be behind what happened. According to her, so does the president. Both of them are suspicious of the dozen boarders. But if they really were up to no good, I can't believe we'd find anything on file that ties them to the Chinese."

"Yet we did."

"Right. It was easy, like you said in the first

place. Except the Chinese are too smart and too good to leave a trail of bread crumbs. Which is why I think something else might be going on here."

"Unless the boarders were just kitchen help," Kali said. "You've built your premise that they weren't on a suspicion. But a company's owner having close government ties proves nothing. And what you say about the Chinese being skilled at espionage undercuts your own theory."

He looked at her. "That's just it. The whole thing makes more sense if someone wants us to point a finger at China."

"Michael—"

"Hold on. I'm not assuming anything. I just want to reason this out," he said. "It doesn't matter whether those kitchen workers were good, bad or neutral. Somebody on the *Stalwart*'s crew had to sign off on bringing them aboard. They'd have to show ID. There would be paperwork. Everyone on the ship has to be documented and legal. You agree?"

Kali thought a moment. "Yes," she said. "I do."

"So my question is who checked their documents?" Carmody said. "Whose job would it have been? Because if that person smells funny, we might just have a whole new trail of crumbs to follow."

Silence.

"I don't know," she said after a moment. "If it's

a member of the regular crew, he or she would have to be someone who works for CloudCable."

Carmody nodded.

"Morse has to know about all this," he said. "We need to tell her. Both of us, together, before we leave for Teterboro."

Grigor strapped the pack over his shoulders and inspected himself in the full-length mirror near the door. He wore a dark blue hooded sweatshirt over a gray T-shirt, khakis and running shoes. A ball cap on his head, tortoise sunglasses with round lenses over his eyes. He was freshly shaven.

His gear was stowed in the pack. The Glock, the Scorpion, everything else he might need for his kill. Also, his computer, passport and a change of clothes.

He turned from the mirror for a last look around the room. It was immaculately clean and tidy. Almost as if he'd never been there. He had even made and smoothed down the bed.

Grigor left the room and went to the elevator and rode it down to the lobby, dropping off his key card at the front desk, leaving the hotel through the Forty-Second Street doors. Outside, he was met by sunshine and a light breeze, yet another beautiful spring day in the city. He took a step or two onto the shaded sidewalk, then paused to check his watch.

Ten thirty.

It would take him about a half hour to reach the Terminal on foot.

He turned west and started walking crosstown, one of countless anonymous pedestrians on the busy street.

Hawaii

Five thousand miles and three time zones west of midtown Manhattan, Jochi and three of his men were hiking down a stony, unmarked trail in the granular darkness. It was four o'clock here, two hours before sunrise, and the island of Oahu was still under the pale gray glow of the waning moon.

Silent but for the scuff and crunch of their footsteps, the men could hear the tide receding from the cove below with a sound like slow, rhythmical sighs. They all wore black windbreakers, cargo pants, backpacks and waterproof boots. All wore LED headlamps to light the trail.

They descended from the top of the ridge in pairs, single file. Each team of two was carrying a pontoon raft between them. Sturdy and maneuverable, the inflatables had rigid rubber hulls and narrow upturned noses for gliding over or through high, rough waves. One of the rafts had a plywood launch ramp inside it.

The big Chevrolet Traverse the men had driven from Honolulu was parked on an overlook above and behind them. They had taken the H-1 east to where it turned into 72 and ran along Hanauma

Bay, then made the sharp right off the main road for the cove.

Though only fifteen miles from the harbor, they seemed a world away. Pocketed between steep volcanic walls, the little sand beach could not be seen from the road. The trail itself had no markers or guardrails and did not appear on any hiking maps. Two hand-painted old wooden signs—washed-out white lettering over cracked and peeling green backgrounds—leaned on crooked posts a hundred feet below the trailhead. One warned *WALK AT YOUR OWN RISK*. The other said *NO PUBLIC ACCESS, NO SWIMMING, DANGEROUS CURRENTS*.

The men were already well past the signs and nearing the bottom of the trail. A careful turn with the rafts hoisted between them, another, and their feet settled down on soft, flat sand.

As they dropped the rafts and formed up around them, Jochi realized the beach was even smaller than his photo intel had indicated. It was twenty yards long and barely a third as wide, a half circle, its diameter defined by the shoreline, its inland curve enclosed by the ridge walls. When the ocean roared in at high tide it would have nowhere to go but up against them. It would slam them with waves and flood every inch of the beach. Anyone on it would be smashed to a pulp against the unyielding rocks and then sucked away by the undertow.

Jochi had coordinated the recon with the tidal

ebb and flow. The water would be lowest in an hour and then gradually begin to rise. He wanted to ride the current out as it receded, then ride it back to shore with the incoming tide. But the timing had to be just right. They needed to return here before the ocean came crashing up hard against the sea cliff. At that point, attempting it would be a death wish.

He looked at the men. "Let's go."

The two with the plywood launch ramp in their raft lifted it out, carried it over to the waterline and set one end on a rocky projection so it sloped down to the lapping surf. Then they picked up the raft and put it on the board and shoved it in.

The other team went next. When both rafts were in the water, all four men waded out and climbed inside them, remaining in their original teams of two.

Jochi splashed over to the first raft, jumped on board and took the folding seat in front. On the rear bench, his men had already slid their lightweight aluminum oars through the rings and dipped the blades into the swells.

The cable landing station was at Kono Head, three miles southwest.

They rowed out to it in the filtered moonlight.

Half an hour later the rafts were bobbing in the Maunalua Bay currents a quarter mile east of the head.

Jochi gazed out toward shore through a pair

of digital day–night field glasses. A single low white-walled flat-roofed modular structure, the Kono Head landing station was on the windward side of the extinct volcano, probably two or three thousand feet east of its furrowed base. It would be easily within range of his nanodrones.

He let the binoculars hang from his neck and reached down to a cargo pocket, unsnapping it against his leg.

The tiny Wasp UAV he extracted was just over six inches long and weighed mere ounces. Its bio-mimetic wings, when unfolded, were deliberately similar to those of its namesake. So were the long aerodynamic contours of its molded plastic body. Speedy and agile, with three cameras behind the tiny pane of its eye, the drone's low visual and acoustic signatures made it difficult for counter-surveillance arrays to pick up. If detected, more-over, its shape would fool even AI-based systems into mistaking it for a flying animal.

Jochi held it between his right thumb and fore-finger, clicking the wings into their open, out-spread position with his opposite hand. Traveling at fifteen knots, with half an hour of flight time, it would conclude its mission and return with min-utes to spare.

He raised the drone up in front of his face and activated it. Its wings fanned rapidly. It tugged and pulled and flapped. He felt little puffs of air beat against his cheeks as it tried to escape his fingertips.

"At the one," he said into his headset.

"Yes."

The response came from a man called Niu in the other raft's front seat. He held a drone identical to Jochi's in his hand.

Jochi gave the count. Both men's fingers parted.

The Wasps leaped up into the darkness and shot off across the water toward shore.

CloudCable's Kono Head landing station, or dry plant, was centered within a square, blacktopped parking area surrounded by wire fencing and only reachable from land over a private access road running due north toward the tuff cone. A quarter mile inland, the access road swung briefly west to skirt the base of the cone, then turned north again to intersect with a narrow, lonely public two-lane.

It was at the bay side that the cable made landfall in a section of beach marked off-limits to visitors. Snaking up from the bay through a hole drilled offshore in forty feet of water, the cable fed into a noncorrosive steel pipe and then ran straight under the beach to the station. A flapper valve at the seaward entry to this duct prevented seawater from entering the heavy galvanized pipe.

The intercontinental cable inside the pipe consisted of seven fiber pairs. Two pairs were owned by Olympia.com, and two more by a business consortium jointly operated by the CIA and NGIA. One pair was reserved for CloudCable's own future capacity, and another for potential sale or leasing to outside telecoms. A seventh and final pair was very quietly reserved for use by the US Office of Naval Intelligence as a data traffic conduit for its IUSS, or Integrated Undersea Surveillance System, a kind of burglar alarm for intruding submarines.

The Kono Head plant was the cable's endpoint in the terrestrial United States. It was also the critical convergence of an expanding, diversified and increasingly interdependent network of subsea lightwave cables—its branches extending east to California, and westward across tens of thousands of miles of sea floor to Malaysia, the Philippines, Taiwan, Hong Kong, Japan and finally Australia.

The facility's interior layout was as boxy and homogeneous as its exterior. Nobody that built landing stations cared about aesthetics. The designers wanted them functional, and they wanted them standardized for personnel rotating from station to station. A schematic of Kono Head would therefore show four typical, environmentally controlled, fire-suppression protected sections: the telecommunications equipment room, power generator room, battery plant and control room.

The latter was staffed around the clock by a handful of technicians who monitored the network for compromises, dataflow interruptions and power outages. At this time of morning, that was an overnight crew of four, though a larger day crew would arrive at nine o'clock. The equipment in the other three rooms ran more or less automatically and only required periodic inspection and maintenance.

Kono Head's buffers against physical intrusion were in compliance with industry guidelines. There was bright outdoor security lighting inside and outside the fence. There was real-time video surveillance of the perimeter. But the security patrol was light, consisting of a half dozen young Army reservists from nearby Shafter Flats. Government risk-assessment studies had determined the attack and intrusion countermeasures in place made a successful attack on the station unlikely.

Jochi thought the assumption ludicrous. And very advantageous to him.

The Wasps flitted over the water at an altitude of three thousand feet. One of them could have done the job, but Jochi had wanted some redundancy. Say his drone stalled in the air. Or whatever. You needed backup in case of a malfunction. He'd gone with two rafts rather than one for the same reason.

The drone he'd released shot left, and the other right, approaching and circling the target area from opposite directions. High in the darkness above it, they captured high-resolution images of the access road, outer fence and the vehicles in the parking lot. They photographed the station's roof and outer walls. They took videos of the guards making their rounds. They covered every yard, every foot, every inch of the facility.

The recon took fifteen minutes. Then the digital gauge on Jochi's pocket controller told him the drones were reaching the extent of their battery life. But that was all right. They had gotten everything he needed.

He and Niu brought them in.

It was nearly dawn when the men reached the mouth of the cove. As they rowed toward the pocket beach, Jochi stared eastward through rising gray curls of mist that seemed as thick and heavy as smoke. Perhaps two degrees above the horizon line, the orange-red sunlight was racing toward him like a sheet of flame over the water.

Smoke and fire, fire and smoke, he thought, unconsciously and rhythmically to the repetitive beating of the oars. *Smoke and fire, fire and smoke.*

The fire seemed very close now.

New York

In New York City, where it was already midday, DeBattista stood outside a Teterboro hangar under a wide-open blue sky, watching a squad of mechanics and fuelers move around the Dassault Falcon 8X they were prepping for Carmody's flight.

He wasn't thrilled about the bargain. Especially considering the financial hit he stood to take.

The Falcon was a stretched-out shiny long-range business aircraft he normally chartered to his biggest payers. Wall Streeters, for instance: hotshot corporate M&A types on the sell side, hedge fund and private equity guys on the buy side, with a smattering of star athletes and movie people thrown in for good measure. In the New York area you had droves of people who pissed pearls before breakfast and shit diamonds at bedtime. Toss in the high net-worthers who didn't want the hassle and costs of maintaining private jets of their own and you had a steady cash flow.

The trijet had set DeBattista's air transport company back fifty-eight million bucks when he added it to his fleet. Another mil or two in yearly operating expenses on top. A huge financial layout, but the profits were stupendous. DeBattista charged a hundred-thousand-dollar minimum for a nonstop to Paris, London or Berlin. For certain exclusive conveniences and amenities, he would double the price of the same trip. With the money-honey niceties in his discreet Love Cloud packages, he liked to say the sky was the limit—ha ha—depending on a client's tastes. But you had to consider the hired help, and the right help didn't come free.

So this latest Carmody thing had the makings of a cash catastrophe, and DeBattista thought it might be hazardous to his health, besides. But he couldn't have refused. If not for Carmody, the Mafia lunatics would have fed his uncle alive to the pigs. Three, four years ago, was it? They had sent him a parrot to deliver the message. *"Sei un uomo morto."* You're a dead man.

Carmody had rewritten that script, given it

a whole different ending. Ask any barman in Salerno or Battipaglia, he'd know the gory story.

DeBattista heard a plane flying overhead, raised his eyes in time to see it pass through a sketchy white wisp of cloud. One of his competitors taking off from an adjacent field, he thought. But fuck them all, big and small. Let them try and outdo his Love Cloud package.

It took a bundle to sustain an air charter outfit, but it took some kind of smarts and balls for somebody with his background to even think he could start one up. In America they usually belonged to holding companies formed by old money *Mayflower* families, people with nothing to do but play with their inherited fortunes. Eye-talians like him and his uncle found a different way, and it wasn't always clean and pretty. But when doors were closed to you because your name ended in a vowel and you had to claw through the barriers by your fingernails, you allowed for getting some dirt under them.

Uncle Enzo had done Carmody some favors of his own, he thought. No small ones either. But suppose Carmody hadn't helped with the Neapolitan zoo crew. Suppose he had told his uncle it was too dangerous. The pigs would have feasted on him.

DeBattista lowered his gaze to the Falcon, watched his maintenance people inspect the aircraft's wing elevators, rudders and tires, watched the fuelers fit their hoses into its turbos. After a minute, he glanced at his Rolex. A few minutes past noon. Carmody had told him to be ready to leave around three o'clock.

He turned toward the trailer that served as his main office. In a couple of hours, he would climb into the Falcon and start his preflight. He trusted all his people, but if he was flying the plane would do his own instrument checks. Still, he had a little while to take care of some odds and ends at his desk... Who the hell knew when he would be back?

The whole thing smelled of calamity. But a debt was a debt, and the DeBattistas always repaid theirs. If Carmody wanted him in the pilot's seat, he would fly it straight to hell, up the devil's ass and out his pisshole.

With a smile.

"It's lunchtime, Ki," Musil said over the phone. He was calling from his fourth-floor office at the Terminal. "Are we still on?"

"All depends," Marton replied. He was in his office one floor below. "You still treating?"

"I am."

"Then, why ask a dumb question?"

Musil laughed. "Meet me out on Tenth. Say, in fifteen minutes? We'll walk right over. The office crowd doesn't usually show for another hour, so we won't have to compete with anyone but the cabbies."

"Huh?"

"You'll find out."

"Looking forward to it," Ki said and paused a second. "I can't believe how long it's been since we've seen each other. Physically and not on a computer screen. I mean, we work in the same building, Jot. How do we never *see* each other these days?"

"As my girls say, first-world problems." Musil laughed again. "Okay. Downstairs. I hope I recognize you."

"Har har. I'll be the short, bald, pudgy Korean guy with the famished look on his face."

Ki hung up. Five minutes later, he left the office, made a pit stop to the men's room, then went up the hall to the elevators. Lunch awaited.

On the building's eighth and topmost floor, Carol Morse had been mulling the problems of China, CloudCable, the *Stalwart* and Fake Gelfland on the one hand, a Russian-built secret city in Crimea on the other, and then Pinnacle showing up in that image search to exponentially complicate an already-nervous situation. All after leaving her third voice message of the day for Alex Michaels, who had seemingly gone MIA at the worst imaginable point in time.

It had added up to a splitting headache.

She was groping in a drawer for some Tylenol when her admin buzzed on the speakerphone.

"Yes?"

"Mr. Carmody and Ms. Alcazar are here to see you."

Morse was surprised. She hadn't been expecting Carmody. And certainly not Kali Alcazar, who had said nary a word to her since arriving in the country months ago. Which made her one among legions, but never mind. She had wanted Carmody to ask Kali for a favor. Maybe they'd turned something up.

She abruptly forgot about the Tylenol.

"Please, send them in."

The door swung open, and Carmody appeared in his motorcycle jacket, tall, bulking and barrel-chested, coming right up to the desk with two long strides, sitting down in front of her without a word. He seemed to fill the entryway, fill the room, fill the chair. His knees were awkwardly bent and poked up higher than they should have, as if he had trouble squeezing himself into it.

She was thinking offices weren't made for men like him.

"Duchess," he said, "we've got news."

So, they had discovered something.

She angled her head to glance past him. Kali had followed him through the door and stood just inside it in riding leather, looking as out of place as Carmody. He had insisted nothing was going on between them, and maybe that was true. Or maybe something was going on, and they didn't realize it. Or he didn't realize it yet. Not that it was really Morse's business. And not that she qualified as an expert at love. And not that she had time to think about any of that right now.

She looked back over at him.

"OK," she said. "Let's hear it."

He nodded and started to talk.

She listened, closely.

Abdul Samad was dropping off a fare on East Twenty-Seventh Street when his wristwatch signaled the midday prayer call. He waited for his passenger to skim her card, thanked her for a generous tip and waited only until she left his cab to hit the off-duty sign and pull into traffic.

Ten minutes later he was heading crosstown in his Toyota passenger van. He yawned, tired. With five hours to go, his break could not have come at a better time. He would make his offering and enjoy a good lunch with his first cousin Haram.

The street was nearly clear of traffic, and he reached Tenth Avenue in minutes. As usual his cousin had reached the restaurant ahead of him, so he double-parked alongside his cab. Grabbing his wireless key fob from the center console, he hustled up the sidewalk toward its door.

As he entered, Abdul saw two of the drivers already at their usual table. Haram, meanwhile, was in the back on the prayer rug, immersed in his devotions.

Abdul spared a glance at the buffet before joining him, hoping the cook would bring out some *aloo bonda* today. He hadn't yesterday, choosing to experiment with *dosai*. *Dosai* after breakfast. An insult! He and the other drivers had made sure to give him an earful.

At the lunch buffet one always knew what to expect. It was an oasis of friendship and harmony—a serene, happy place amid the craziness of driving a taxi on the streets of New York—and the food was what held it all together. Why change things on a whim?

No one came to the Share Punjabi restaurant looking for surprises.

Grigor was across the street from the Terminal when he saw Musil exit through its Tenth Avenue doors. It was five minutes past noon. Roughly the same time he had taken his lunch for the past two days. Most people were creatures of habit. That was the known and expected element. But today Musil was leaving with another man. He was an unknown and unexpected variable.

They turned right, in front of the building, Musil on the inside of the sidewalk, his companion to his left on the outside.

Grigor took out his phone to snap some photos, holding down its shutter button for three seconds. The two men walked one block south to the corner of West Fifty-Fourth, then crossed to his side of the street, turned right again and continued downtown. He walked about a half block behind them, his long legs keeping an even pace as he checked the phone. Its camera had taken over a dozen rapid-fire photos of the men. In most they were partially blocked from the lens by the moving northbound traffic and other pedestrians. But one clearly showed the person with Musil.

He tapped the phone to access his database of stolen law-enforcement agency files. Tapped again to open the biometric search engine and then submitted his photo for a facial-recognition check. The database relied on periodic security breaches by hackers and was far from exhaustive. There was no guarantee it would draw a match. But he thought his chances were at least forty percent. Not good, but fair.

In this instance, he came out on top. It was an FBI personnel file, probably from the same hack that had produced Musil's information. Though the photo was several years old, the man was easily recognizable as the same person walking alongside Musil. *Ki Lung Marton.*

Grigor scanned the file, glancing up ahead to make sure he didn't lose the two. He wondered where they were going and after a minute found out. Midway down West Fifty-Third Street, they turned into the restaurant he'd seen the taxi driver enter the day before. Coincidental on the surface, but again Grigor's mind automatically weighed the odds.

If they were having lunch, they would probably choose somewhere within walking distance so as not to waste time. Say within three to five blocks north or south, given the average hour's break. He estimated there were four restaurants or cafés per block on each side of the avenue. Thus, twenty-four within three blocks, thirty-two within four, and forty within five. Making the chances of Share Punjabi being their destination about one in sixteen once they turned south in front of the Terminal.

Again, not a bad shot mathematically. But by luck or likelihood, Grigor thought, things were stacking up nicely to his advantage.

He walked on past the restaurant toward the taxi stand.

13

Morse had never been a fan of the word *takeaway*. It suggested that it was necessary, or at least preferable, for a given event, report, article, speech, what have you, to have a salient point, or set of points, to make it worth stowing away in your memory. To her that was a very limiting perspective—and one that very often led to unforced errors. What at first looked incidental sometimes turned out to be essential. And changing circumstances could cast the seemingly important into total irrelevancy in a heartbeat.

In her opinion it was best to steer clear of looking for takeaways and keep an open, probing mind when evaluating things. A prime example being the complicated CloudCable–Seven Winds tangle Carmody had just presented.

"If I understand correctly, what you're telling me is your personnel file reinforces the suspicion that our Seven Winds twelve were Chinese threat actors," she said.

"Or it would, if the system wasn't so much of a snap to hack," Carmody said.

"I was getting to that," she said. "I'm not a computer person. So maybe it's why I have trouble understanding how an easier-than-expected hack of a human resources database turns into someone deliberately planting the file."

"*Possibly* deliberately," Carmody said.

She nodded.

"Right," she said. "But I wonder how that's really a considered opinion. We're talking about a company that provides cruise ships with kitchen help. That isn't the type we would normally equate with high-level network security."

Kali was still standing inside the office door.

"Be smart," she said.

Morse looked at her. "What?"

"The assessment was mine," she said. "I *am* a computer person."

A thin smile spread across Morse's lips.

"So we all know," she said.

Kali showed no expression.

"OK," Morse said. "Say something's very unkosher about the twelve. And say Seven Winds and its Chinese parent company were complicit in putting them aboard the *Stalwart*. That sounds like an international conspiracy to attack an American ship. Why would they plant the file for us as an Easter egg?"

"We didn't say it was planted," Carmody said. "Maybe HR thought it was put away safe and sound. Could be somebody fiddled with their system to lower the defenses."

"A third party? That's what you're suggesting to me?"

"It's possible."

Morse looked at him. "So someone hacks their system to make it easy for *us* to hack it and find the file," she said. "Pulls the strings to jerk around China and the United States. That's your hypothetical scenario?"

"Yeah," he said. "A double-blind."

Morse thought for a long moment, then shook her head.

"It would be very goddamned clever," she said. "And sinister."

"There's plenty of clever and sinister to go around."

"And you're convinced there had to be an insider aboard *Stalwart*?"

He nodded. "When twelve new crew members come shipboard in a foreign port, it triggers all sorts of automatic security procedures. Especially when they're citizens of another country. *Chinese* citizens would get serious background checks."

Morse looked at him.

"Who's to say it didn't happen?" she said. "Anyone who went to the trouble of putting them on board would make sure they had the right passports, work visas, that sort of thing."

Carmody shook his head. "That wouldn't be enough. *Stalwart* was a US cable layer. It was working on a project that was partially government funded, with CIA spooks along for the ride. There would be strict anti-terrorism protocols." He paused. "These twelve were total blanks. No résumés, no nothing. They would never cut the mustard."

"You're positive."

"Yeah," he said. "In the Navy, the person in charge is called a boarding officer. On a civilian ship, a boarding agent. Same difference," he said. "Everything flows through him. He'll run his checks ahead of time to make sure there's nothing peculiar. He sees they transferred from a Chinese company just two days before *Stalwart* hauled in, then sees they have no résumés, he'll red-flag them on the spot. And make sure to notify his boss."

"CloudCable."

"Right."

Morse said, "So if the agent didn't flag them, we need to know why not. And if he did, and CloudCable approved them, we need to know why."

Carmody nodded.

"The project's managing director in New Hampshire, Olsen, could have given us that information," Kali said. "But he chose otherwise."

Morse looked at her, then at Carmody, then at both of them.

"Suppose I tell you Agent Musil's been looking into some odd circumstances surrounding a *Stalwart* crew member named Stephen Gelfland, who, it so happens, turns out to be the boarding agent," she said. "Then suppose I tell you one of our analysts ran a photo of him—or someone claiming to be him—through our face-rec database. And things got even odder."

Carmody bent forward with his arms across his knees. Morse thought again that he didn't seem especially comfortable. With him on it, the chair almost looked like it came from a child's room.

"Odder how?" he asked.

"The impostor's photo drew a hit," she said. "But we haven't been able to access the file. It's sealed."

"By?"

"Alex Michaels," she said. "I've been trying to get in touch with him."

He digested that, his eyes on her face. "How long were you going to wait to tell us about this?"

"Never mind. I'm telling you now," she said. "There's a project. Classified, not ours. Russian. It's called Pinnacle. I can't say I know everything about it…"

She let the sentence hang there. Kali had suddenly caught her attention by moving away from the door and deeper into the room. She glanced around, saw a chair against the wall and pulled it up alongside Carmody.

"I can," she said.

"All right, big question." Ki leaned forward over his plate, speaking in a hushed voice. "What's Pinnacle?"

"I don't know," Musil said.

"You have *any* idea?"

"No," Musil said. "Do you?"

Ki shook his head, forking some creamed, pungently seasoned spinach into his mouth. It was a quarter past noon, and they were at one of the small tables along the wall at Share Punjabi, their plates heaped with food, two tall mango lassis on the table between them.

"Man, this is great." Ki smacked his lips. "Spicy, but great."

Musil smiled. "Enjoy."

Ki reached for his lassi, wanting to calm his overheated taste buds before he dug back into his buffet selections.

"There has to be an image of our Fake Gelfland, origin unknown, inside that file," he said and drank. "Maybe more than one."

"Probably," Musil said. "And if it's restricted access, I think it holds something apart from just photos."

"Information about our mystery man."

"And possibly other things connected to him."

Ki nodded his agreement.

"I can't figure it, though," he said. "Michaels could have cloaked the file from the search engine. Instead, he locks it up tight but leaves it out there for somebody like me to find. Seems like a contradiction."

Musil spooned some chutney onto a piece of flatbread.

"Not really," he said. "It's obvious he isn't interested in hiding its existence from us. He just wants to personally authorize who opens it."

"OK," Ki said. "Why?"

"Why leave it in plain sight? Or why keep it locked?"

"Both."

"In plain sight because he thinks it might become important in an investigation. Locked because it contains sensitive material he's trying to prevent from circulating."

"Politically sensitive?"

"That's usually the reason. But there could be another reason. Or several. We were in the FBI long enough to know how it works."

They ate. Musil watched a bearded guy in a knitted white skullcap enter the restaurant, approach a group of men at a table in the center aisle, exchange familiar greetings and toss his jacket onto a vacant chair. Then he went to the niche in back, took off his shoes, and knelt on the prayer rug.

"When will you find out what Michaels has to

say about the file?" Ki asked. "Assuming the big-wigs share that with you."

"I don't know," he said. "Soon, I hope."

Ki nodded, eyed the mound of tandoori chicken on his plate and picked up a drumstick.

"On another note, how are you doing?" Musil asked.

"Right at this moment?"

Musil watched him gnaw with relish on his drumstick. "I know what eating does for your state of mind," he said. "But in general."

Ki took longer than he needed to chew and swallow.

"I'm up and down," he said after a minute. "Mark and I were always together. There'll be a part of a song, a TV ad we hated, and I'll remember us groaning about it. Something dumb like that. Or I'll pass the couch on the way into the kitchen and think I see him out the corner of my eye. And then, pow, it hits me that he's gone."

"What do you do when that happens?"

"God's honest truth?"

"Yes."

"I sink into a deep hole. It takes me a while to pull myself out."

Musil set his fork down onto his plate. "I'd like you to try something for me, Ki-Man."

"From the buffet?"

Musil didn't smile. "Seriously. Would you?"

Ki looked at him over a tandoori wing.

"Tell me what it is," he said. "I'll tell you if I'm game."

Musil nodded.

"Every morning when you wake up, I want you think of five things you're grateful for. Only five. Before you even get out of bed."

Ki was quiet a bit. "Can I make it two?"

"Five."

"Three?"

"Five."

"Any other requirements?"

"That's it."

Ki said, "When would I kick off this New Age dharmic self-help regime?"

"Tomorrow. Officially. But you can start practicing right away."

Ki finished what was left of the chicken wing and dabbed his fingers on his napkin.

"OK, dude," he said. "I got this."

Musil smiled. "Excellent," he said.

They sat there eating in silence a while. The waiter came around with a tray of samosas and dropped one into each of their dishes. The man in the prayer niche bowed forward in prostration, his forehead touching the rug, then gradually straightened up. After a minute he put on his shoes and joined his friends at the long cafeteria table.

It was now about a quarter to one, with the restaurant's daily wave of office workers flowing through its door, people of every skin tone and discernible ethnicity. Musil took a moment to soak it all in. The atmosphere was warm and accepting and everything he loved about the city.

He looked at Ki and said, "My friend, we need to do this more often."

"So we always agree before life gets in the way." Ki shrugged. "I'm digging the moment. My brother Jot and great eats."

Musil nodded.

"A nice start," he said.

Ki nodded.

"Better chow down. Lunchtime's almost over," he said, and shoveled more food into his mouth.

Grigor hovered near the taxi stand for several minutes after the double-parked cabbie entered Share Punjabi. Then he stepped into the street and went around the front of his vehicle to the driver's door.

The van was an older model Toyota, which was one reason Grigor had chosen it. Most new vehicles with keyless entry systems were equipped with anti-hacking systems. But that had been far less common just three or four years back.

Standing outside the door, he reached into his pocket for the twenty-thousand-dollar transponder Kosov had included with his mission kit. It was the same size and shape as the bug detector but with a plain black plastic casing. The only external feature was a small button on one side.

Grigor held it between himself and the door and thumbed down the button. The restaurant was a hole-in-the-wall, only a few hundred feet away, and not very deep. He was betting the cabbie and his entry fob were well within range.

He was right. It took all of a second for his transponder to intercept, boost and relay the fob's coded signal to a receiver inside the van.

A glance through the door's tinted window and Grigor saw its lock knob slide up.

He pulled the door open. No one on the street took any notice. He was a taxi driver getting into his vehicle, part of the scenery, an invisible man.

Sliding behind the wheel, Grigor adjusted the seat to give himself some leg room, stepped on the brake and pushed the Start button. The engine awoke with a sigh.

In the Share Punjabi, Musil glanced toward the door at the men and women threading in from the sidewalk. It was almost lunchtime for the office crowd. The restaurant was getting noisier as it filled up.

"Man," Ki said, "those are some blue-ribbon champion loud asses."

"Or possibly we're just quiet."

Ki looked at him. "There you go doing it again."

"There I go doing what again?"

"Always seeing the best in things."

Musil shrugged. "Why not?" he said. "They seem happy. I like to see happy people. It's better than seeing sad ones."

Ki paused with his spoon over his dessert dish. "You've got a point there."

Musil plucked their check off the table. It was almost one; they were running late.

"Finish up," he said. "I'll take care of this so we can get back to headquarters."

The cabbie named Abdul speared a sugary ball of *gulab jamun* with his fork. To his great joy and satisfaction, he had found a huge hot tray of samosas at the buffet today...as well as this, his favorite dessert.

He took a huge bite, pushed the rest into his mouth and made a contented sound in his throat. Then he looked across the table at his cousin. Haram was reaching into his pants for his wallet.

"Going already? What's the hurry?"

Haram slipped a few bills from the wallet, leaving them on the table as a tip.

"Hurry?" he said. "I've been here over an hour. It's getting late!"

Abdul had to admit it was and nodded in reluctant agreement. He would need to move his double-parked van so Haram could pull out of his spot at the taxi stand.

He glanced over at the cashier. The only person near the counter was a guy in a black turban, and he seemed to have already taken care of his check. Abdul thought he might be waiting for somebody.

He grabbed his jacket off the back of his chair, thinking he might as well pay before he got stuck there in a long line.

"I'll leave with you," he said to his cousin.

* * *

Grigor checked the dash clock. It read two minutes past one, and Musil and the analyst had not yet come out of the restaurant.

They were taking longer than expected.

He felt a rare twinge of impatience. If the cab driver left before they did, he would have to vacate the taxi and immediately go to his fallback. He couldn't just sit here until the driver returned to find him inside. But he knew it would be quicker, cleaner and easier to get things done right now. This was a golden opportunity, one with a high probability of success. He was intent on taking advantage of it.

Grigor waited, double-parked at the cab stand about thirty feet down from the restaurant.

It was now five past one. The restaurant's door opened and closed. People went in and out.

But not Musil.

Grigor sat looking out the windshield, one hand on the wheel, the other on the gear shift. He wanted to be ready when the moment arrived.

He waited. Another minute passed. Another.

More people came and left.

He waited.

Then the door opened again, and he straightened in his seat. They had finally appeared. The analyst first, Musil following him out a split second later.

Grigor's attention tunneled in on them as they turned right and uptown. They had a three-block walk to their headquarters. There were three corners where they might cross to the west side of the avenue. It didn't matter which corner they chose. One was the same as the next to him. He would cruise slowly along behind them, staying in the empty bus lane nearest the curb, waiting until they stepped into the pedestrian crossing.

And then he would take them out. Both of them. He couldn't pick and choose even if he wanted. When the weapon was a five-thousand-pound moving vehicle, it was not going to be a surgical strike. But that was fine with him. The men worked for the same organization. They had also worked together in the FBI. In his experience, they were likely to be sharing information on the CloudCable probe. It was best not to leave one alive.

Grigor touched a steering wheel control and engaged the passenger van's Sport mode. That would relax the throttle and improve its handling during acceleration.

His wait was over.

Shifting into Drive, he pulled smoothly away from taxi stand and into the northbound bus lane.

They had walked a block and a half uptown on the east side of Tenth when Ki Marton noticed the traffic light changing up ahead at the corner of Fifty-Fourth Street.

He was on the outer part of the sidewalk, Musil to his right on the inside.

He slapped Musil's shoulder and motioned toward the corner.

"Let's catch the light!" he said and quickened his pace.

Musil hurried up alongside him.

Abdul noticed his taxi van was gone the instant he left the restaurant.

He froze next to Haram blinking in stunned disbelief. Taxi vans didn't simply disappear. They did not roll off on their own. Nor were they usually stolen from cab stands on busy midtown streets in broad daylight. With five other cabs at the stand.

When one left the cab with the wireless key in his pocket, the reasonable and firm assumption was that the vehicle would stay put.

Plus, he was double-parked. A thief would have no way to know the cab he had pulled alongside was his cousin's, who happened to be inside the Share Punjabi buffet eating lunch with him. Far more likely that the driver had only stepped out for a minute to pick something up and would rush back so as not to block the other cab from pulling out. Even the most skilled and brazen car thief would choose an easier target of opportunity. He would not want to risk the cabbie showing up before he could drive away.

And so Abdul stopped outside the restaurant's front door. Stunned. Frozen. Disbelieving.

Then he felt Haram's hand clamp around his arm and tug. He had swiveled his head around

toward West Fifty-Fourth Street and was pointing in that same direction with his other hand, his
finger furiously jabbing the air.

"Look!" he said. "Is that yours?"

Abdul turned, and his jaw dropped.

It *was* his cab. In the bus lane, moving slowly
toward the corner.

He took off running after it.

Grigor inched toward the men at a slow crawl.
His heart rate was even. His breathing was quiet
and regular. They were only a few yards ahead of
him now, nearing the corner of West Fifty-Fourth
Street.

Still as a viper eyeing its prey, he watched as
the men stepped into the street. There were a few
pedestrians crossing ahead of them, but no one
around them. Offering him a clear, open lane.

Grigor slid forward…and then heard the shouting behind him. It was muffled by the taxi's
rolled-up windows, but loud enough for him to
pick up its excited tone. He glanced into the rearview mirror and saw the taxi driver in the white
skullcap running toward him, waving his arms
frantically in the air, a second man close behind.

Icy calm, Grigor toed the gas to speed up a
notch, pulling away from them. Just up ahead, the
corner traffic light was changing, the signal about
to go from red to yellow to green. He saw Musil
and the analyst hurry to make the light, turn and
step out into the crossing.

This was his moment. He pressed the gas pedal to the floor.

The weaponized taxi van accelerated rapidly, heading toward them straight as a missile.

Two seconds after that, it struck.

Measured in physical reaction time, the speed of thought is between two hundred and seventy and five hundred feet per second. Even at the lower value, Ki's brain would have sent signals to his body over three times faster than the passenger van coming toward him. As an analyst with a trained, supple, sharply honed mind, his thoughts probably clipped along at the high end of the speed scale.

In the crosswalk between Musil and the yellow taxi van, he had enough time to hear the loud surge of its revving engine to his left, glance in that direction and then see the van hurtling up the avenue from almost half a block down, sprung high off the ground, its front end broad, thick and massive and bearing straight at them.

Neurons fired.

Muscles responded.

The speed of thought.

"Jot!" he shouted and pivoted slightly toward his friend, arms extended, his outspread hands slamming into Musil's arm below the shoulder. They pushed him hard and back toward the east side of the avenue, the side they had just stepped off moments ago.

Ki felt Musil stagger away from him, saw pedestrians scatter wildly in the street, heard people screaming and horns honking and tires screeching, and above it all heard the loud, swollen vroom of the accelerating passenger van as it came on. High, broad, thick, massive, surging and deadly.

Ki stood at five-six, and the taxi's elevated front bumper struck him just below the hip, pushing his legs up to its fifty-mile-an-hour velocity. The initial impact carried them forward while his upper body and head remained relatively motionless. The physical stress on his skeleton instantly snapped his spine and split his pelvic bone down the middle. A millisecond later he was pitched off his feet. His body twisted halfway around as it flew over the front bumper and hood, his head smashing into the windshield, partially shattering its glass before the van's continued linear momentum sent him flying up across the roof, where he tumbled backward like a broken mannequin to land on the street behind it.

Meanwhile, Musil found himself sprawled facedown near the curb. As he'd stumbled off balance, a large running body had slammed into him, knocking him hard to the pavement. Now he boosted himself up to his feet, his *dastār* gone, his long black hair spilling down into his eyes. Blood was running down his face from a cut on his forehead.

He looked around for Ki but didn't see him. The taxi van was also gone—he didn't know where.

Around him the avenue was all clamor and commotion. Shrieks, wails, horns. People running wildly through the intersection. Pouring out of hastily stopped cars. Digging phones out of their pockets, crying, calling the police.

Ki.

Where was he?

Musil looked left, looked right, didn't see him. He spun around, searching the avenue. Didn't see him. Then he noticed the pedestrians gathered in front of a stopped car about ten yards down the street. Ten or fifteen of them. His eyes homed in on a woman with wide, panicky eyes and her hands on her head…

He pushed through the crowd toward the knot of pedestrians and into it, then saw Ki on his back a few feet away. There was blood all over his face and clothes. His head and limbs were bent where they shouldn't have been. One guy with a phone to his ear was shouting for someone to send an ambulance.

Musil waded forward and reached Ki and knelt. He registered that his glasses were gone and insanely looked around for them, his eyes scouring the blacktop. Then he got a grip and forgot them.

Ki was bleeding from his ears and nose and mouth. His jacket was twisted around his chest.

Musil leaned over him.

"Ki," he said. "It's Jot. I'm with you."

Ki stared upward. Musil fought the urge to lift

his head off the ground. Moving it might do more harm than good.

Then, sirens. The high-low of police cars. The piercing wail of ambulances.

Musil bent closer.

"You'll be OK," he said. "Hang on. They'll get you to a hospital."

Ki stared. His eyes wide open but unfocused. Musil wasn't sure he could see him. Or that he knew what he was seeing if he could. He seemed to be in shock.

Then his hand came up. A flap of skin hanging from the back of it. Musil glimpsed something white through the peeled, torn flesh. Bone, tendon, he didn't know. He didn't know. Tears sprang from his eyes and ran hotly down his cheeks.

"Ki."

The hand fell onto Musil's wrist and clenched it. *"Ki..."*

He arched convulsively off the street. His back bowed. His mouth opened and closed, opened, closed. A thin, rattling breath escaped it.

Musil swiped moisture from his eyes with his free hand. Then bent lower, so his lips were almost brushing Ki's ear. He gathered himself.

"Dear friend, my dear friend...find peace," he said, his voice a trembling whisper. His eyes clouding up again, then overflowing, the tears streaming down his cheeks. "Anguish shall be dispelled from your body... Rise above the limits of time… Rise in the company of the blessed… *Waheguru, Waheguru, Waheguru…*"

Ki's fingers went slack.

Grigor shot past West Fifty-Fifth and the Terminal in the taxi van, then swung around the corner of West Fifty-Sixth, speeding east down the one-way street. He tore past brownstone apartment buildings and scaffoldings and a coned-off road trench. He saw construction workers in hard hats and orange safety vests turn to look his way. Then he saw a delivery truck stopped ahead of him at the traffic light on the corner of Ninth Avenue.

He braked hard an instant before smashing into it. Snatched his pack off the passenger seat, grabbed the door handle. Then launched out onto the street and ran, leaving the taxi there with the door flung wide open.

He ran down Ninth, cut right, ran another block downtown to Fifty-Fifth, and cut left toward Eighth Avenue, tossing his cap and sunglasses into a trash receptacle. After a minute, he slowed to a hurried walk. No one noticed him on the busy side street. He could hear sirens howling and shrieking in the air.

14

April 19, 2024
CIA Headquarters, Langley, Virginia/New York

Langley

It was almost twenty after one when Michaels's car returned him to the Visitor's Control Center. He trotted inside, slid his badge under the window to the security guard, went to retrieve his phone from his locker and immediately saw the missed call and voice message notifications on his lock screen.

Morse must have tried him a half dozen times.

He stepped outside, holding a finger up to his driver. He wanted to play the messages before getting in the car.

"Alex, it's Carol Morse. Call me ASAP. It's urgent."

"Hi, Alex. Morse again. Thought I'd give you another try. Same message as before. Thanks."

"Hi, it's Morse again. Sorry to bug you, but it's urgent that we talk."

"Alex. You know who this is. Listen, it's the CloudCable thing. Leo's men had an odd face-rec hit. A file came up. It's the one, and that worries me. Waiting to hear back from you."

Michaels stood outside the VCC with the phone in his hand, a surprised and apprehensive look on his face.

It's the one.

He trotted up to the Mercedes and gestured for his driver to lower the window. "Better wait in the lot, Chris," he said, wagging the phone. "This could take a few minutes."

The driver nodded and swung into the large visitor's parking area to his left.

Michaels tapped in Carol's number.

Kali had barely started to talk when the admin knocked at the door. Three sharp raps. Morse glanced across the room, surprised by the interruption. What would make her break into a meeting? Carmody and Kali swiveled around in their seats to look.

"Come in."

She stepped into the office. One look at her told Morse something was terribly wrong.

"Emma, what's going on?"

She stood there mutely, her eyes wide and agitated.

"Emma?"

"We just received an emergency crossconnect with NYPD." The admin's breath trembled. "It happened right outside. On Tenth."

"*What* happened?"

"They think it's an accident. A taxi, it hit one of ours. Ki Marton. He was out there with Agent Musil. The avenue's full of police and EMTs." She cleared her throat. "I *know* Ki."

Morse stared at her. She knew him too. For years. Ki was Leo's ASAC back at FBI Cyber. One of the men who migrated over to the Force with him.

She sat there facing Emma, Kali and Carmody doing the same, not a sound in the office around them. It occurred to her almost semiconsciously that she couldn't hear any sirens. The Terminal's foot-thick walls stopped all noise coming up from the street.

Finally, she broke the silence.

"Emma, do you know his condition?"

The admin looked at her from across the room. Nodded.

And started crying uncontrollably.

"You sure gave that sugar cone no mercy," Leo said over his empty ice-cream cup. "Guess I don't have to ask if you liked it."

Rachel pushed what was left of the cone into her mouth.

"It's the best," she said. "Totally."

He smiled. It was about half past one, and they were at a small round table in the Chelsea Market's common area, tourists and shoppers streaming everywhere around them under its high, vaulted roof.

"Rach," he said, "we haven't talked much about you coming to live with me. But I thought about it all the time I was in the hospital. Every day. I just figured it should wait till I got better."

She looked at him. "I was really scared when you got hurt," she said. "I didn't know if it would be like it was with Mom. That I would never see you again."

Leo felt a sharp twinge of guilt.

"I'm sorry," he said. "You were getting settled in with your aunt. Starting a new school. I figured I'd butt out instead of making you feel bad for me."

Rachel was quiet. "It's OK," she said.

"No, I made a mistake," he said. "I should've called more often."

They sat there a moment.

"I'd like you to really think about whether you want to come live with me," he said.

"And Mack," she said.

"And Mack," he said.

She held her eyes on him.

"Do *you* really want me to live with you, Leo?"

"More than anything," he said. "But I can get

grouchy. And Mack poops on the floor sometimes."

"On the *floor*?"

"Sometimes. In the kitchen." He shrugged. "It
comes up easy. A paper towel and some spray
cleaner do the trick."

She giggled and pulled a face. "Gross," she said.

Leo smiled again and realized he was having
fun. He guessed it was a little unexpected, considering how uptight he had felt asking Rachel's
aunt if she could spend her school lunch break
with him.

"Just so you know," he said, "you wouldn't be
on turtle poop duty. I—"

The phone rang in his pants pocket. He pulled
it out, saw that it was Carol and thought at once
that she might have something to tell him about
Pinnacle. Whatever it was.

"One minute, Rach," he said and swiped to answer. Then, into the phone, "Carol, what's up?"

Silence. He waited a second. He thought he
could hear her breathing at the other end.

"Carol? You there?"

Another moment's silence.

"Leo, you should come back to HQ," she said
finally. "There's been…something terrible's happened. It's Ki Marton."

"What are you talking about? *What* happened
to Ki?"

A pause.

"Carol?"

"He was killed, Leo. A hit-and-run right outside on Tenth. Musil was with him."

He felt the blood drain out of his veins.

"I'll be there soon as I can," he said and disconnected, staring numbly into Rachel's ten-year-old face.

She looked back at him, her eyes filled with open curiosity and worry.

"Hon, we have to go," he said.

At one thirty-eight, Grigor entered a place called Caswell's Ale House on West Fifty-Third Street, sat down at the bar and put his backpack on the floor at the foot of the stool.

He glanced up at the menu board. The tavern was about three-quarters full, and he could hear sirens sporadically through the door as its lunchtime patrons went in and out. The sound was several blocks west, and no one in the bar paid attention to them. This was New York City.

After three or four minutes, the server came over, and Grigor ordered a hamburger and dark ale. Then he took out a cheap burner phone he had purchased at a chain drugstore near his hotel.

Using a GoRide shuttle account activated under the alias Luis Castro, he arranged for a car to pick him up at the tavern in about fifteen minutes. His request was for two stops. The first was at a location he'd scouted out in Flushing, Queens, only blocks from the Woodmere Middle School. The second destination was LaGuardia Airport in East

Elmhurst, four miles and a fifteen-minute drive west across the bay.

He had no intention of going to the airport.

The request submitted, Grigor set the phone down on the counter. The server came over with his order. He thanked her and ate.

Cordoned off by police sawhorses, the four-block stretch of Tenth Avenue between West Fifty-Second and West Fifty-Sixth Streets was jumbled with flashing patrol cars, EMS vehicles and a large mobile crisis-response truck. There were cops at the barricades and everywhere else.

Morse left the Terminal with Carmody and Kali and then went downtown in the middle of the street. They got less than half a block before a pair of uniforms stepped in front of them.

"No one's allowed here," one of them said. The name on her badge was J. Williams. "You'll have to turn around."

Morse waved her Net Force ID, nodding back toward headquarters. "We're Department of Internet Security. One of our people was killed. I need to find the man who was with him, Agent Musil."

Williams eyed the card in her hand. "I'm sorry, I can't let anyone thr—"

"Who's in charge of the scene?" Morse interrupted.

The other cop stepped up. His chest was stuck out. The badge on it said he was P. Votto. "There a problem?" he asked.

Morse saw Carmody move toward him and cut between them. She held the ID up in Votto's face.

"I just told your partner. We're looking for one of ours. His name is Musil."

"Look, we've got orders. You have to turn around."

Morse drilled him with a stare.

"Do want me to call the commissioner? I can do it right now. And I swear to Christ I'll make sure you're suspended without pay. Indefinitely."

Morse watched him fold. She saw it in his eyes, and she saw it in his sinking chest and in how the badge sunk with it. She gave him a silent ten-count to save face.

At eight, Votto stepped aside and gestured toward an ambulance a half block up. "I think he's in that one."

Morse nodded.

"Thank you, Officer," she said and led the way over to it.

The Fifty-Fourth Street intersection was busy with cops and forensic techs marking the street, writing notes, drawing up diagrams and taking photographs and measurements. There was a lot of string and tape and spray paint. The EMS vehicle was just on the other side of the crossing. Beyond it, a group of police were assembled around a row of yellow cabs parked at the curb.

Morse went up to the ambulance. Musil was seated on the rear step while a paramedic examined him. His hair was loose, and his clothes were bloodstained and dirty.

He looked straight at her as she approached.

"Director Morse," he said.

She nodded. "Are you OK?"

"Yes." He swallowed. "Ki Marton is dead."

"I know," she said. "I'm sorry."

"We had lunch," he said. "I heard him shout my name. Then I saw the taxi. A van. Ki pushed me out of its way."

"He saved your life."

"Yes."

She took a breath. "Leo told me Ki was the best. All those years at the FBI, he said he made him look good."

Musil nodded. She saw a lump form in his throat and waited while the paramedic bandaged a cut on his arm.

"Jot," she said after a minute, "what happened to the driver?"

"I don't know. He never stopped."

"Do you know if the cops have him?"

"No. They didn't say."

"I'll ask."

Musil nodded and was silent.

After a moment Morse said, "He must have lost control of the cab."

"I don't know," Musil said. "He came straight at us."

"Are you sure?"

"Yes. I thought he sped up. I could hear his engine."

Morse looked at him. Then looked around at

a seeming commotion at the taxi stand down the block. *Then* she almost incidentally realized that Carmody and Kali were no longer with her and looked around to see where they had gone.

A second later she saw that they had split off from her and were back at the corner intersection, Sergeant Votto moving toward them in a hurry.

Carmody was looking over the painted markings in the crosswalk when Votto came bulling toward him through the aggregate of police and medical first responders. He raised his eyes to the sergeant's face.

"You going to tell me to play somewhere else again?"

The cop just stood there. He was a couple of inches shorter than Carmody but still over six feet tall and built like a guy who could bench-press three hundred pounds without breaking a sweat.

"The blonde lady asked to go to the ambulance, you got through," he said. "But this is an active scene. You can't stand around here." He nodded past Carmody at Kali, who had drifted toward the curb. "Neither can she."

Carmody pointed down at a large red *X* on the blacktop. "Votto, is this where the taxi hit our guy?"

The cop looked at him.

"Yeah."

Carmody nodded. "There's another paint mark a good ten, twelve yards over that way," he said and motioned down the block. "That where he landed?"

"Yeah."

"So he flew back over the cab's roof."

"Yeah."

Carmody looked at him.

"Anybody else killed?"

"No," the sergeant said. "We saw quite a few bumps and bruises. But nothing serious. Thank God."

Votto's belt radio squawked with overlapping communications. He listened a moment, didn't hear his code, then turned his attention back to Carmody.

"I'm guessing you're with Net Force, like the blonde."

"Uh-huh."

He gestured toward Kali. "Your friend over there too?"

"Close enough."

Votto nodded. There was more chatter on his radio. He gave it another perfunctory listen and then phased it out.

"You got a name?"

"Carmody."

"Look, Carmody," he said, "I'm not trying to be a hard-on."

"Didn't say you were."

The cop expelled a breath through his mouth.

"Guess you didn't," he said. And paused again. "You lose one of your own, it's tough letting somebody else handle things. But you have to leave it to us."

Carmody didn't answer him. After a second, he motioned back down at the ground.

"There are no skid marks from the cab's tires," he said. "When a driver hits his brakes to stop, his wheels lock. His wheels lock, there's friction between the tire and the street. There's friction, the tire rubber heats up and transfers a residue to the blacktop."

Votto didn't say anything.

"The cabbie never hit the brake pedal," Carmody said. "His wheels kept spinning. There was zero drag between the rubber and the road. So no marks."

Votto still didn't say anything.

"Another thing," Carmody said. "When somebody flies backward over a moving vehicle, it usually happens for two reasons. One, its front end is higher than his center of gravity. Figure the bumper of the taxi was about level with our guy's stomach, maybe a little higher, so that part jibes. But you know the second reason?"

Votto slowly shook his head.

"The taxi was accelerating. If it's decelerating when it hits someone, it pushes him forward, or rolls over him, or maybe carries him along under its wheels. But when the driver's foot is on the gas and the vehicle is speeding up, it tosses him up and backward. Like a wild bull in a ring when it charges the matador."

Votto looked at him for a long moment.

"Were you a cop in another life?"

"No."

"Then, what?"

"Air Force," Carmody said. "Twenty-Second Special Tacs."

"Iraq?"

"Different places."

"And after you got out of the service?"

"I can't talk about after," Carmody said.

Votto shrugged, then glanced past him and down the block.

"Those cabbies park outside the restaurant over there every day around noon," he said. "It's got a prayer rug in back. They go over to it, do their thing, then have lunch together and go back on shift. Usually, they're inside an hour or so."

Carmody nodded.

"One of them had his passenger van stolen," Votto said. "Whoever took it hit your guy and then left it a few blocks east of here. In the middle of the street."

"What's a few blocks east to you?"

"Fifty-Sixth," the cop said. "Around Ninth."

Carmody nodded. "Those cab drivers wouldn't leave their motors running. Not if they're going to be inside the place an hour."

"Probably not."

"Was there a spare key in the van?"

"No. It's keyless."

"People still leave spares. Most often in the center console."

"The driver claims he didn't."

Carmody regarded him a moment. "So somebody starts up the cab, plows through this crosswalk, rounds the next corner, drives an avenue and runs off."

"Right."

"Like that somebody did what he did with a purpose."

"Maybe."

"Any sign of him?"

"Not far as I know. But Fifty-Sixth is a crowded street. He could've stopped at the light and booked it before anyone noticed."

"And the van's still there?"

"I heard Dispatch says the tows are on the way. But it'll sit a while longer so the evidence techs can finish their on-site. In case your people want a look for themselves."

"Thanks."

Votto shrugged. "You didn't get that piece of information from me," he said and paused. "I hope the cocksucker who did this pays."

Carmody nodded, turned to look for Kali and saw her crouched near the foot of the crossing.

"See you around," he told the cop, and strode over to her.

"Find something?"

She stood up and showed him.

"This was lying on the street," she said. "It's a *dastār*. A Sikh turban."

He grunted. "DeBattista's plane is waiting for us," he said. "We're supposed to fly in an hour."

She nodded.

"Don't think we'll make it," he said.

She nodded again.

"You were way ahead of me on that, weren't you?" he said.

Kali didn't answer. After a second she brushed off the turban and folded it neatly in her hands.

"I should return this to Musil," she said, and walked toward the ambulance.

At two o'clock in the afternoon, the request-a-ride driver pulled his blue Mazda3 sedan into a quiet, dead-end street in Flushing, then rolled slowly toward a large, well-maintained bungalow that was the last house before the cul-de-sac. A For Sale by Owner sign stood in the lawn. The rooms visible through the half-drawn window shades looked empty and bare.

In the passenger seat, Grigor as Luis Castro played with a paper clip he had nicked off the hostess's stand at the ale house, straightening it and twisting it between his fingers.

"Would you please back in?" he said as they neared the driveway. He dropped the clip into his pocket. "I need to get some luggage out of the place."

The GoRide driver nodded, drove slightly past

the house, and nosed up to the weedy cul-de-sac for a good angle. Then he reversed into the driveway.

"Moving out of town, sir?" he asked.

"Yes." Grigor used a faint Andalusian accent. Specifically, northern Sevillian with its swallowed letter *s*. Practice. "I didn't want to sell. It's private and quiet here. But my parents are ill, and it's time to live closer."

The driver nodded and stopped outside the garage.

"I get it. It's kinda the same with my mom these days."

"*Asi que va*…so it goes. We all get older."

Grigor reached for his door handle, hesitated. "Would you mind if I put everything into the trunk? My backpack too? So it can all stay together."

The driver popped open the trunk latch. The phone app had identified him as Terrence. He was about thirty, with brown skin and black hair done in short, tight braids.

"Why not?" he said. "I'll help with it."

He got out, went around back, opened the rear driver's-side door and pulled the pack off the seat as Grigor exited from the opposite side.

"Ah, heavy!" he laughed, carrying it in both hands. "Guess you have a long trip!"

Grigor smiled and raised the trunk lid for him. "You're very kind, Terrence."

The driver leaned forward to put the pack inside.

Moving swiftly up behind him, Grigor grabbed a fistful of his hair with his left hand and pulled his head back so hard that it almost met his collarbone. Then he slammed the lead sap in his opposite hand sideways into his right temple—three rapid blows with its edge. Grigor felt the driver's skull crunch in, its bones splintering sharply to rupture the underlying temporal arteries.

The driver's eyes rolled up in their sockets as Grigor struck his shattered skull twice more to be thorough. Then he shoved his body forward into the trunk, jamming in the legs. The hemorrhage of blood drowning his brain would kill him within minutes if he wasn't already dead.

Grigor quickly attended to the rest. He felt in the driver's pocket for his key chain and snatched it out. He lifted his pack up from the ground, tossed it back inside the car and got in behind the wheel. He pulled the driver's cell phone off its cradle and logged him out of GoRide. Then he took the paper clip out of his pocket, used it to eject its SIM card and flicked the card out into the grass. The phone was now off-line, along with any tracking applications that might have run in the background.

Grigor shut the Mazda's door but did not immediately pull from the driveway. He had one last thing to take care of before he left here.

Reaching into a pocket for his satphone, he placed his call.

* * *

Moments after the paramedics finished with him, Musil stood outside the EMS vehicle, staring dully down the block toward the taxi stand. Carol Morse was now with the police talking to the cabbies and other witnesses on the sidewalk.

"Agent."

He glanced around toward the voice, saw Kali suddenly alongside him. She appeared to have come from the direction of the crosswalk.

After a second, he realized she was carrying his *dastār*. She held it out to him, folded in her upturned palms, like an offering.

"I believe this is yours," she said.

"Thank you," he said and took it from her.

Kali nodded. "In Sikh tradition, the color black represents the surrender of one's ego. Isn't it so?"

He looked at her.

"Yes," he said.

"I've noticed you always wear a black *dastār*. Without exception."

A beat of silence.

"Yes," he said.

She dipped her head slightly.

"Student of the Ten Gurus, warrior of light, protector of the right, the meek and the weak," she said with her head still lowered, "your friend was fortunate to have you guide his passing."

Musil stood there in silence for a long minute. His mouth opened and closed.

"This is a surprise," he said at last.

Kali looked up at him.

"Life is full of them," she said.

A few yards down the street, Morse was at the sidewalk cab stand listening to the cabbie Abdul Samad tell his story to a responding police officer for the third time.

There hadn't been that much to it the first or second times, and the same was definitely true now. He had double-parked alongside the taxi belonging to his cousin Haram and then gone into the Share Punjabi to have lunch with several other taxi drivers—a group that included Haram, who was still out here with him, corroborating his every word. His daily routine was to drop off his jacket at the table to claim a chair, say *dhuhr*, the midday ritual prayer, in the niche at the rear of the place, then sit and eat for roughly the next forty minutes.

"When Haram got up to pay, I went with him, and we left together," he told the cop.

"Because your van was blocking him into the spot."

"Yes."

"And then?"

"I saw my taxi moving away."

"In the bus lane."

"Yes, Officer. There was a man inside. I saw him and ran after it."

"But you say you didn't get a good look at him."

"No. He drove away very fast."

Morse had been silent up to that point, not

wanting to ruffle the interviewer. But she chose that moment to jump in.

"Sir, could you tell me again what you *did* see of him?" she asked. "Think carefully."

Abdul turned to her. "He wore a cap. Like a baseball cap."

"And can you describe him at all?"

"He was white. A thin face. I remember he sat like this." The cabbie stiffened his shoulders exaggeratedly. "So straight, you know? Like wood."

Morse nodded, wishing Leo would show up. Fifteen years of marriage to him, she'd picked up some of his interviewing skills by osmosis. But it felt like a poor approximation. She had never come close to him, even before her career path with the Company led her from investigations to a supervisory position.

She was trying to think of anything else worth going over with Abdul when the cell phone trilled in her belt holster.

She took it out, checked its display and answered.

"Alex," she said, "I've been trying to reach you for hours."

"I know. I listened to your messages," he said. "I was at Langley."

She nodded her understanding. "No devices."

"Right," he said. "I phoned your office from outside the visitor's center. Didn't reach you, left a message and decided to ride back to DC. When

I still couldn't get hold of you, I finally decided to give your cell a shot." He paused. "Are you OK?"

She took a few seconds to collect her thoughts. "We have a situation here, Alex."

"What's happening?"

"I can't explain this minute. But about Pinnacle... I need access. Something came up in the *Stalwart* probe and—"

"Carol, I sent you the unlocked file."

Her eyebrow went up. "When?"

"As soon as I returned to my office. It's FYEO-encrypted. I'm leaving you to decide who else sees it."

She stood there a minute.

"All right," she said. "Thanks, Alex. I'll get back to you within the hour. We need to talk."

Michaels didn't immediately hang up. She could feel his concern in the long silence on the line.

"I'll wait to hear from you," he said.

At the Woodmere Middle School, Principal Bernard Hausman was ten minutes from what promised to be a testy interdepartmental meeting when his assistant buzzed on the intercom.

He pushed Talk. "What's up, Giovanna?"

"I have Mr. Musil on the phone. He's one of our parents."

Which Hausman knew. Besides both his daughters being honor students, Musil had been something of a celebrity since last summer's craziness put him on the news. They'd had several conversations before and after.

He checked his watch. "His timing couldn't be worse," he said. "I have three chairs about to march in here screaming their heads off about the budget."

"I know, Bernie. I already suggested he leave a message. But he says it's urgent."

Hausman sighed.

"OK, put him through," he said and wondered guiltily if he would be as accommodating to a parent who wasn't the toast of the town.

A moment later Musil came on the phone. "Principal Hausman?"

"Hello, sir. Everything well with you?"

Musil took a breath.

"I have a difficult situation," he said. "There's been an accident where I work. On Tenth Avenue. A taxi driver lost control of his vehicle, and my colleague was killed. We were together when it happened."

"My God. I hadn't heard. Are you all right?"

"Yes, thankfully," Musil said. "Principal Hausman, I don't want the girls finding out about this in class. You know how it is with the internet. So I need to ask that they be discharged early."

"Of course, I understand. Will you be picking them up?"

"That's the problem. My wife is away. And I'm not sure how soon I can leave the office," Musil said. "I've arranged for a GoRide to bring them home from school. A family member will be waiting for them."

Hausman shook his head. "Sir, I do understand. But we require that students leaving early are released to a parent or guardian."

"I know. That's why I wanted to speak to you personally."

Hausman thought a minute. He didn't feel Musil's request was really that unreasonable under the circumstances. The man was in law enforcement and knew his business. Moreover, he had his own concerns about the internet. He didn't want to be the uncompassionate jerk whose name went viral for denying a hero's request.

"Can you give me the GoRide information?" he asked, picking up a pen and memo pad.

"Yes, the driver's name will be Terrence. I request him frequently. He's very reliable."

"And the car type?"

"A blue Mazda sedan...a recent model, I think."

"OK. I'll be in a meeting for the rest of the afternoon. But have him call my assistant Giovanna when he arrives. She'll escort Jani and Raysa to the car."

An audible sigh of relief.

"Principal Hausman, I'm profoundly grateful you could make an exception."

"No problem. I'm just glad you weren't hurt." Hausman glanced at his watch again. "Sir, that meeting's about to get started. But I'd like to send you my best thoughts. There's anything else you need, don't hesitate to let me know."

"Yes. Thank you. Goodbye."

Musil hung up. Hausman hung up. Then Giovanna buzzed.

"Sir, the chairs are here for your two fifteen."

When it rains, it pours, and I'm always stuck with no umbrella, Hausman thought.

And pulled out his meeting notes.

Grigor ended the connection with Hausman and snapped his phone into the empty dash cradle. He had been a flawless Amenjot Musil.

He felt heady and exhilarated. Almost out of body. While he would have preferred taking Musil with his first strike, things were still on course and clipping along. Also, the analyst had been a potential problem in his own right.

It was best that he'd been liquidated.

Grigor sat very still behind the wheel. There was something about successfully converting a plan into action, an indescribable high. Like he was transforming matter into energy and riding the wave. Like he was freed light.

He gave himself a minute to savor the feeling. Then he took a deep breath, pushed the ignition button and steered the Mazda from the driveway onto the street.

He was on his way to pick up the kids.

* * *

Carmody went to join Kali outside the ambulance. He looked at her and then at Musil.

"How you doing?" he said.

Musil did a half nod, half shrug. Carmody could tell he wasn't close to half OK.

"I've seen you around," he said. "Don't think we've been introduced."

Musil nodded. He held the recovered *dastār* in his right hand.

"I'm Carmody."

"Jot."

"My sympathies about your friend. I hear he was the best."

"Thank you."

They bumped fists.

"I was just at the crosswalk," Carmody said. "You up to talking?"

"Yes."

"I didn't see any tire marks over there," Carmody said. "It means the driver never applied his brakes. Never tried to swerve out of the way."

Musil nodded.

"I thought so," he said. "I told Director Morse."

"Something else," Carmody said. "Having to do with Ki. Still all right with this?"

"Please, go ahead."

"His body was thrown backward. Over the taxi's roof. That tells us it was accelerating. Probably doing fifty, sixty miles an hour in midtown traffic."

Musil nodded. "He came right at us."

"So it seems," Carmody said. "You get a look at the driver?"

"No. I had no time."

Carmody stood quietly alongside Kali for a second, then cocked his chin down the avenue toward the Share Punjabi. Morse was still at the taxi stand with the police and drivers.

"A cop back at the crossing told me the van was stolen from a cabbie in the restaurant. He says it's got a keyless ignition. Claims he had the only key with him. That there are no spares."

"Then, how would someone start it up?" Musil said. "He would need a transponder. Something to relay the signal."

"Exactly."

Musil looked at him. "They're very expensive. Tens of thousands of dollars on the black market. And they have a short range."

"Probably the thief scouted out the territory in advance," Carmody said. "I don't know how else he'd be sure where the cab driver was. Which seems like a lot of time, effort and money just to drive the cab a couple of blocks and ditch it."

"What do you mean?"

"He left it sitting at a traffic light. Practically around the corner."

Musil let that sink in. "Do you think he deliberately planned to hit us?"

"I think you were targeted."

"Why?"

Carmody said, "It doesn't really matter. Like it doesn't matter if it was you or Ki. Or both of you. He's still out there. And he knows what he's doing." He paused. "We have to pull in. Assume he'll find some other way to come after you."

Musil looked thoughtfully at the ground. He almost seemed lost in his own world. But after a minute he suddenly snapped his head up. He glanced from Carmody to Kali and back at Carmody, the skin tightening on his face, shrinking in around his eyes and cheekbones.

Some other way.

"Blessed Lord," he said. "My children."

15

Grigor pulled up outside the Woodmere Middle School at a quarter past two in the afternoon. He called the direct number Hausman had given for his assistant, told her he was there and waited with the engine idling.

Within five minutes, Giovanna came out a side entrance with Musil's daughters. She spotted the Mazda at once and brought them over.

"Terrence?" she said.

"Yes, ma'am." Grigor exited onto the sidewalk, smiling at the girls. "Raysa, Jani, if you're more comfortable without your backpacks, I'll help you carry them upstairs once you're home."

They happily shrugged out of their straps. He took both packs, leaned in through his door and set them on the front passenger seat.

Jani looked up at him. "Did our dad tell you our names?"

"Yes." Smiling again. "He's even showed me pictures."

He held the rear door open as they got in, the older sister first, Raysa next. Then he shut it and turned to the principal's assistant.

"Would you like me to call Mr. Musil so he knows I've picked them up?" he said.

"Oh, yes, that would be great. If you don't mind."

Grigor nodded. "No problem at all," he said. "Have a wonderful day."

A moment later, he got into the driver's seat.

"Are we both buckled up?" he asked.

"Yes!" the girls answered together.

He smiled.

"That's two for the price of one," he said and angled into the street.

Giovanna watched him drive up the block and round the corner. Then she turned back into the school, thinking it wasn't too often you got someone as pleasant and professional as Terrence from GoRide.

No wonder Mr. Musil kept him on his repeat list.

Leo was cabbing it up to the Terminal after having dropped Rachel off at her aunt's when he saw the police barricades ahead of him on Tenth Avenue. He told the driver to pull over, skimmed his credit card and got out, weaving through streams of pedestrians.

As he reached the roadblock on Fifty-Third, he

saw Morse a few yards beyond it with a bunch of policemen and civilians, all of them on the sidewalk near a line of parked taxis. He'd always been able to spot her from a distance. It was partly her blond hair, but it was also her tall, straight posture. There was never any mistaking her in a crowd.

He pulled out his phone, called her and waved. "Car! I'm over to your right."

She turned, looked down the avenue and waved back, running toward him. She cut past a sawhorse, ran another half block, and then they were facing each other in the middle of the street.

She stood there looking at him, seeing the sorrow in his eyes, seeing the strain on his features, not really knowing what to say. She knew how much Ki had meant to him.

"Car," he said and swallowed.

"Leo…"

Their eyes met.

And the next thing she knew they had their arms tightly around each other, and he was sobbing with his face in the hollow of her neck, the tears hot and wet.

Standing near the ambulance with Carmody and Kali, Musil yanked his phone from his pocket.

"School lets out in less than an hour," he said. "I need to contact the principal. Have him see that my daughters stay until I pick them up."

Carmody said, "Do they have cells?"

"Yes."

"Why not just call them?"

"The phones are off while they're in class," Musil said. "It's the rule."

Carmody was quiet. Kali nodded to Musil.

"Call," she said. "Right now."

"Woodmere Middle, principal's office," Giovanna said. She had just sat back down at her desk after coming upstairs. "How can I help you?"

"Hello, I'm Amenjot Musil. My daughters Jani and Raysa are students at your school."

She wondered if she'd missed something. Maybe he didn't recognize her voice, which was strange since they had spoken less than an hour ago. But you never knew.

"Mr. Musil…this is Giovanna Walsh. Mr. Hausman's assistant."

"Yes, may I speak with him? It's important."

"Sir, his meeting's scheduled to run until late this afternoon—"

"I'm coming for my children. It's almost three o'clock. Can you see that they stay in the building after the bell rings? And that there's a security officer with them?"

Giovanna blinked. Things had gone from strange to totally off-the-wall in five seconds flat.

"I don't understand," she said. "I thought…you asked us to let them out early…"

"What do you mean? I haven't spoken to you."

"Mr. Musil, I'm very confused. I just brought

them downstairs to the GoRide. The way you and Principal Hausman arranged."

Dead silence on the line. Giovanna felt a sudden and profound sense of misgiving. She wasn't sure why. But it permeated her like a cold mist.

"Mr. Musil? Is everything all ri—"

"I need you to put the principal on the line. It can't wait."

"Yes, I'll buzz him. Give me a minute."

"Tell him it's an emergency," he said. "My girls are in danger. I need to find out what's going on."

The Mazda3's dashboard clock said it was two thirty on the dot as Grigor swung into the dead-end street.

Raysa looked out the window, a confused expression on her face. The turn had been unexpected.

"This isn't the way my dad takes us," she said.

He flicked her a glance in the rearview mirror.

"We're making a stop here first," he said, smiling. "I told you about it, didn't I?"

Raysa shook her head.

"No," she said. "You didn't tell us."

"I must have forgotten," he said, driving on. "Well, it won't take long."

She looked up ahead. There were only five or six houses on the block, and the car had passed them all except for the last one before the dead end. It was on the right side of the road and had a sign out front that read *For Sale by Owner*.

"Are you going over there?" Jani asked, pointing at the place.

Grigor nodded his head.

"Yes," he said. "I just have to pick something up."

The two girls exchanged glances. Then Jani leaned forward in her seat. The house looked empty and gave her a creepy feeling.

She took hold of Raysa's hand and squeezed it. Raysa squeezed back.

"Our father says we should go straight home when he isn't with us," she told him. "He never turns this way."

Grigor was driving on toward the house.

"I'm sure he won't mind this one time," he said. "We have to go there before going anywhere else."

Jani felt unease trickle own her spine as he reached the driveway and turned in. It didn't look as if the owner mentioned in the sign still lived here.

Raysa shrank closer to her sister so their knees almost touched, their hands briefly unlocking as she squirmed on the car seat. But then their fingers found each other's again and held on even tighter.

"There's no one here," she said. "Can't you take us home first? Then come back?"

Grigor pulled up to the garage with the lowered door, cut the ignition and slid a hand under his hooded sweatshirt. An instant later he drew his Glock 43X from its holster, swiveling around to point it between the two front seats at the girls.

He saw their eyes widen with fear and smiled.

"Don't either of you move," he said. "I'll explain everything."

* * *

"He has Raysa and Jani," Musil said. His voice was a dry, reedy rasp. "I don't know what he wants. But he has my daughters."

Kali and Carmody stood there looking at him. It was moments after he'd gotten off the phone with their school.

He looked down at his cell, tapped an icon, studied the screen.

"Checking their location trackers?"

Musil nodded, looked at the screen another couple of seconds, expelled a breath.

"Nothing," he said.

"You told me they have to stay off in class. Maybe they're still off."

Musil didn't answer. Then he pocketed the phone and looked around at the nearby police cars. "We should tell them."

"No," Carmody said.

"He has my daughters."

"That's why we keep them out of it for now."

"They have manpower that we don't."

"And we can do things they can't." Carmody kept his voice low. "I don't want them stepping on us."

Musil looked at him. "We don't even know what he wants."

"Right," Carmody said. "But we know he wants something. And that means you'll hear from him."

Musil shook his head. "He could bring the girls anywhere in the meantime."

"Not in that GoRide," Carmody said. "It's too easy to find, and he'll know it."

Musil thought a moment. "He was able to impersonate me. Well enough to fool a man I've met before. Someone that good could have prepared a change of cars."

"Or a place nearby where he intends to lay low," Carmody said. "We can still get a fix on those phones. On or off."

"Don't you think he would discard them?"

"I think we need to get back to the Terminal and find out."

Musil nodded. Then had a realization push suddenly into his brain. "My wife. I have to tell her. She's out of town."

"Where?"

"Milwaukee."

"Work or family?"

"She's visiting her brother."

"He able to protect her?"

Musil nodded. "Sayad was in the Army."

"Then she ought to stay put. She doesn't have to know about the girls yet."

"I won't lie to her."

"I'm not saying you lie. Just hold off telling her. Do that and she'll want to come home. She's safer there right now."

Musil put a hand up to his forehead and rubbed.

"He killed Ki."

"Yeah."

"He has my daughters."

"Yeah."

"I can't lose them. We have to get them back."

Carmody looked at him.

"Trust me," he said. "We will."

"The first thing I'm going to explain," Grigor said, "is that I don't allow my passengers to have cell phones."

He held his pistol steady, its silenced barrel nosing out at the girls between the Mazda's front seats.

Jani stared at him. Her spine felt like a pole made of ice. She heard her sister sobbing beside her and kept holding her hand.

"No need for tears," Grigor said. "I just want to know if either of you has a phone."

Neither of them answered.

He leaned forward, held the barrel three inches from Jani's face and made a wiggling motion with it.

"Tell me," he said.

She tightened her hand around Raysa's.

"Tell me."

Jani sat there staring at him, the cold spreading out from her back to her ribs and circling around her chest, making her shiver all over. But she didn't answer.

Keeping his pale blue eyes on her face, Grigor thrust his arm farther out between the seats and angled the gun toward Raysa, pushing the *o* of the silencer's bore up against the right side of her head. She made a high, mewling sound, fresh tears squirting from her eyes.

"Yes or no, big sister," he said.

"Please leave her alone—"

"Then, tell me. Last chance."

Jani looked at him. "Yes," she said, her lips trembling. "I have one. I have a phone."

"Where is it?"

"In my backpack."

"Where in your backpack?"

"In the outside pouch."

He glanced over at the two packs in the front passenger seat. "Are you sure? Because I'll be very disappointed if it isn't there."

"I'm sure."

He pulled the silencer away from Raysa's head so he could maneuver in front but kept his weapon trained on the girls between the seats. Then he turned to look at the pack Jani had been wearing. It was on its back where he had deposited it in the passenger seat.

He rolled it over. "There are two pouches," he said. "Top or bottom?"

"The top."

Grigor unbuckled its strap with his left hand, opened the pouch flap and saw the phone. It was in a special sleeve.

He pulled it out, quickly looking it over in his hand. It had been switched off, probably a school requirement.

"Very good," he said to the girls.

They sat there petrified with fear, Raysa weeping fitfully.

He gave her a stony look. "Now yours," he said. "Where is it?"

She opened her mouth to answer but couldn't manage to wring the words out through her tears.

"She doesn't have one," Jani said. "Our mom and dad say she's too young."

"Really?"

She nodded.

Grigor abruptly leaned closer again and pushed the gun against her head, forcing it backward. His eyes remained on Raysa.

"Is she telling truth?" he asked.

Raysa nodded, tears flowing down her cheeks.

"Not good enough," he said and shook his head. "Talk to me. Go on. You have such a pretty voice."

Her lips opened and closed as she struggled to force the words out between heavy, convulsive sobs. It seemed to take all her strength, but at last she managed it.

"Jani's telling the truth," she bawled thickly. "I don't have a phone."

Grigor kept his eyes on her for a moment longer. Then he drew the gun back from her sister's forehead.

"OK," he said. "I like girls who tell the truth."

Seconds passed. Still facing them, Grigor pushed his door open wide enough to toss Jani's phone onto the grass bordering the driveway. He was aware its location could be traced even with the cellular connection disabled, but the clandestine tools to do that took some time to set up. He doubted Musil already knew his daughters had been taken…and even if he did, he wouldn't have known for long.

Aiming the gun through the partly open door, he fired once, blowing the cell phone to bits. The discharge hardly disturbed the quiet. No one heard. The properties on the block were widely spaced. This being the last before the cul-de-sac, it was even more isolated than the rest. A few birds squalled into the air, and that was all.

Grigor shut the door, turning to face the girls again, putting the Glock back on them.

"Here's the next thing I want to explain," he said. "You see the garage in front of us? I know, it's hard to miss. But nod yes or no, anyway. So I know you're paying attention."

They nodded. He smiled.

"Good," he said. "Listen carefully. I'm going to let you both out of the car and then open the garage. You'll hold hands and walk inside. There's a door to your right and you will stop in front of it and wait for me. Follow?"

They nodded. He smiled again.

"You really are learning," he said and paused a moment. "You know, I went to a special school, for special children. We lived there and learned special things. And I was the best student until I wasn't. If you keep behaving, I might tell you the story. But right now you're getting out."

Grigor exited the car, opened the rear passenger door and motioned them onto the driveway.

He held the Glock in the kangaroo pocket of his sweatshirt.

"All right," he said. "Go on."

The girls clasped hands. As they started toward the garage, Grigor slid back into the Mazda and reached under his hoodie for the remote he'd taken from Kaplan, the homeowner. The door rose with a rattle, and they entered and moved to the right.

A minute later he brought the car in, turned off the engine, got out, lowered the garage door and reached past Jani and Raysa to open the fire door. It was unlocked, exactly as he had left it.

He twisted the knob, and it swung inward. Beyond it was the unoccupied kitchen.

The Glock out of his pocket again, he stepped to one side of the entry and turned to the girls.

"Go inside," he said flatly.

Jani let go of her sister's hand and then walked through the door. Raysa went next, her cheeks sticky with tears as she came into the kitchen.

"Walk," Grigor said, gesturing with the gun. He was still out in the garage.

Jani took hold of Raysa's hand. It was trembling. She moved close to her and felt her arm shaking against hers.

They started deeper into the house, Grigor behind them.

"We'll be OK," she told her sister, whispering it too quietly for him to hear.

16

April 19, 2024
New York

The Net Force CyberOperations Training Center occupied an entire floor of the Terminal, its spacious classrooms, labs and auditoriums capable of accommodating multiple instructors' classes and boot campers at once. Alex Michaels's hiring drive had been a runaway success, exceeding even his optimistic expectations, and the influx of applicants from colleges around the country had created an almost two-year-long waiting list.

Today, however, the CTC was empty and quiet around Natasha Mori, giving the auditorium a hollow, cavernous feel. She had come in to prepare her orientation spiel for the incoming group and also to put some distance between herself and her apartment. After Chacagua Island, no one was going to dun her if she took a few days off. But she didn't want to stay home with her thoughts. She had more than filled her quota for that lately, thanks. With Bryan's mom up in Maine taking care of him after his surgery, and her sorta-kinda roomie Duncan Ulysses apparently pulling one of his disappearing acts, she had felt cooped up and restless.

And so here she was being productive and pacing the auditorium in an augmented reality headset, one of multiple designs that Michaels, her former professor, had patented over the past five years. Lightweight and portable, it wasn't the most full-featured of his designs. The holos lacked nuances of detail. But it did what it was supposed to do pretty well, offering her a convincing environment that was a composite of the computer-generated and the real.

For the moment Natasha was staying out of the center of the auditorium, wanting a view of the lecture area from its perimeters. She wore a faded denim jacket over a long loose purple tunic, black leggings and iridescent multicolor Converse high-tops. Her choppy white hair—tipped with black here and there, seemingly randomly, but not really—roostered out from under the headset's elastic head straps.

Augmented reality.

Holographically projected into her retinas were rows of chairs arranged in a wide horseshoe, as well as the platform where she would stand facing the group between its branches. She had already tried out several alternative seating layouts—wide fan, three-quarter arena, end stage, a bunch more—

leaving some in their boilerplate configurations, tinkering with others. She had used the headset's interactive software to play with the holo's lighting and ambience, raising and dimming the brightness of the room, adding and removing potential stage backdrops and displays. Forty-two seats, one for every person scheduled to attend the session.

After checking things out from various angles, she had pretty much settled on the horseshoe lay-out. It would bring her closest to the recruits and also provide excellent sightlines, which translated into eye contact, which would help her to connect with them and get group discussions going.

Natasha went around to the heel end of the horseshoe, then walked into the hole. She could hear her sneaker soles brushing softly on the her-ringbone hardwood floor, hear the low, cycling sigh of the HEPA system, hear herself breathing its filtered, temperature-controlled air. Her imagi-nation augmented the augmented reality, adding the rustle of bodies in chairs, the patter of fingers on keyboards and touch screens, the occasional semiobsolete scratch of pens on sheets of note-book paper. And her mind being what it was, the racket of somebody getting up for an inevitable pee run. The room prep was all about optimizing dynamics and energy, making it not so different from planning a show at Club Fallout. Just with-out accounting for the beats, dancing and Duncan, her musical partner in crime.

The very *MIA* Dunc, that was. She had seen

neither hide nor hair of him since her return from Chacagua Island. But he would sometimes drop off the radar, usually with a swipe right, and they did have a couple of weeks to go until their next set of gigs. So she wasn't hitting the panic button just yet.

Natasha used the wireless controller in her hand to make some adjustments to the holo, then moved around inside the horseshoe, deciding the arrangement could still use some tweaks. Writing ledges, possibly? Contoured seats? Maybe she'd added too much space between them...

She was inputting her latest round of changes, when a door opened at the auditorium's rear. Still playing with the control unit, she looked across the room as someone walked in, then realized it was Kali Alcazar. Black jeans and leather jacket, she strode up to the toe of the horseshoe without a word, then plunged straight through it, wading through the rows of ghost seats.

Natasha pulled off her headset. "Hey, slice, you totally just blew my illusion."

Kali didn't answer. She came straight up to her, tapped her shoulder.

"I need you to come with me," she said.

"Come where?"

"Morse's office."

"*Morse?* What's this about?"

Kali looked at her.

"Pinnacle," she said.

Silence. Natasha's eyes widened. "How do you know about that?"

"I'll explain when there's time. Lives are at stake, Natasha."

She opened her mouth, couldn't think of anything to say, and finally nodded.

A moment later they were hurrying out of the auditorium together.

Natasha followed Kali to Carol Morse's office, abruptly halting just inside the door.

The room was crowded. Leo Harris and Jot Musil were in chairs at Morse's desk, with Morse herself standing to their right under a wall monitor. The only one there Natasha hadn't technically met was the guy on the other side of the entry. Carmody. But she'd seen him around HQ the past few months, and heard he was connected to the *technologie vampiri* business, and recognized him from the rooftop the other day, when he had been waiting for Kali to step off the vertipad. Now he stood there looking huge in a motorcycle jacket, his arms folded across his chest.

She hadn't expected a roomful of people. Hadn't thought to find anyone in the office besides Morse. Seeing them all gathered here was a shock. But what had really stopped her cold in her tracks was the image on the display.

"What's going on?" She stood flat-footed, glancing sharply at Morse. "Nobody told me this would be a fucking house party."

"I'm sorry, Natasha—"

"Sorry? My life is my life. That's our *deal*."

Morse looked at her. "What we discuss stays with the people in this room," she said. "But we need you to answer some questions. Give me a minute and you'll understand."

Almost against her will, Natasha glanced back up at the photograph filling the wide-screen display. Dark trails seemed to come off it. The alkaline smell of charcoal ashes stung her nostrils. Synesthesia was a genetic condition that involved a sort of cross-wiring of the senses, and she had manifested it before she was eight. Someone with tetrachromacy had an extra color channel in the eye, allowing him or her to pick up a far wider and more subtle palette of hues than most people. Natasha had experienced that rare mutation almost out of the womb. The odds of having both conditions—of being a combined synesthete and tetrachromat—were almost nil. But she had defied those odds and won the mixed-sense sweepstakes.

Sometimes she considered it a gift. Sometimes it seemed good and sweet and beautiful, like in that Skittles slogan about tasting the rainbow.

Not right now, though. Right now the photo was pinging her with all kinds of mixed-sensory unpleasantness.

At a glance it resembled any class picture in any country in the world, except for the variance in the students' ages. They ranged from young children to adolescents. There were four rows of them, five or six in a row, twenty-seven in all. The older, taller ones were standing in the back two rows. The shorter ones at the front were in chairs.

The group was almost evenly divided between boys and girls. The boys wore gray trousers, gray sweaters, white shirts and red neckties. The girls wore gray skirts and vests, white blouses and red crisscross snap ties. There were triangular patches on their sweaters and vests, left side, above the heart.

Natasha's twelve-year-old self sat in the first row of the photo, second from the left. White hair, talc-white skin, long, knobby white arms and legs. Her large, deep-set eyes without expression. Her smile flat and lifeless.

The smile had been an alien thing on her face, disconnected from her feelings, something she'd put on every morning like the school uniform. She'd gotten more than her share of scrutiny from the instructors and scientists because of her mutation. She had wanted to avoid drawing equal attention to her unhappiness.

"Everyone stick with me while I lay this out," Morse said now. "Take a look at the breast patches. I'll get right to what's written at the bottom of each crest."

Natasha didn't need to look. She was all too familiar with it. The triangular red border, the white field inside it, the red double-chevrons pointing upward like inverted *V*s against the white. At the vertex of the larger, outer chevron, a five-pointed red star. Stitched above the base of the triangle, also in red, was a single set of Cyrillic characters.

"The word is *Vershina*," Morse said. "It translates as *summit*…or *pinnacle*. Not coincidentally, that's the name of a secret Russian program dating back to Stalin. The goal was to create the ideal human specimen through genetic selection, then mold them into apex spies and soldiers. They called it *forced evolution*. The guy who came up with it was a Darwin fan, a zoologist who bred and studied foxes. He figured he could domesticate them over successive generations and make them more like dogs. Trainable, eager to obey commands. His theory being that if it worked, he could eventually do the same with humans."

Natasha took a breath. She hated remembering the program. And she still felt ambushed by Morse. But she couldn't ignore the grave faces in the room.

"Dmitry Belyayev," she said. "That was the scientist's name. His title was Director of the Institute of Cytology and Genetics. He died fifteen years before I was born." She paused. "At the Pinnacle school, they called us tame foxes in his honor. Cute."

"Give them credit," Morse said. "Belyayev was mostly a quack. But while he was training his furry animals, the KGB found real scientists who gave the program legitimacy. They did their first in vitro fertilization in the early sixties. In the late eighties they were splicing chromosomes. That was the critical development. By 1990 or so, they were genetically engineering human zygotes at one of their *ZATO*s, or secret cities." She turned to Natasha. "I think you should explain about the project leader."

She inhaled again.

"His name was Ivan Mori. My father. I was a Pinnacle baby. He modified one of my mother's eggs and then reimplanted it. That's why I'm in that class shot. But if we were the successes, I won't get into the failures. It's too fucking horrible to mention."

Nobody spoke. Morse did something with her control and the class picture shrank into a window about half the total size of the screen. Then she did something else and a second window opened underneath it.

It showed a collection of photos, all of the same man.

Natasha recognized him at once, his image provoking a powerful mixed-sensory reaction in her. She saw a murky brown aura in front of the display that tasted like a soggy wool coat sleeve on a day smelling of cold winter rain. Other colors, tastes and smells barraged her, none good.

"That man...we think he has my daughters," Musil said flatly. "Jani and Raysa. They're fourteen and ten. We think he's taken them."

Natasha turned to him. "Oh, no," she said.

He just sat there looking drained.

She briefly raised her eyes back to her class picture. In the top row, last on the right, was a boy of seventeen or so. He had short, light brown hair. A plain face, his eyes neither large nor small. The nose was thin, the chin narrow and slightly undershot. He was the oldest-looking kid in the group, and the tallest. Nothing else stood out about his appearance...except for the cruel twist in his smile as he looked into the camera.

Natasha stared at his face. She could clearly see he was the same person as the man in the pictures at the bottom. Younger, but recognizably the same person.

"It's Grigor," she said. "Grigor Malkira."

"Tell us about him," Morse said. "Everything you can."

She nodded.

"I was young when we first met," she said. "Really young. My father left Russia, and Grigor and I wound up in the same orphanage. That's where a lot of us where warehoused. It was years before they sent me to the secret city where they trained the Pinnacle kids. Okean Ninety-Five. I met him again there."

"The photographs on the bottom...they're supposed to be someone named Stephen Gelfland," Musil said, speaking slowly, as if some massive gravity was pressing down on his words. "He was hired to work aboard a ship. The CS *Stalwart*."

"The cable ship?"

"Yes," he said. "I think Grigor killed him last November. Before it sailed. I think he stole his identity and took his place on the crew."

"And replaced him in all those photos at the bottom."

"With deepfakes, yes. On every passport and driver's license photo accessible online. Every electronic archive." Musil looked at her. "Ki Marton, one of our analysts, ran the images through our own facial-recognition database. The Pinnacle file came up. But when he tried to open the file it was locked. By Director Michaels."

Natasha gave a nod. "The prof did it for me. To *help* me. So I could stay in America. It was part of the deal."

"With Russia," Harris said.

"Yeah," she said. "You'd have to ask him about the rest. I can't talk about it."

"That also part of the deal?"

She nodded again.

Musil said, "Natasha... Ki was killed less than an hour ago. He was my friend. We were together when it happened."

Natasha looked shocked. "I *knew* Ki. He would speak to my classes." She hesitated, shaking her head. "I'm so sorry."

Musil breathed deeply.

"I was probably the real target," he said. "I've been looking into Gelfland's disappearance. Spoken to people about him."

Natasha was thinking hard. "Your daughters," she said. "How did he—"

"Malkira, if that's who it was, called their school. He asked to have them dismissed early and picked them up in a car," he said. "I know the principal. We've met many times. But he was convinced he was talking to me."

She looked at him for a long moment. "At Pinnacle they didn't always know how we would turn out. *Mostly*, they didn't. It was like they mixed the ingredients together in a test tube, shook them up and waited to see what developed. After we were born, they brought us to the secret city and put us on different tracks. They trained and educated us based on our abilities." She paused. "I can see things other people can't. Do different things. Like, I'm also a massive hyperpolyglot. A language accumulator. I hear somebody say a few sentences in German or Dutch or whatever and pick it up. My brain just computes and extrapolates. Phonetics, syntax, everything."

"And Malkira?" This from Carmody behind her. She turned to him.

"Grigor's next level," she said. "Better than me. He can sound like anyone. Act like anyone. But he isn't doing impersonations. He sponges up dialects. Voices. How people walk. It's like he's a chameleon. Or an octopus. The way they make themselves invisible."

"Aggressive mimicry," Morse said. "That's the term in the Pinnacle file."

Natasha nodded. "And the thing is…" She swallowed dryly. "We all learned to kill. They trained us like animals. I don't know how else to say it. That's how it was. I hated it. But not Grigor. He liked to hurt people. Even at the orphanage, before the training. I was a little girl…and he hurt me, OK?"

No one spoke for a very long moment. She took a breath.

"What you're saying fits Grigor. I mean, to the letter," she said. "That call to the principal. And turning into Gelfland. He could do it. I don't know about deepfakes across the internet. But he'd have help with them."

"Russia again," Harris said. "That's who we're talking about. Who would have sent him here."

"Yeah."

He started to say something, seemed to reconsider.

"What is it, Leo?" Morse asked.

He tugged his ear. "Just thinking."

She stood there with her eyes on him. No one spoke. He looked around the room.

"So, what now?" he said.

Musil's cell phone rang in his pocket before anybody could answer.

Grigor sat on a lawn chair in the bungalow's vacant sunroom, the girls in a corner facing him on two identical chairs. His right leg was bent upward, his right arm straight across the knee. It made a comfortable, steady base for the Glock in his hand. A fulcrum on which he could angle the gun smoothly from side to side.

At the moment, he was keeping it still, its barrel aimed at a point perfectly between them. He held the satellite phone in his left hand to his ear.

"Hello, Agent Musil," he said, in their father's voice. "Agent Musil speaking."

"Where are my daughters?"

"'Where are my daughters?'" Grigor repeated. The voice could have been a perfect digital recording of Musil, an instant playback. After a half second's pause, he shifted to his own voice. "My apologies. Birds like to flap their wings. I don't mean to provoke."

"Where are they?" Musil said.

Grigor swung the gun left toward the older girl, then right onto the younger, then left again. He had told them not to move, and they were being cooperative, though he'd allowed the older one to put a soothing arm around her sister.

"I may or may not be looking at their pretty faces," he said. "It's quite possible I have a gun on them. You can be certain they aren't dead yet."

"I want to speak to them," Musil said.

"Time for that in a while."

"I want to speak to them."

Grigor was quiet.

"I imagine you're in an office," he said. "After the excitement on Tenth Avenue, you would have contacted your children's school to check on their safety. But when you heard I pulled them out of class—or should I say *you* pulled them out?—you probably ran to your colleagues for help. And now I assume you're all huddled in that very imposing headquarters building."

"Put my daughters on the phone."

Grigor looked at them over the gun barrel.

"I want to tell you it can't be tracked," he said.

"My phone, that is. And your daughter's phone is gone. Just so you don't waste your time."

"What do you want from me?"

Grigor was silent a moment.

"You should understand something," he said. "I have your children. I can kill them or not. It makes no difference to me. But it does to you. Which means I'm in control."

Musil didn't answer. Grigor liked that. It was a silent concession.

"You went looking into things and lit a fire, and someone saw smoke," he said. "I'm the fire-fighter. I was sent to put it out. I think you know what that means without my saying it. I don't want to upset your little lambs. But I think you know."

"I want to speak to my daughters."

Grigor glanced at the window shade, fully drawn now as if to seal the room away from the rest of the world. Hawaii was waiting. He had big things to do there. But outside was outside, and inside was inside, and he could not afford to look past the present moment.

He lowered the phone from his ear, looked at the older girl.

"Mittha," he said, using the pet name he had read off Musil's lips outside the school. He waved her toward him with a wobble of the gun. "Come here. Your father wants to talk."

She stared at him a moment from the corner of the wall. Then she dropped her arm from around Raysa's shoulders and stood up and came toward him, her head and back straight, trying to look brave, marching like a soldier.

He waited for her to get about two-thirds of the way across the room.

"OK, far enough," he said. "I want you to tell your father you love him. Just that. I…love…you…Daddy. One more word, and I'll shoot out your sister's front teeth."

Jani stood there looking scared and forlorn but composed. He pressed the speaker button and held out the phone and nodded.

"I love you, Daddy," she said, clearly.

Grigor took the phone off Speaker. "Back to your sister," he said, wobbling the gun on his knee again.

He watched her return to the corner, put the phone up to his ear. "Agent Musil?"

"Yes."

"You asked to hear your daughter, and you heard her," he said. "Would you prefer I don't kill her? And the little one?"

Silence.

"Musil?"

"I don't want you to hurt them," Musil said.

Grigor nodded.

"Then listen carefully to what I want."

Musil's line went dead. Malkira had disconnected.

He sat a moment, everyone in the room looking at him in silence. Then he half turned toward Harris.

"My daughter's phone," he said. "He told me he took it from her."

Leo looked at him.

"Both girls have phones," Musil said.

"Trey, c'mere!" exclaimed the tech from her console.

Her name was Wonder Castro, and she had been trying to find the Musil girls utilizing the Force's Needlefish phone tracking system.

"One sec," he said, noting her urgent tone.

Trey was her colleague Trevon Raymore. He had been across the aisle at his own console, attempting a standard GPS trace.

Phone surveillance experts with the organization's Operational Technology Resources (OTTER) unit, they were installed—Trey preferred to say *shit-pitted*—in a basement sublevel some two hundred feet below the administrative section where Carol Morse, Leo Harris and more of the big wheels were officed. With renovations to the warehouse still incomplete, their work space was only reachable by creaking, archaic early-twentieth-century freight elevators and plunging, claustrophobic stairwells...but its equipment and systems were state of the art.

Raymore jumped out of his seat, hurried over to Castro's station and looked at her map screen. It really didn't look a bit different from his or any other conventional GPS-based navigational map.

But what made it very different was the *un*conventional software beneath its digital hood.

Tracking a mobile phone with the Global Positioning System was old hat. Cellular towers received signals from GPS satellites, which in turn retransmitted those signals to phones within range. The phone's location could be determined by triangulating its position relative to those towers. As its user moved away from one set of towers and within range of another, his or her movements could be followed on a map.

But turn off the phone and the job got stickier. When a phone was powered off, it did not receive cellular signals, and GPS tracking didn't work, period.

Needlefish, however, did not need GPS to track a phone. It did not require cellular data to work. Instead, it employed a far more complex and sophisticated side-channel method that interpreted readings from sensor arrays inside the phone.

Mobile devices were jam-packed with them. Every phone had a gyroscope, thermometer sensors, a magnetometer, an accelerometer, a proximity sensor, touch-screen sensors, ambient-light sensors and as many as four microphones, to name a bunch. These sensors might rest, but they never slept. The gyro was an exceptionally busy little bugger. A phone's compass app relied on it to provide directions. Also, the gyro—along with the accelerometer, which measured the speed of a phone's movement—was responsible for rotating a screen image whenever someone changed its orientation…say, to watch a video horizontally in landscape mode.

This pair of sensors—accelerometer and gyroscope—were Needlefish's embedded moles inside a phone. By accessing its compass app through an installed code, it could detect whether the phone moved a few degrees right or left, or up or down. The technology itself wasn't new. It had been around for about a decade. But years of advances in the field of artificial intelligence had been needed before it could be used to actually pinpoint a phone's whereabouts.

What the AI did was see how all those movements corresponded with specific locations on a map and then make some reasonable deductions. So three jinks fifteen degrees to the right, a dip in the road, another jink here, a sloping slide there, and finally a big, wide one-eighty turn and a halt, all within fifteen seconds, might *look* like someone in Mumbai, India, took New Panvel traffic circle to the Birmole Hospital parking area, after turning off Matheran Road to the southwest.

But it wasn't cut-and-dry. Sometimes the same set of jinks, dips, slips and slides corresponded to multiple city or town layouts. Sometimes the geomapping wasn't too accurate or up-to-date. There were construction detours, road closings, exit openings. A road that dipped down low last week might have been filled in and leveled since. Or maybe someone had randomly made those very movements while scooting around the Arctic tundra on a snowmobile. It happened. So what Needlefish did was kick out the leading candidates and rate them in order of likelihood. It's *probably* that traffic circle in Mumbai. But it very well could be we're looking at an approach to the Arc de Triomphe roundabout. And we can't rule out Mohanlal roundabout in Doha, Qatar, though it's a third-place long shot.

It helped if you were able to exclude certain locations. Say you were confident the parties you were tracking weren't in Qatar. Or France. Then you could tell Needlefish to leave those places off its candidate list. And even better if you could narrow the search to a specific country, district or city.

Which was what Castro and Raymore had been able to do looking for Musil's daughters.

They knew from the jump that the kids were in New York. They also knew the girls had started out at the Woodmere Middle School in the borough of Queens. And they knew that all five city boroughs had highly exact and current street maps and satellite imagery. These factors bumped up Needlefish's location accuracy to a tick under one hundred percent.

Assuming there was a phone to locate.

That had been the big question mark hanging over the techs. If there was no phone, any Needlefish search was moot. Musil had told them the girls' abductor had claimed it was discarded or destroyed…but it was within that very claim that he found a small kernel of optimism.

Your daughter's phone is gone, the man had said.

Phone, singular.

Not *phones*.

According to Musil, his daughters always went to school with *two* phones between them. One each.

They had kept their hopes in check. The kidnapper very well could have misspoken. Musil had also acknowledged that he might not have heard him correctly. He might have taken both phones. Therefore nobody got too excited.

Until now, with Castro looking at her map and excitedly calling Raymore over to her station, and the two of them staring at her display.

"Do you see what I see?" Castro said.

"Pa rum pum pum pum," he said, nodding.

She didn't catch the reference. But he wasn't keeping score.

"I see," he said.

They looked at each other, almost giddy.

"This has to be it," she said.

Two minutes later, Castro's Needlefish map replaced the photos on Morse's wall screen.

"I know that neighborhood," Musil said, looking at it. "If it's where my daughters are, it would be minutes from their school."

"Malkira might be playing us," Harris said. "He could've planted one of their phones there to throw us off."

"Or not," Carmody said.

Musil's face was tense and thoughtful in equal measure. They had shifted to the map's satellite view, and he was looking at an aerial photo image of the tagged house: a single-family bungalow on a dead-end street named Meadows Court.

"My daughters know they have Needlefish on their phones," he said. "After last August, Raysa started having nightmares. She was terrified someone would take her away and we wouldn't find her."

"Like you found that little boy in the park," Harris said.

Musil nodded.

"She saw the news stories. She knew Anton Ciobanu would have killed him. I installed the software to set her mind at ease," Musil said. "I told her she had nothing to worry about. That I would know where she was even if the city went dark and the phone service went out again. I remind her every morning when I drop them off."

"So you think she held on to it?"

"Or hid it. I don't know how she could do either. But she would try before letting anyone take it from her."

The room was quiet. After a moment Carmody pushed himself off the wall.

"Time for us to quit standing around and do something," he said.

17

Dragonfly leaped up from the Terminal vertipad at three fifteen.

It quickly rose to a thousand feet and swung east across Manhattan, skirting the southern border of Central Park, then climbing another thousand feet into the air to cruise at twice the legal altitude of civilian helicopters. Crossing a narrow strip of the East River, its flight path bisected Roosevelt Island lengthwise, then took a sharp dogleg north and east above the tidal strait spanned by the Hell Gate Bridge.

Ten minutes after takeoff the VTOL shot over eastern Queens. Overflying power plants and smokestacks and the remnants of the old waterfront manufacturing district, it took seven more minutes to cross the residential grid of Jackson Heights and reach Flushing Bay.

In his cockpit, Lucas tapped a button on a touch-screen panel. The modular rack unit on the right side of his fuselage had been installed just minutes before takeoff. Eight screwlike connectors and it was on.

Now he felt *Dragonfly* give the merest of shivers as the *Little Wing* drone was ejected from its rack pod.

A small autonomous aircraft launching from a larger one is a major aerodynamic challenge. The obstacles to its success only increase if its parent aircraft is hurtling through the air at three hundred miles an hour. It has to instantly overcome the speed and direction of the wind drag and its own weight, among other powerful forces trying to swat it out of the sky.

This drone was a marvel of flight engineering and nanocomputer technology. Three feet long, tubular, with a cone-shaped nose, it tumbled and spun in the crosswinds a moment, its slender wings completely folded in on themselves. But after a second or so the drone's twin-bladed tail prop boosted it away from *Dragonfly*, and they telescoped outward to their full eight-foot span.

Self-stabilized and oriented, *Little Wing* dashed across the bay, locked in on the phone signal Needlefish had been picking up.

Watching the drone fly off through his windscreen, Lucas nodded, mouthed a silent prayer for those little girls and then radioed the Terminal.

"Baby's on the way," he said into his headset.

Carol Morse and Leo Harris sat watching the drone's streaming video imagery on her wall screen as it flew toward its destination. They were alone in front of her desk, their chairs close together. The others had cleared the room almost half an hour ago.

Morse drank some lukewarm coffee from her Yeti, reached over to set it down on the desktop and happened to notice Leo's wan, tired features. Regarding him a second, she tapped his wrist to get his attention, motioned to her wireless headset and switched it off.

He did the same and looked at her.

"You OK?" she said.

"No, Car. I'm not."

"Me neither."

Harris nodded slowly.

"Ki's dead," he said. "Some Russian super-whatever killed him and took Musil's kids. And I can't figure out why."

She nodded. "You're thinking Musil isn't all of Net Force. We're a government organization. Someone would pick up where he left off."

"And Malkira would know," Leo said. "This isn't his first time around the block."

"Agreed."

He looked at her.

"Something else," he said. "We all think Mal-kira was on the *Stalwart* to make sure the Chinese ops got aboard. But how's that jibe with him being Russian?"

Morse was nodding again. "I've asked myself the same thing, Leo," she said. "Especially because Carmody and Kali showed up here today with evidence supporting a Chinese connection."

"What kind?"

"A personnel file. They pulled it from Seven Winds Malaysia's HR system. It links that kitchen crew to the same Chinese government officials Alex told us about," she said. "But there's a catch. They're convinced the file was planted. Or at least that someone wanted it to be found by us."

He looked at her.

"You think Russia's behind all of this? Trying to make China look bad?"

"I might," Morse said. "Except that still doesn't explain those Chinese ops. Or our photint showing that China's fishing militia probably helped take the ship. *Or* President Tsao coming within an inch of accusing *Stalwart* of espionage to POTUS."

Leo looked at her. They had to get back to *Little Wing*'s feed.

"It could be Russia. It could be China. It could be both or neither or somebody else," he said. "We got all these pieces of a puzzle and don't know how they fit together."

Morse nodded. "We'll find out, Leo," she said.

"Won't bring Ki back."

"No," she said. "It won't."

Silence.

Morse started to reach her hand out toward his, caught herself, and just looked at him, realizing he'd noticed. It could have been an awkward moment. She knew it would have been if she tried to pretend it didn't happen. Or if he tried. But they weren't going to fool each other. They had been married for fifteen years.

Morse nodded almost imperceptibly. He nodded back. It was an unspoken acknowledgment. She was another man's wife now, the mother of his children.

They turned their headsets on and raised their eyes to the screen.

The drone was getting close.

It was a small, quiet space tucked away down at the end of a long, branching fifth-floor corridor. A hundred years ago it might have been used to store maintenance supplies. The walls were exposed brick. There was a desk with a computer, a couple of wooden chairs, and a table under a high skylight. Someone had put a bamboo plant in a white vase on the table and it was thriving.

Kali had found the room on one of her first visits to the Terminal and liked its solitude. Once or twice, she had freshened the water in the vase.

She entered now, sat down at the desk and turned on the computer. Natasha Mori followed her through the door carrying two brown cardboard cups. She set one in front of Kali and stood near the desk with the other.

"Thank you," Kali said.

Natasha said, "It's sucky pod brew. Your punishment for letting me tag along."

Kali switched on the computer. Natasha looked at her.

"It's probably none of my business," she said, "but I figured you'd head out with your guy."

Kali turned to face her as the monitor brightened up.

"He isn't my guy," she said.

Natasha grinned. "Then, how'd you know who I meant?"

Kali looked at her silently. Natasha hesitated.

"Moving on," she said, "what are we doing in here?"

"A search," Kali said.

"Of?"

"I'm starting with Jinggu Technologies. A Chinese official, Deng Yannan, is listed as the owner. It's a parent company of Seven Winds."

"The one that put those people aboard the cable ship. The ones you think Grigor signed off on."

"Yes."

Natasha nodded. She slid a chair up alongside Kali and sat down. "When you say *starting*..."

"I type in a search term and let the results guide me," Kali said. "I want to fully understand Malkira's reasons for returning to the States."

"Because why would he do it unless there's a

bigger reason than getting rid of one snoopy investigator? It isn't like he's just some mob hit man."

"Yes."

Natasha nodded. "So…you free-associate when you search?"

"Yes."

"Web browser as Ouija board. Cool concept," Natasha said. "I'm the same. With my analytical software. And when I make music. Everything, really. It's all improvisational. Like spirit writing. Thoughts come to you out of nowhere."

Kali looked at her. Natasha sipped her coffee. Kali looked at her another moment.

"He's the best at what he does," she said finally. "I need to do what I do best."

Natasha nodded again. Then she put her coffee down on the desk beside Kali's, tilting her chin to the screen.

"We should get this shit started," she said.

Carmody accelerated as he shot off the bridge on the R 18, then cut left heading toward Queens Boulevard. Black helmet, jacket and leather gloves, his black riding pants thick at the knees and tucked into his boots. Traffic was heavy as usual, but he weaved speedily through it, white-lining the lane dividers as he raced past the clumps of plodding vehicles. Drivers honked their horns, shouted curses out their windows, and flashed their middle fingers, but he ignored them. New Yorkers seemed to aggressively compete for every square inch of space. He didn't like it, didn't have time to waste on petty battles. He'd been in too many real ones where men and women working together selflessly could mean the difference between life and death.

Two innocent kids had been taken hostage by a human killing machine. Carmody didn't care what Malkira wanted or where he came from. He barely cared about Malkira at all.

For him, right *now*, it was about those kids.

He whipped onto the highway ramp and opened his throttle, following the route map the OTTER techs were relaying to his head-up.

"You all there?" he said into his helmet mic.

"We see you nice and clear."

"Good, stay with me," he said and roared east.

It was three thirty in the afternoon in New York and therefore nine thirty in the morning on the island of Oahu, when Grigor sent a secure, self-deleting text message to Jochi from his satphone. He stood in the sunroom of the house near the overgrown cul-de-sac. The Musil girls were in the beach chairs. His Glock was just forward of his right hip in a concealed-carry holster. His message was typed thus in simplified Chinese:

沉默之龙

Phonetically the characters spelled out the phrase *quien long*. The English translation was *silent dragon*. Broken down to its original pictographic components, it would more accurately translate as *dragon hiding in deep water*.

Grigor counted in his head. Ten seconds later his outgoing message vanished from the conversation and Jochi's response appeared:

火

Phonetically it was pronounced *HU-a*. Read either as a pictogram or standard character, it translated into English as *fire*.

Grigor counted to ten in his head again. The character vanished from his phone's display. He returned it to his pocket.

It was 3:31 p.m.

He looked at the girls, his lips in the sidewise twist that was Grigor Malkira smiling without a mask. Events would move rapidly now.

Jot Musil merged onto I-678 in his Acura and checked the dash clock. Three thirty-five. He had left the Terminal fifteen minutes before Carmody. He believed it was time enough.

Come alone. If I have the slightest suspicion anyone is even close, I will kill your older daughter where both you and the younger one can see. It will be a 9 mm frangible round in her right eye, and that would be a mess.

Musil drove along. The traffic here was lighter than it had been driving off the bridge. He wasn't far now. Four miles, possibly five.

He glanced unconsciously at the large brown envelope beside him on the passenger seat.

I want all the data you've compiled on me. Bring a hard copy, no electronic files. I want to know everything you've learned.

Musil snapped his eyes back to the windshield. He had been quietly reciting his cherished *banis*, the words of strength and healing taken from the hymns of the everlasting Gurus. He did not fear for himself. He feared for his children, for what would happen to them if he got things wrong. He feared for his wife and what would happen to her. He thought of his hurried conversation with Saya on the phone that morning and could not remember if he had said he loved her before hanging up. He normally would have. His father had been a man of his generation from Bareta in eastern Punjab. He had been a hard worker and treated his family with reserved kindness. He had never expressed his feelings in words. He had never openly shown affection. As a child, Musil had longed for a simple embrace. He had tried to learn from that.

He hoped he had told Saya he loved her. He had been in a rush to get the girls ready for school and wasn't sure.

He thought of Malkira's instructions again.

When you arrive, I want you to pull into the cul-de-sac at the end of the street. Stay inside the car until I call you on the phone. I will tell you exactly what you need to do before I can let your daughters go.

Musil drove. In another two miles he would merge onto Whitestone Parkway and then onto the local streets. He was minutes away.

Little Wing reached the inlet to the cul-de-sac at twenty-six hundred feet. Guided by the sensor readings from Raysa Musil's cell phone, it went gliding high above the street toward their source. Lucas's mission log would categorize the flight as a DILR—detect, identify, locate and report—which precisely described its actions. His log would also note its arrival time as 3:37 p.m.

The bird was sharp-eyed and exceptionally smart. Sharp-eyed was par for the course: virtually all military and law-enforcement drones carried high-res imaging suites. But *Little Wing* owed its outstanding braininess to a core machine-learning processor that enabled it to independently distinguish targets of interest from ground clutter, and then collect its intel based on a scalable list of priorities. It could tell a vehicle from a clump of brush, and a fire hydrant from a person—and *then* decide when one guy was of greater interest than the next. If it simultaneously spotted somebody walking his Jack terrier and another man running past him with his heels on fire, it would tag the runner for a first-look investigation. But if a guy on the same street burst from a house with a submachine gun, the drone would push him up to the top of its priority list. These graduated, near-instantaneous judgment calls required a superior level of machine cognition—the ability to draw probable conclusions from its observations, to interpret the data it gathered and react on the spot.

Keen vision, common sense and a yen for mobile communication devices. The drone was built for hunting people, and people usually carried phones. Since every mobile phone had a distinct electromagnetic footprint—making it a reliable giveaway of someone's position—they were foremost objects of attention.

Little Wing therefore carried an antenna array that could track a phone's EM emissions to within inches of its position. If it detected one in its recon box, it would zone in from a high altitude, identify its make and model, and tag its location on its video and pictures.

Lucas saw the results of the bird's phone sweep on his head-up within a minute of receiving its first imagery of the bungalow and grounds.

It had located two, and within a hundred feet of each other. One, a popular Android, was clearly Raysa Musil's based on the tracking software installed by her father. *Little Wing*'s geolocators put it in an attached garage. The second was about two hundred feet away from the garage inside the bungalow. The bird had instantly matched its radiation signature to the spectra associated with a satellite phone—labeling it as an ISAT produced by Russia's Morsviasputnik telecom.

"Six, you looped in on these readings?"

Six. Carmody's call sign.

"Got them, yeah."

Flogging the R 18 along the highway, Carmody glanced at the imagery on his head-up and made some rapid assessments. The ISAT had to be Malkira's, likely putting him inside the house. Also, there was no vehicle in the driveway. Which meant he had pulled the car into the garage. Which in turn meant Raysa Musil's phone was probably inside the car.

He was thinking she'd stashed it out of sight. Maybe under the seat. Or maybe in the gap between the seat and lower backrest. If Malkira had faked being a rideshare driver, he would have let the girls into the rear as part of his charade. And he couldn't constantly keep his eyes on them while driving the car. Raysa could have waited till he wasn't looking and hidden it. Unless he'd killed her while she was in the car, then left the body inside with the phone. Or killed her in the house and carried her back to the car.

Carmody knew both were possible scenarios. But he was betting on her still being alive. Malkira had more to gain from that, so far. Though, that would change very soon.

Hard on the route map, he swung off the Whitestone at the Linden Place exit, leaning tightly into the curve of the ramp. He was less than a mile from finding out if he was right or wrong.

Crouched on the balls of his feet, Grigor wound the industrial tape around Raysa's ankles once, then twice, the *rrrrip* of the adhesive surface pulling from the spool loud and harsh in the room. He gave the tape another couple of turns, pressing it down with his fingertips as he went along. Then he sliced it from the roll with his ceramic knife, stood up and walked around in front of the two girls to examine his work, standing between them and the window.

They were side-by-side in the lawn chairs, Raysa's left armrest against Jani's right, both chairs about ten feet back from the window.

Grigor had trussed and gagged the girls so they couldn't move or make anything but muffled, almost inaudible sounds, stuffing a wadded handkerchief into each their mouths and wrapped the tape around the top of it to hold the fabric in place. Their arms were behind their backs, bound at the wrists with the tape.

He found the stark differences between the girls interesting. The older one's large brown eyes were wide above the tape, and she looked confused and afraid but not docile. He saw anger in the way she focused her stare on him.

Not so for the younger doe. She had stopped sobbing a while ago and seemed almost unresponsive, a withdrawn look in her eyes. Grigor recognized trauma when he saw it. She was a slight, weak little thing.

He stood there looking the girls over, hands on his hips. He was fully armed, the Glock in its waistband holster, the Scorpion EVO slung over his shoulder. He wore two open-top five-in-line magazine pouches, one on each side of his waist. The pistol clips were on the right. The ones on the left contained the EVO's heavier 147-grain full metal jacket ammunition.

After a minute he turned to the picture window. The shade was still drawn. Grigor stood behind it, moved it slightly aside with two fingers to look out, and waited.

Musil turned the car into the cul-de-sac. Up ahead he could see a yellow reflectorized sign marking the bulbous end of the roadway. Past it was a wood-slat fence.

The few homes on the street stood far apart on spacious lawns. They were all large bungalows with wide, enclosed porches. A century earlier, Meadows Court had been a bedroom community outside the developed portions of the city. It remained quiet and almost rural as if existing in its own slow backwater of time.

The last house on the street stood on the right near the dirt and brush terminus. There was a large for-sale-by-owner notice in the front yard. Musil knew it was where Grigor Malkira was holding his children. Raysa's phone, acting as a beacon, had pinpointed the location.

He did not glance over at the house as he drove past. It was unbearably hard to restrain himself. But he knew Malkira would be watching.

Musil pulled onto the dirt, eased forward until

his front grille was almost up against the fence, and cut his engine. He bowed his head slightly and mouthed the *banis*.

His phone rang. He glanced over to where it sat in the center console. The display said *Unknown Caller*. He lifted it out of the tray.

"I'm here," he answered.

"I see that," Malkira said. "You've followed my instructions?"

"Yes."

"You're alone."

"Yes."

"You brought the file."

"Yes."

"And I can trust you have no electronics."

"Yes."

Silence.

"You believe in God, do you?"

"Yes. I want to see my children."

"Soon enough. Were you praying just now?"

Musil didn't answer.

"Were you praying?"

"Yes."

"For?"

Musil breathed. "I appealed to the Lord of Justice for his help and support. I asked that my family be allowed to live in peace."

"I can do anything I want to your pretty young daughters. I can boil them to death in scalding bathwater. I can make it so their brains have to be scraped off the walls," Malkira said. "Don't you think that gives me a say?"

"I have faith in his guidance."

Silence again.

"Get out of the car," Malkira said. "Walk up the driveway to the garage. When its door opens, you'll step inside and wait."

"Will I see my children?"

"Have faith," Malkira said, and ended the connection.

Carmody shot out of the highway exit, taking Thirty-Second Avenue east in light neighborhood traffic. He rode on for several blocks, then saw the corner of Meadows Court straight ahead to his left, perpendicular to the avenue. As he continued past the cul-de-sac's inlet, he glanced over his shoulder at the tree-lined residential street.

Musil's car was there. Parked at the dead end.

He slowed down, turned right off the avenue at the next corner, took another right and then hung a third to put himself back on Meadows Court a block south of the inlet. There was no one ahead of him, no one behind him. The only person out was a mail carrier pushing his delivery cart up the sidewalk.

Halfway down the block, Carmody pulled alongside a parked car, stopped and waited. He sat with his hands loose around his grips, the bike purring softly as a kitten underneath him. Its electronic injection system kept the two-stroke sipping fuel, so there was no need to blip the throttle.

He waited. After a minute his head-up gave him an aerial of Musil exiting the Acura, *Little Wing*'s livestream providing a close-in view. He saw him walk from the dead-end area to the driveway on his left. Saw him turn into it and continue up toward the garage. With the drone hovering almost directly above the garage roof, Carmody did not have an angle of the door rising open. But he saw Musil briefly pause in front, step forward and disappear inside.

This was it—*almost.*

"Spotter up," he said into his mic.

"Roger," Lucas answered up above.

Carmody waited in the motorcycle's saddle, everything around him still and quiet.

Calm before the storm, he thought.

In *Dragonfly*'s passenger compartment, Dixon popped the right-hand door latch and slid open the door, feeling an immediate rush of wind on his cheeks. He mounted his sling in ninety seconds, attaching its vertical straps to the cargo hooks, then adjusting the D-rings on its horizontal line.

His .300 Winchester Magnum rifle was on the floor in its hard case, the Leupold optic already affixed, a five-round magazine pushed into the well. For ammo he was using Hornady 150-grain SST Interlocks hand-loaded with Hodgdon's blue, liking the flake's slow burn for long-range velocity.

He turned, crossed the cabin and removed the bottom cushion from one of the vacant seats. He carried it over to the door and set it down. Then he lifted the WinMag out of the case, got as comfortable as possible on the seat cushion and secured the rifle in the rig.

"Ready back here," he said into his headset.

"OK, I'm moving into position." This was from Lucas up in the cockpit. "When this bird drops, it drops fast, so do your best not to fall out."

Dixon glanced down the aisle through the open cockpit door at Lucas's back.

"Thanks for the advice," he said.

Lucas rotated in his seat and gave him a thumbs-up.

"No problem, hero," he said. "It's a long way down to the ground."

Musil entered the garage and heard its roll-down door activate behind him. He had seen the Mazda parked inside from the driveway and stopped for a quick look around. The garage was otherwise empty, its shelves and pegboards bare, no tools, no spare tires, no lawn mower, no coiled-up garden hose, no dirty work boots flopped over against a wall, nothing.

As the garage door lowered behind him, he saw the fire door on his right in the common wall with the house. His eyes held there as the mechanized garage door rattled shut and cut off the sunlight.

He stood waiting in the dark. He heard the hard, rapid stroking of his heart in his chest and breathed deeply to slow it down. In through the nose, holding the air in his lungs, exhaling through his mouth. His nostrils had picked up a faint soapy smell, mixed with chemical traces. Epoxy. *For Sale by Owner.* The garage was emptied out, its concrete floor cleaned of oil stains and resurfaced. Fixed up for potential buyers.

Musil stood there. He couldn't see anything. He couldn't hear anything but the slow, deep, rhythmic, repetitive in-and-out of his breath. He imagined his daughters on the other side of the fire door, separated from him by a few short yards. He pictured them in the house, frightened and helpless, and fought down the irrational impulse to try kicking his way through to reach them. That wouldn't work. That would only get them killed. He had to stay calm.

He inhaled, exhaled. Slowly, deeply.

The fire door opened, swinging into the garage.

Grigor Malkira stood framed inside the entryway, a pistol extended in his hand.

Musil stared at his face. It was the face from the photos. The one Ki had traced to Pinnacle.

Fake Gelfland.

"You wanted me," Malkira said, softly. "Here I am."

Musil watched him. He saw a second firearm at his side, strapped over his shoulder. A carbine.

"I assume that's the file," Malkira said, nodding toward the envelope in his hand.

"Yes."

"Good. Put it on the floor and leave it there."

Musil did as he was told.

Grigor smiled. It was like a thin tail coiling upward on his lips.

"All the lies," he said. "Next I want you to remove your turban."

Musil looked at him.

"No disrespect," Malkira said. "I'm just making sure you aren't hiding anything like a bug or a weapon."

Musil breathed. After a moment he took the *dastār* off his head and tossed it underhand onto the floor between them.

"Good. Now your shirt. Pull it out of your waist, unbutton it, and open it wide."

He opened his shirt. Malkira nodded.

"Shoes, next. Kick them off."

Musil did it.

"Good job, Agent," he said. "Last thing. You're going to drop your pants and shorts and then turn in a full circle for me."

"I want to see my daughters."

Malkira jabbed the pistol at him. "Shut up and follow instructions."

Musil opened the button of his waistband, unzipped his fly and pulled down his pants and shorts. Then he spun around and stood there facing Malkira again in only his shirt and socks, almost naked in the dim garage.

"All right, little man," Malkira said. "You can pull your pants up. Slowly."

He did it.

Malkira watched him. "To answer your question," he said, "I'm here to slow things down while other things speed up. Call me a balance." He paused. "I'm also here to kill you."

"Don't hurt my daughters."

"That will depend on whether you brought anyone with you."

"I came alone."

Malkira's smile curled more tightly on one side. "You're a good father. I envy your girls. Mine gave me up to an awful place. Ask Natasha Mori."

Musil breathed. Malkira held the gun steady on him.

"She's like me, you know. Motherless. Fatherless. Bred to kill. They blocked her instincts. Her appetites. She was too much for them to handle. But I knew her before. I know better than anyone. And your people will find out. You won't be there to warn them. She'll eat their hearts out of their chests. Their blood will flow down her pale lips. When she wakes up."

Musil said nothing. Malkira moved back and sideways into the house, one nimble step. Then he waved him over to the door with the gun.

"Suppose we go see your daughters," he said.

Lucas knew the drone couldn't see through walls—not *exactly*.

Thermal imaging technologies had come a long way, and *Little Wing*'s camera was sensitive even at a great altitude. It could inspect a site with astounding clarity in pitch-darkness. It could rapidly switch between wide and narrow fields of view, magnify what it saw at a very high resolution and downlink its pictures over large distances without appreciable degradation. It really was a powerful eye in the sky.

But glass rejected huge swathes of the IR spectrum. The thick, insulated sides of a building also blocked clear and distinct infrared images. The beams could only go so deep before they decayed. Thermal cameras were limited by physics.

Lucas knew *Little Wing* didn't have physics-defying supervision. Exactly. But he had served with the Army's Task Force 160—the Night Stalkers—right up until retiring from the service and knew it came damn close.

Because it could pick up unique heat signatures on the other side of walls and use its artificial intelligence to interpret those signatures, no matter how vague. Or to put it another way, it could review the characteristics of a splash of heat, then look at other splashes in a given space around it and compare them to emissions from elsewhere in the room. With that done, it could match them against its extensive in-memory database to tell them apart, as it would when deciding whether it was looking at the bonnet of a fire hydrant or a human head.

But the drone wasn't wholly unique in that capability. Others had it. What made *Little Wing* a phenom among drones was that it could go several steps beyond the rest and instantly create visual simulacra of emissions sources and their surroundings. A virtual reality depiction of the room behind the walls, based on what it figured out about the heat patterns inside it.

In his cockpit, Lucas made the sign of the cross as the drone's camera lens rotated toward the front of the house. His face felt taut and his neck stiff. He'd been nowhere near as tense in Syria once upon a time, using a close relative of *Little Wing* to take out ISIS butchers in their hideaways.

But this mission was also nowhere the same.

This one was about saving two young children and their father.

And suddenly, now, Lucas could see the kids in his head-up. See the layout of the room around them, like an interior designer's floor plan, but brushstroked with texture and color. The scene *Little Wing* generated wasn't a hundred percent realistic. Nor were its versions of people. But they were easily good enough. He saw the girls in chairs to one side of the window, their wrists and ankles taped. And entering the picture from the right—

His stomach clutching, he straightened behind his controls and said, "Six. From the garage. You see what's going down?"

"Roger," Carmody replied. "This is it."

Grigor entered the living room a step behind Musil, his elbow locked around his neck, holding the Glock up to his head. He had pivoted around his back as he stepped through the fire door, moving in on the agent with the gun.

The girls turned their heads to look from their chairs. Bound, gagged, terrified. Musil saw the helpless bewilderment in their eyes. He had never seen anything worse.

Grigor pressed his forearm into his windpipe, cutting off his air.

"You hunted me," he said. His voice quiet and level. "Now you pay the price."

Musil struggled to answer. Grigor's arm choked the words off in his throat. He tried again, croaked, "You said...wouldn't..."

"I won't hurt them." Grigor finished the sentence. "You die. They watch. And live to remember."

Which was only a half lie. Kill the parent, exterminate the line. *Zu Zhu* to the ancient Chinese, ironically.

But father first. Grigor wanted them to see his head explode. That part was true.

He screwed the gun into Musil's left ear. Musil heard the noise out on the street with his right, *rrrrRRRRRRR...*

We have to get them back.

Trust me.

He knew what to do.

It was everything Carmody hated and mistrusted. The windowed video on his visor looked like some kind of computer animation. Like the head-spinning, stomach-turning HIVE simulations. Its depth of field was off. Its imaging was scrubbed of texture. It wasn't precisely real.

He relied on his ability to see the world as it

was. *Banked* on it. But he was compromising with a machine approximation. Ceding part of himself to something that came close but wasn't quite. The decision-making part of his brain rebelled. His hand didn't want to crank the motorcycle's throttle.

He needed to overcome his own resistance. Trust something outside the range of his immediate and unaided perceptions. The eye of a fucking drone.

Carmody shot through the intersection into the cul-de-sac, coming on with a roar. The houses blurred by, the trees, the grass. Between heartbeats, he imagined windows opening, heads poking out, people wondering about the racket. Then the dead-end sign was just ahead of him. The sun winking off the reflector lenses below it. And sticking up from the yard on his right, the For Sale by Owner sign.

Carmody barked out a voice command and the sim instantaneously expanded to fill the upper half of his visor. He pulled hard on the bars, right, scrambling over the curb and onto the grass. The bungalow was in front of him, the holly bushes outside its wide sunroom window climbing to the lower sash. Its upper sash divided into multiple rows of panes, a drawn white shade behind them.

He could see through the shade. A kind of video game representation of the room with the girls in the chairs to the right. Musil to the left, Grigor Malkira behind him. All of them real and not real.

Carmody twisted the throttle some more, dropped his clutch, felt the air vibrate around him from the surging engine. The bike reared up like a stallion, stayed up going toward the holly bushes.

Gritting his teeth, he plunged into and over them toward the sunroom window.

The sound of the accelerating motorcycle was Musil's cue. Carmody had started either from the corner or the opposite side of the intersection. The cul-de-sac was three hundred feet long from inlet to dead end. Sixty miles an hour, ninety feet per second.

That had given him three seconds.

Grigor also heard the gaining growl of the engine, but he hadn't expected it. There was a skipped second before he reacted. Musil had taken advantage of it and planted his feet and brought his chin down against Grigor's arm.

The bend of Musil's neck left just enough space between the arm and his windpipe to allow for a single breath. The sudden downward motion of his head caused the bore of the silencer to slip out of his ear. He made the most of the opening and brought both hands up, bending his elbows like he was grabbing a pull-up bar. Then he locked one hand around Grigor's arm and the other around his wrist and turned slightly into him, his hip against his body, sidestepping to give himself a little more space.

The move joggled Grigor's balance. His arm was

still hooked around Musil's throat, but his choke hold loosened another hair. Musil had breathed and driven his right fist hard into his groin. As Grigor sank down an inch or so, he followed through with the same arm, jabbing its elbow up into the hollow of his ribs.

Grigor had stumbled back a half step, already recovering, raising the Glock in his fist, aiming past Musil at Raysa and Jani.

Three seconds.

Then the sunroom window exploded inward.

Carmody launched over the shrubbery with the bike almost vertical, the spin of its rear wheel shaving buds off the topmost branches in a flying flutter of green. He crashed through the window, sailing into the house airborne. Shards of glass spilled down from the upper sash in a noisy jangle. Spears of wood blew out around him as the muntins cracked and snapped and mixed with the cascade of shattered window glass.

An instant later Carmody came down in the middle of the sunroom, still up on his back tire, hitting the floor with a jolt. Musil and Grigor were to his left, the two captive girls in the lawn chairs to his right. Leaning deep in their direction, Carmody let go of the handlebars and launched sideways off his saddle just as the bike's front wheel came down to the floor.

The Motorrad bounced, leaned, overbalanced and pancaked. Carmody pulled in his arms and tucked his knees up to his chest as he hit the floor, rolling toward the girls on his back and shoulders, almost bowling into their chairs. Flat on its side, spinning end over end, the Motorrad skidded toward the wall like a hockey puck, plowing into it, smashing partway through into the next room.

Carmody came up out of the roll in a crouch, facing the wreckage of the thin partition wall. As he reached under his jacket for his Sig, he had a split second to notice the gaping hole left by the motorcycle's impact. The bike's front fork was on the other side of the wall under a heap of gritty debris. The rear tire was sticking out into the sunroom, still spinning slowly amid chunks of timber and plasterboard.

A split second. Then the Sig was out of its holster, Carmody swiveling ninety degrees on his knees toward Musil and Grigor.

They were tussling about ten feet away. Musil had his back to Carmody, his long hair flying wildly around his head. Free of Grigor's chokehold, he had locked his hands around his gun arm, grabbing it above the wrist, trying to pin his body so he couldn't move it, trying to tear the Glock free of his hand. Taller than Musil by a head, Grigor was turned toward Carmody and the girls.

Then his eyes landed on Carmody's weapon. He reacted instantly, levering his arm upward even as Musil continued to grip it with both hands, aiming the gun over Musil's shoulder at Carmody.

No. Not at him. He saw Grigor's level stare and knew.

The girls.

He snapped the Sig up in his hand, aiming at Grigor's face.

Carmody was quick. Air Force doctors had scored his fast-twitch reflexes at plus-seventy above normal. Olympic athletes doped to reach plus-thirty. Statistics about the upper ranges only went to plus-fifty. One in a hundred million people scored that high. His plus-seventy was off the charts.

Grigor might have been quicker. He read the trajectory of Carmody's gun coming up in his hand and once again moved like lightning. With his free hand, he grabbed Musil's shirt and shoved him hard toward Carmody. Musil stumbled backward over drifts of wood and glass, his body directly in front of Carmody. He held his fire.

Grigor used the advantage. His eyes on Carmody now, he triggered the Glock twice before he turned toward the door to the living room.

The first bullet missed. The second round tore through Carmody's jacket into his left triceps. His arm hot, he saw that Musil had flailed out of the way, and fired back. But Grigor was already through the door. The shot hit the wall that had been behind him a moment ago.

Musil scrambled over to Carmody.

"You're hit," he said.

Carmody boosted himself to his feet. "Go to your kids."

"You can't follow him. *You're hit.*"

Carmody waved him toward the girls with his free hand.

"Go!" he shouted, and turned toward the ragged hole the Motorrad had plowed into the wall, lunging around the bike and through the opening in pursuit.

Grigor sprinted across the living room, grabbed his pack off the floor without skipping a step, then cut right down a short hall. He pushed through the main back door, then the screen door, and was out in the backyard. He turned left toward the stockade fence bordering the dead end, took a running leap, and vaulted over it, his long legs completely clearing the top of the fence.

He landed in a level, weedy space between the fence and the metal rail that extended from the dead end of the road. It was about twenty feet deep. Beyond the rail, the slope was rocky and steep, going down to the street at a forty-five-degree angle. But its base wasn't more than thirty feet below him. Glancing down, he could see traffic through the brush and stunted trees.

Grigor hurried across the open space in weeds up to his knees. Not slowing down, he shoved his pistol into his waistband, put his carbine into the pack and shouldered its straps. Musil had surprised him by not coming alone. He hadn't expected that. Or the lunatic on the motorcycle. How had he known exactly where they were inside the bungalow? Grigor had checked to see if Musil was wired up. It couldn't have been that.

A thought struck him and he glanced skyward, his legs rustling through the weeds. He didn't see anything up above him. Which didn't mean there wasn't anything.

But he couldn't think about that now. He had carefully planned his escape contingency. Execution was still the critical thing.

He reached the rail and hopped over onto the slope.

"Six—target's turned left. There's a fence, you see?"

Carmody rogered Lucas as he burst out the screen door, then removed and tossed his motorcycle helmet. He would lose the drone's livestream. It would cut him off from *Dragonfly*. Without it he was on his own. But he would have his peripheral vision. His full range of senses. A fair trade-off.

He ran toward the stockade fence, long strides. Malkira couldn't have cleared it more than ten seconds ago.

It was about five feet high. Carmody's left arm was bleeding and numb, so he shoved his gun into his pants, grabbed the top of a board with his right hand, planted a foot on the side of the fence, and hauled his weight up and over.

Malkira had already crossed the weed-grown

space between the fence and the rail extending from the dead end. Carmody spotted him scampering downhill on the far side of the barrier, only the back of his head visible over the crest of the slope.

Carmody drew his gun again, sprinted up to the rail through the weeds, and hopped it. The ridge dropped sharply to the street below. It was clogged with brush. The footing was loose and rocky. By the time he landed, Grigor was better than a third of the way to the bottom.

He yanked the Sig out of his waistband and fired. But he didn't have a decent angle, and his shot went high. Grigor half spun in response, whipping the barrel of his carbine around his back as he scrabbled toward the base of the slope.

Bullets sprayed the upper hillside. Soil and pebbles spurted up an inch to Carmody's left. He dove into the weeds to the right and then rolled onto his back, tumbling over his wounded arm with a grunt of pain.

Another volley clipped the weeds around him. Carmody slid about six feet downhill on his rump, rocks, twigs and soil scraping up under his jacket and shirt. Then he sprang to his feet and triggered a three-round burst through the scrawny trees, aiming for the middle of Grigor's backpack. It was a broad target, bright yellow against the green and brown scrub. But his over-the-top angle hadn't improved, and Grigor was jostling down the ridge fast, and the trees and bushes gave him cover.

Carmody still managed to hit him right of center. Or maybe just hit the pack. He couldn't tell. He saw its fabric puff out over his hip, then saw Grigor lose traction on the crumbly soil. He went onto his bottom just as Carmody had seconds before, scuffing and skidding several feet down toward the street below.

Carmody scrambled after him through the snarled, matted growth. He was about fifteen feet above and behind him. Grigor had managed to stop his slide near the base of the slope, grabbing onto a spindly, outthrust branch for purchase.

A moment later Carmody saw his free hand go into one of the pack's outer pockets and then reappear holding a small round object. At a glance it looked like a green golf ball. Except the ring and lever told him it wasn't.

Grigor inserted two fingers into the ring and yanked it to pull the safety pin. He released the lever and threw it overhand to give it a high point of release. It was barely out of his fingers as he turned to run.

Carmody saw the grenade sail uphill, rotating in the air as it arced toward him. Then it dropped onto the slope and blew.

Grigor scraped and clawed his way down the slope as the minifrag detonated behind him. He felt a searing, penetrating pain in his side. A slickness under his backpack and shirt. He knew he'd been shot, though he had barely realized when the bullet struck. It was almost as if someone had playfully slapped the pack. The round must have hit it low, drilled through its fabric and entered his body below the ribs. A few inches higher and it would have set off the remaining grenades in the backpack's upper panel. Lit him up like a torch.

Still, the bullet had done enough damage. He thought it might have gone deep, buried itself inside him below the ribs. But he would have to wait to check it out.

He reached the base of the hill, crossed a narrow dirt strip to the pavement and turned right on Thirty-Ninth Avenue, hurrying toward the thoroughfare he'd scouted out days before. The avenue was packed with noisy rush-hour traffic, and the 115-decibel pop of the grenade had gone ignored or unnoticed by drivers and pedestrians. An engine backfire would have been louder.

When he came to the corner, he hooked right again and then abruptly merged into the thick crowd on Main Street. People were streaming around him in all directions, elbow to elbow. It was a world apart from the sleepy cul-de-sac only a block or so west. A mash-up of ethnic restaurants, small businesses and outdoor food markets. The store signs were in half a dozen different languages. Spanish, Hindi, Arabic, Chinese and Vietnamese.

Grigor lost himself in the press of bodies, walking south. Glancing up at the sky, he saw an aircraft roughly overhead. Lower than any plane, higher than most helicopters. He estimated its height at two or three thousand feet. It had to be a rotorcraft. But he didn't hear the distinctive whacking of copter blades. It made no noise at all. Or none that reached below.

He continued up Main Street, weaving through the crowd. The mass of pedestrians thickened as he hastened farther south. There were gyms and nail salons and banks and walk-in medical clinics, and people were flowing in and out of them. He pushed and bumped through the close press of bodies, wincing whenever anyone jostled his side. The wound wasn't bleeding profusely—not yet—which was a sign the bullet had missed his major blood vessels. But it could easily have punctured an organ and done internal damage. The bleeding was certain to get worse unless he took care of it soon.

A dozen yards along he looked up again. The rotorcraft was still in a hovering pattern. Not stationary but steady and circular. He was positive it was either searching for him or had already spotted him. Which didn't really matter. Both possibilities were about to become moot. He was about to lose the aircraft.

The 7 train line was just ahead now. He saw a station entrance with green metal railings and sets of concrete stairs leading underground. About a half block beyond was a second entrance, one with escalators instead of stairs.

It would be easier to take an escalator down to

the platform. He wanted to limit his movements and save his strength.

Grigor passed the stairway and hurried up the street to the escalator. He turned into its entrance, took hold of the rail to steady himself, stepped onto the treaded metal riser and started to move.

A second later, he disappeared beneath the sidewalk.

The minifrag might have sounded like a backfiring automobile exhaust. But its high-explosive fill and the fifteen-foot radius of its shrapnel spray made it surpassingly lethal.

The instant he saw it arcing toward him, Carmody knew he had between three and five seconds. Minus three, minus five. The timed fuse would be one or the other. Then the primer would ignite the tetryl and the blast wave would drive the casing's metal fragments upward and outward in every direction.

But three seconds could be a long time when the adrenaline was pumping. If the shrapnel field was flying up and out, he had to go down and away.

Knees bent, head low between his arms, Carmody lunged into a forward roll down the hillside about two seconds before it dropped. It was basic training all over again, except he was on a slope instead of a gymnasium floor. His leg muscles gave him the initial propulsion. His size and weight and forward momentum took care of the rest.

He went tumbling toward the base of the ridge, crashing through the tangled brush, rolling over rocks, dirt and root clumps. The breath woofed out of him. His left arm felt like a white-hot blade was stuck in it. Behind him the hillside coughed dirt and twigs into the air. He heard the crack of shrapnel carving into bark and bouncing off rocks.

And then he was at the bottom, in a patch of dirt verging on the sidewalk. He sprang to his feet, realized he was on an avenue full of cars and people, the Sig in his hand. An old Asian woman with a shopping bag noticed it and hustled past him. A guy behind her too. They both pretended not to see.

Carmody tucked the gun into his pants, looked left and right for Malkira. He didn't see any sign of him and almost wished for a second he hadn't ditched his helmet. *Dragonfly* was up above him somewhere. He couldn't see or hear it, but it was up there. Lucas and his drone would be able to track Malkira within the search box. Visually and through his satphone emissions.

He looked this way and that again. Nothing. He frowned and looked at the ground for possible footprints. Nothing…at first. Then his eyes narrowed.

Something had caught his eye peripherally to his right. He went over to it, looked down, squatted for a closer inspection.

There was fresh blood in the dirt. Not a lot, but a few scattered droplets. He kept looking at the ground and saw one or two more drops farther to his right. Each smaller than a nail head. Then another tiny splash at the edge of the sidewalk. And another beyond it that was actually on the pavement and about the size of a dime.

Carmody stood up quickly, turned right on the sidewalk and ran in the direction of the blood trail.

Lucas shook his head and sighed with his hands on the controls. His HUD readouts were blank. The sidewalk might as well have swallowed Malkira. Obviously, he'd done his homework. The 7 line was one of the busiest in the city, and its eastbound trains would have poured thousands of people onto Main Street at rush hour. Despite having him in their sights when he'd made for the station, they had been unable to take him out in that close crowd.

He glanced over his shoulder at Dixon. He had shut the door and was packing up his WinMag.

"Fucker lost us," he said and blew more air. "Those trains run every four, five minutes this time of day."

Dixon looked at him. "You know how wild dogs and wolves go after their prey?"

Lucas shook his head.

"They aren't built for speed," Dixon said. "They're persistence hunters. They'll track an animal for miles until they wear it out."

Lucas looked at him. "Carmody?" he asked.

Dixon nodded and closed the rifle's hard case.

"I always tell people," he said.

* * *

Carmody stopped among the swarm of pedestrians on Main and looked up. He had spotted *Dragonfly* in the air immediately after rounding the corner a block back. Now, minutes later, Lucas was pulling off south and west toward Manhattan.

He lowered his gaze. People moved past him like water around a boulder. Like he was too massive an obstacle to budge, so they naturally split left and right to get around him.

Grigor Malkira was gone. Carmody hadn't had a chance once he got ahead of him on this street. It wasn't just the moving bodies. There were too many places to duck out of sight. Too many escape routes. Buses, cars, a subway station.

Carmody turned back toward Thirty-Eighth Avenue and then walked toward the hill behind the cul-de-sac. His arm felt like dead weight, but climbing it was his best shortcut to the house. So he would climb.

He wanted to see how Musil and his girls were doing. And he wanted a look at that GoRide car in the garage.

Grigor changed trains several times. He was confident he hadn't been followed. But he wanted to be as cautious as possible.

He took the 7 local four stops and changed to the express. He stayed on that train for three long stops and switched to the E train into Manhattan. He rode the E to Penn Station and Thirty-Fourth

Street, then bought a ticket for the AirTrain to Newark Liberty in New Jersey.

When he arrived at the airport, Grigor intended to briefly check into a hotel. He needed a place to hole up for a few hours. He needed to get rid of the knapsack with its weapons, ammunition and explosive mixtures—and make sure there were no chemical traces on his body. And he needed to take care of his wound.

There would be no stopping again once he reached Hawaii.

18

New York

"So," Natasha said, looking at the computer monitor. "What's here for us?"

"I'm gathering information," Kali said.

"Shocker. About?"

Kali didn't answer. Though Natasha wondered if she even heard the question. She was clearly focused on what was in front of her. One thing their Ouija web search had quickly demonstrated was that if you knew what you were looking for and where to search for it, it didn't always take a complicated hack to mine solid gold information from the internet.

The web page Kali had clicked on was called Global Ship Finder, and it was the second site she had visited in the past few minutes. The first—and the one that led her directly to it—was a database of foreign importers and exporters named Asian TradeWizard Worldwide. Backtracking another step, TradeWizard had come up among a long list of hits when Kali googled the keywords *US China trade resources.* As far as Natasha could tell, she had navigated to it at random from among the rest.

Asian TradeWizard's menu bar was pretty basic. Its drop-downs were *Home, International Sellers, International Buyers* and *Transactions.*

In a search box on the *Sellers* page, Kali had typed *Jinggu Technologies.* The filtering search box underneath it offered only a single company product: core steel piping.

Next, Kali had moved her cursor back to the menu bar and clicked on *Transactions.* That took her to a new page. Its top two search boxes were side-by-side near the top: Importer and Exporter.

For *Ship-from,* she typed *Jinggu.* For *Ship-to,* she entered *CloudCable.*

When she clicked the search button, a list of purchase orders appeared. These specified the quantity of each order, its departure date and location, and its delivery date and location. The transactions went back half a decade, but Kali was able to narrow her results to the current year.

There had been three shipments since January. All originated at the Port of Dalian, Liaoning, and were received at Honolulu Harbor, Port of Hawaii. The first had left China on January 5, 2023, and arrived in Hawaii on February 13. A second had departed August 20, 2023 and was delivered September 26. A third cargo had left on March 12 and arrived in Hawaii just the day before, on April 19.

"That's a shitload of pipes," Natasha commented.

Kali had turned to her. "Jinggu is the parent of Seven Winds. It has ties to the Chinese government," she said. "The piping is used exclusively in marine cable networks. And Jinggu is Cloud-Cable's sole provider."

"Seriously?"

A nod. "That came up when Carmody and I were in Morse's office this morning," Kali said. "But it's no secret. There are filings. Bills of lading. Most are public record."

Natasha had thought about that.

"Jinggu's kinda like a spider in the middle of a big web," she said. "All the threads lead to it. Or maybe I should say all the steel pipes."

Kali hadn't commented. Instead, she copied the dates to the computer's notepad, exited the website and did a second Google search. This time she had entered the words *cargo ship tracker*.

Again, a column of several hyperlinks came up. And again, she had made her choice.

Which was how they got to the Global Ship Finder site they were on now. Scanning the home page, Natasha saw that the menu bar's drop-downs read, left to right, *Vessels & Cargo*, *Ports*, *Live Ship Tracking* and *Real-time Location Maps*.

"OK, wild guess," she said. "You want to find

out what ship delivered the pipes. Or that last batch of pipes, anyway. Right?"

Kali nodded. "The ship and the shipping company."

"Can you tell me why? Or are we still free-styling?"

Kali didn't answer. She was back to looking at the computer screen.

"Nope, Tash, I cannot tell you because you're being ignored," Natasha muttered to herself.

A minute passed. Kali clicked on *Vessels & Cargo* to open a new page. It had several search boxes. One instructed the visitor to search for a ship's name and owner by its nine-digit Maritime Mobile Service Identity code, or International Maritime Organization number. There were additional filtering boxes that could narrow the name search to a specific type of vessel, the flag under which it was sailing and the freight carried aboard. She could use one or any combination of the four for her search.

"Too bad there's no date filter," Natasha said. "Major fail."

Kali nodded. "We'll try another site if we have to. But first I want to see what turns up here."

She started her search leaving the MMSI and IMO boxes empty. In the flag box, she typed *People's Republic of China*. In the cargo box, she input the words *marine cable piping*.

Nothing came up.

She made the search more general, typed *cable piping*.

Nothing.

She typed *piping*.

That was too broad. The site kicked out over twelve thousand results. China was the biggest exporter of steel and steel pipes in the world.

Kali sat looking at the screen. Typed *marine cable tubing*.

No results.

She typed *cable tubing*.

Still nothing.

"Try *marine cable conduit*," Natasha said. "Every conduit's a pipe, but not every pipe's a conduit. If that's a bust, it's time to try a thesaurus. Or one of those other sites."

Neither proved necessary.

Kali typed in Natasha's search term, and the screen automatically jump-linked to another page in the website with its own URL. There were still over three thousand hits, but this time there was also a date filter.

She entered the most recent set of dates and departure–arrival locations. What came up was:

Vessel Name: PRCMV *Xingyun Liwu*
Type: Container
Built: 2021
Shipper: Guiding Star Marine Logistics Co., Ltd.

"Lucky Gift," Natasha said.

Kali looked at her.

"*Xingyun Liwu* is Mandarin. And that's how it

translates," Natasha said. "The name of the ship is *Lucky Gift*."

Kali looked at her another second and nodded.

"We should find out who owns Guiding Star… and see how it connects the rest of the Jinggu spiderweb," she said.

Somebody on Meadows Court had called NYPD. Carmody supposed it could have been his crashing a motorcycle through the bungalow's window, or the shooting inside, or the frag grenade exploding on the hillside. It was all just a hair louder than an alarm clock going off on the dozy street.

Be that as it may, he had barely jumped the fence into the backyard when he saw a middle-aged guy with a detective's badge on his sport jacket a few feet away. He snapped his head around to Carmody, his hand dropping to the vicinity of the holster bulge in his jacket.

"Stop right there," he said. "Who the fuck are you?"

"My name's Carmody. Net Force."

The guy grunted. "Got identification?"

"Who's asking?"

"I'm Detective Lombardi."

"Sorry, Lombardi." Carmody raised his open palms chest high as he approached. "I don't."

"What do you mean?"

"I don't carry ID."

"Are you kidding me?"

Carmody shook his head.

"Not worth taking a chance the bad guys get hold of it," he said. "Where's Agent Musil? His girls?"

"Out front," Lombardi said. He motioned toward Carmody's left arm with his chin. The leather sleeve was punctured and slick with blood. "What happened to you?"

"I fell off my ten-speed."

"Must've been one hard fall. You hit a nail or something?"

Carmody looked at him.

"Musil and those kids. They OK?"

"Yeah. Thank God."

Carmody nodded. Lombardi nodded back.

"I got a call from on high about you," he said. "Your people already arrived."

"So why're we wasting time back here?"

Lombardi looked at him. "You come crawling out of the bushes. How am I fucking supposed to know you from Wayne Newton?"

"Wayne Newton?"

"Whoever," Lombardi said. "This is your scene. The body's ours for the morgue."

Carmody raised an eyebrow. "What body?"

"The one in the trunk of the car," Lombardi said. "Looks like he was a rideshare driver."

"How do you know?"

"Because there's a GoRide sticker in his window. And because he kept his registration and insurance card in his glove box, and we ran a check. Some people actually carry their docs."

Carmody stood there a second and said, "I want a look at him."

Lombardi gave a philosophical shrug.

"Your scene, like I told you," he said. "I'll bring you over to the garage so nobody else wastes your precious time."

Carmody followed him around to the front of the bungalow. He saw half a dozen police cruisers with flashing roof racks outside. Also, a crime scene van. And a white Net Force cyber-triage van. The cops were kind of loitering around. The techs looked more purposeful rolling their equipment carts to and from their vehicles.

They went to the garage. Carmody saw at once that the trunk of the car was open. Lombardi brought him over, the photographers and evidence collectors around it parting ranks to open a lane for them.

Carmody bent over the trunk and saw a young man stuffed inside with the side of his head caved in. The trunk liner under the head was saturated and gummy with drying blood.

Carmody looked at Lombardi. "You have his name?"

"Terrence Josephs," Lombardi said. "Twenty-two years old. Guy's barely ripe. Looks like somebody hit him with a brick."

"You know where he made his last pickup?"

Lombardi shook his head. "His phone's gone. Or whatever device he used to log his rides."

"We'll need to contact GoRide to find out."

"Already did," Lombardi said. "I'm waiting for

a callback. Don't think it'll take long. This isn't the kind of situation where they make a stink about sharing the info."

"You'll let me know?"

"Sure. Give me your cell number. Or do you not carry a phone either?"

Carmody nodded and gave it to him. Then he turned and looked out the garage door. Musil was standing near the Seeker with his girls.

"There's a totaled motorcycle inside the bungalow," Lombardi said. "Expensive BMW. Looks like somebody rode it clear through the window."

Carmody didn't say anything.

"I notice you're wearing a biker jacket," Lombardi said.

"So?"

Lombardi shrugged.

"That's a helluva ten-speed you ride," he said. "Very Steve McQueen."

Carmody looked at him.

"Beats Wayne Newton," he said.

The bathroom tiles were spotted with blood. Grigor had found a cheap motel within a five-minute shuttle ride of the airport terminal, booked a corner room on the second floor, and dropped off his backpack. He'd seen a gas station and convenience store across the street from the motel and gone there to buy a first aid kit. It contained sterile gauze, cleansing wipes, a tube of antibiotic ointment and medical tape.

Now he sat on a chair opposite the bathroom's full-length door mirror, wearing only a bloody towel around his waist. His shirt and jacket were soaked red on the side where he was shot, but he had wanted to prevent his pants from getting stained as well.

The entry wound was about a quarter inch in circumference. Smaller than the slug by almost a third. When a bullet punctured human flesh, the skin pulled in around the hole it left behind. It was a natural healing mechanism. The body trying to close the wound.

Grigor didn't think his bleeding was too bad. In fact, it had slowed over the past few hours, convincing him he would not need to stitch the wound shut. If he cleaned and packed it well enough, the flow would stop.

He reached down into the open first aid kit on the floor and used its wipes and ointment to sanitize the wound. Then he got out the roll of gauze, cut a long length with his knife, and folded it into a neat, thick square. He placed it atop the wound and breathed through clenched teeth as he applied steady pressure with his fingertips. Blood squeezed up under the gauze, streamed down his waist and dribbled to the floor, adding new splotches to those on the tiles. But he wanted the gauze to seal the hole in his flesh.

With the gauze pressed down hard on the pad, he reached for the tape and wrapped it around his middle. Two loops, then a third, using nearly the entire roll.

Afterward, he sat breathing deeply and slowly as the pain ebbed from his side. Grigor assumed the bullet had struck a rib after plowing through soft tissue. Otherwise it would have passed straight through him. Probably it had broken apart. But there was no way of knowing how extensively his organs had been damaged in its path. Or which organs. Their internal bleeding was probably worse than what he saw on the outside. Blood could leak into his abdomen and chest. What he had done here was only a stopgap. He would need surgery to remove the fragments and repair whatever injuries they caused.

Still, he thought he would be all right for a while. His flight was in just over two hours. He could rest on board the plane and then conclude his assignment. After that, he would take fuller care of the injury.

Grigor stood up, examined his dressing and gave a satisfied nod. It was clean and tight. He would wipe the blood off the bathroom floor, dispose of the washcloth and towels and get dressed. Then find something to eat before boarding.

In twelve hours, he would be in Oahu. He could manage. The end was close.

Finding out who owned Guiding Star Marine Logistics was as easy for Kali and Natasha as clicking on its company website.

The site opened in English, but was available in Chinese, Russian and French. Based in Shanghai,

China, with offices in Jilin City, Guiding Star was listed as being under the sole proprietorship of its founder, a man named Zhou Bohai.

The About drop-down offered a summary of Bohai's family history and the company origins, which were essentially inseparable. Although Guiding Star had been established in 1986 as a marine freight venture, the Zhou family had proudly claimed its place as a regional shipping giant since the early nineteenth century, when the clan's ancestral patriarch opened an overland trade route to Russia along a portion of the old Silk Road.

Natasha read silently along with Kali as she scrolled down the page, then scrolled back up to a family photograph at the top. According to the credit, it was taken in 2017. Bohai was a bald, jowly man of forty-five or fifty standing with a group of about a dozen relatives: his parents, his siblings and their spouses. The caption below the photo identified each family member and, parenthetically, their relationships to Bohai. On his left in the middle row was a thin, attractive woman about ten years his junior.

Kali tapped a finger to her image on the computer monitor.

"Do you see this woman? The caption names her as Deng Jing. Zhou Bohai's sister," she said. "She's the owner of Seven Winds. The man to Jing's right is her husband, Yannan."

Natasha looked at her. "Wait, back up, head spinning," she said. "The owner of the company that shipped the pipes CloudCable buys from China, Zhou Bohai, is the *brother-in-law* of the guy whose company makes them?"

Kali nodded yes. "Deng Yannan. Owner of Jinggu."

"And Bohai's *sister* and Yannan's wife is Deng Jing, whose company got those twelve very suspect kitchen staffers from Jinggu?"

Kali nodded. "Seven Winds."

"And Seven Winds sent that dirty dozen aboard the *Stalwart*. Where they were ridiculously approved by Grigor. Who was impersonating the ship's boarding agent Stephen Gelfland. Who disappeared last year before the ship sailed and was never seen or heard from again. Kind of exactly like the *Stalwart*."

Kali nodded again. "Guiding Star's shipment of pipes left Shanghai several weeks before the *Stalwart*'s disappearance. Aboard the *Xingyun Liwu*. The *Lucky Gift*. The largest container ship in its fleet."

"And the *Lucky Gift* docked at Honolulu Harbor yesterday."

"Yes."

"And today someone we think is Grigor, who somehow or other got off the *Stalwart*, tried to murder Jot Musil. The agent who's been investigating what happened to the ship," Natasha said. "And who by no coincidence is also investigating what happened to Stephen Gelfland."

"Yes," Kali said. "And we know what's gone on since."

Natasha looked at her. "You think maybe somebody here should be checking out the *Lucky Gift*? Like, at warp fucking flying Hawaiian speed?"

Kali sat in the silent room a moment.

"I do," she said.

Carmody got a lift back to the Terminal in the rear of the Seeker van. There was no digital evidence for it to collect at the scene, so it hadn't stuck around long. The techs told him Harris had sent it out just in case.

Meanwhile, the cops gave Jot Musil and his kids a ride home. Musil had wanted the girls to pick up some of their things before bringing them to a relative's. It was too dangerous for them to stay at their own place with Malkira unaccounted for.

The Seeker was a full cyberforensics laboratory on wheels. Its rear section had creamy fluorescent lighting and looked like the inside of a starship. Computer equipment, control panels, counters and swivel chairs lined the walls. The air was filtered and recycled. Three techs had come out with it. As the van rolled toward Manhattan, Carmody sat in one of the available chairs thinking about things and trying to keep his left arm as still as possible.

They had not yet reached the Queensboro Bridge when his phone rang. The number wasn't familiar, but on a hunch he decided to answer. The hunch proved correct.

"Carmody. It's Lombardi."

"What've you got?"

"You're killing me with pleasantries," Lombardi said. "Wendell Balen. That's the name your man used to book his GoRide."

"You have the trip history?"

"His request was made at one thirty. Pickup spot was a pub called Caswell's. It's on West Fifty-Third off Seventh Avenue."

Carmody was thinking that was just a couple of blocks from where Malkira had ditched the taxi van.

"Balen asked for a couple of stops," Lombardi said. "One was the bungalow on Meadows Court. The next drop-off was LaGuardia Airport. But I assume that was bullshit. He was never really going there."

"You have the pickup time?"

"The driver arrived at the pub at one twenty-eight."

"So he would have gotten to the bungalow around two, two fifteen."

"In decent traffic, yeah. Probably your man had it all set up ahead of time. Killed Josephs right there in the driveway, stashed him in the trunk, drove to the middle school for the kids. It's maybe five minutes away."

"Anything else?"

"I'm assuming the Balen name is an alias. Not that you're going to tell me if I'm right."

Carmody was silent.

"Thought so," Lombardi said. "The credit card

he used is legit, though. Opened in twenty twenty-two. The GoRide account was just opened today."

"Does it have Wendell Balen's address information?"

"GoRide just needs a valid email," Lombardi said. "I can tell you rideshare a lot when you aren't crashing expensive motorcycles through windows."

Carmody was quiet another second. "If the card's for real, the issuer would have a mailing address on file for Balen. Other information from when the account was opened. Somebody had to fill out an application."

"Right."

Carmody grunted. "Got anything else on Balen for me?"

"If I say a case is yours, it's yours," Lombardi said. "I'm not looking for extra work."

Carmody sat quietly as the van rolled on.

"OK," he said. "Thanks for the call."

"Don't mention it, McQueen. You ever feel like telling me what all this is about, I'll cover the beers."

"One or several?"

"Hey, I live my whole life in Queens, it makes me a Mets fan. Doesn't necessarily make me a fucking cheapskate too."

Carmody nodded with the phone to his ear.

"Good to know," he said.

"Some guys have all the luck," said the doctor. The name on her tag was Lina Rae, and she was an acute care surgeon at Mount Sinai West in Hell's Kitchen, about four blocks north of the Terminal.

"When's getting shot ever lucky?" Carmody asked.

He was sitting on a cot in the ER, shirtless, Rae inspecting the dressing she had applied to his forearm with the help of one of the nurses. The privacy curtains were drawn, and an antibiotic solution was dripping into his arm from an IV bag.

"When the bullet misses your artery and doesn't hit bone or nerve tissue because your triceps belongs on a plow horse, leaving very little collateral damage besides the wound," Rae said. "The X-rays show I got most of it out. But I think there are still pieces in your arm."

"You think?"

"You have enough shrapnel inside you to trigger a metal detector. Some of what's in your arm is embedded in scar tissue, so I'm guessing it's been there a while. But I can't absolutely differentiate the new from the old without more scans."

Carmody grunted and glanced up at the IV bag. It had emptied by about a third since she had spiked the back of his left hand. He put his right thumb and forefinger around the needle cap.

"What are you doing?" Rae asked.

"Unhooking."

"You can't do that," she said.

He pulled out the needle, hung the line on the pole and smiled at her. "Wasn't so hard."

She frowned. "You haven't gotten the full round of amoxi. I'd also like you to stay for observation. At least a couple of hours."

He stood up. His T-shirt and jacket hung over the back of a chair near the cot. He reached for the shirt and started putting it on with one hand. It was a clumsy struggle without being able to completely raise and extend his left arm. But he managed to twist and turn and tug it down over his head.

Rae poked her head through the curtain. A moment later, Kali entered the little space.

"Thought you were out in the waiting room," Carmody said.

"I was." She got the jacket off the chair and held it so he could get an arm into the sleeve. "I thought you might need some help."

"I don't."

"Of course not," she said, and went around behind him to assist with the other arm.

Rae was looking at him.

"You weren't admitted, Mr. Carmody, so I can't stop you from leaving as an outpatient," she said. "I strongly recommend that you avoid strenuous activity for a few days. Rest overnight. I'd like to see you back here in a week or so. But I know I won't."

"How can you tell?"

Rae looked at Kali over his shoulder. Kali returned the glance and finished getting him into the jacket.

"Thank you for your patience, Doctor," she said. "Will that be it?"

Rae nodded.

"That's it," she said.

It was six fifteen as Kali and Carmody left the emergency room and turned downtown toward headquarters, the sun in deep decline across the river, the daylight grainy and diffuse over Tenth Avenue. The wailing patrol cars and ambulances that arrived after Ki Marton was killed had left. Traffic had thinned. The office crowd had nearly evaporated. From several blocks north of the hit-and-run, Carmody couldn't see the chalk markings near the crosswalk, but he knew they were still there. It would take a while before they were erased by tires and rain.

His cell rang in his pocket. He thought for a second that it might be Lombardi again. It was Morse.

"Are you feeling all right?" she asked.

"Not really," Carmody said. "What's up?"

"We have something on the Wendell Balen AKA," Morse said. "How close are you?"

Carmody looked a block or two ahead to the Terminal. "If you toss a water balloon off the roof, I'd get plopped."

"I won't add insult to injury," she said. "Hurry up to my office. You're going to want to hear this."

"So talk," Carmody said. "Wendell Balen."

He sat backward in a chair in Carol Morse's office, his legs spread. Morse was sitting behind her desk, Kali and Leo Harris on his side of it.

"The credit card outfit gave us their information," Morse said. "It was good of them. Even with identity theft laws and exigent circumstances, they could have made us wait for the paperwork."

"What about Balen?" Carmody said.

"The card is for his business account. A Durham, North Carolina, address. I had our people check it out, and it's valid. His company is Fancy Food Marketing. Wholesale imports and exports. Balen founded it about eight years ago."

"We get his contact information?"

She nodded. "I was able to reach his warehouse and talk to a company officer who was working late. She told me Balen's been traveling for the past month." A pause. "That's what he does. Travels and makes deals. His current trip is to Ukraine. Specifically, Crimea."

Carmody looked at her. "You're kidding."

Morse shook her head. "Our government slapped a partial embargo on trade with Crimea. Because of the Russian occupation. But the ban exempts certain food and agriculture products, and Balen applied for a license. His secretary said he's there buying some kind of honey. For distribution to foodie shops here in this country."

"Present tense?"

"That's the kicker. His trip was combined business and vacation. He left for Europe last month.

The last time he checked in with his company was two weeks ago. From Simferopol."

"Seems a while."

"The secretary thought so. But it *was* partly a vacation."

"Balen have family?"

"He's divorced, no kids. Lives alone. Travels solo. Ring a bell?"

"It's Stephen Gelfland all over again," Leo said. "Bet anything his picture was also deepfaked on the internet."

"It was on his passport," Morse said. "We've already checked out DoS records."

Leo looked at her. "I don't know where the Chinese fit into the picture. But Crimea, Malkira, the hacks…this whole thing says Russia."

"And the Wolf," Kali said.

"That's an assumption," Morse said.

"No. Drajan Petrovik has the resources and technical ability for the operation. He's been with the Russians since escaping Romania. And deepfake hacks were a speciality of his partner. Emil Vasile."

"The guy Dixon killed in Bucharest," Carmody said.

Kali nodded. "They were close when I knew them. Like brothers. He would have taught Drajan."

Morse looked at her. "And you waited till now to tell us?"

Kali said nothing.

"Why?" Morse said.

Kali said nothing.

Carmody said, "Let's drop it for now."

"No," Morse said. "Ki Marton is dead. One of my agents was nearly killed with him. Musil's daughters were fucking kidnapped. And *you're* sitting here with a hole in your arm." She looked at Kali, her eyes furious. "Why didn't you tell us about Petrovik's acquired deepfake skills before?"

Kali exhaled. A long, slow breath.

"Because he is my responsibility," she said. "Because his cyberattack on New York is partly my responsibility. And the destruction of Janus Base in Romania. Drajan accomplished both using code he stole from me."

Morse looked at her. "You could have shared all that with us months ago. It could have helped us stop him."

"Until a few hours ago, I expected to be flying to Crimea to do that," Kali said. "I couldn't be sure any information I shared with you was safe from him."

Morse shook her head. "No. That doesn't wash. Screw you and your secrets. I should have listened to Howard all along."

Silence in the room. Kali crossed her arms and looked at her. "Think whatever you choose. It's your right."

"Duchess, my two cents," Carmody said, "I think Petrovik wants scenes like this. Wants everyone and everything in the world going at it. China, Russia, the United States. All of us in this room. I think he wants to see the sky fall down."

"You don't know that," Morse said. "It's an opinion again."

"Maybe. But it's his MO. Based on what I do know."

Morse took a breath, turning to Kali again. "I presume you haven't had a chance to tell Mike about the cargo ship?"

She shook her head.

Carmody looked from one to the other. "What are you talking about?"

"In a minute," Morse said. "Let's get back to Wendell Balen. I told you he contacted his secretary two weeks ago. He'd cut the specialty honey deal, and was supposed to be heading back to the States to meet with potential retail distributors. New York was first up in his itinerary. Then Hawaii."

Carmody was quiet a moment. Then he said, "You think Malkira might be headed there?"

Morse looked at him.

"He's already on his way," she said.

19

Teterboro Airport, New Jersey

Nick DeBattista was about to head home from the airport for the night when his phone rang.

"Great Circle Charter."

"Nick. Carmody."

"Great. I'm hanging up."

"I need to get to Hawaii."

"I'm hanging up."

"There'll be the same number of passengers as before."

"What *before*? There was no *before*. I got my Falcon ready for you at a huge financial loss to myself. I won't even give you the dollar figure. But you crapped out."

"When can you have it ready for me?"

"Fuck you, Carmody. I was flying you to Romania today. I had my fucking bags packed."

"Nick—"

"Don't *Nick* me. You think I run a bus line for old ladies playing the slots in Atlantic City? You were getting a Falcon. Practically a fighter jet. A fucking Mach nine-two-five fighter jet. For free."

"Nick, I need it tonight."

"Yeah, well, of course. I just told you. It isn't happening."

"What time can you have it ready?"

"Take care, Carmody. Enjoy the rest of your life. And go fuck yourself while you're at it."

"Nick. I need to get to Hawaii right away. I need the plane. And this time I can get you paid."

DeBattista stared out the window of his office trailer, the receiver to his ear.

"You hit the lottery or something?"

"I'm talking government funds."

"Seriously?"

"I'll tell you who to bill. You settle up with them."

DeBattista was silent. The sky to the west was streaked with orange and purple. The day was almost over. He had planned to go home, order in for dinner, pour a couple of glasses of wine and maybe listen to some relaxing opera music for the rest of the night.

But figure this run was officially for Uncle Sam, he could bitch about the short notice and add a nice, big pile of official bucks to his usual rates.

"Where in Hawaii you going?" he asked.

"Oahu."

He did some rough mental calculations.

"It's after six o'clock. The Falcon's all fueled up. But I'm doing my preflights from scratch. I don't give a fuck if you like it or not. That's how it goes with me, dig?"

"Yeah."

"We leave at ten tonight. I'll have you there by seven in the morning."

"OK."

"That's nine hours. Nobody else could do it in less than eleven."

"OK."

"Don't be late," DeBattista said.

He hung up without another word, looking across the room at his luggage bag. He had already stowed it on the plane when Carmody canceled before, and here it was back in the office, and it aggravated him. He really didn't appreciate being jerked around. But he knew Carmody. He'd heard his tone of voice on the phone, and it sounded like there was some major shit going down. Pissed off or not, he'd probably have flown him for free, not that he would ever let him know.

DeBattista rose to turn off the lights and lock up the trailer. Ten minutes later he was rolling his bag back out to the hangar in the cool early dusk.

Fourteen miles across the Hudson River, Carmody walked toward the entrance to a metal skybridge connecting the Terminal's main building to its smaller adjunct, where he had arranged to meet Dixon, Long and Kali down on the ground floor. With its tin ceiling and crank windows, the skybridge dated back to when a New York traffic jam meant the milkman's horse cart had lost an axle and stalled the ice wagon behind it on the cobblestones.

The Fusion Center leading to the skybridge was filled with workstations arranged along spacious aisles. Men and women with FBI, NYPD and Homeland Security ID tags mingled with Net Force personnel at the computers and wall screens. This was where they came to pool their resources when conducting investigations requiring interagency cooperation.

Carmody was surprised to see Jot Musil as he reached the skybridge's door.

"What are you doing here?" he said.

"Looking for you." Musil stepped over to him. "One of the security people said he'd seen you come up."

Carmody cocked a thumb back over his shoulder. "There's an empty office. I had to make a call."

Musil nodded. Carmody looked at him.

"What I meant," he said, "was that I thought you would be home with your girls."

Musil nodded again. He had showered the grit out of his hair and changed his clothes. But he looked wiped out.

"Jani and Raysa are at their uncle and aunt's," he said. "Morse arranged for an ESU detail to watch the house. Police special operations."

"Good," Carmody said. "It would be better if their dad's around to hug them."

Musil bowed his head slightly.

"You saved their lives," he said. "Thank you."

"You had a part in it."

"Without you, Malkira would have killed us all."

"Maybe." Carmody shrugged. "I still don't understand why you came here tonight."

"Morse told me you have an idea where he's gone."

"She say what we're thinking about that?"

Musil shook his head. "She wouldn't be specific. She feels the same as you do. That I should go home and leave it to you."

"She's right."

"No," Musil said. "It isn't over. Malkira's out there somewhere. He could try to hurt my girls again."

"I'll see that he won't."

"I want to help."

Carmody looked at him. "I already have my team," he said. "We're leaving tonight."

"Where to?"

"Hawaii," Carmody said. "Six thousand miles from here. Your family needs you to be with them."

"If Grigor Malkira has left New York, he's no threat to them right now."

Carmody was quiet a moment.

"Something big is going on. It's more than him. It's the *Stalwart*, and it's a whole lot of other stuff."

"I know."

"I know you know. I'm just saying that whatever we're headed into is going to be dangerous as hell."

"I need to help."

"Stay here with your family."

Musil shook his head.

"It would be the easier choice," he said. "But you were a soldier. You are a warrior. You know that sometimes you can't stay. Sometimes you have to leave to protect them."

Carmody was quiet, his eyes holding steadily on his face. Several long seconds passed. At last, he nodded his head toward the entrance to the skybridge.

"Come on," he said. "They're waiting downstairs."

Carmody and Musil crossed the skybridge to the adjunct, then got in an elevator and took it down as far as it went.

They stepped out into a corridor with a uniformed guard at its head. On his shoulder was the Quickdraw patch of Net Force's rapid response team.

Quickdraw was primarily meant to do its work overseas. In founding principle, the Force did not have the same legal jurisdiction to conduct armed missions within the United States as the FBI, Homeland Security or local police departments. Under the umbrella of protective operations, however, it could do so in support of those agencies, as well as the National Guard and Coast Guard. It therefore had some flexibility participating in law-enforcement and intelligence operations.

It was prepared, in other words.

Carmody nodded at the guard, and they stepped past him to a large steel door. It was a foot thick and insulated for fire protection. The metal security notices on and above it stated no unauthorized personnel were permitted into the area beyond. A key code and biometric identification were required for entry.

Carmody touched his thumb to the reader and tapped in the code. He and Musil walked through.

Each of the rooms lining the corridor beyond required additional biometric entry. Equipment storage was a broad category, but they were designed according to a similar interior blueprint. Their shelving and cabinets were mounted onto motor-powered, cantilevered carriage and rail systems, so there were no fixed aisles. Touch-pad controls on the face panels of the shelves moved the units together and apart like huge metal book covers. Some of the rooms were filled with advanced communications, surveillance and computing technology.

Carol Morse, Dixon, Schultz, Kali and Natasha Mori were waiting in the Terminal's armory. Its stainless steel shelves pulled out and opened wide and shifted around to reveal racks and cabinets designed for long guns, assault rifles, explosive projectile weapons and pistols. There was a steel armorer's desk and workbench. There was shelving stacked with cases of ammunition. There was an explosives storage unit. An optics unit. A walk-in unit containing body armor.

Carmody entered a step ahead of Musil and looked at everyone's faces.

"Gang's all here," he said.

The black Rhino GX SUV arrived at Great Circle's private terminal at a quarter past nine. The edge lights were on along the runway, and the Falcon sat warming up in the brightness of the floods.

The Rhino rolled up onto the apron, coming almost planeside before it stopped. Carmody and his group got out the rear, Morse staying in front with the driver.

Outside the aircraft, DeBattista was talking to a couple of his mechanics and the driver of a wheeled cargo belt loader. He broke off his conversation as Carmody walked up to him.

"Tell me I'm not dreaming." DeBattista pinched his arm. "You actually showed on time."

Carmody looked at him. "I wish you liked me better."

"Ask me if I give a shit," DeBattista said. "So what's going aboard with you?"

"A couple wooden crates. A few small bags."

"What's in the bags?"

"Mostly clothes."

"And the crates?"

"Odds and ends."

DeBattista looked over at the group standing by the Rhino.

"I didn't know Dixon and Schultz were with you."

"Well, now you do."

"Who are the other ones?"

"Friends."

DeBattista's gaze held on Kali. "I like the friend with the dark hair."

"Put your eyes back in your head," Carmody said. "You'll need them to fly the plane."

"She the one who lets you ride her motorcycle?"

"She did."

"Don't tell me."

Carmody shrugged. "Accidents happen."

DeBattista looked at him.

"Those *odds and ends*," he said. "They going to blow us out of the air?"

"Only if they get tossed around."

"Oh, well, hey." DeBattista gestured toward the guy in the cargo loader. "Eddie will take care of the bags and crates. You can all get aboard in the meantime. Wheels up in twenty minutes."

"OK."

Carmody went back to the Rhino and held a finger up to Kali, Natasha, Dixon, Schultz and

Musil. Then he went around to Morse's window and waited as she lowered it.

"Well, you're off," she said.

"Almost."

"Captain Harper will meet you at Barbers Point."

"Right."

"You'll coordinate with him. There's to be no independent action."

"You bet."

Morse looked at him for a long moment. "How's your arm?"

"The one without the bullet hole's terrific."

She smiled.

"Godspeed, Mike. Keep me updated."

Carmody nodded and stepped back from the door. Morse's window rose. He rejoined the others, and they walked across the tarmac and went up the boarding ladder into the plane.

New York is six hours ahead of Hawaii on the world clock, and it was a quarter to eleven on Friday night when Grigor Malkira's plane landed at Daniel K. Inouye International Airport. A moderate tailwind had shaved forty minutes off the trip.

Outside the terminal, he got into a yellow cab and took it to Honolulu Harbor. There was almost no traffic on the Nimitz Highway, and the ride was fast.

"Drop me off in the parking area behind Pier 1," he told the driver.

"Where exactly, sir? It's pretty big."

"I'll let you know."

The cab driver nodded and turned into the expansive lot. Grigor directed him to a low flat white-walled commercial office building near the waterfront.

Jochi was waiting outside alone.

"This is it," Grigor told the driver. "Right here."

The driver stopped to let him out. He saw Jochi's tall, broad silhouette a few yards away in the darkness and looked nervous. Grigor paid his fare in cash, exited the cab and watched him turn quickly back toward the road.

The night was clear with light breezes off the water. He inhaled the briny air.

"How was your flight?" Jochi asked.

"It got me here."

Jochi grunted, nodded to his left. The colossal hulk of the *Xingyun Liwu* was visible just east of the white building.

"We're nearly ready," he said.

Grigor looked at him.

"Take me to the ship," he said. "I want to see for myself."

Kali sat quietly beside Carmody in the Falcon's passenger cabin. Their rotating chairs were like personal islands. They were huge and cushiony and dove-colored, with wraparound backs and high wing arms. The carpeting was a plush camel tone. There were lounges and tables and a dining area, and there was a galley with a full bar and wine refrigerator and shelves of fluted glasses. The lavatory floors were tiled in white marble.

The group was spread out in the cabin. Schultz and Dixon were at a table playing cards. Natasha had stretched out on a lounge and gone to sleep. Carmody glanced over at Kali and noticed she was looking at Musil. He was in a chair about a mile up toward the front of the cabin, wide awake, seemingly preoccupied with his thoughts. He had said little to anyone since they left the Terminal.

"Brave guy," Carmody said to her.

She nodded. "He is committed to his values," she said. "You didn't tell me he was coming with us."

"He just showed up at the Terminal. I tried to talk him into staying home."

"And he talked you out of it."

Carmody nodded. "I guess he hit a soft spot. Said something about warriors leaving the people they love to protect them." He paused. "Imagine how it used to be. Before cell phones. Before the internet. Soldiers, thousands of miles away from their wives and kids. By the time they got news from each other it was two months out of date."

Kali looked at him and drew closer and placed a hand on top of his on his armrest, her fingertips curling around to the fleshy part of his palm. His hand was twice the size of hers. He closed it around her fingers and squeezed them very gently.

"Kali—"

"Shhh... Michael."

He looked at her. Her hand in his on the armrest. She leaned over and touched her lips to his and held them there a long second. Her mouth was barely open. Their breaths overlapped and intermingled. She moved her head sideways and inhaled through her nose and smelled his cheek. He felt her inhalation against his skin. He felt her closeness. It tickled slightly and made his throat tighten up. She leaned back.

They sat with their hands together on the armrest another moment and then slowly pulled them apart.

"I think we need to talk," he said.

She looked into his eyes and nodded.

"In time," she said.

It was after midnight when President Annemarie Fucillo's cell phone rang in the Oval Office study. Not the phone provided by the Secret Service but the one she had owned for years before being elected chief executive—the flip phone people in the White House called the First Phone, to go with the First Cat. After a bit of wrangling, she had hashed out a compromise with her security team, permitting a few modifications to its O/S and settings, and agreeing to use it only to communicate with senior advisers and a nucleus of her closest friends. The tweaks and limited usage made it about as secure as her official phone. But when she answered it, she knew she wouldn't live to regret hearing from the caller.

In this instance, it was Carol Morse. Who had been a trusted friend and confidant long before she became one of Fucillo's primary appointments at Net Force. And who had just hours ago lost a man to a mysterious hit-and-run.

"Carol! How are you?"

"I'm fine, Marie…"

Fucillo was thinking she didn't sound fine. She was also thinking Morse was not a hopeless insomniac like herself, and that her calling at this hour was anything but the norm.

"You've had a rough day," Fucillo said.

"Not too many are easy lately," Morse said. "A lot's happening here. You'll find out the details in your morning briefing. But I didn't want to put off updating you."

Fucillo nodded. "OK, shoot," she said, and sat listening to everything Morse had to tell her about the *Stalwart* disappearance, Grigor Malkira, the kidnapping of Musil's daughters, and the connection it all seemingly had to a container ship docked in Hawaii.

"Do you honestly think there's something aboard that ship we should worry about?"

"We'll find out," Morse said. "But nothing feels right. The Chinese are definitely involved. The question is how? Is it their government? Or parties *inside* the government?"

"Which makes all the difference."

"Yes."

"Especially if those parties have ties to Russia."

"And that's how this fish smells."

Fucillo was quiet a moment on the phone. "I wish we had hard evidence that Moscow's somehow in the middle of this," she said. "Something I could hold up to see how they react."

"So do I. And maybe we can find it," Morse said. "In the meantime, I'm thinking President Tsao might want to chat with his sister and brother-in-law. *Whatever* is going on, that couple is in it up to their necks."

"Would you suggest I speak with Tsao about them?"

"If you're really asking, I would advise it," Morse said. "Both our countries have too much to lose if things play out badly."

Fucillo nodded to herself.

"I'll make the call," she said, and paused. "Aside from all this—you're really OK?"

Morse was quiet.

"Carol?"

"There's some personal stuff," she said.

Fucillo sat a moment, her forehead scrunching with concern.

"We should have lunch very soon," she said.

Once aboard the *Xingyun Liwu*, Jochi led Grigor forward on the weather deck past tiers of containers stacked as high as four-story buildings. Washed with light, the latitudinal and longitudinal aisles between the stacks were wide enough for two cars driving side by side, and with ample clearance.

There were four deck hatches, one for each of the stowage holds running the length of the ship on its lower deck. All were covered with multiple steel panels controlled by pneumatic lifting mechanisms. Hatch Number One was behind the ship's forepeak, just aft of the bow.

Jochi stopped near the sign marking it off on deck, pulled a red LED light wand from inside his jacket and held it up over his head. Sixty feet above him in a modular hut, a man toggled a switch on his instrument console.

The hatch cover's steel panels slowly began to move upward with a mechanical grinding noise. They rose vertically twenty feet above the deck, then slid back to open the colossal hatch, folding together like giant playing cards. Simple cargo elevators led straight down into the hold from three of the open hatch's four sides.

Jochi motioned to the one nearest him. It was a few feet over to his right.

"Be careful," he said. "It's quite a plunge."

He stepped onto the platform, waited for Grigor and pressed a button. It started to descend.

A vertical shaft running through the ship from top to bottom, Hatch Number One went straight down for hundreds of feet into the *Xingyun Liwu*'s deepest bowels. Grigor held the elevator's curved metal guard rail, peering into the expansive converted boat bay below. It was very well and evenly illuminated, allowing him to see the fast attack boats waiting three in line on their launch ramp.

Chinese Gahjae-class semisubmersibles, they were gray and wedge-shaped, like shark heads.

The platform reached bottom and halted with a decisive bounce, prompting a hot jab of pain in Grigor's abdomen. His face gave no hint of it.

Jochi got off the platform. Grigor let go of the handrail and followed. He saw men moving around the boats.

He walked along the side of the ramp with Jochi, looking them over. They were small—fifty feet from bow to stern—and could be operated with a crew of two or three, each vessel carrying several additional passengers.

"The guard at Kono Head changes at five thirty in the morning," Jochi said. "Sunrise is at six o'clock. We'll deploy at four."

Grigor looked at him. "No," he said. "We need to go sooner. Can you do that?"

"How much sooner?"

Grigor glanced at his watch. "It's ten to midnight. I'll give your men an hour. Then we'll get the boats out of here and into position."

Jochi was surprised.

"What brings this on?"

"I have my reasons," Grigor said. "Tell me the top speed of these boats."

"Upward of fifty knots. That's on the surface."

"And under?"

"About half."

"At how many feet?"

"Between sixty or seventy. They aren't made for great depth."

Grigor calculated mentally. A statute mile of 5,280 feet measured distances over land. A nautical mile was 6,076 feet. And one knot as a rate of speed equaled a nautical mile per hour. So the conversion differential was 1.15.

It was simple multiplication. The Gahjaes could travel nearly sixty miles an hour at the land rate. About thirty submerged. And thirty was slower than he preferred. But what they lost in velocity would be gained in stealth.

Grigor didn't want to stick around the ship. All along he had thought himself well ahead of the people investigating the *Stalwart*. But he'd also thought Musil would come to the bungalow alone. He had prepared for the eventuality that he wouldn't as a precaution. But *only* as a precaution.

He had been wrong about Musil, misjudged him, very possibly taken him too lightly. The truth, though, was that he was more concerned about the madman who had crashed through the bungalow's window. Literally crashed his plan. Although, the truth was there was no planning for someone like that. No fooling himself about him. Grigor had seen the look in his eyes. It told him who he was dealing with. He would find his way here before too long. Which meant he had to move quickly to outpace him.

"I want to wash up," he said. "Change into fresh clothes. Get something to eat. Can you arrange it?"

"Yes. I'll see to everything."

Grigor nodded. "Also, I need some first aid supplies."

"Are you all right?"

"I have a cut," Grigor said. "It's nothing."

Jochi eyed him a moment.

"The crew cabins are on the other side of the bulkhead," he said and nodded aft. "You can use mine for privacy."

He turned and walked along the line of fast boats toward the steel bulkhead door. Grigor followed, his side pulsing, the taste of copper on his tongue. With Jochi's back to him, he wiped his arm across his mouth and gave it a secretive glance.

There was blood on it.

20

April 19–20, 2024
Hawaii

The Falcon descended into Kalaeloa Airport shortly before one in the morning. The tower had directed DeBattista to an extension situated at the far southwestern edge of the island and reserved for the Fourteenth District Coast Guard. The fleet of aircraft on the tarmac, all white with orange bands, consisted of several Ocean Sentry medium-range patrol planes, a long-range sub-chaser, a Lockheed HC-130H search and rescue aircraft, an MH-65 Dolphin helicopter, a Hercules transport and some amphibious water jumpers.

Three JLTVs were waiting near the runway with their lights on, a group of men and women in blue uniforms standing outside them. Carmody climbed down the ladder ahead of the others, looked around for the one with five stripes on his insignia, and saw him approach with his arm extended.

"I'm Captain Aaron Harper," he said. "Welcome to Oahu. Hell of a sweet plane you've got there."

Carmody shook his hand.

"Beats flying coach," he said. "You and your people look plenty awake for this hour."

Harper smiled. "A call from the director of Net Force is enough to knock all the tired out of me," he said. "Can't say it wasn't a surprise. But from what I understand, there's a chance we'll have to hit the ground running."

Carmody nodded. Thirty or thirty-five, Harper was thin and tall, with short sandy-blond hair, alert eyes and sharp cheekbones. He looked and sounded like he was from Missouri and belonged on a white horse.

"How much did Carol Morse tell you about why we're here?" Carmody asked.

"Actually, I spoke with Director Michaels," Harper said. "To be honest, he didn't say a whole lot. I was told we need to take a close look at a cargo ship in the harbor. He was clear it couldn't wait."

Carmody nodded again. Behind him, everyone was getting off the plane.

"There someplace we can talk?" he said.

"We'll bring you and your people to the station. It's four minutes from here if we putter over." He motioned toward a JLTV. "Come on, I'm driving that one."

Carmody fell in alongside him.

"Sure," he said.

They reached the complex in three minutes. Harper hadn't quite puttered.

United States Coast Guard Air Station Barbers Point edged on a wide strip of beach across the water from a humpbacked coral atoll. The JLTVs turned into an entry road bordered by tall royal palms, passed a checkpoint booth with an orange stucco roof and pulled up to one of the buildings.

Carmody exited a moment ahead of Harper and stood facing west. He felt the nearness of the sea. He saw the dark outline of the atoll rising in the distance. He remembered his long days on the beaches outside Lanai City when he was nine and ten and eleven. Sometimes he would grab some of the boys from school, hike out to the dunes and climb up to the old concrete pillbox with the American flag painted on its side, pretending they were soldiers, there to defend the shore against evil invaders. Sometimes he went alone to look for shells and starfish or sit for hours to watch the clouds and identify them by their shapes.

He realized Kali had come up to him.

"This place reminds me of Malta," she said. "It has a life apart."

Carmody looked at her. "I grew up not far from

here," he said. "Lanai's about eighty miles due east. There's a ferry across."

She nodded silently. Harper had gotten out his door, and they turned to join him. Then the three of them went over to the others gathering outside the JLTVs.

"We prepared a conference room," Harper said. "There's coffee and snacks."

Carmody looked at him. "Musubi?"

"Homemade," Harper said. "This is Hawaii."

Carmody smiled a little. "Keep it up and you'll be stuck with me," he said.

The twelve stepped down into the Gahjaes through hatches on their upper decks, giving each boat an infiltration team of four. Their Chinese marine night camouflage was lightweight, with patterns of black and gray. The loose-fitting jackets left room for them to wear their body armor without restricted movement. They wore ballistic helmets, balaclavas, and flip-down night-vision goggles.

The men were all armed to the teeth. They carried the TP9s they had used to take the *Stalwart*. They carried Glock 19 Gen4 handguns with flashlights and laser sights. They all had pouches filled with smoke and explosive throwables. Most carried People's Liberation Army–issue QJZ-39 lightweight heavy machine guns, several had brought Beretta 40 mm projectile launchers, and one man in each team bore a Hawk Type 97 semiautomatic combat shotgun, manufactured in China like the machine guns.

Jochi lowered himself aboard the second boat, Niu the third. Grigor waited until the rest were inside and then slipped into the first boat in line. He had the same uniform and gear as the others. Additionally, he carried the dagger Jochi had prepared for him, its blade coated with tetrodotoxin—one of the most lethal poisons known to man. Three milligrams were enough to freeze the muscles that controlled the breathing reflex.

The launch took under ten minutes. With the Gahjaes fully crewed, one of the boat bay operators used a touch screen to open a hatch above the water's surface. Another touch of his panel and two robotic side brackets locked round the first boat, one on each side of its hull. Articulated like human arms, they moved the boat down the ramp's keel rollers to the hatch, then gently prodded it into the harbor water.

It slid down beneath the surface and disappeared, followed by the second boat, and then the third.

They turned out of the channel into deep water, following the curve of the island, bearing northeast toward the cove at Kono Beach.

The nine people around the conference table in leather chairs included the entire Net Force contingent, Captain Harper, and a pair of his aides: a lieutenant named Kara Lee and a lieutenant JG named Matt Baylor. A refreshments room had been set up down the hall with coffee, tea, bottled water, muffins, sliced mango and pineapples, and the station cook's vaunted musubi.

Carmody took about twenty minutes to bring Harper's group up to snuff. They mostly listened, asking very few questions. It was about two in the morning when he finished.

"So we're trying to find out what happened to Grigor Malkira, and we're trying to find out what might be aboard that container ship," Harper said. "And its purpose."

"Boiling it all down, yeah," Carmody said.

"One thing," Harper said. "How could he have gotten past airport security at this end?"

"Easy," Carmody said. "He probably had a backup alias. Malkira gets off the plane, the TSA guards ask for his ID, he shows them the second set. As far as TSA's concerned, valid documents are enough. They're looking for Wendell Balen. He's already somebody else. Nine times out of ten they won't check the passenger list to see if that second person really boarded at the gate."

"How about the police? Wouldn't there be a BOLO if Michaels put them on notice?"

"They require written legal authorization to access the list, and that has to go through the airline's legal department," Musil said. "They would have no chance of accessing today's list at short notice. Not this time of night when the offices are closed. And passport chips are normally impossible to fake. If he had an alternate and it passed as authentic, he would have walked out of the airport without a problem."

Harper lifted a water bottle off the table and drank.

"Pardon my French, but I don't need any of that shit to board the ship," he said. "The Coast Guard has sweeping constitutional authority. They can't stop us."

"You'd better plan on everyone on it carrying guns," Natasha said. "If Grigor's with them, they'll be waiting with a plan."

There was a short silence. Harper looked down the table to where she sat next to Kali.

"Michaels told me a little about him," he said. "We'll be prepared."

Carmody asked, "What's the number of crew on one of those boats?"

"Between twenty-five and thirty, usually," Harper said.

"So few? Even for one that big?"

Lee was nodding in the affirmative. "My father worked on containers until he retired. All a cargo ship does is go from here to there. It isn't on military or scientific operations. Or laying cable like the *Stalwart*. It just needs a minimal crew complement according to international manning regulations."

"That's if they're just moving cargo," Schultz said. "We don't know what else they've got aboard."

"My guess is they wouldn't overload it," Carmody said. "If thirty's about right, they won't risk too many more. They'd try to make everything look normal so nobody pays attention to them." He looked intently at Harper. "Can you muster up fifteen of your best? Even this time of night?"

"You're in luck. We've got a new PSU—Port Security Unit—here at Barbers. I can give you more than that if you need them."

Carmody shook his head. "Fifteen's plenty. More's a crowd."

Harper nodded. "OK," he said. "What else?"

"A couple of harbor patrol boats. Something up in the air. So we make an instant impression." Carmody paused. "That's it, unless you have any other thoughts."

Harper was quiet a moment.

"Maybe one," he said.

Submarines were fairly slow travelers. This was true of even the most streamlined nuclear-powered boats, which could reach a maximum speed of fifty miles per hour or so. Such was the drag of water on the vessel's outer skin—*water resistance*, in layman's terms—that it could not go any faster without sustaining critical structural damage. The H2O molecules rubbing up against it created friction, and the friction would slow it down...and even tear it apart if it accelerated past a certain speed threshold.

The drone submarine was radically different. This was because of several innovations creating an effect known as supercavitation, a process by which pressurized gas ejected from rapidly spinning nozzles in the forward section of the vessel formed a kind of bubble, or envelope, around its entire hull, nose to tail.

Because of that bubble, the skin of a supercavitating submarine would never come in contact with the water. Thus, there was no friction. No drag. Nothing to keep it from shooting through the ocean like a submerged rocket.

The initial classified research for the technology making this possible had been conducted between 2000 and 2014 in the People's Republic of China—specifically at the state-funded Harbin Institute of Technology's Complex Flow and Heat Transfer Lab. The head of the development team was one Li Fengchen, a professor of fluid machinery and engineering. Subsequent work was done over the next decade both at Harbin and the Beijing Institute of Technology.

By the time Russia hacked the sub's design specification in 2023, Chinese scientists had overcome nearly all the obstacles to its construction and operation.

In Crimea, the Russians went about building their own.

At fifty miles per hour, a conventional nuclear submarine would need over a week to travel from the Crimean Peninsula to Hawaii.

The drone, traveling at roughly a thousand miles an hour—its midrange speed, which was faster than the speed of sound in dry air—had come close within seven *hours* of its launch.

Its voyage from the Simferopol bunker had first led it south through the Black Sea into the narrow Bosporus between Bulgaria and Turkey into the Sea of Marmara. From there it swung sharply west into the Mediterranean, skirting past Laconia in southern Greece, then making a linear fifteen-hundred-mile traverse above Africa's northern coast to enter the Tyrrhenian Sea between Tunisia and the boot of Italy. Off Valencia, Spain, it had curved south and west past the heaving limestone massif at Gibraltar to spit itself out into the open North Atlantic.

Then a southward turn between the Portuguese Azores and the Gold and Ivory Coasts of West Africa. Down into the South Atlantic, east around Cape Town, and north past Madagascar into the Indian Ocean. Four thousand miles farther east in a smooth, easy arc that took it through the Torres Strait above Australia into the Coral Sea and then the North Pacific. There the submarine bore north by northeast past the Solomon Islands, the Republic of Nauru and the Marshall Islands, to finally come to rest underwater, hovering at a depth of three thousand feet north of the Kure and Midway Atolls.If someone had drawn vertical north–south ruler lines connecting the two atolls to the submarine's location on the map, and then a horizontal east–west line between the atolls, it would have formed an isosceles triangle with the drone at its vertex.

And there it lurked roughly two hundred-fifty

miles southwest of Oahu, Hawaii, waiting for a signal to get back on the move. And strike.

It was half past two in the morning when the Dolphin jumped into the sky from Air Station Barbers Point, then banked slightly east over Mamala Bay. Notified in advance of its flight, the control tower at Pearl Harbor-Hickam radioed the pilot to confirm he had a clear lane to Honolulu Harbor.

Also at two thirty, a pair of twenty-nine-foot small-crew United States Coast Guard cutters swung from their berths at Hickam into Kalihi Channel. Rounding the east side of Sand Island, they buzzed down to the Pier 1 anchorage and moved into position alongside the *Xingyun Liwu*.

Their searchlights speared the ship's hull. Overhead, the Dolphin spun toward the ship and hovered in place above its deck, bathing its stacks of containers in the glare of high-intensity xenon floods.

The three orange-and-white USCG land vehicles—two Lenco BearCats followed by a thirteen-ton computer/communications truck—left Barbers Point first and arrived last. They had made the big loop north on the H-1, swinging below Ewa-Schofield Junction and then down past Pearl Harbor and the Shafter Flats barracks to the quay.

The BearCats' rack lights were flashing carnival patterns into the darkness as their rear hatches opened and the boarding team poured out. Carmody, Dixon, Schultz, and Musil arrived in the lead BearCat, along with Harper and seven of his men. The other eight from PSU Hawaii exited the second BearCat. Kali and Natasha Mori were in the C2 truck with its driver and three additional technical personnel.

The coast guards were in ballistic helmets, camouflage and vests. They carried M4A1 carbines, Remington 12-gauges and compact versions of the Sig P226 in Carmody's sidearm holster. Carmody's group wore midnight-black stealthsuits and carried M249 light machine guns with Bluetooth-enabled optics. They had HIVE-compatible A/R flip-down goggles on their helmets. All had secure channel radio-over-IP headsets.

Carmody looked up at the *Xingyun Liwu*'s starboard hull. A metal gangway ran from the dock to deck. He turned to Harper.

"OK, let's do this," he said.

The gangway had about seventy risers, one for every foot of height. He led the men up, Harper behind him, then the rest. The clanging of their boots was loud in the night.

Carmody sprang off the gangway and was momentarily blinded by the light shafting down from the Dolphin. Then his eyes adjusted. Men were bustling around the deck in a state of stunned confusion, shouting at each other and the boarders.

"Who speaks English?" he shouted.

No answer.

"Who speaks English?"

No answer.

"Who speaks English?"

"I do. What's going on? Who are you?"

Carmody turned. The man was in officer's whites, a diamond and three bars on his epaulets. *Chief Officer.* His shirt was sticking out of his pants on one side: he must have hurried out of bed to get dressed.

"Where's your captain?"

"He's asleep."

"Bullshit. Get him up here."

"What do you want? You have no right to board this vessel."

"We're the only ones here with rights," Carmody said. "So get your captain. Tell him it's the United States Coast Guard. Tell him we're searching the ship with or without his permission. He's got two minutes."

21

April 20, 2024
Hawaii

The Gahjaes remained submerged until they were well past the mouth of the Hanauma Bay crescent and about five hundred yards from Kono Head. Jochi knew the juts and spurs of the coastline west of the head were mostly too rugged to allow for landing. But he had reconnoitered a small notch near Kahauloa Cove where the current swirled into the rocks and became trapped in a kind of button-hook, forming a calm, sheltered tidal pool.

Releasing ballast now, the boats surfaced, pulled into the notch and stopped in the shallows. They had gone as far as possible without running aground.

After a minute their hatches opened, and Grigor, Jochi and the men got out. Knee-deep in water, loaded with gear, they waded through the tide pool onto the little beachhead and began their short hike east toward the landing station.

As they climbed up over the rocks, the Gahjaes left the notch and turned in the same direction. They rode low in the water, fanning out to avoid each other's wakes, staying close to the dark and jagged shore.

The *Xingyun Liwu*'s captain did not quite show up in two minutes, but he made it close. Carmody saw him standing near Hatch Number One when his boarding party reached it.

"Tell me why you're here," he demanded in British-accented English. He was a large, erect figure in full uniform. "My ship is under the Chinese flag. A sovereign vessel. You have no right to bring weapons aboard."

Carmody stepped up to him. "What's your name?"

"Captain Chen. Why are you here?"

"Save it, Captain." Carmody motioned to the hatch cover. "What's below this thing?"

Chen said nothing.

"I asked you a question."

Chen said nothing. Carmody looked at him. He was tired of asking things twice.

"Open it up," he said.

Chen instantly looked flustered.

"It is a storage hold," he said. "For equipment."

"We'll see."

Chen crossed his arms. He was growing more rattled and overcompensating for it.

"I cannot allow you into the ship's holds," he

said, digging in. "Not without approval from my employers."

Carmody looked at him.

"The hatch," he said. "Last chance."

"It's impossible. If you return tomorrow morning, I'll try to arrange——"

Before he could finish, Carmody stepped forward, bunched Chen's collar into his left hand and smashed the back of his right hand across the man's jaw. Then he shoved him hard with both hands so he stumbled backward and fell to the deck.

Chen wiped the blood from his mouth. Carmody peripherally saw Harper straighten with disapproval. Or maybe he just sensed his tension. Or maybe the air transmitted it.

He didn't care. Grigor Malkira had killed a man and abducted two children. He was here in Hawaii and connected to this ship.

He looked down at Chen, clutching his Sig.

"Tell somebody to open the fucking hatch," he said.

The thirteen men brought ashore by the Gahjaes rounded the bottom of the tuff cone twenty or thirty yards north of the landing station, scampering down onto the private access lane below the spot where it met the local route.

Grigor was behind Jochi, letting him be his guide as they picked their way over the gray igneous bluff above the notch. He could see the station's perimeter fence up ahead in the darkness.

Jochi paused and opened a shoulder pack. Inside was a Wi-Fi jammer the size and shape of a walkie-talkie. He thumbed it on and pulled out its telescopic antenna. The device would block the signals from the wireless security cameras and insert its own false signal into the network. A person monitoring their feeds would never detect any interruptions. What appeared to be a livestream actually would be a minutes-old delay.

They hurried closer to the facility, Grigor in the lead. After another ten yards he signaled a second halt. There was a security guard patrolling inside the fence. He was a short distance off, coming around from the left.

He pulled his silenced Glock 19 and stole forward alone. He felt only a mild stiffness across his side from his bullet wound. No pain. He knew it was the adrenaline. He also knew that could mask any further damage the lead fragments caused inside him. He would take the bargain.

Seconds passed. Grigor waited as the night guard came closer. Then he raised the pistol to place the laser dot in the middle of his face and fired once through the fence. The guard went straight down.

A wave, and the men sprinted forward. One produced a pair of bolt cutters to clip the wire mesh. It took less than three minutes to get through.

They sprinted across the parking lot toward the back of the plain single-story building. There were about thirteen or fourteen vehicles outside. They would belong to both CloudCable's employees and its outsourced security detail.

Another guard appeared around the east corner. He was walking slowly, relaxed, unaware of any threat. He looked surprised when Jochi shot him in the heart.

They left his body on the ground where it fell.

The nanodrones had photographed a back door to their left. They rushed over to it single file, hugging the building's wall. Grigor stood back, nodded to one of the men with a combat shotgun. He raised the weapon and fired at the lock plate. It discharged with a loud whump, the plate blowing to pieces.

Grigor moved in and smashed the door open with his foot, a high kick at the shattered metal plate.

Inside was a bright, spacious hallway running the width of the building. A third security guard came running out of a crosscorridor. He'd heard the volley and brought his pistol up in his hands.

Grigor shot him with his carbine at close range, a quick burst stitching across his middle, almost cutting him in two.

Behind him Jochi and the men spread out, left and right, then down the branching corridors. Grigor brought three of them with him and followed the room signs: *Telecommunications Equipment, Power Generator, Battery Plant, Control.*

He ran toward the control room. Guns chattered in the corridors; the men were clearing out the building. He heard voices. Shouts. Some of them questioning. Some panicked and desperate. He heard more flurries of gunfire. A woman screamed. There was another burst, and the scream died.

The control room had double swinging doors. He shouldered it open and tossed off a flashbang grenade. Then he plunged through into the smoke.

Inside he saw a security guard and an engineer in a white frock. The guard's hands were clapped over his eyes like he'd been blinded by the detonation. Grigor ran up to him, put the carbine's muzzle to his forehead and fired. Blood and brains sprayed out behind him in a fan. He crumpled to the floor.

The engineer was squatting beneath a desk, her eyes wide and white. "Don't hurt me," she said. "I have three children."

Her voice trembled. Grigor saw the skin fluttering in the hollow of her throat.

"Where are the network and switching controls?" He kept the rifle pointed at her. "Tell me, and I'll pretend I didn't see you."

She gestured vaguely to the right. "It's against the wall. The big console. Please don't hurt me."

"It shouldn't hurt," Grigor said and squeezed the trigger.

He hastened to the controls and left the woman there under the desk, her body riddled with bullets.

The Gahjaes lined up three abreast in the bay off Kono Head, twenty yards apart, their bows turned seaward. The boat in the middle was pointed straight ahead, due south like a compass needle and perpendicular to the shore. The two flanking boats were at forty-five-degree angles, one nosed east, the other west. Their central machine guns were manned. Each ship had a sailor at its torpedo controls. The multiple rocket-powered grenade launchers in their crew compartments could be picked up and fired in seconds.

The cable landing station was secure. Kono Head was theirs. If anything tried to get past them, they would blow it out of the water.

Aboard the *Xingyun Liwu*, Carmody stood at the edge of the hatch as the cover panels groaned, grated and clanked open on their rail mechanisms, rising up and folding back to their vertical positions. The hatch was around a hundred feet long and fifty wide. He was thinking a midsize truck could have fit on any one of the panels.

He glanced down and around its lip and saw the three rail elevators leading below. Then he looked at the men clustered near the hatch. They included Schultz, Dixon, Musil, Harper and three or four of Harper's port security guys. The group also included a nervous-looking Captain Chen. Four or five other members of the Coast Guard PSU had gathered the crew amidships and were keeping watch on them. The rest were searching the deck.

"OK," he said to Dixon. "You and Schultz take

one elevator. Musil and Harper the other." He looked at Chen. "You'll go with me."

Chen's mouth was still bleeding, and his lip had swollen up.

"You are not Coast Guard," he said thickly. "Who are you?"

"Doesn't make a difference."

"Only the Coast Guard has authority," Chen said. "I do not have to comply with your orders."

"That's arguable. But say you're right. I can still throw you down the hatch, and it's a long way to the bottom. You want to try me?"

Chen looked at him. Carmody kept the Sig level with his chest. Chen reluctantly nodded and stepped onto the elevator platform.

A moment later Carmody got on with him. Schultz and Dixon got on their platform. Harper ordered his men to stand by on deck and got on with Musil.

They all rode down into the hold at once.

Grigor sat at the console in the landing station's control room, reached into a pouch for the pocket SSD, and touched a fingertip to its biometric lock. The tiny authentication light flashed from red to green. Like a traffic light. *Go.*

He jacked the drive into an open port and typed. Even with its rapid upload speed, there was a large amount of data to decrypt and transfer. Depending on the computer's processing capacity, he might need a half hour or longer to complete the upload and confirm the underwater sensors were activated.

Footsteps to his left. He spun in his chair, his rifle coming up.

Jochi stood looking at him.

"What is it?" Grigor asked.

"We've zeroed out the personnel," Jochi said. "The guards. The engineers. A maintenance woman."

"You're positive?"

Jochi nodded. "There were fifteen altogether. I had the men put the bodies in one room."

"Those guards outside too?"

"Yes."

Grigor nodded. "All right," he said. "Stay alert. Don't get sloppy. This is going to take a while."

The elevator was about a quarter of the way down into the hold when Carmody realized he wasn't descending into a hold at all. The light was soft and scattered and came from all directions, but it was also without shadows. He could clearly see the space below him.

There were walls lined with flat panel displays. There was what looked like a long boat ramp with rollers. There were robotic arms.

He looked up at Chen. The captain's expression was one of open fear and dread. He looked like someone whose life's biggest secret had just been exposed.

"What is this?" Carmody said.

The captain didn't reply.

Carmody saw a big red emergency stop button under the handrail and hit it with the base of his fist. He grabbed Chen by the shoulders and jammed him back against the rail with his chest. They were seventy feet above the bottom of the hold. Or whatever it was.

"Tell me," he said.

The captain didn't reply.

Carmody grabbed Chen's nose and gripped it in his fist and pressed his thumb into the side of the bone and twisted. Hard to the left, then hard to the right. He felt the nasal bone crack under the flat of his thumb. Blood squirted from the captain's nostrils and he mooed in a way that might have been comical under very different circumstances.

"Tell me."

Tears squirted from Chen's eyes, but he didn't reply. Carmody continued pinching with his fingers and twisted again. Blood gushed out. The nose was no longer intact. It felt soft and crumbly and loose in his hand. Like when he was young and would freeze a Turkish Taffy bar and smack it against the counter to break it into little pieces.

"Tell me."

Chen whimpered and blubbered but didn't reply. Carmody muscled against him and heaved him up so he was balanced on the rail, the metal bar across his back, his feet off the platform. He pushed so the man's weight tilted precariously back over the rail into space and the only thing keeping him from falling was Carmody's own pressing weight and mass.

"Listen," he said. "I saw two little girls taped to chairs with gags in their mouths. I saw a man try to kill their father right in front of their eyes. I want to find that sick bastard. I want to know what he's doing in this country. And I'm running out of time. If you don't tell me, you're worse than useless. You're getting in my way. And I promise I'll throw you over the side to get you out of it. So talk. Or don't. Your decision."

Chen looked up at him. The lower half of his face was a mire of blood. He coughed up red saliva.

"They will kill me. Do you understand?" he said. Wetly, like he was gargling. "I'll be killed. My men too."

"Maybe," Carmody said. "And maybe I'll see you aren't."

Chen looked up at him.

"This is a space for boats. A bay."

"They aren't here."

"No. They left."

"How long ago?"

"About an hour."

"Where are they?"

Chen looked up. Carmody stared into his eyes.

"I'm waiting," he said. "Talk."

Chen talked.

22

Harper and Carmody stood on the quay outside the Pier 2 cruise ship terminal in the harbor, a few yards north of Pier 1 and the *Xingyun Liwu*. The terminal's windows were dark now at three in the morning. The Coast Guard had commandeered its docking facilities, while the MH-65 continued to spin in place above the container ship. On adjoining Pier 1, the ship's crew members were being marched into Coast Guard vans and driven off to a Navy detention facility at Hickam.

Carmody looked over the extraordinary vessel alongside the dock. He had never seen anything like it. About sixty feet long, it sat between two large outspread manta-type wings with tubular nacelles at their bottoms. Its hull panels were angled and faceted, like on a stealth bomber, and made of some dark gray nonreflective metal alloy. Its broad windshield was tinted so no one could see inside. The craft could have been a starfighter in a science fiction movie.

"Your one thought," he said to Harper.

"I tend to think big," Harper said. "There's only a single Ghost. It's a prototype. I hear they're messing with different versions, but we have the original at Barbers. We've been running it through trials for a couple of years."

"You actually know how to pilot it?"

"I have people that do," he said. "My job is to act important and bark orders."

Carmody looked at him. Lights from the official vehicles on the adjoining pier strobed over both their faces.

"According to Chen there are three fast attack boats," he said. "We can't send drones or helicopters to check their position. We can't risk tipping them off. So we just have to assume they're guarding the beach at Kono Head."

Harper nodded.

"I can handle the seaward approach," he said. "You need extra resources?"

"I've got enough people."

Harper paused.

"No one answered the phone at the landing station," he said. "We could try messaging them. But I know we wouldn't get through that way either. All it would do is the same thing you worry about with drones and copters. Give the bad guys advance notice."

Carmody nodded.

"What bothers me is that they might have hostages," Harper said. "I estimate there are between twelve and twenty people at the landing station. That's staff and security combined. If we move in like gangbusters, we could lose all of them."

Carmody shook his head.

"Malkira doesn't take hostages with intentions of letting them go," he said. "I told you about those kids in New York. He was going to kill them. He was going to kill their father. He killed one of our analysts, and he killed some poor GoRide guy. Most likely, he killed whoever owned that bungalow. And Stephen Gelfland, Wendell Balen… God knows how many others. If anyone's still alive in that building, he'll kill them too. Unless we get them out of there first."

Harper was quiet again. "We still don't know what Malkira and his men want," he said. "You take Chen's word when he says he doesn't either?"

"Not his word," Carmody said. "But I believe him because it's basic information security. And because it makes sense. Keep it compartmentalized so nobody can sing out the whole story. Chen only knows his part in things. There must be engineers in that crew who know theirs. And somebody in that bunch has to know why it's carrying a deepwater submersible. In a fucking moon pool."

They were silent. A couple of the Coast Guard vans with detainees were pulling off the dock toward the road. The helicopter chopped overhead.

Harper hesitated. Then he said, "I'm going to tell you something," he said. "Kono landing station is a data traffic center for all kinds of spooks. The CIA, National Geospatial Intelligence, quite a few people know about it. But what most people don't know, and what you don't either, is that it's also used by ONI."

"Naval Intelligence."

Harper nodded. "It's part of a first alert system against enemy submarines. The Integrated Undersea Surveillance System."

"And they leave it guarded by a handful of reserve guys with pistols?"

"There's a memorial right here at Pearl Harbor to the same lack of vigilance on December 7, 1941. Like there's a 9/11 museum at the WTC in New York. Like there should be something for January 6, '21 at the Capitol."

Carmody said, "Say Malkira shuts down the facility. What happens?"

"Probably a big disruption to civilian telecommunications on the islands. Maybe problems for the spooks too. But the IUSS should be OK. There's built-in redundancy in its system." Harper considered for a moment. "The real threat point isn't a shutdown, Carmody. It's somebody corrupting the network with a hack. That could put it under hostile control…and the computers in there are sitting ducks."

"Then, we need to assume that's why Malkira's there," Carmody said. "Let's send your sub-chasers out on patrol. And flip what I was thinking about the ground station. *We* need to be the ones to take it off-line. Cut the power. So he can't get at the computers."

Harper shook his head. "Taking it off the power grid's doable. We can have somebody at Hawaiian Electric flip the circuit breakers. But there's a backup generator at the station that can run the computers for days," he said. "It's the size of a bus and meant to keep running in a total blackout. I don't know how we can knock it out. Not from outside the facility."

"I do," Carmody said.

It was 3:30 in the morning when the two P-8 Poseidon jets took wing from Pearl Harbor-Hickam. Flown by pilots from the navy's VP-4 "Skinny Dragon" maritime patrol squadron, the 737 derivatives were joined by a sturdy, fifty-foot long MQ-4C Triton drone capable of staying in the air for twenty-four hours on recon-surveillance missions.

Their sensor suites—and in the case of the Poseidons, weapons packages—varied, but their assignment was singular: they were submarine hunters designed to protect the coastal United States from enemy attack.

This morning they had roughly two-thousand miles of ocean to patrol.

With its outspread wings skimming along inches below the water's surface, the Ghost left Honolulu

Harbor doing a slow and steady five or six knots. As it made the swing west past Kahanamoku and Waikiki Beaches, the craft began to accelerate, building even more speed as it went by Diamond Head, and the man-made loko kuapa fishpond and Hawaii Kai development.

By the time it crossed the Kui Channel and Hanauma Bay—where the Gahjaes had surfaced hours before—the Ghost was doing better than ten knots. Its wings were pulled inward and close together, rising high off the water, lifting the hull up as well.

At fifteen knots it began hydroplaning a dozen feet above the chop, almost soundless, the nacelles powering it along with a pair of three-thousand-horsepower turboshaft engines.

Inside the craft, Harper and his crew experienced none of the usual shaking, rocking and swaying of conventional speedboats. In fact, they hardly sensed any motion at all. If they felt they were riding on air, it was because they were. Propellers at the front of the Ghost's nacelles were generating a churning cushion of air bubbles underneath it, stabilizing the hull and eliminating friction with the water.

Kono Head was about twenty-five miles up the coast from Pier 1. Shortly before four o'clock in the morning, fifteen minutes after Harper had climbed aboard the Ghost and launched, it came flying toward Kono doing a swift, almost soundless fifty-five knots, racing along atop its churning bed of foam.

Inland to the northwest, meanwhile, Carmody's team had arrived at the landing station's rear flank. They were also on the hurried move.

"Annemarie," Morse said into her phone.

"Carol," Fucillo said into hers. She glanced at her clock on the Resolute desk. Nine-thirty in the morning, they had spoken just hours ago. And Carol's voice carried the weight of an iron anvil. This couldn't be good news. "What's going on?"

"We have an urgent situation in Hawaii," Morse said, and explained.

The two-lane ran full circle around the base of the Kono Head tuff cone, eventually linking up to wider and busier traffic arteries to the north and west. The two JLTVs sped over Honolulu Harbor on the H-1 and made a couple of turns to get on the loop, dropping Carmody's team off on the west side of the crater, right on the slope above and behind the cable landing station. The Coast Guard drivers immediately U-turned and pulled into a scenic lookout about an eighth of a mile back to wait.

Carmody was with Dixon, Schultz and Musil. He knew it would be four of them on the ground against Malkira's unknown number of bastards. But he'd led the two Fox Team members for years and trusted them with his life. Plus, Musil was no slouch. By reputation, and from what Carmody had seen of him. In his view, Malkira could have five times as many men and still be at a disadvantage.

At the southern shoulder of the road, Carmody paused and looked straight down into the parking lot through his goggles. He saw three men out back, spread out across the building's rear wall in the darkness. Another two on the east side of the facility. They were wearing camos and night goggles and full face masks. He assumed there were more on the east side, but it was partly blocked from his viewpoint. He would worry about the ones inside later.

"Outlier?" he said over the RoIP. "You with me?"

"Yes." Kali's voice in his ear.

"All right," he said. "Cut the juice."

Kali sat typing at a keyboard in the C2 truck parked alongside the *Xingyun Liwu*. Harper had been able to quickly acquire the passwords for the landing station's internal systems. Only a half dozen of CloudCable employees shared them, and of those two were presently on shift in the building. She could remotely access the controls for its thirty-ton backup generator with a simple command, ensuring it stayed off when main power was cut to the building.

That was the easy part. The hard part was keeping it off.

Natasha sat beside her and watched. From what she had gleaned, the emergency generator would have to automatically sync itself to the main grid's output before going online. In the United States that output was a standard sixty hertz. To produce that much power, a big steel rod in the generator's prime mover had to rotate six hundred times a minute.

Under normal conditions, the backup generator would run at a very low output so it could sync up quickly if the electricity went down. But Kali was unsyncing it. Corrupting its logic. When the main power was cut, the generator would go offline instead of online. When it went offline, the pistons that turned the humongous steel rod would slow down rather than speed up to get in synch. Then when she put it back online, it would overwork in its rush to sync back up.

According to Kali the amount of internal stress that created would tear it apart.

"Like some dopey little kid who loses his mom in a crowd," Natasha thought aloud.

Kali glanced over from the computer screen. "What?"

"When he realizes she's a half block away, and tries to catch up, he falls and skins his knees," Natasha said. "Except a generator that weighs more than a tank falls a whole freaking lot harder."

Kali fixed her gaze on Natasha for a fraction of a second, then turned back to the screen without a word.

Typing.

Grigor's upload was at seventy percent when the facility lost power. Four or five seconds later, he heard a loud, grinding clatter from elsewhere in the building.

The backup generator, he thought.

He looked around from his chair, his jaw tightening up. His eyes were much quicker to adapt to darkness than the average person's. But he could see very little around him. The overhead LEDs were out. The desk lights. The computer monitor in front of him, along with all the rest of the display screens, and all the indicator lights and readouts on all the control panels in the room. He couldn't hear the low sigh of the HVAC system. He couldn't hear the low ambient hum of electricity passing through capacitors and transformers. There was only dead silence to match the enveloping darkness.

He swiveled to the double doors, barely able to make out the high rectangular shapes of their windows. The corridor outside was pitch-black. The entire station.

Everything was dark.

Grigor pulled the SSD drive from its cable, hastily stuffing it back into its pouch. Then he flipped down his thermal goggles and sprang to his feet. Jochi burst through the doors a second later, his goggles also lowered over his eyes.

"What's going on?" he asked excitedly.

Grigor heard the rattle of semiautomatic gunfire outside.

"There's your answer," he said, raising his TP9. "Come with me."

* * *

It was four-thirty in the afternoon in Crimea when Drajan Petrovik's encrypted link to the SSD drive alerted him to the halted upload.

He turned from his monitor in the control room, where he was surrounded by a half dozen officers from its Unit 74455 Center for Special Technologies. All were Koschei's people, utterly loyal to him, handpicked to operate in the gray margins of the Directorate's authority. All had undergone a specialized training regimen for the operation and were unimaginative but capable.

They were looking at their computers in confusion. Drajan could feel their sudden anxiety. For his part, this was an unexpected and unwanted development. But his goal in the operation differed from theirs. He could be cooler about it. So long as it brought Kali to him.

A woman came over from her station across the room. The lead project manager, she was blonde and attractive. Her name was Alina Bailik.

"Drajan…what is happening?" She motioned to his screen. "Look there. The transfer isn't half complete."

Her tone was confidential. They had been having an affair for the past two months. Quintessa's possessiveness only made her more desirable to him. The lure of the forbidden.

"Koschei will be here in minutes," he said to her. "Hopefully it's a brief interruption. But the rest is up to him."

Bailik looked at him. "It has taken us months to put things in place. How can this be?"

He met her gaze.

"Everything is a gamble," he said, and shrugged. "It's that simple."

A moment passed. She breathed deeply.

"If only I could be so calm," she said. "I envy you, Drajan."

He thought about that for a fleeting second.

"I wouldn't," he said.

The *Ghost*'s pilot and copilot saw the fast attack boats on their thermal display, positioned in a defensive line about thirty yards offshore.

"There they are, sir!" said the pilot. His name was Linick.

Seated behind the men in the command module, Harper looked at his overhead display. Its augmented reality night vision imagery highlighted the Chinese watercraft against their darker surroundings with bright colored outlines. They were three abreast, the bows of the two flanking vessels pointed slightly east and west to cover all the seaward approaches to the beach.

Harper thought fast. Ideally you wanted to strike your target where it offered the largest profile, which was broadside. But he was not going to wait for the boats to open fire.

"Ready Torpedo One. Hit the guy in the middle Let's see if his friends take the bait."

"Roger." This from the co-pilot, Strauss.

Linick gripped his joystick, racing ahead toward shore. Beside him, Strauss wasn't mucking around with instruments and readings. At high speed and close range, he used his sailor's eye and the aug-reality monitor like a hunter using a scope. Then he pressed a red toggle on his panel.

Harper felt the *Ghost* shudder a little as one of its lightweight Mark 54 torpedoes discharged from a tube on the side of the hull. Locked on, moving at almost sixty-five knots, it closed fast, bearing steadily toward its target at the head of a long, churning wake.

Strauss didn't miss. The torpedo struck with a loud *whoom* that he and the others could hear as well as feel through the *Ghost*'s hull. Then a high sheet of foam reared up from the water's surface as the boat blew, consumed by a gaseous orange knot of flame.

Harper saw its two companion vessels peel off to the left and right and initially thought they were taking flight. But the *Ghost*'s ARNV mast provided a three-sixty field of view, and a glance at his overhead told him otherwise.

After shooting in opposite directions for a hundred yards or so, the one on the left had about-faced, slowed in the water, and released its torpedoes full salvo. A pair of them launched from their tubes.

Harper stared at his screen as they came racing toward the *Ghost*. They were seconds from impact and in line to slam it dead-on.

* * *

Carmody's team split up on his signal, scampering downslope into the parking lot as the explosion roared from the beach. He and Dixon descended on the east side of the landing station, Musil and Schultz on the west side, to his left.

They ran across the lot, triple-time, heads low, their rifles in firing position. Coming at the men outside the station from two sides would divide their attention—and the blast still echoing in the air from the direction of the bay had added to the confusion and distraction.

Carmody saw one of the guys behind the building turn toward him, raising his carbine. He triggered his M249 first, and the guy went down.

Suddenly the lot was with thick with gunfire. Racing ahead, he heard Dixon's rifle chatter to his right, then saw a second guy fold to the blacktop. That made two of the three men out back.

Schultz and Musil scratched the third, hitting him with twin volleys that spun him around on his feet. He fell with his own gun spitting harmlessly into the air, a spasmodic trigger pull.

Carmody ran on. He heard another explosive blast from the beach, then the chop of heavy machine guns. Harper was doing his dance with the Gahjaes out on the water.

Another few yards now. Carmody had nearly reached the station when the pair he'd seen on its west side squirted around the angle of the wall, firing away with their rifles. But Schultz tossed a grenade, and it banged and they spilled to the ground.

Carmody glanced over to his right, at the far end of the building. He hadn't been able to see whether there were men on that side. But he figured there would be and estimated he only had a couple of seconds.

"Dix." He tapped his goggles with two fingers, pointing to his eyes, then motioned to the right with his rifle. Dixon nodded, and they waited.

He'd guessed correctly. Two more guys in camouflage came hooking around the corner. Carmody could see one of them about to lob something. He and Dixon opened fire, aiming high, above any possible body armor. A spray of bullets disintegrated their heads.

Then they were at the back door, Dixon beside him on the right, Schultz and Musil sprinting up on his left through the acrid nitrite smoke of the grenade.

Carmody looked at the door. It hung partway open. The lock plate had been chewed up by what he guessed was a shotgun round.

He signaled again. Schultz crowded against the building wall on the opposite side of the entry, Musil close behind him. On his side it was Dixon and himself.

Schultz tossed a flashbang through the door. It popped loudly inside the building. A second later Musil ran in with his rifle outthrust. Schultz followed, then Dixon.

Carmody was stepping through behind the others when he heard something behind him. Footsteps. Rapid, scuffling, more than one set.

He spun around, looking toward the east end of the building.

Two men were racing away from the facility. Probably they'd left through a side door. But how they got out didn't matter. They were out. Running across the lot toward the low, rocky slope climbing up to the two-lane.

One was tall, bulky, built like an ox. He recognized the other at once. The thin, long arms. The legs like stalks.

Malkira.

Carmody gave Dixon a heads up over the RoIP, told him to take over for him, and hurried off after them.

On board the *Ghost*, Harper was thinking the *Gahjae*'s crew had taken his bait hook, line and sinker. Their torpedoes were right on course. But they couldn't hurt what they couldn't hit. High off the water on its wing struts, his craft was hovering well above the fish as they shot ineffectually through its cushion of foam into the darkness.

Meanwhile, the *Gahjae* had throttled back in the water to release them. Making it eminently vulnerable to his own torpedoes.

"Turn wide to port… Get our nose on her!" he ordered. "Stand by, number two!"

"Yes, sir!" Strauss said.

The *Ghost* went around the Chinese boat in a long, looping turn.

"Number two—fire!"

"Aye!"

The *Ghost*'s second Mark 54 hit the Galijae amidship, colliding with its hull at a textbook perfect ninety-degrees. There was a flash in the night, a roar, and it was gone, blown out of the water.

Two down, Harper thought.

He checked his screen. The *Ghost*'s three-sixty view field showed the third fast boat racing away from them a hundred fifty yards to the east.

"Linick, see that last one?"

"Check."

"Get after it. Full throttle."

"Roger"

"LeMahieu?"

Doug LeMahieu, the fourth member of the crew, was aft in his seat manning the Vulcan Gatling gun.

"Yes, sir."

"Objective's yours. Fire at will. They aren't running out on our party."

The *Ghost* surged after the fast boat, practically flying over the water. At his station, LeMahieu began chopping out .20 mm ammunition.

Harper grabbed his bullhorn microphone.

"Halt and surrender!" he shouted. "This is your only warning!"

The fast boat kept racing eastward in the dark, but the *Ghost*'s near-frictionless speed vastly overmatched it. Within a minute it had chased down the smaller craft like a fox after a hare, pulling within fifty yards, LeMahieu slamming it with bullets at a rate of six thousand rounds per minute. Chunks of its hull blasted into the air. Flames spouted from its deck. Finally it stopped dead, leaning to one side at an extreme angle.

"Come up onto the deck with your hands in the air," Harper boomed through the horn. "You have thirty seconds before we open fire."

He silently counted down. The fast boat sat at its precarious tilt, taking on water. No one came topside. He kept counting down.

Fifteen seconds into his count the Chinese craft blew from within, self-destructing with a flash that momentarily blanked his display and pushed a whipping, thumping wave of seawater over the *Ghost*'s hull. But it remained balanced on its foils thanks to twenty-odd gyroscopic stabilizers under the keel.

Harper kept his eyes intently on his monitor once it cleared of glare, observing the wreckage of the boat on the surface. His impulse was to order Linick to move in and see if there were any survivors, unlikely as that might be. The crew obviously hadn't wanted to be taken alive, and he doubted anyone could have made it through the blast.

After a minute, he went ahead and looked anyway.

"Oh, shit. Oh, Jesus God," said the pilot, Lt. Jase Waller, the P-8's commander. "Archer, you see what I see?"

Archer was Captain Ty Archer, his co-pilot.

He looked at their display. Relayed to the cabin by a member of the three-man sensor team in the rear of the plane—Airman Aldrich, Sensor One—the Triton drone's optical real times were picking up fluctuations in the surface current consistent with a submarine to a near hundred percent probability. Triton's magnetic anomaly detector had reinforced that appraisal with its own readings.

Something was clearly down there. And that wasn't all. Like a high-tech Etch-a-Sketch, the integrated AI aboard the drone had drawn a picture of the sub on-screen, and it was a class apart from any boat in its digital memory archive. In essence, what they had was an underwater UFO. A big one. And one that definitely wasn't of American origin.

"Roger—what the hell do we do?"

Archer checked his distance readouts. Triton was now about three hundred miles southwest of Oahu. Their own position was a hundred miles closer to the island. They could cover the distance to the boat in minutes.

"We get over there, drop our sonobuoys and contact base," he said. "Then we wait to see if we're going to be heroes."

It was four-thirty in the morning.

President Fucillo took the call through a White House operator at four forty-five. On the private line with her was Admiral Francis P. Kealey, Commander of the US Pacific Fleet at his Pearl Har-

bor headquarters complex. Also patched in from
their residences were SoS Tanner Woodrbridge
and NSA Josh Urias.

"OK, everybody's here," Fucillo said. "Get right
to it, Frank."

"Yes, Madam," he said. "One of our Tritons has
located a submarine. About three hundred miles
southwest of Oahu. Shallow depth—six hundred
feet. It's presently stationary."

"Have you identified it?"

. "The boat's signature is anomalous. But we're
certain it's a Chinese drone."

"Because?"

"Fourteenth District put two subchasers and a
UAV in the air when the Kono Head landing station was hit. All three have the new multifunction
radar pods. Also one of the planes is already on-
site and dropped its sonobuoys. A hundred and
forty of them. It gave us a clear acoustic profile
and we ran it by ONI." A pause. "Beijing calls
it the Silent Dragon. It's the damn hypersonic
they've crowed about for years."

"Nuclear capabilities, yes or no?"

"Yes, Madam. That's the bad news. Probably it
has Yu-9s. Light torpedoes. They've got two fifty-
kilogram warheads—and the way they work gives
them a wide blast radius. One would erase the island. I don't want to think what two would do."

Fucillo took a breath.

"What do you think it's waiting for?"

"Best guess—the group that broke into Kono's

there to take out the Sentient offshore surveillance system. So we can't track the sub if it moves within range of the coast."

"Which is?"

"About twenty miles. Could be closer to thirty."

"Options, Frank."

"Our planes have Mark Fifty-fours aboard. They're ASW torpedoes. Best we've got. This is why we build them."

Fucillo nodded.

"Take that damn thing out before it comes an inch closer," she said.

Koschei had approached the control room in heady spirits, though that mood would dissolve before he entered. He had moments ago concluded a satellite call with his imbedded people in the Chinese government. But what began as his update on Silent Dragon's status had turned—if just briefly—into a conversation about their mutual vision of the future.

They had spoken of a new power structure in Beijing after the weak-minded President Tsao was gone. He would truthfully deny having ordered the strike on Pearl Harbor, would prostrate himself to the Americans, but it would be too late. The United Sates would be forced to retaliate in kind. Not to the extent of an all-out war. But with a force that would shake Tsao out of the office he believed was his for life.

Koschei and his allies had discussed their shared

opportunity when the dust settled. They had talked about their nations coexisting in a comprehensive economic partnership, with a full political and strategic convergence of purpose. In his enthusiasm, General Huang had even spoken of the bear and dragon rising atop America's bones. While that seemed a touch melodramatic, Koschei had seen it as a valid metaphor. Sino-Russian competitiveness had hurt both nations for decades, but they had far too much in common to let that go on to their detriment. Hundreds of billions in trade every year, an aversion to American cultural and political interference… It was high time their nations acted together to assert primacy over the West and take charge of global affairs.

Heady indeed, and Koschei had stepped through the heart of the mountain to the control room with a subtle hop in his normally even, regular step.

That changed the instant its door slid open and he saw the grim faces of the technicians turning in his direction.

Half a minute passed. He stood looking inside, his eyes moving from one to the other, seeking out Drajan Petrovik. The project manager, Alina Bailik, stood beside him.

He walked over to them. "What's going on?"

"Malkira broke off the upload," Drajan said. "Sentient's underwater sensors are still active."

Koschei was silent as that sank in, his brows coming together over his eyes like thick, dark clouds.

"Has there been word from Grigor?"

"Nothing."

Another silence. Koschie looked at Bailik. "How far would the submarine travel before they destroy it?"

"We can't know with certainty," she said. "I doubt we can push it to cavitation speed quickly enough to avoid their aircraft. There isn't time for a run-up. But we could set it on an evasive course. At three hundred miles from the target, there's a fair chance of bringing it within firing range."

"And if not? They'll blow it out of the water."

"You worry too much," Drajan interjected. "The submarine is of Chinese design. Built with Chinese technology. The Americans would dredge up its wreckage and still point their fingers where you want them pointed. It would be unfortunate to lose the boat. But the core goal is still achieved."

Koschei stood there with his eyes on Drajan's face. Then he gave a slow, heavy nod.

"Send it," he said.

Grigor Malkira and the other man were all the way up the slope before Carmody reached them. They had started out with a fifty-yard lead, and he'd been unable to close the distance in time. He saw them running to the top, then lost sight of them as they clambered over.

He went up after them. The draw was about fifteen feet high, not much of a climb. A minute and he was standing on the road shoulder.

He looked left, right. Didn't see them. He looked

across the road at the base of the tuff cone, craned his neck to look up the slope. Still no sign of them. He thought a minute. They could be up or down the road. But he didn't think so. They had no escape vehicle. They had come on boats. If they stuck to the road on foot, it would be too easy to follow and find them.

He stared at the cone. It was probably fifteen hundred feet wide. Maybe two hundred feet high. Sheer and rugged on the side facing him. But he was betting they had gone up. There had to be a path around the base.

Which side? Left or right?

He thought quickly. It wasn't quite a fifty-fifty choice. Left, east, was the windward side of the cone, facing the bays and coves down toward Waikiki and Honolulu. It would have more exposure to the elements than the western side, which curved inland. That meant more rain hitting it. More water running down the slope. More erosion. That side was likelier to have a path.

Carmody turned left on the road and got lucky. The trail was only a few yards east around the foot of the cone. He saw freshly crumbled sand, gravel and volcanic ash on the blacktop underneath it.

Then he looked up and saw them. They were about sixty feet above him. Climbing the slope. Not clawing, not scrambling. Upright, on their feet. But not exactly racing along either.

Carmody flipped up his goggles. Daylight was

leaking into the sky and he didn't need them. He ran up onto the cone behind the two men.

The slope was more precipitous than it appeared from the base. After a few yards the trail turned sharply, made a sheer jump, then made another abrupt turn. Carmody zigged and zagged between large humps of stone. He lost sight of the men, saw them again. They weren't gaining on him, but they weren't losing ground either.

He didn't see them looking back at him. But they had to know he was behind them. There was no stealth up here. No being quiet. Not for any of them. The slope was crinkled and broken like the hide of an ancient elephant. Their soles crunched on dust and ash and fragments. Tumbled rocks and pebbles were everywhere. On the trail, alongside it. They rolled and shifted and dribbled and skittered underfoot.

Carmody gulped air, ran through a switchback, cutting one way, then another. The two men vanished above him. Reappeared. He thought he might have picked up a few yards on them. Then he hit another switchback and they were gone again.

He ran between two curving walls of stone. They bulged out on either side of the trail like swollen bellies, narrowing it around him. Then the slope banked steeply upward between them. Carmody had to scramble on all fours to a massive slab of rock on the left side of the trail. He found a handhold there and hauled himself up to his feet.

He was climbing past the slab when an arm

suddenly came out from behind it, locked around his throat and dragged him backward hard, nearly pulling him off his feet. It was thick and muscular and strong as steel.

And it was choking off his breath.

"Sir, the object's on the move," Sensor One said over the *Poseidon*'s phones.

"You're positive?" said Lieutenant Waller up front in the cabin.

"Yes, sir. Speed sixteen knots and accelerating. Bearing north by northeast."

Straight for Oahu.

Waller inhaled. He was a third-generation air jock. His British grandfather had flown a Dambuster Lanc in the Second World War. His father an F-15 over the Balkans. Until now his navy career had consisted of breezy six-month deployments to Guam and Pearl. Eclipsed wasn't the word. But lightning had struck with a summons to the airfield, then moments ago a direct order from COMPACFLT.

He exhaled. It did nothing to slow his heart rate. "Fire Control?"

That was FC Natalie Daubach.

"We have a lock," she reported. "But it's gaining fast. Up to twenty-four knots…thirty… This thing's really gaining speed—"

"Then what are you waiting for? Fire."

"Yes, sir…"

"Now!"

Ten seconds later she released the torpedo.

* * *

Carmody brought his hands up to the arm clamped around his throat, trying to pry it away. It didn't budge. Malkira's companion had been perfectly positioned for an ambush. The guy was even bigger than he was, and his left arm was still weak from the bullet wound. He spun Carmody halfway around on the trail. Jerking him from behind. Twisting him. This way, that, like he was a rag doll. The slope slid out from under his boots. Another twist. Another jerk. This way. That. His fist pounded the side of Carmody's face. It felt like a mallet.

Then Carmody saw Malkira above him. About ten feet up the slope. Just standing there in the middle of the trail.

He had something in his hand. Long, bright, silver, reflective.

A knife.

"Jochi, get him up here."

He moved up the trail, forcing Carmody along in front of him, pushing him forward with his chest. Carmody dug his heels into the dirt. The guy held him in his vice lock and kept pushing and punching his face.

Malkira took a step toward him. He was holding the knife low. About level with his hip. His arm cocked at the elbow. He was going to uppercut him with the blade.

Carmody knew what he needed to do. But he couldn't do it too soon. It had to be timed right.

He waited until the knife was coming up in Grigor's hand. Not giving him a chance to stop his upward stabbing motion. Then he pivoted to the left, using his hip, using his shoulder, using his legs, bringing the big ox behind him around his right side, counterclockwise, between the arcing blade and his own body.

It didn't cut the ox too deeply. He was strong enough to stop his off balance momentum so the edge of the blade just grazed him through his right sleeve. He spun around and hurled himself on top of Carmody, body-slamming him, knocking him backward off his feet and down onto the trail. His face was in Carmody's face. His beard was squashed into his mouth. He brought his hands down around Carmody's throat. Carmody brought his hands up around the guy's throat. But the guy had him pinned with his weight. Had him crushed into the dirt and rocks. The guy had all the advantage.

Then something happened Carmody couldn't have explained.

The ox's eyes suddenly widened and rolled upward. His mouth contorted into a warped circle. His face twitched. The muscles under the skin of his forehead and cheeks seemed to move independently of each other, like they were pulling part. He made a gasping sound and then a wheeze and then a thin, high whistle like his throat had closed up in three distinct, spasmodic stages. Veins bulged out in his forehead. A thick gob of saliva ran down from his mouth into Carmody's face. Then it started gushing out of his mouth.

Carmody kept his hands clenched around his throat. Its muscles were pulsing and stiff.

The guy took another whistling breath and thrashed on top of him. His arms flailed. His legs kicked out like he was swimming.

Carmody pushed up hard, rolled the man sideways and off him. He went over onto his back and lay there juddering and twitching and flopping like a fish out of water. His face was bluish-purple. His tongue was swollen grotesquely and lolling out of his mouth. His head was banging against the ground with some strange serial muscle contractions. Carmody stood up, covered with dust, and drew his pistol from his holster. He spared a second to think about the knife blade and wonder what the hell might have been on it. Then he shot the guy once in the forehead and looked up the trail for Grigor.

He saw him right away in the ghostly predawn light, about forty feet above him, nearing the rim of the crater. The trail running up to the rim curved around a knobby projection and then rose straight and steep to the top. Grigor was scrambling to reach it, climbing like a crab on all fours.

Carmody had no clear shot at him from his angle. He wasn't going to hit him, and he didn't try. He holstered his gun and went after him.

Seen on Fucillo's livestream, the spray from the MK-48's underwater explosion looked oddly like a huge white flower blossoming open in the darkness.

"Madam President, we have a hit," Admiral Kealey said a second later. She could see him from headquarters, Pearl Harbor, on a separate screen. "Thank dear, sweet God."

Seconded. Fucillo sat very still as her advisers broke into cheers and applause through some of the Situation Room's other video displays—Woodridge howling so loudly through the speakers it hurt her ears. The events in Hawaii had developed so quickly there had been no time for them to gather in person, putting her alone in the room except for some hastily roused young White House staffers. They were also clapping their hands in monumental relief.

She gave them a minute to settle down, then turned to the one nearest her at the table.

"OK, Jimmy," she said. "We're just getting warmed up. I want President Tsao on the line. Right now."

Carmody climbed and clawed and scrabbled up the tuff cone's slope. Sweat spilled down his face and into his eyes. He took off his helmet and tossed it to the ground. It was nothing but an impediment to him right now.

He climbed faster, his feet slipping on the dirt. He could see that Grigor had a rifle on his shoulder. Once he reached the rim, he would have a perfect vantage for firing it downslope. Carmody would be a sitting duck on the trail below him.

He climbed. He was getting closer to Grigor.

Maybe ten yards behind him now. The slope grew almost vertical as it neared the brow of the crater. He climbed. Gaining maybe another five yards.

Then Grigor was just above him. He pushed himself up the trail, harder, faster. He was drenched in perspiration. His chest hurt from bruises and exertion.

Grigor was almost at the brow. He reached one hand over it and dug his fingers into the tuff and was hauling himself up onto it.

Carmody lunged. He grabbed Grigor's legs with one hand, then the other, and pulled himself up along and over them. Grigor tried to kick him off, but Carmody held on and climbed up onto his back, pinning him down, his chest pressing against Grigor's shoulder pack.

For a moment Grigor lay flat on his belly. But only for a moment. Then he heaved up and rolled around with surprising strength, and all at once he was on his back with Carmody on top of him, the two of them face-to-face on the rim of the crater.

He punched Carmody's arm where he'd been shot. Carmody returned the favor, grabbed the right side of Grigor's abdomen and dug in his fingers. He felt the soggy warmth of the bandages under his shirt and grabbed his side more tightly, as though he was trying to tear out a chunk of his flesh.

Grigor groaned softly. He clawed for a rock and picked it up and smashed it against the back of Carmody's head and then repeatedly pounded it against his shoulder above the gunshot wound. Carmody felt it open up wide. Felt blood pouring out of it. Now his scalp was bleeding too. He clenched his teeth and got his fingers deeper into Grigor's side. The shirt there was permeated with blood. His fingers were wet and slippery.

They were still face-to-face. Eye to eye. Their noses almost touching. Carmody realized Grigor had let go of the rock in his hand. He was going for something under his shirt.

The knife. Grigor had gotten his fist around the handle.

Carmody grabbed his wrist to try and hold it down. But Grigor again surprised him with his strength. His arm came up, slowly, straining against Carmody's downward pressure. The blade rising in his fist like a silver fang, its tip inches from Carmody's cheek.

Carmody hauled himself to his knees, pulling his head away from the knife, jerking Grigor up by the shirt so he was in a sitting position. Carmody was now kneeling between Grigor's legs. They were still facing each other. He still had one hand around his wrist. He slid his hand an inch down to get it over his knife hand, then twisted the hand back on itself until the blade was turned all the way around and pointing at Grigor's throat.

Grigor stared into his eyes.

"Don't," he said. "I can tell you things. About Pinnacle. The Wolf. *Don't.*"

"OK," Carmody said and forced the knife into

the right side of his neck, using Grigor's own hand to push it in deep, burying it until the handle was flush with his skin, and the tip of the blade was poking out the left side.

Grigor produced a thick, moist sound from his wide-open mouth, sitting there on the rim of the crater, the knife transfixing his throat. Carmody hauled himself to his feet. He grabbed the straps of Grigor's pack, found the buckles and snapped them open. He shucked the pack off Grigor and tossed it behind him onto the path. Then he bent, clamped his hands over Grigor's shoulders and pulled him up to a standing position.

Grigor's legs were limp. Blood was pouring down his chin from his nose and mouth. Carmody held him up on his feet a second with the knife in his throat. Then he shoved him over the crater's rim and into its rocky bowl two hundred feet below.

The sun was up, banding the sky with orange and yellow above the crater's edge. Carmody turned, sat down with his head resting back against the slope and thought as dawn turned into full daylight. After a while, he grabbed Grigor's pack off the ground, stood up and started back down the trail.

23

Washington, DC/Hawaii
April 20, 2024

SECRET/ORCON/NOFORN

EYES ONLY

DO NOT COPY

OFFICIAL MEMORANDUM OF TELEPHONE CONVERSATION

SUBJECT: Telephone Conversation with President Tsao He Feng of People's Republic of China

PARTICIPANTS: President Annemarie Fucillo of USA, President Tsao of PRC

Notetaker (Situation Room): Carmen Seager

DATE, TIME April 20, 2024, 12:06—12:16 a.m. EDT

PLACE: White House Oval Office

"President Tsao. Annemarie Fucillo."

"Yes. Of course. It's an unexpected pleasure to hear your voice so soon after our last conversation."

"I'm sure."

"Madam President, it is my understanding that there is an urgent matter you wish to discuss."

"That's accurate. And I'm going to get right to it. Because I want you to know that my country came very close to being attacked by a Chinese-designed submarine within the last hour."

"One moment, please. I assure you, my country had no—"

"I choose my words with great care, Mr. President. You'll note I did not say the sub was one of yours. I said, specifically, it was of your country's design. There is a difference. I want to make it clear that my people believe there are entities within your government who were involved. But I am also going to tell you that we do not think you were personally responsible."

"Madam...what you are alleging is inconceivable. And incredible."

"So you say. But my intelligence folks are very thorough. I'm convinced their appraisal is sound. It is our strong, undivided view that those behind the strike were working with outside threat actors to undermine your authority with malicious intent and instigate a military conflict between our two nations."

(PAUSE IN THE CONVERSATION)

"Madam President, true or not, these stunning

allegations need explanation. I have a need to know who you believe these individuals to be."

"On that we're in full agreement. And I'm prepared to share our information once this call ends. But Mr. President, I have to be straightforward with you. Speaking as a friend, we have a complicated situation. There may be dangerous forces at work that are disassociated from any government. Yours, mine or others. If we're going to get to the bottom of it, we'll have to trust each other. Establish a closer relationship moving forward, predicated on a thorough accounting of the circumstances behind the *Stalwart's* disappearance. I want the truth. Should the worst have happened—and I pray it hasn't—I expect those responsible to be brought to justice. All this could be painful for both of us. But the positive, I mean it sincerely, is that it would send an unequivocal message to those parties that their plan has backfired. That instead of bringing us to war, it has brought us closer together in an atmosphere of mutual cooperation. Your thoughts?"

(EXTENDED PAUSE)

"Madam President, I think we will need a public gesture."

"Say, a joint press conference at the White House?"

"Yes."

"You'll agree to that right now? Without precondition?"

"Yes."

"Then, sir, we're on. And let me tell you that is music to my ears."

* * *

It was almost six o'clock when Carmody returned to the landing station. He'd heard sirens yowling and helicopters chopping in the air the whole way down the cone and could see why. The parking lot was filled end to end with Coast Guard and Navy police vehicles. Not to mention the personnel who had come inside them.

Lee and Baylor from the Fourteenth District were there, and they got him past the checkpoints. He tracked down Dixon inside the facility.

"You and the rest OK?" he said.

Dixon nodded.

"They're back at the air station," he said. "I figured I'd stick around and wait for you."

"How did you know I would make it back?"

Dixon shrugged.

"You're predictable," he said and paused. "There were four mooks inside the building. Fifteen bodies. They slaughtered the whole staff."

Carmody winced.

"Malkira won't be killing anyone else," he said.

Dixon nodded. "There's more we don't know than we do about him," he said. "And not just him. I feel like we still need all kinds of answers."

Carmody held up the backpack. "Something tells me we might find some in here," he said.

An hour later, Carmody got out of a JLTV at Barbers Point to find DeBattista on the field watching a team of Coast Guard runway jocks prep the Falcon for takeoff.

"Man," he said, "you look like shit."

"Thanks," Carmody said.

DeBattista smiled a little. "It's all right. You can catch some beauty sleep on the way home."

Carmody was quiet. DeBattista stood there a moment, then snapped his fingers.

"Almost forgot," he said. "Your friend's been asking around for you. The looker, I mean."

"Her name's Kali," Carmody said. "Thought you told me you were going to keep your eyeballs in their sockets."

DeBattista feigned looking wounded.

"I meant the other looker," he said.

Carmody found Natasha Mori in the conference room where they had met with Harper and his aides the night before. She was at the table looking pensive over a cup of coffee.

"I heard you wanted to see me," he said.

She regarded him but said nothing. He stepped in from the entryway.

"You OK?" he said.

Natasha hesitated.

"She's gone," she said.

He looked at her. "Who's gone?"

"Kali."

Carmody felt like he wasn't tracking.

"What are you talking about? We take off in an hour." He cocked a thumb over his shoulder toward the airfield. "The plane's out there getting fueled up."

"I know," Natasha said. "She said you would understand."

He suddenly felt even more confused.

"Understand what?"

"Why she couldn't go back to New York with us." Natasha shook her head. "She said to tell you sometimes people have to leave. And she just left."

Carmody looked at her in silence.

His jaw clenched. His heart froze.

Then it plunged to the center of the earth and kept dropping.

* * * * *

Don't miss the other books in the bestselling Net Force thriller series!

e-novella

e-novella

Available now!